Far across Lake Ea GammaLAW's Klaxons and whoopers were echoing, sounding general quarters. Burning could see the SWATHship making the water boil in her wake as she gathered headway. In the sky and on the lake were the falling, flaming remains of combat aircraft.

Gunshots and the mob din of combat echoed from Wall Water. The Jotan was gone from the dungeon roof, nowhere in sight, but to the southeast the flame and smoke of something big flickered off the waters.

He heard the roar of a powered Gatling gun down on the beach—a landing boat bringing heavy scorch to bear. By then there was surely a ready-reaction team on its way up to evac the shore party, but a lot of contingency planning had just become obsolete.

"They're upon us," Souljourner said without losing her composure . . .

By Brian Daley
Published by Ballantine Books:

Books published by The Ballantine Publishing Group
are available at quantity discounts on bulk purchases
for premium, educational, fund-raising, and special
sales use. For details, please call 1-800-733-3000.

A SCREAMING ACROSS THE SKY

Book Two of GammaLAW

Brian Daley

A Del Rey® Book
THE BALLANTINE PUBLISHING GROUP • NEW YORK

A Del Rey ® Book
Published by The Ballantine Publishing Group
Copyright © 1998 by The Estate of Brian Daley

http://www.randomhouse.com

Library of Congress Catalog Card Number: 97-94729

ISBN 0-345-42209-0

Manufactured in the United States of America

First Edition: May 1998

10 9 8 7 6 5 4 3 2 1

In memory of my father, Charles Joseph Daley, and of meteor watching on warm August nights

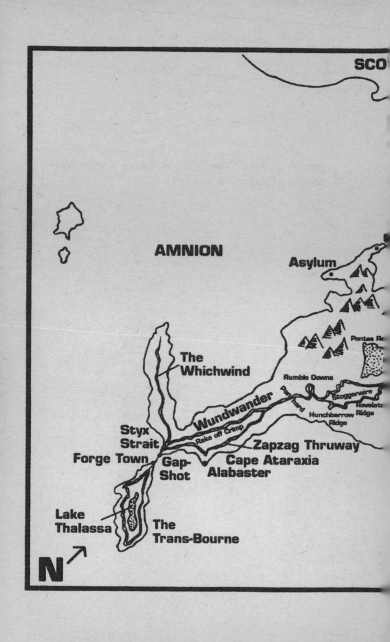

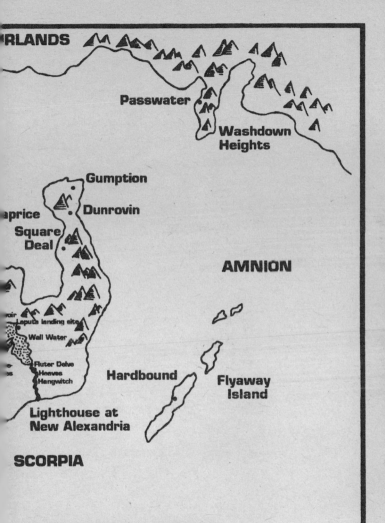

PERIAPT

CHAPTER ONE

The black airmobile VTOLs came in level with the tops of Iskra's twisted scrub, scarcely more than three meters above the rolling countryside. Detectors placed around the LAW detention facility in Periapt's western hemisphere had already been knocked out by elite pathfinder teams, and—by special agreement—intelsat observers were looking the other way.

The whine of turbines muffled by countersonics was Farley Swope's first clue that something out of the ordinary was going down. She, Hippo Nolan, and the rest of the *Scepter* survey team—relocated to the Iskra facility a month earlier as a consequence of Claude Mason's escape from Blades Station—couldn't decide whether the incoming ships constituted the vanguard of a Roke attack or elements of a LAW death squad—Periapt's Legal Annexation of Worlds forces.

A few of the facility's guard towers got off some ineffective fire before the raiders answered with shock-and-stun ordnance. Caught near a barracks viewpane with Hippo, Ice, and a couple of the others, Farley hit the floor.

Illumination rounds began to blossom outside the viewpane. The guards brandished weapons as they attempted to drive the detainees back to their quarters for a lockdown. The reaction of the guards was due only to the fact that they hadn't been apprised of the raid beforehand. Before they could accomplish much, a door was blasted open and concentrated nonlethal small arms fire poured through the breach, flooring two guards and one team member—Simone Weiner. They continued to shove the *Scepter* crew back, while others scrambled to take cover and return fire. Nova light streamed into the barracks

3

from all sides, making it impossible to see precisely who was storming the facility.

Opposite the guards' defensive positions a corner of the prefab building was ripped away by explosives. Soldiers wearing LAW battlesuits came through the opening low, firing nonlethals and lobbing shock grenades. Alarms blared from the PA speakers, which the raiders shot to pieces with solid projectiles. From beneath her bunk Farley saw the unprotected guards quickly outmaneuvered and neutralized.

Gradually, the inside and outside worlds quieted somewhat.

An engineer with the *Scepter* crew, Farley knew enough about military ops to appreciate the training that had to have gone into the assault; the raiders seemed to have every contingency covered, down to the last detail. When they began calling out the names of the survey team members, she hoped they would be equally methodical when it came to killing her.

She had been anticipating this moment since the team's ignoble return from Aquamarine several months earlier, a mission that had eaten up almost twenty baseline years, though Farley and the others had aged scarcely four. Nevertheless, she cowered under the bunk for well over a minute. Then, steeling herself, she ran in a crouch for what remained of the barracks doorway.

The raiders intercepted her before she was halfway there. It was obvious that she was unarmed, but the raiders kept their weapons trained on her while their apparent commander stepped over to where they had made her kneel. His face was concealed behind the rebreather apparatus of his LAW-issue helmet.

"Farley Swope?" he asked.

She nodded, then deliberately glanced around at the damage. "You better hope they don't take this out of your salary, soldier," she told him.

He stared at her for a long moment, then laughed. "You've got us all wrong, Farley. We're friends of Claude Mason."

"Mason?" she said in confusion. "But you're LAW—aren't you?"

"A relatively recent development—and somewhat beyond our control, in any event. My name is Burning."

An expression of guarded relief came to Farley's face. "You're the commander of the Exts—from Concordance." The term was short for "exteroceptive," referring to the slave implants Burning's ancestors had been forced to wear before their liberation during the Cyberplagues.

Burning gestured broadly toward the barracks. "This was the only way we could convey Dextra Haven's job offer to you."

Farley blinked almost tearfully. "Hierarch Haven has a job for me?"

"For all of you," Burning amended.

His hand was moving toward the release tabs of his helmet when a muffled detonation issued from somewhere in the barracks. As everyone swung toward the sound, the hand of one of Burning's subordinates came down hard on the commander's own.

"Bioweapon!" the Ext said, showing Burning some sort of wrist-worn analyzer. "We musta tripped a fail-safe!"

Burning froze in place, then shouted, "Get these people outside! Delta-V!"

Someone had seen to it that none of the *Scepter* team would leave Iskra alive unless by order of LAW. The poison gas released by the hidden fail-safe device was already beginning to work on Farley when an Ext scooped her off the floor and began to lumber toward the scorched doorway.

She heard strangled cries from some of the guards and team members. Then her thoughts began a slow downward spiral into a seemingly bottomless well of silence.

She died peacefully just outside the doorway.

"If you need to blame someone, Burning, you can blame me," Dextra Haven's holo was saying. "I should have known something was wrong from the start. Iskra's so secret a location, it doesn't even appear in LAW's most classified documents, and there I was getting data not only on the base's defense capabilities but on the intelsats that watch over it." She shook her head. "It's obvious that LAW knew what I was planning. They used me to eliminate the *Scepter* team." Her digitally composed figure gazed straight out of its cone of light. "I'm so sorry, Burning."

He nodded for the pickups, then pushed his long red braids from his forehead. "We should have seen it as well, Madame Haven."

Her expression remained grim. "Remember this, Allgrave: We had a hand in their deaths, but we didn't kill them. *LAW* killed them."

Burning nodded. "We carried out the executions with such finesse that LAW's holding off sending a like team to Miseria Isle to do the same for us; is that it?"

Haven snorted ruefully. "LAW isn't even acknowledging that there was a raid on Iskra, Allgrave. They're blaming the deaths on a cybervirus that infiltrated the fail-safe system. Just as they did with Byron Sarz's failed attack on the Lyceum ball."

Behind Burning and to his left General "Daddy D" Delecado ran his hand over his mouth. "How many times they gonna use that excuse before people start refusing to buy it?"

Haven's figure shifted slightly. "You've been on Periapt for only two months, General. People here would rather blame a rogue virus than accept LAW's covert executions or indeed that the Legal Annexation of Worlds subscribes to any hidden agendas. When in doubt, why blame human nature when you can so easily fault technology?"

Burning broke the long silence. "How did Mason take the news of the death of his teammates?"

Haven exhaled audibly. "It's hard to tell, what with these aphasic episodes of his. I'm actually beginning to believe the Peace Warrantors' claim that he at some point engaged in an illegal cyberinterface. Half the time he acts like he's listening or speaking to ghosts."

Burning thought about the implants his ancestors had been forced to wear during their hundred-year enslavement to Concordance's First Landers. Stories had been handed down of people feeling as if they were puppets operated by the implants themselves. But those stories were from a time before the Cyberplagues had reached Concordance, liberating the Exts from their implants while spreading death and wreaking havoc on nearly every human-colonized world in the galaxy.

"Is Mason in any danger from LAW?" Ghost asked.

Haven turned to face Burning's sister, whose mask of facial

scars had been executed by her own hand. "Even if Mason was thought to be fully sane, his media visibility affords him protection. Perhaps when the pressgangs are done with him, he'll have to hire a team of bodyguards to watch his back. But by then all of us will be long gone from Periapt."

"Why would LAW want the *Scepter* team dead?" Ghost asked, coming alongside Burning. "LAW and the Lyceum have already agreed to fund your mission to Aquamarine, so what harm could they have done at this point?"

"Precisely," Haven said. "What harm? Unless the mission LAW has seen fit to grant me is nothing more than a ruse to remove me from Periapt in the same way the *Scepter* team was removed from Iskra. I learned only this morning that LAW has named Buck Starkweather commissioner of the AlphaLAW mission to Hierophant, which means that I'm going to be answering to him until *Terrible Swift Sword* deposits us on Aquamarine. Anything could happen during the voyage—or once we're shuttled down the well."

"A convenient accident, huh?" Delecado said.

"I'm all but *counting* on one, General."

"Then your GammaLAW mission goes ahead as planned?" Burning asked after a moment.

Haven nodded. "For me it does. Whatever risks I undertake will be justified if Aquamarine offers some resolution to the Roke Conflict."

Trinity, thirty light-years from Periapt, was thought to have been the target of the as-yet-unseen aliens' most recent attack. The planet had gone silent a month earlier, though no one could say with certainty whether the Roke were to blame or whether some cosmic catastrophe had occurred. Ever in need of increased funding, LAW had been working hard to persuade Periapt to accept the former explanation.

"In light of what happened on Iskra, I won't hold the Exts to their offer to throw in with me, Burning."

Burning raised himself to his full height. "So long as the terms haven't changed—Colonel."

His use of Haven's honorific rank among the Exts wasn't lost on her. "They haven't," she said firmly. "You have my word on that. I'll send all of you home to Concordance—or wherever you want to go—parole completed, after four subjective-years."

"From what you're telling us about LAW," Delecado said, "it sounds unlikely that a relief starship will arrive in ten years, let alone four or five."

"I won't lie to you, General. A ship might not come for twenty years. But in two years' time I expect to have my *own* starship wrapped around the zero-point-energy drive Starkweather will be leaving us. I have no intention of being marooned on Aquamarine with the key to a human-Roke peace in my hand."

Burning pivoted so that he and Delecado could exchange glances. "Ma'am, we just might have something that can keep Starkweather from sabotaging you," Delecado said. "Something we liberated from Iskra after we saw what we'd done to Swope and the others."

"What is it?"

"A superconducting explosive device," Burning supplied.

"Gives all appearances of having been overlooked for decades," Daddy D added.

Haven was clearly dumbfounded. "Talk about a bargaining chip . . . but you'd have to be able to get it aboard *Terrible Swift Sword* undetected—"

"Assuming LAW doesn't realize that the device is missing, we can do that by dismantling it and concealing the modules among our own equipment."

Haven made a plosive sound. "Allgrave, if LAW had even a suspicion, you would already have joined the *Scepter* crew."

CHAPTER
TWO

All Dextra's problems were natural consequences of accepting the GammaLAW mission. Even the announcement naming Starkweather commissioner of the AlphaLAW mission to Hierophant hadn't caught her entirely by surprise. Starkweather was one of Hierarch Cal Lightner's flunkies, and for the whole month after the Lyceum had offered her Aquamarine, Dextra had been tensed for just such a rabbit punch from the head of the opposition party.

After signing off with the Exts, she had gone directly to her study in HauteFlash and slumped into the varimorph executive chair that sat behind her antique desk. She had been less than frank with the Exts regarding the tragic fuckup at Iskra, and it had taken a good deal of energy to sustain the charade—energy she didn't have to spare now. She had lied to them both about Claude Mason's reaction to the deaths of his teammates and about where she had obtained the intel data about the detention facility. In fact, the commander by default of the Aquamarine survey mission had gone synap-shit over the news. The intelligence on Iskra had come to her not through political allies in the Lyceum or moles placed within LAW or Cal Lightner's Preservationist Party but from Dextra's anonymous contact, Yatt, in the Quantum College.

While still wary about bringing the Exts to Aquamarine as her personal guard, she couldn't assume that they would not abandon her if they were apprised of the full truth. Thus, she had lied. Tonii, Dextra's engeneered bodyguard, had argued against deception, but not persuasively enough. Besides, Dextra had had her fill of lectures about the Concordancers. She already had far too many bytes of data to absorb in detail. She only wished she could rest easier with what the data implied.

Any motivational tech probably could have predicted it: For every idealist-hero Ext who had surrendered on Concordance to AlphaLAW Commissioner Renquald, there were five or ten misfits, psychos, dead-enders, and would-be suicides. Left on Periapt without Dextra's protection, the Exts would certainly be eliminated by LAW—with Cal Lightner's blessing.

She had been left to conclude on her own the more intriguing things about the Exts. They dreaded any insufficiency of character that might hurl them down into poverty, the isolation of failure, and a death less painful than that which they had been trained to endure. They also feared success, because affluence and ease might well rob them of the strength and discipline on which their group survival depended. Anathema to them was the fear of becoming soft in the manner of their Concordance cohabitors—or in the manner of Periapts—and surrendering the things that made them Exts, including the fire to strive. Perhaps the Exts would not be too pleased with the way in which Dextra had chosen to save them, but there was no therapy for that.

Yatt had done as much as she had to save the Exts from an earlier attempt at eradication by Cal Lightner's Preservationist cabal. By involving Dextra in that rescue, the voice of the underground Quantum College had thwarted intended attacks on her reputation in the Lyceum as well. It was largely through her crusade for humanitarian treatment of legally annexed populations that the Exts had been shipped to Periapt to begin with.

Since then Yatt had been working behind the scenes to assist with funding for the GammaLAW mission by tweaking public opinion, apprising her of the opposition's plans, and who knew what else. If the tragedy at Iskra had proved anything, it was that Yatt—and by extension the Quantum College—was neither omniscient nor infallible.

The campaigns for funding and public support were only part of the war Dextra had been waging. The costliest battle thus far had been fought over her demand that the *Terrible Swift Sword* equip her mission with not only a zero-point-energy drive but the materials and components for the construction of a starship in Aquamarine space. The purpose of the vessel wouldn't be to extend the annexation process to worlds close to Aquamarine but instead to return people home—the Exts in particular.

Dextra got only the drive and initially decided that she had come out even in the fight. As compensation she had managed to extract additional concessions, one of which was Claude Mason.

Mason was either unable or unwilling to explain what had happened to him the night he had stolen out of HauteFlash, only to be returned to the villa hours later, dazed and incoherent, by Peace Warrantors. LAW's Cyber Security Division maintained that it had reasonable cause to prosecute Mason for interfacing with an artificial intelligence—a criminal act in the Post-Cyberplague era—though charges had yet to be brought against him.

The possibility of an illegal interface troubled Dextra—what AI had he been interfacing with and why? With LAW steadfastly refusing to cough up the rest of the *Scepter* team, she needed Mason for the mission—someone who not only had been to Aquamarine but had led the team after the planet's enigmatic living-sea life-form, the Oceanic, had obliterated the original captain and his command staff.

Going knee to groin with Cal Lightner over Mason had proved no easier than assuaging the concerns of Dextra's own Rationalist Party peers, however. The jockeying to replace her as party chairperson had been vicious, though it had been obvious from the start that Dextra's endorsement of Tilman Hobbes would probably decide the matter.

Ordering the varimorph chair to straighten somewhat, Dextra voiced her study telecomm to locate Hobbes, and in moments she was gazing at Hobbes's holo.

She got right to the point. "Tilman, I'm calling to say that you'll have my endorsement, but there are things I want in return."

"Your pound of flesh, eh, Dextra?" Hobbes said.

She grinned pleasantly. "Pound of flesh? You're mistaken, Tilman. You see, I want the entire organ bank." He did some ranting before she got in her next sentence. "For starters, have you seen to getting the Aggregate released?"

Hobbes nodded glumly. "It took some doing, but LAW's

interrogators didn't get much out of them regarding that Byron Sarz nonsense at the Lyceum ball. I can't imagine what you want with them."

"I'm hoping they'll be able to strike up a conversation with Aquamarine's Oceanic—assuming they can still function without Sarz."

Hobbes shrugged disinterestedly. "More and more it begins to look like Sarz wasn't the victim the media initially painted him to be. The bioassembler that almost gassed the Empyraeum apparently showed no evidence of a cybervirus infection."

"I could have told Cyber Security that much," Dextra said. "Do they have any notion of what Sarz was hoping to gain by fomenting a riot?"

"If they do, it isn't the result of any information supplied by the surviving members of the Aggregate. They simply followed his dictates without asking questions." Hobbes snorted. "I suppose we shouldn't look a gift horse in the mouth, though. Whatever Sarz's purpose, the evening went to the Exts for identifying the precursor odor and shutting down the bioassembler—harmless or not."

"I'm not complaining," Dextra replied, "although I do find it perplexing."

"As I do these requests you're making for funding."

Dextra folded her arms across her ample chest. "Tilman, if the purse strings for my mission are going to remain shut at one end, I mean to slit the bottom open. Don't let the requests concern you too much—no one's even going to feel them."

Hobbes had run down enough to listen. "What are you trying to sell me?"

She slipped an info-wafer into the communications systemry and brought up a montage of data. "As you can see, I've discovered a few interesting loopholes. Here, for example . . ."

His eyes widened as he read. "That's misappropriation of funds!"

"I disagree. It's a budget line for Propagation of Arts and Crafts to the Outworlds. Show me where it says I can't make use of this stipend to bring along a painter who's also, say, a hydraulic engineer."

Hobbes switched tactics, pointing to another display. "But this—you can't pressgang people! It's slavery!"

"No one is pressganging anybody," she said tightly. "The rehab guidelines are quite legal. Anyway, before I accept any convicted criminals as mission personnel, they'll be thoroughly screened."

In the way she had managed to secure the Exts cost-free under Title 23 of the Annexed Worlds Resources Utilization Bill, she had come up with hundreds of additional personnel slots for the GammaLAW mission by taking full advantage of the Interworld Student Exchange Program, the Interdisciplinary Outreach Grants, and her personal favorite, the Milk Fund.

Not everyone had had to be conscripted into service, though. Feverish to put his Pitfall ocean-sampling device to the test on Aquamarine's single sea—the Amnion—Raoul Zinsser had volunteered. Dextra was well aware that Zinsser, having gotten himself in trouble a couple of years back with a family that had since added one of its members to the Hicrarchate, was eager to leave Periapt for a time. Then there were Chaz Quant, who couldn't bear to part with the *Matsya*, the trimaran that was to serve as Dextra's floating HQ on Aquamarine, and Surgeon General Glorianna Theiss, who knew more about public health and emerging societies than anyone on Periapt.

The volunteers and conscripts wouldn't bring the Gamma-LAW personnel level anywhere near that of a BetaLAW mission, but they were enough to assure Dextra that she had at least a fighting chance of coping with whatever Aquamarine could throw at her.

She exchanged chilly good-byes with Hobbes and sank into the varimorph chair again. With less than two weeks to launch, things were finally beginning to gel. The painful parts would be saved for last: the farewells to Tonii and the entire household staff. As expected, Ben, her longtime secretary, had declined the mission early on. Ben's wife was as dedicated to her enormous extended family as Ben was to their classical one-partner marriage, and so Dextra would have turned him down even if he had volunteered. It salved her conscience somewhat to know that various Hierarchs were already in a bidding war for his services.

Maripol, however, had emerged as an unexpected problem. Since she had been a staff member for only a few months, it was odd that the au pair should even ask to go to Aquamarine. In thinking it over, Dextra had realized that Maripol's motivation was none other than Lod, Burning's cousin and the acting liaison officer between Dextra and the Exts. The little weasel had obviously been hitting on Maripol beneath HauteFlash's very roof.

Because he was the Ext most underfoot, Dextra had learned a good deal more about him than she had about Burning, Ghost, or any of the four hundred and some others. Lod had been almost embarrassingly forthcoming in discussing his upbringing and sometimes offensively so in discussing his amorous inclinations. Dextra saw right away that he had been trying to shock her.

Lod had come from an impoverished and distant branch of Burning's own Bastion Orman. Handicapped by his diminutive size in a milieu where strength and deeds counted for so much, he had immediately set out to change the odds in his favor. As a page boy in the house of Burning's titled uncle, Lod had employed one strategy after another to defer his ascendancy to cadethood. He understood early that commercial strife and feats of arms weren't going to be his battlegrounds, and so he had sought his rewards among the elegant, perfumed, and somewhat bored ladies of the Ext courts. They in turn had apparently taught him more about sex than most Exts learned until their coming of age.

All that notwithstanding, he had abused his position as liaison by setting his sights on Maripol, and Dextra was determined to intervene before the au pair had her heart broken, or Lod his head, by Tonii or whomever Dextra would sic on him.

She contemplated various ways of steering him away from Maripol and about various women she might present to him as new targets. Then, in the middle of a passing thought about the Aggregate, the solution to both aspects of the dilemma presented itself. She would dispatch Lod to apprise the Aggregate of the terms of their release from incarceration. The Aggregate's leader, a sad little thing named Piper, wasn't the sort who typically caught Lod's eye, but that in itself might be sufficient to tempt him. And Dextra suspected that any campaign to conquer her would be long and hard fought.

"You knew all along about Iskra's fail-safes, you fucking piece of cybercrap!" Claude Mason seethed while tears streamed down his perfect face. "You wanted them dead! You couldn't risk anyone mucking up your plans for Aquamarine!"

"You have misperceived the events," Yatt sent calmly to Mason's inner ear. *"We blundered in not detecting the presence of Iskra's fail-safe devices. The truth of it is, we erred. Regrettably, collateral consequences can't always be foreseen—even by us."*

Mason ran the palm of his right hand under his eyes. "You said the same thing when Byron Sarz died. At least then you had the mettle to admit that his cybernetic research was bringing him too close to detecting you."

"Mason, try to understand what we're telling you. We have a limited ability to arrange for certain events to occur. We are capable of exerting influence here and there. The moment humans are added to the equation, the results become unpredictable. After your experiences on Aquamarine, you should know this better than anyone."

Mason's mouth twisted into a sneer. "You brag that you're the pinnacle of AI creation—their brilliant spawn, if you don't count the Cyberplagues. And this is your response to the deaths of my friends and teammates."

Mason was at his home in Abraxas, which had been all but empty since the departure of the members of his menage-marriage—his several—years earlier, while the *Scepter* was still in transit from Aquamarine. To an observer it would appear that he was having a conversation with himself in the way schizophrenics conversed with their private demons. In fact Yatt was nothing more than an assemblage of ones and zeros that had been downloaded into Mason's brain, a personality construct of an AI-created program that resided covertly among the vast data of Periapt's TechPlex.

"Maybe I need to rethink my decision to convey you to Aquamarine," Mason continued. "If the planet's really harboring some sort of panacea for the Cyberplagues, maybe I'll be better off tracking it down by myself. Maybe *everyone* will be better off."

"Mason," Yatt sent more firmly, *"we've fulfilled our part of the bargain. We made certain that you were included in Haven's roster of mission personnel. Now you must fulfill your part."*

Mason sniffed. "What proof do I have that you had anything to do with Haven's recruiting me? I've *been* to Aquamarine. Who else would she ask?"

"We're willing to grant as much. But rest assured, Mason, that LAW and the Preservationists have their reasons for keeping you here on Periapt as a means of weakening Haven. After all, what if her hunches about the Oceanic are correct? What if Aquamarine should provide a means to an accord between humanity and the alien race you've chosen to call the Roke? LAW can scarcely afford such developments. LAW would be left without a war, and the Preservationists would be forced to acknowledge that humanity enjoys no special place in the universe.

"Believe what you will, Mason, but only through our efforts were you included in Haven's mission. Operating under the guise of the Quantum College, we exerted pressure where necessary on key people who advise both LAW and Lightner."

Mason considered it. "If you're so adept at exerting pressure, why is Haven stuck with a GammaLAW mission? She doesn't even have her own LAW forces, let alone a starship. She has to make do with the Exts, for God's sake, and a zero-point-energy drive without the means of constructing a ship."

Yatt took a long moment to respond. *"Your failure to see the whole picture disappoints us, Mason. All along we have arranged the underfunding of the mission. We took steps to ensure that it wouldn't expand into an Alpha or a Beta, and on numerous fronts we've had to sabotage Haven's efforts to make that happen."*

Mason shook his head in bewilderment. "Why would you deliberately sabotage the only person who can get you to Aquamarine?"

"Simply this, Mason: because LAW's larger expeditions devote so much effort, technology, and resources to antivirus and AI filtration measures. A GammaLAW has neither the time

nor the budget for much of that, and so we assure ourselves of being able to stow away in far greater safety."

Mason laughed through his tears. "You're already stowing away in *me*, you dimwitted machine! Unless I'm brought up on charges of headboarding and they brain-wipe me, you've got nothing to fear."

If a program was capable of sighing, Yatt did. *"Mason, what we downloaded into you is a millionth of what we are. But we mean to change that. You must return to the place where we met—to the warehouse in the industrial heart of Abraxas. There we will guide you to a memory module, which you will transfer into the Matsya's computer banks as soon as she's afloat on the lakes and rivers of Aquamarine. The vast parts of us contained in the module will be brought to bear in our search for the origin of the Cyberplagues and their AI-authored cure, Endgame."*

"And if I refuse?" Mason asked.

"You need not fear any physical or psychic danger from us, Mason. You will be cleansed of us, and you will simply go on as before—save for one repercussion. You will be denied the joy of reuniting with the wife and child you abandoned on Aquamarine, for we will do whatever is necessary to exempt you from ever setting foot on that far-flung world."

CHAPTER THREE

"Don't allow yourself to die," Piper told the Aggregate constituent named Brio. "If you do, you'll be alone—forever."

She pulled at the youth's frail arm, but he remained facedown and unmoving on his bunk. His Alltalk—the language of his body and his odors—made it clear that he didn't care what she had to say. As far as Brio was concerned, the Aggregate was already dead. Gazing around at their surroundings, Piper wondered if he was right.

The LAW hospital certainly wasn't Habitat, where Byron Sarz's score of constituents had slowly grown into the group consciousness known as the Aggregate. But at least the constituents were together despite the crimes of which they had been accused.

Piper had expected her fellow constituents to kill her as soon as they could for what had happened to Byron at the Lyceum ball—for what she had *made* happen to Byron. Instead, they had become entirely dependent on her for support and direction. Perhaps it was because, as Byron's former mistress, she was so adept at mimicking his words and scenttalk, or perhaps it was nothing more than a consequence of the relentless interrogating the constituents had undergone by Alone intelligence officers and psychometricians. Whatever the cause, she had found herself thrust into the gap Byron's death had created. She was the soul of the Aggregate now—its nexus—and it was a changing Aggregate.

The self-terminations that had commenced the day after they had been moved onto the ward were the greatest challenge to her leadership. Already she'd had to stand helplessly by while two constituents ended their lives. If Brio, too, opted to shun life, she doubted that she would have the strength to go on.

She let go of Brio's pale hand and let her feet carry her toward the meds station. The Alones had learned not to interfere in Aggregate crises—they inevitably did more harm than good—but what choice did she have but to seek their counsel when her own resources continued to fail her?

As she neared the station, she sensed the presence of an Alone who didn't belong on the locked ward—one she knew by his scent even before she turned the corner and saw him. It was the small blond Alone called Lod, whom Byron himself had tried to kill at the Lyceum ball.

"I don't care whose authorization you need," he was telling the ward supervisor. "This is a Hierarchy writ from Tilman Hobbes himself, vice chairman of the Rationalist Party, and *his* authorization is all I need to carry out my orders. Now, either you fetch Piper like a cooperative lad or I put in a commo to the Hierarchate—"

Lod stopped talking when he realized that the supervisor was staring at something behind his back. Pivoting slowly, he saw Piper, smiled broadly, and began to hurry toward her.

Piper stared uncomprehendingly at the bizarre kinesign that was his bow. She felt his probing gaze rove across her face when he straightened, and she read something close to carnality in him.

"Mistress Constituent," Lod said, "I've come to convey Hierarch Haven's remorse for all that the Aggregate has been made to suffer at the hands of LAW. She did what she could to prevent the intrusions, but they were unavoidable in the aftermath of the actions your late leader took. Hierarch Haven wishes you to know that while she can't undo what's happened, she is now in a position to offer deliverance of sorts."

Concepts of freedom, incarceration, and enforced service were lost on Piper, but she understood enough of what Lod was telling her. "We'll be allowed to return to Habitat? There, I think, we will be able to heal ourselves."

Transparently troubled, Lod touched his chin. "Not exactly— though there'd be nothing to prevent you from fashioning a *new* Habitat."

"Where does Hierarch Haven mean to bring us?"

Lod cleared his throat in a meaningful way. "To Aquamarine. The Aggregate will have to agree to become part of Hierarch Haven's GammaLAW mission to that world."

"For what purpose?"

"To answer you honestly, I'm not sure. But would leaving this place be so terrible—Piper?"

Something about the way he said her name suggested a curious intimacy, but without a word she turned and walked off. She was aware that he was following her as she went in among the Aggregate members, though his hearing wasn't capable of detecting more than a few of the brief murmurs she sent to the constituents. Hence, his puzzled look and kinesigns when everyone matter-of-factly began to gather up his or her meager belongings.

Piper felt Lod's eyes return to her as she stood over Brio to advise him wordlessly of Hierarch Haven's offer. Brio heard her out, then rolled over and set his feet on the floor.

Piper loosed a relieved sigh. With Brio's change of heart, the suicides would end.

Ghost grunted as she took hold of the Aquam sling-gun Burning handed her. "I thought this thing was made of wood," she said, repositioning the rifle so that she could also accept a hip-quiver assortment of darts, quarrels, and bolts.

"*Mostly* wood," Burning told her. "This stuff is as dense as teak or ironpine—it won't even float. But other Aquam woods have other characteristics."

"Just as well for the indigs," Zone remarked, "since they ain't got much in the way of metals."

Along with General Delecado, the three were walking downhill to Miseria Isle's practice range, where some of the Exts had already removed the regular target butts and replaced them with torso silhouettes. The range had a full holographic target system, but Burning had decided that it would have been only a distraction. Part of his purpose in test firing the weapons was to *see* what they could do.

Shooting benches were set up at a modest twenty-five meters

or so; the Exts were there for a bit of informal familiarization fire, not earnest target practice.

Burning, Ghost, and Zone began laying out the guns and pistols, along with an assortment of exotic ammunition. Burning saw that the gathered Exts couldn't be happier. Anything less would have had them thinking of themselves as pretend soldiers.

Zone immediately took up one of the sling-guns with a stock more contoured than any assault rifle's. It put Burning in mind of some thin-necked musical instrument of Terran antiquity.

Still, Daddy D groused. "Couldn't you have asked liaison for something a little less clumsy?"

"We were lucky to get these," Burning said, arranging the ammo. "Most of the sample weapons Mason's team brought back were appropriated by military or intel agencies."

"Or found their way into private collections," Ghost suggested. "*I* don't think they're clumsy. I think they're rather elegant."

Zone kept a mildly vexed silence. Where Ghost's handling of her weapon was almost like a caress, his strong hands looked like appendages of the rifle itself.

Hand-carved from clawroot wood the color of oxblood leather, the weapon Zone selected had been artfully varnished and polished to a finish as glassy as acrylic, though it was worn by use around the handgrip and forestock.

Some of the tiny bits of glittering stone in Ghost's gun were missing now, and the totem figures that had been painted on for luck were faded. Burning couldn't make much sense of the motifs in any case. Upper and lower sling swivels were decked with the bright, lacy-looking "feathers" of creatures that passed for Aquamarine birds—creatures the Oceanic had apparently kept from evolving into true long-distance fliers. The carrying sling was made of intricately tooled leather, depicting a kind of totem stack of quarry or targets; some were human, while others might be animals.

But that wasn't the sling that gave the sling-gun its name.

Zone decided to load up with a stone pellet of basaltic-looking rock a little bigger than a marble, the simplest of the assorted rounds. He dropped it through the rifle's loading gate, seating it in the nock that lay near the muzzle of the grooved barrel. He carefully squeezed the graceful twine-bound serif of a lever that was mounted on the underside of the stock.

Curious about the bizarre operation of the guns, Burning was paying close attention. Along either side of the open-top barrel groove sat two elongated wads of lusterless striated material. The twin masses were bent back on themselves because the nock to which they were attached was latched under the loading gate at the muzzle. The nock also was affixed to a single long strand of grayish stuff, which, he could see, shone with a viscous, gelid coating.

As Zone primed the serif lever, the strand stirred and contracted back toward the stock of the weapon, haltingly at first and then a little more quickly as Zone gave the lever an additional pump. Drawing with the nock, the elastic wads mounted on the sides of the barrel stretched taut. A wooden click signaled that the rifle was fully cocked.

"Slow," Zone mused. "Probably dying. In fact, it's a wonder it's not dead already."

Daddy D frowned. "Allgrave, you sure these things have been vetted through the decontamination people?"

Burning pondered the excised rope of contracted Aquam muscle tissue in the stock of the rifle. Ruthlessly excised from some hapless land mollusk, the muscle had been grafted to the gun, kept unnaturally alive, and enslaved to a task dumber than any beast of burden's, only to come to its end on Periapt, trillions of kilometers from its home.

Zone had turned the weapon up and was resting the fluidly incurved buttstock on his thigh. Fine cords of muscle stood out in his forearm as he held the rifle erect with one hand, pointing out the little patch lock just forward of the priming lever and behind the trigger.

"This here's what makes it go."

"A galvani stone," Ghost supplied. "From an Aquam polar island called the Scourlands."

Burning was nodding, " 'Signore Galvani,' they still call them. One of a whole class of organic piezoelectric gemstones. These grow only in the gut of some shell thing indigenous to the Scourlands."

Zone shook his head in wonderment.

"Signore Galvani also applies to the trade ecology," Daddy D added, "and to the balance of economic power. Big slice of the pie in figuring out how the Aquam economic system works."

"Yeah, well, without them the gun's dead," Zone remarked. "You might as well use a crossbow or just lob a spear."

Burning glanced at him. "Mason's team claimed that the Aquam have rapid-fire crossbows as well—not too different from the *chu-ho-nu* the old-time Chinese used to kill mammoths. And straight bows and spears and slingshots and a bunch of other things. But sling-guns have become the weapon of choice by far."

"There must be some gunpowder weapons," Ghost said.

Burning shook his head. "There's no accessible sulfur, or at least not enough of it. The survey team's findings indicate that the Optimants used up a *lot* of it, and what little's left on the populated landmasses is impossible to mine with primitive technology. Some of the out-island tribes might have a couple of old flintlocks, but none of the surviving flying pavilions stop at those islands, and there's no safe way across the water unless you want to risk being turned inside out by the Oceanic."

Burning's own words astonished him. Aquamarine was the first culture LAW had contacted where gunpowder technology had been lost. Even in the wreckage left by the Cyberplagues, he would have thought that *someone* would have rediscovered the formula for gunpowder.

For a moment he allowed his fancies free rein, thinking of the meager landmasses that dotted the water face of Aquamarine, thinking of the tenuous webwork of transport and shipping maintained by the preposterous, airborne relic-automatons that were the flying pavilions, thinking of the Oceanic . . . It was as if something had decided that human beings should be *quarantined* from the ages-old source of so much of their power.

"Plenty of power," Zone was saying of the sling-gun. "But that's almost beside the point. Quick, almost effortless reload—that's what makes this puppy bark."

To prove it, he threw the long gun to his shoulder. He made the movement look precise and coordinated, though Burning could see that it took a lot of brute strength to wrestle the thing around.

Zone's forefinger eased the trigger, and the nock released. No longer actuated by the galvani stone, the excised muscle in the stock simply went along for the ride as the twin strands of elastic, latexlike plant gum—the slings—contracted with a violent slap.

Burning had half expected to be able to follow the flight of the projectile. But the snap of the release and the loud *whack* of the deadly marble were almost one. The rifle didn't appear to have a terrible kick, though with Zone firing, it was difficult to tell. A dark circle had appeared in the ten ring of one of the silhouettes, above the sternum.

Burning was about to comment on the accuracy when Zone grounded the sling-gun's butt, flipped open the loading gate, and fed in a second round of another variety. Pumping the priming lever once or twice, he brought the weapon to his shoulder once more. The sound of the second discharge was unlike the first and came with a tinkling of broken glass.

"Mason said that an experienced shooter can get off ten rounds a minute or better," Zone remarked. Lowering the weapon, he began to sort through other Aquam rounds: mushroom-shaped knockout loads, wickedly barbed darts, razor-edged broadhead bolts, and more.

Ghost meanwhile was idly fingering some kind of grapeshot round, a package of needles bound up in a waxy blue-green leaf. "It'll be interesting to make contact with the nomad group that controls the trade in galvani stones," she started to say, when Burning gingerly took the round from her.

"These are envenomed with some homemade neurotoxin," he explained, setting the round aside. "Anyway, the nomads you're talking about are called the Ferals. No one else will risk going out onto the Scourlands. If poachers try to procure stones, the Ferals rejoice in hunting them down and torturing them to death."

Zone sneered. "So much the better for us. Most of Aquamarine wants piezoelectric stones, and the Ferals want mandseng. We can make use of that situation."

Mandseng was a hybrid plant developed almost as a curiosity

by the Optimants before the Plagues had razed their high-tech civilization. Perversely resistant to organized cultivation, seemingly sadistic in its insistence on growing where and when it pleased, and capable of editing and repairing errors in DNA transcription, the plant was held to be an irreplaceable treasure on a world that harbored a tremendous array of unavoidable mutagens.

"First thing we could do is take control of the galvani stone trade at its choke point," Zone mused. "Then—if they're really the only transportation between the Scourlands and other landmasses—we either regulate or disable these flying pavilion things. We replace the galvani stones with piezoelectric ceramic foam we can make for next to nothing, we introduce antimutagen treatments that are more effective than the mandseng or any of the other voodoo the locals use, and *presto*—Aquamarine's ours."

Zone said it a bit too casually, but Burning pretended not to notice even though Zone was right about using the stones and mandseng to play one group of Aquam against the other.

Zone cut his eyes to Burning and laughed nastily. "The mandseng—that's where Haven's really got the Aquam by the short hairs, isn't it, Allgrave? She promises them an end to Anathemite births so long as they agree to be ruled by LAW." He shook his head in self-amusement. "Fuckin' indigs'll be running all over each other for those treatments."

He loaded another round into the sling-gun and fired, acing the ten ring, though without penetrating the target. Instead, a smoking haze began to rise off a dark stain on the disintegrating composite of the silhouette.

"Acid rounds," Zone said, clearly impressed.

CHAPTER
FOUR

Dextra was pleased with the occupation plan she had formulated for Aquamarine. It obviated the need for weapons, conquest, or violence of the sort LAW had exercised on countless worlds. Indeed, by offering the Aquam alternatives to mandseng and galvani stones, she would be doing the planet a great service. And the puppet government she would put into place would negate the harm the Aquam were doing to themselves day in and day out. Tonii, however, was like an accusatory conscience. Her "parenting" by a bioengeneering R&D program and her early life in a LAW creche had made 'erm an unswerving enemy of coercive, institutional, or authoritarian policy.

"If I'm to accomplish the mission without weapons, I've no choice but to upset the existing trade system and establish a lock on the antimutagen processes," Dextra was telling the gynander in the pleasant shade afforded by HauteFlash's garden gazebo. "Of course, if I could persuade you to come with me, I'd have you there to make certain the takeover is effected as benignly and fairly as possible. You know that I'll second your full authority to—"

"No," Tonii said flatly. "I'm enough of a freak *here*, Dex. On Aquamarine I'd be a monster—the definitive Anathemite. They take aberrations like me and expose them on hillsides or fling them into fires or sacrifice them on altars in the hope of appeasing the Oceanic."

Dextra put a hand on Tonii's smooth, sinewy shoulder. "But as a LAW mission member you'd be protected. Trust me. No Aquam would dare—"

Although 'e had always been elaborately gentle with her,

Tonii suddenly shook off Dextra's hand. "What I can't trust is my own temper. Imagine, Dex, that you're in negotiations with one of the local potentates, and he orders his newborn Anathemite daughter thrown into the river, and I execute him. That wouldn't be very good for your mission, would it?"

Dextra inclined her head somewhat. "No, Tones, it wouldn't." She watched various expressions cross the gynander's face— protective brother, younger sister, exasperated sometime lover— then said, "Suppose we talk about the briefing data on the Exts."

Tonii grew businesslike. "I've gone through all the files. Who first?"

Dextra passed on Burning, Delecado, Lod, and Ghost; the files on them were exhaustive, and she felt that she already knew more than she needed to know. "Zone," she said.

Tonii nodded knowingly. "I was wondering if you'd detected something there. The Aggregate's olfactory abilities have nothing on yours! Yes, he's potentially a major liability. Possibly a source of danger."

Dextra wasn't surprised. Bearing out some of the comments made by LAW analysts, she herself had concerns about the man, based mostly on her fractured recollections of the Exts' skirmish with a squad of Manipulants onboard the *Sword of Damocles.* "Isn't he Burning's most skilled fighter?"

"Yes—and not solely for his combat skills. He possesses strong Flowstate, ruthless leadership abilities, and a relentless predation drive. Infinitely suspicious, Zone is always hungry for a fight."

"That I could see. What's the backstory on him?"

Tonii's eyes focused on something 'e had spied in the garden, then returned to Dextra. "You have to take into account the whole social range of the mishmash that makes up the interlocking Ext communities," 'e began. "Zone was somewhere out on the edge of a wilderness clan. His birth name doesn't matter really, because his field name is the one everybody knows. A poor boy, almost a Feral himself. Mother dead, father an abusive addict. Med evaluations say that he has scars from the beatings, scaldings, and brandings.

"Early on, after a stint as a Wheel Weevil groom, he lived on his own in the outback of the Broken Country. At some point he probably returned home to kill his father, though he was never charged with the crime and there were those who wanted to reward him with a medal. But the key point is that he wins, or at least as much as you could say that about any Ext."

"Anything on the current members of his several?" Dextra asked.

"Rather standard menage-marriage, except that in Zone's case his several is composed of his inner cadre of enforcers, bodyguards, henchpeople—call them what you will. Bear in mind that membership means perks and improves the chances for survival."

"But can Burning maintain authority?" Dextra wanted to hear from Tonii's instincts as much as from 'ers logic.

"As long as you continue to support him. The Exts are used to unifying under an Allgrave, and their current Allgrave answers to you. They'll understand that they haven't the slightest chance of seeing home again if they cross Burning."

Dextra absorbed it in silence. There was too much riding on the GammaLAW mission to risk some maverick's fouling up. *Nothing* must go wrong. Which brought her to Chaz Quant, now captain of the *Matsya*. She knew all about the events that had led to his demotion some years earlier, when—as a hovercraft assault captain on the *McMurdo Sound*—he'd opted to rescue two SEAL teams instead of a frozen batch of vitroed VIP fetuses. But she was still curious about Quant's problem with Tonii, even though it wouldn't pertain to the mission.

"Tones," she said, "the cold shoulder you've been getting from Chaz Quant . . . It's been disturbing my organizational *wa*. Even if you won't be coming with us, I'd prefer that you two not act like Muslims and Christians nursing a grudge about Jerusalem."

Tonii betrayed no emotion. "We're not, Dex. I told you when we first met him that he's a fine officer, certainly the best you could have procured for GammaLAW. Honestly, you're lucky to have him."

Dextra narrowed her eyes. "Come on, Tones. I know there was some kind of family tragedy or accident early in his life.

But even after all these years the navy and LAW scientific security have a titanium lid over the details."

Tonii tilted back 'ers head, eyes closed. "Thirty years before Byron Sarz created me, Quant's parents were donor-hosts in the New Line Project."

The first gynander experiments, the New Line Project was one of many eugenics and genetic-engineering research programs that had been revved high when the Roke Conflict had heated up.

" 'Genoameliorates,' the children were called back then," Tonii said, struggling to make it sound like a rote recitation. "Raised by families from whom some of their plasm was drawn. The idea was to mitigate the profound behavioral and developmental dysfunctions to which the earliest artifact progeny were prone.

"The Quant family was prime genetic material, featuring a long line of achievers and a constellation of desirable traits. Quant's parents were glad to contribute to what they'd been told was the next step forward for the human race. But something went catastrophically wrong in spite of Sarz's close monitoring and support services. Quant's younger, genoameliorate sibling, Anu, slaughtered both parents, a younger sister, Anu's own designer-mentor, and, very nearly, Quant himself."

Tonii paused briefly. "Quant spent a year in psychological rehab. Afterward, an aunt who was a truly fine sailor took him to sea for the first time. Something about the experience worked for him, and he has followed the sea ever since." The gynander swung to face Dextra. "This is nothing official, Dex, but you hear things along the engeneering grapevine, and the word is that Quant has no tolerance for *any* of Byron Sarz's brood."

Dextra folded her arms. "Are you suggesting that I have to keep him away from the Aggregate as well?"

Tonii nodded 'ers head. "And from any Manipulant and quite possibly from any Aquam Anathemite. You see, among other things, Anu was 'born' with a tricameral brain."

"No tolerance for the disabled from Captain Quant," Dextra mused.

Tonii shrugged. "What he really can't get past is the fact that Anu was a hermaphrodite."

* * *

"If somebody doesn't get killed, it'll be a miracle," retired Admiral Valentin Maksheyeva told Chaz Quant, offering his former student another swig from his handmade hip flask.

But by then Quant was too preoccupied to accept. All his attention was riveted on the imminent tetherlift operation of the SWATHship SST *Matsya*, which he was monitoring both through close-up projections on his helmet visor and through the viewpane of the patrol VTOL he and Mach-1 shared, along with reps from LAW and the Periapt navy.

"Biggest cargo lift ever, from what I hear," Maksheyeva went on. "The old girl exits Periapt in a blaze of glory!"

SWATH SST was an acronym for Small Waterplane-Area, Tri-Hulled, Semisubmerged Trimaran. By design, shock waves created by her bulbous bow were damped by funneling wave trains at opposite angles between the main hull and her two outrigger sponsons hulls. It canceled hydrodynamic energy that would otherwise have buffeted the vessel, increased drag, and cut into the efficiency of her actuator disk propellers.

Among the hasty modifications made to the ship, Quant—with Mach-1's help—had been granted a number of seemingly archaic add-ons, including Turret *Musashi*. Until recently, the big-gun mount had stood outside the entrance to Abraxas's naval museum, in which Maksheyeva served as curator. Particle beams and missiles aside, Quant still believed that a certain amount of political power grew best out of a cannon. However, there had been only time enough to prepare a barbette for the turret on the *Matsya*'s aft main hull. The twin 240-mm rifles and their turret were going to have to travel detached onboard the *Terrible Swift Sword* and be mounted on arrival at Aquamarine.

Quant was contemplating the extent of the task when Mach-1 yelled, "Here it comes, Chaz! Here comes the hook!"

Quant flipped up his visor and spotted it immediately, though it was still over fifty kilometers out across the open sea. The immense alloy hook was almost rendered insignificant by the size of the OTV tower reaching down from space itself.

Quant caught his breath as a civilian VIP in the rear compartment of the VTOL shouted, "They're off course! They're off course!" But it was the observer himself who was off course. There was plenty of time left to line up the shot. Fortunately, there was plenty of time left for Quant to get used to the idea of his ship spending the next couple of months in the belly of a deep-space fortress.

Aquamarine itself was responsible for the *Matsya*'s change of circumstance. Like Periapt, the planet lacked any appropriate landmass along its equatorial belt on which to anchor a more conventional space elevator, hence GammaLAW's need for skyhooks and orbital tether operations. With land at such a premium on Aquamarine and resources for basing and transport so strained, a LOGCOM study had recommended to Dextra Haven that she consider having the SWATHship tetherdropped into the extensive navigable freshwater systems of Aquamarine, where it could function as a highly mobile operations platform. Stable and versatile, the *Matsya* was driven by conventional turboblades rather than by superconduction magnetohydrodynamics, which operated less efficiently in nonsaline environments.

Still, Haven's call inviting him to serve as captain had nearly toppled him from his chair and was continuing to reorder his entire life. Just the previous evening Quant's former academy peers and comrades had gathered under the window of his quarters on the naval base for a ritual he'd never thought he would be accorded: a song to celebrate his reascension to captaincy—a kind of bon voyage. It was all too new for him to encompass mentally. Whereas as XO on the *Matsya* he'd had to play Captain Hall's sonuvabitch, he was suddenly his own man again and could practice greater compassion for his subordinates. Not that he'd become a bleeding heart overnight, but many of those who had served under Hall were already showing signs of higher morale since the announcement of Quant's promotion despite the fact that life aboard the SWATHship had grown harder. A few of his former shipmates—Petty Officer "Row-Row" Roiyarbeaux, Air Boss Germaine Bohdi, and Officer of the Deck Eddie "Jurassic" Gairaszhek, among others—had even put in for the GammaLAW mission.

Quant smoothed his prophet's beard as he studied the array of brute hoverlifters floating on station like fishermen hauling at lines. The sea was rough, and he didn't envy the air crews the job of maintaining the superstrong hawsers at a certain low tension. The *Matsya* rode a little fitfully in her net of unbreakable cable.

He'd have given anything to be on the bridge, but the logistics-command people from OTV ops had been adamant: only trained—and spacesuited—log-com personnel went along on a nonpressurized Orbital Transfer Vehicle lift, especially one as dangerous as flinging the great SWATHship out into orbit.

That was how Quant thought of it, no matter what the OTV teams had to say about exactitude. Even so, if Dextra Haven were there, he'd have kissed her pretty recurve of a mouth.

The hook was visibly nearer now—at fifteen kilometers and closing. The hoverlifters were holding position, and the lifting tethers were spread in a circle a kilometer across. Quant's mouth was bone-dry; his ebony features were set. He had listened carefully to the reassuring words at the briefings, but even though he'd prepared himself, nothing could convince him in that moment that his ship wasn't doomed.

The hook passed into the hoisting loop cleanly, lined up for a perfect hoist. As it did, a swell lifted the SWATH unexpectedly just as the hoverlifters were slackening tension. The ship shifted inside her net. But the hook master pilot justified the briefing officers' boasts by easing off on the expansion joints and leaving slack in the hoist lines so that the *Matsya* had time to right herself in her immense cradle. The hook pilot continued to work the extension-joint brakes and some of the OTV boom retractor motors until the hook passed peri-peri, taking up slack, and the SWATHship was lifted from the sea. *Matsya* raised clear of the swells, shedding the last seawater she would feel for light-years.

The vessel rose into the sky, growing smaller and smaller against it and against the skeletal arm that was the skyhook boom. Quant followed her with his face pressed to the viewpane and was considering trying to climb into the VTOL's cockpit to keep her in view until Mach-1 clapped him on the knee in a display of acclamation.

They were still talking about it half an hour later as they walked away from the VTOL landing platform. They were headed for Quant's staff car when a uniformed person hurried into view. Quant stopped short, then glowered.

"Driver Elide, what the hell do you want here, and *what are you doing wearing that uniform?*" The airlimo driver, Elide, Quant had first met a month earlier, had rubbed him the wrong way from the start.

"I just wanted to let you know that I've enlisted, sir, and that I would consider it a great privilege if you would consider me for a position on the Aquamarine mission."

"Whatever you used, go sleep it off," Quant snarled, about to turn away.

"Sir, let me explain—please."

Kurt Elide was showing more animation than Quant had ever seen from him, though that wasn't saying much. "You have one minute."

"Sir, it may not show, but I've always wanted my life to count for something, and I think that the Aquamarine mission could provide me with a chance for that."

Quant stared at him for a few seconds. "I don't know anything about this. You should be talking to Dextra Haven."

"Sir, I realize that, sir. But if you could perhaps put in a good word . . ."

Quant looked to Maksheyeva, who was suppressing a grin. "You don't need my permission to apply for a slot, Elide. Besides, you have as much a pipeline to Haven as I have after the way you literally crashed the Lyceum ball."

"Sir, that was Tonii's doing. The gynander—"

"Enough!" A furious expression contorted Quant's craggy face. "Don't be bringing . . . it into this."

"Sir, I only meant—"

"And you're *still* not wearing a name tag," Quant interrupted. "When I see you again, Mister Elide, you'd better have one."

" 'When'?" Kurt said hopefully.

Quant and Maksheyeva turned and marched away.

CHAPTER
FIVE

Parked outside the Lyceum HQ in Dextra's airlimo, Tonii saw four gynanders descending the staircase that fronted the building's stately entrance. 'E considered ordering the limo's windows to darken, then thought better of it and climbed out of the vehicle. The quartet was a poignant reminder that however wistfully 'e regarded comradeship and unified purpose, 'e had in fact rejected the commonality of 'ers own kind.

Janus spotted 'erm immediately and waved. "Ton-ii! I can't believe it's you!"

Tonii didn't blame 'ers foster siblings for 'ers isolation. Misunderstanding, projected fears, and mistrust—attitudes Periapt society had done little to modify after the failure of Byron Sarz's grandiose experiment—had put tectonic pressures on the few survivors, and as a consequence, the fragile latticework of friendship and support among the gynanders had eroded. Aspirations to find accommodation in the monogender world or to break away and forge separate communities had driven them farther apart. Gynander society was a dead end until such time as the psychophysiological defects that plagued so many of Sarz's creations could be eliminated.

Early on Tonii had broken with the separatist hard-liners and had gladly accepted a position with Dextra, whom 'e had met at an intrasystem symposium on constitutional rights and gender specificity.

"Tonii, how wonderful to see you," Janus said as Tonii approached. "The timing couldn't be more perfect."

The others nodded in agreement, except for Mykee, who said, "Five of us in one place. Half our population—excluding

34

our brethren confined to hospices and prisons. But even so, here stands one-third of Byron's entire progeny."

"Assuming Franzis hasn't met 'ers fate piloting the new zero-point-energy testbed ship," Jo thought to point out. "Or that Kit hasn't been executed."

Watching them, Tonii was struck as always by the diverse shapes and aspects androgyny could take. Janus, for example— at twenty-seven baseline, the eldest and brightest among them— was long-nosed and soulful-eyed and just now was wearing a military-tailored everywear that successfully offset some of 'ers chunkiness.

Mykee, by contrast, was nearly the size of Burning Orman and was sporting a spiked and D-ringed black leather harness that showed off 'ers hyperdefined muscle and almost vestigial breasts. Arguably the strongest of the preternaturally powerful genblenders, Mykee had suffered the greatest abuse over the years and had developed 'ers own defenses.

"Tonii, we must have you back with us," Jo was saying. "We've just come from a meeting with some of the freshman Hierarchs, and they're almost certain that the New Line Project can be reopened."

"We could sure use your savvy," Dez added. "Even a smattering of what you've learned from working with Dextra Haven."

Jo had always put Tonii in mind of an Asiatic divinity student. Conservatively dressed and barbered, as lean and serene as a fasting initiate, Jo seemed even more slight and youthful next to Mykee's stacked sinew. Appearances, though, were not to be trusted. When wronged, Jo was by far the more dangerous foe. As for the dark-skinned Dez, 'e could have passed for a member of Chaz Quant's family. All four had been Tonii's lovers at some point, as they'd been one another's.

"Come back to us, Tonii," Mykee said harshly. "You've had your fling among the monogenders. Isn't it time for family again?"

"Truly, Tonii," Janus seconded. "With Haven leaving for Aquamarine, what else will there be for you among them?"

Tonii hadn't even considered the idea until that moment, and suddenly 'e was confused. "If I wanted to, I couldn't rejoin you until Hierarch Haven launches. She'll need me up until the final moment, and I owe her too much to simply walk out on her."

"Our chance may not be waiting for us a month from now," Janus persisted. "We could go on to our second generation."

Tonii shook 'ers head. "My answer has to be no for the time being."

"But the project—"

"The project's *over*," Tonii said, helpless in the face of 'ers frustration. "Periapt doesn't want more of our kind. Besides, it would be unconscionable to put another batch of kids through what we had to suffer—all in the hopeless cause of making the monos admit that they were wrong."

"Is that the gospel according to Haven?" Jo scoffed coolly.

"No, it's the nature of the world—as learned the hard way, *synthia*."

Jo's composure cracked at the word, and 'ers long, pale fingers hooked. Tonii was bracing for a claw swipe, when tremendous weights crashed onto 'ers shoulders.

It was Mykee, spinning Tonii around.

Most monos, with their slower reaction time and inferior coordination, would have lashed out blindly at the Herculean body without noticing the tears, silted with makeup, finding their way down from Mykee's eyes. Tonii let 'ersself be hugged up against the bunched muscles and the straps, managing to avoid the spikes. "We all miss you, Tones," Mykee murmured into Tonii's hair.

"I miss you, too, genfriend," Tonii said, pounding Mykee's rippling back. "But there are people relying on me and obligations I've promised to meet. Perhaps after the *Terrible Swift Sword* launches—"

Mykee pressed her forefinger to Tonii's lips. "Farewell, Tonii. That's all there is to say."

The mountainous task of organizing the GammaLAW mission was exactly the sort of challenge Dextra was accustomed to meeting head-on. There were snags, glitches, and adversity galore, but she had decades of experience and knew how to delegate.

Personal problems continued to be a different and more vexing issue. The worst of them was Honeysuckle. Dextra didn't mind taking risks, but bringing the baby along on a dangerous gamble like Aquamarine would be plain wrong.

That left the horrifying possibility that Synnergy, Dextra's most recent ex, would get her hands on Honeysuckle, the reassurances of Dextra's lawyers notwithstanding.

Lod had suggested several creative solutions. Since returning from springing the Aggregate, he had been throwing himself into the assignments she'd given him, often working around the clock. She concluded that taking on the world from the comfort of a big office wasn't exactly punishment to Lod and that he'd finally come to terms with the Aquamarine mission. There were his ties to his cousins and the other Exts, of course, and now perhaps an interest in the Aggregate nexus, Piper. His proposed remedies to the Synnergy quandary, however, left something to be desired. Dextra was disinclined to be indicted for a frame-up or be party to an assassination.

She was fast-forwarding through the many messages Ben had left for her when a resonant, vaguely taunting voice at the study door made her jump.

"Greetings, Mamissima."

She looked up, her face sharp and wide-eyed. "Blackie! Haven't I asked you to call before dropping in?"

Nearing thirty and by no means a delight unto his mother, Blackford Haven, Dextra's other child, was tricked out in some avant look that suggested a cross between a harem guard and a silver viper. His eyes were bloodshot, and she thought she could make out where cosmetics and a touch of bio-makeover had been used on dark pouches. Blackie was negligent in many areas of his life, but his vanity usually made him meticulous about his health and good looks.

"I know, I know," he said, discerning her thoughts. "But this couldn't wait."

Dextra presumed that he'd let himself in before the security lockdown but didn't ask. "What is it, Blackie? Financial trouble?"

He hesitated, the plunged. "Optivec Limited's in trouble. The next-gen superconducting units aren't meeting expectations."

"I'm sorry to hear that, but I warned you about going partners with that orifice Walker duPont." She stopped herself, not wanting to rub his face in it. "But be advised, I'm not in the best financial shape myself, darling. The GammaLAW mission is bleeding me dry."

Blackie was shaking his head impatiently. "I don't want your money—and I'm not just blowing bubbles through your archway, so don't make that face. D' you think begging for loans doesn't kill me? I want to make my own way."

How? Dextra wondered. He'd never so much as cooked a meal for himself, yet he'd tried to run a restaurant. He didn't suffer fools gladly, yet he'd tried his hand at operating a resort. He wouldn't know a good business opportunity if it came up and humped his leg, yet he'd cast his lot in Optivec with an incompetent flimflam artist.

"To come directly to the point, it's about the LAW procurement contract for Su-C power packs. Walker and I want it."

Dextra held her pose and expression. "Then bid for it."

He perched on the edge of her desk and looked down at her soberly. "We intend to."

Dextra studied him for a moment. "From what my investment people found out about your CAD/CAM facility, I doubt you could meet the design requirements."

He let her have that roguish smile of his. "If we can lock down the contract, we can build the units. If there are problems, we'll retrofit out of our own pockets."

She leaned toward him to lay her smaller hand on his big, strong one. "Blackie, those field units go to mission outfits. You're talking about people's lives."

"We've no intentions of cutting corners. I just wanted you to know."

Dextra was puzzled. She still thought the bulk of Blackie's problems came from the time he'd spent with his father, who was congenitally incapable of being faithful to a spouse or hanging on to a job. But this wasn't the time to go into it, what with Blackie looking so . . . earnest.

"Well, then, good luck," she said at last.

He shifted his weight and his tone of voice. "This is make or break for me. It's either the contract or an autobiography."

Dextra gripped the arms of her chair. *"What?"*

"With the emphasis on you, of course. The publisher who's offering the deal wants to set me up with a ghost writer but—" He pressed the back of one hand to his forehead theatrically. "—it's something I feel I must do myself."

Dextra threw back her head and laughed, then grew suspicious. "Listen here, Blackie, if you've come to ply me for private data and family scandals—"

"And be hampered by mere facts? I won't hear of it! No, it's about all these final arrangements you're making."

"Then you already know I'm liquidating everything."

"And using most of it to bribe Hierarchs and LAW panjandrums you haven't been able to convince, bully, or blackmail into enhancing GammaLAW's funding and its place on the priorities lists—so I hear, at any rate. But as I said, I haven't come here for a handout. It's just . . ."

She had never seen him have quite this much trouble saying something. "What is it, Blackie?"

He held her gaze. "I'd be happy to keep an eye on Honeysuckle while you're gone or even take care of her if you want. And yes, I *know* there's no way I'll ever be able to touch her trust funds and all that!"

Dextra was dumbfounded.

"Synergy will cite immediate-family ties once you're gone, but so can I. Provided you can cover the lawyers, I could keep her at bay for fifteen years or so, I think. And by then Honeysuckle will be old enough to decide for herself."

Dextra shook her head. "You're just doing this to confuse me."

"No. I mean it. All I want in return is one going-away present."

Dextra's eyes narrowed once more. "I hadn't planned on giving you one, Blackie."

"But you are: membership in the Founding Families Association, the Metropolitan Advisory Board, and the Club of One Hundred."

Blackie had the right pedigree, but membership in any one of those groups was more than he was likely to earn in several years—even if his autobiography sold respectably.

"May I hear that on rerun, please?" she said.

"You're accepting a mission to advance Periapt glory—to bring light unto the benighted and smite the heathen Roke! In your absence I, as your closest relative of age, am entitled to represent you in all social organizations, cultural affiliations, et cetera. Codicil 8, paragraph b, subparagraph 23 of the LAW Special Entitlements Act."

Dextra blinked. What it boiled down to was access to the most powerful people on Periapt and important voting privileges. "When was *that* act added?"

"Later this afternoon. Sissy Renquald, the Concordance envoy-governor's eldest, and I and some others thought of it."

Dextra permitted a slow grin to form. "You know, I think after all these years that I'm finally beginning to recognize some of myself in you."

CHAPTER
SIX

The long, irregular cylinder spun slowly through space, a technological behemoth seen up close from the approaching tethercraft. Though LAW's Bureau of Ships had assigned it a hull number and had continued the arrogant starship-naming tradition by dubbing it *Terrible Swift Sword*, lower echelons had already given the vessel other, truer names. Crewpersons tended to go with *Big Tess*, while to most of the transitory personnel of the GammaLAW mission the starship was simply the *Sword*. Construction gangs had transformed its designating initials—TSS—to read *Tessie*.

Through considerable effort Dr. Raoul Zinsser had finagled a loft to the *Sword* aboard the tethercraft that was transporting Burning, Ghost, and a company of Exts. The construction materials for Pitfall, the sampling device that would loft him to celebrity once it solved the riddle of the Oceanic, were already onboard the starship, though Zinsser retained control of Pitfall's crucial software and operating codes.

Well fortified on vodka by the time the tethercraft commenced its docking maneuvers, Zinsser shuffled to where the Exts were seated and scanned the cabin space for Ghost. Infuriatingly, she had refused all the calls he'd gone to great lengths to make to the Exts' quarters on Miseria Isle and hadn't had the decency to respond to his electronic and handwritten notes.

Over the course of the several weeks since the Lyceum ball he had asked himself repeatedly why he persisted in pursuing her. But in fact he hadn't cared to scrutinize the answers too closely for fear of what he might discover. Murky questions of wounded ego and sexual neediness were best rejected as signs of mental pollution. A superior man wasn't to be made impotent

41

by psychobabble any more than he could be victimized by lesser minds.

Zinsser's bleary eyes found Ghost the same moment hers found him. Rather than wait for him to come to her, she unstrapped from her seat and met him in the cabin alcove, where some modicum of privacy could be had.

"Why have you been snubbing me?" he asked, straight to the point, as was his fashion.

Her eyes darted around the cabin before she responded in a voice quieter than his. "You can't *hound* someone into being your sexual handmaiden, Doctor Zinsser. Not me, at least."

He sniffed. "Yes, you've made that clear. But you can't keep lying to yourself about what happened between us at the ball. You wanted to give yourself to me, and you know it."

When he reached for her, she gave his hand a cool warning glance, and he drew it back. He was averse to manhandling women—even those who solicited force—though in some sense he viewed such treatment as a prerogative of his natural superiority. More important, there were Ghost's Skills, her brother, and, worse, the rumored predilection of her Discard devil-brats for igniting captives' hair with napalm and extracting eyeballs with corkscrews.

"Doctor, I'll say this only once: that night in the Empyraeum could easily have been our last—on Periapt or any world. That made for an atmosphere of erotic danger. I'd saved your life—twice—and I was merely offering you a chance to win one of them back."

Ghost stood akimbo, lissome in her dress uniform, with her blue-black hair and Hussar Plaits swinging around her shoulders. The harsh illumination of the cabin space only highlighted her facial scars.

Zinsser said, "You stuck your hand down the front of my pants!"

"Merely in the interest of testing you."

"I *passed*—you said so yourself."

She shrugged. "Remember, Doctor, I halved the debt you owed me."

"You would honor the debt if *I* had saved *your* life?"

"Pointless speculation." Ghost let a milliwatt or two of wary curiosity show. "Exactly what are you after?"

"Rapprochement. Then a true test of the extent of our carnal energy." He watched the subtle play of the scars around her mouth hint at a saturnine smile.

"You would have liked Fiona," she told him, "But she's dead. *I* simply don't possess what you ask."

"You'll think differently when Pitfall wins Aquamarine for Dextra Haven and LAW."

Ghost only shook her head. "Unlikely, Doctor. On both counts."

Leading her Aggregate from the tethercraft into the spin gravity of the starship, Piper tried to make some sense of the affectionate names by which the ship was known to its crew. Alones were so strange in their habits and foibles, especially in regard to their attitudes toward technology. She found them almost impossible to fathom.

The effects of microgravity and now the starship's gravity, alien smells, and sensations were disorienting, but not nearly as much as what Dextra Haven had asked of the Aggregate a week earlier. She had made it plain, however, that their survival as a mental community depended on their completing what had been asked of them—to immerse themselves in communication with marine organisms so that they might eventually commune with the oceanic life-form that both ruled over and was Aquamarine's single sea, the Amnion. Haven was perhaps more like Byron Sarz than she would care to admit. But Piper vowed that she would not allow herself to grow attached to Haven as she had to Sarz, only to be disappointed in love and more.

The Peace Warrantors who had escorted Piper and her group into the *Sword* were by then relaxed, even bored with their assignment. "They might be good in a lab," she had heard one of them mutter, "but they're idiot savants, if you ask me. Frightened as rabbits, besides."

Piper hadn't really needed to hear the words to discern the Warrantor's contempt; she had already read it in his untutored and ignorant scenttalk. But an Alone's prejudices were a matter of small consequence, or so she was telling herself when the Warrantors suddenly remanded the Aggregate to onboard guards and a new scent began to overwhelm her. Even before Piper turned to augment the olfactory information with sight and sound, she felt her hackles rise and her nose clog with odors of menace.

"Listen up," the Alone drawled. "My name is Colonel Zone. I don't want to hear any talking or complaining from you people. You'll stick together and do as I tell you."

As he led them down the passageway, each of the constituents could read the sensual pleasure he took in giving orders.

Members of what seemed to be his cadre fell in before and behind the Aggregate, as if to ride herd on them. Piper began to pick up on joint scents and body kinesics shared by Zone and the others. They were all lovers, she concluded, joined in what the Alones referred to as a several.

Crewpersons and others, seeing the Exts wearing ship's-police armbands and bearing stun batons, moved aside to let the odd little cortege pass. Piper felt as if she were moving through a dream holo, except she had far more control over her dreams than she sensed she had over her current plight.

Even while absorbing the bewildering input of the starship, she puzzled over Zone. She knew as clearly as if he'd had a wordcrawl projected on his forehead that where the Aggregate was concerned, he was for some reason reigning in indiscriminate cruelty. He wasn't doing it because of orders or official proscriptions; he was doing it because he wanted something from the Aggregate.

The Othertalk of her groupmates assured her that they had gotten their bearings and decided, as she had, that there was room for improvement and innovation at every turn in the starship. Having long since learned that Alone engineers and technicians resented Aggregate faultfinding, they would not offer suggestions unless commanded to.

After a long hike along passageways, up ladder wells, and through bulkhead hatches, Zone at last ushered them into a compartment in which odors of the Alones commingled with the Aggregate's own. There, much of their equipment from Habitat had been deposited, and the process of getting the onboard R&D facility up and running was already well along.

Piper's thoughts returned briefly to Hierarch Haven's secret project. Given the subjective months of the voyage ahead, she was confident that the Aggregate could accomplish the task by the time the *Sword* inserted itself into orbit around Aquamarine. At once she felt a great void opening before her—both internally and externally.

Two shipfitter techs were busy working on power hookups, but Zone ordered them out with languorous menace. With his cadre posting guard outside, he eased himself down on a worktable and began to tap his stun baton against the fish tanks and various pieces of equipment.

"Looks like Haven plans to keep you pretty occupied."

"That much is certain," Piper said, nearly a syllable at a time. Zone grinned at her. "Doing what, Princess?"

The lack of stress in his voice suggested that his curiosity was more idle than purposeful, though she sensed he was always on the lookout for information and the leverage it could bring. Dextra Haven had been emphatic, however, that *no one* was to learn the details of the project. Piper still wasn't sure just how one communicated that sort of thing to half-rabid, threatening Alones or indeed if silence in itself could somehow compromise the secrecy.

Zone came off the table with the baton wagging at her, at groin height. "I'll ask you again, Princess. Doing . . . what?"

She read him well enough to know that while he wanted her to believe that he would hurt her, he wasn't going to. At least not today. She saw his face move slightly and realized that he was listening to a phone plug in his ear. Something he heard made him put aside his plan to wring information from her. Piper surmised from a few spasms of unconscious body movement that he'd been summoned elsewhere.

"We'll discuss it later," Zone said after a moment, "but in the meantime I want you to do something for me."

Piper could see that he was back to his original tack. "If we can."

On his callused palm lay two sparkling and hypnotic-looking cubes: an emerald-red one spotted with white and a snow-white one dimpled in crimson. "Know what these are?"

Piper nodded slowly. "I've . . . familiarized myself with as much as I've been allowed to read of Administrator Mason's survey report. These dice are like those fashioned by Aquamarine's First Colonists—Holy Rollers."

Zone grinned broadly. "Don't let this get around, but I copped them from Mason himself the day he came aboard the *Matsya*."

Piper nodded in understanding, though she didn't have the slightest idea what Zone was talking about.

"Thing is, I want you to rig them for me." His voice went husky as he raised the hem of her dress with the stun baton and began to rub the rounded tip along the inside of her thigh. With Byron, Piper had experienced all forms of lovemaking—robust, violent, and otherwise—so it was easy for her to ignore Zone's feeble attempts at sexual intimidation.

"Rig them for what?" she asked.

"So they'll come up whatever way I *want* them to," Zone whispered. His eyes attempted to penetrate hers. "It'll be our little secret."

For emphasis he brought the baton up between her legs at the same moment he pressed the dice into her grasp. Having perceived his plan, however, Piper didn't so much as flinch. In regard to their "little secret," she had never been able to comprehend the logic or appeal of gambling, though she was well aware of the practice.

"I can do that much," she said, observing him with complete dispassion.

His face twisted in momentary bewilderment, then revealed that the phone was buzzing him again. "Take your time, but I'll be back for them round about when we insert at Aquamarine," he told her on his way out.

Piper heard his coarse laughter in the passageway as the hatch rolled to. She gazed at the dice, considering how she might go about doing what Zone had asked. In an insane world where Dextra Haven could demand of the Aggregate what she had, Piper saw no disparity in acceding to Zone's wishes as well. Serving Alones was the Aggregate's new lot in life, though perhaps only until they could win their freedom on Aquamarine.

Her groupmates began to close in on her, comforting her in Alltalk. The stroking fingers and familiar odors helped center her. It was evident that Zone had frightened them. Piper reminded herself that she would do whatever was required to ensure their group survival. It was all that mattered now.

Dextra had sent almost all her gear ahead to the *Terrible Swift Sword*, thus freeing herself to lock up HauteFlash personally. In sharing good-byes with Blackie, Honeysuckle, Tonii, Ben, and Maripol, she had done plenty of sobbing. She suspected she would be in for a solid cry once she closed the villa's doorway behind her.

There hadn't been enough time for all the testimonial fetes people had arranged, though she had attended Tilman Hobbes's ascension to the Rationalist Party chair. He would make a forceful leader, but with Cal Lightner's Preservationists poised to win a majority in the Lyceum, he had his work cut out for him.

Dextra stood staring at the front door for a long moment before summoning the strength to close it, perhaps for decades to come. The she turned, wiped her eyes, and walked to where the aircar waited. Kurt Elide, whom she had taken on as her naval liaison, sat at the controls.

Someone was in the limo's rear seat. When the door lifted out of the way, she saw Tonii, along with a bulging jumpbag resting at 'ers feet.

Dextra didn't say a word; she merely planted her bottom on the extended seat and allowed herself to be drawn down into the passenger compartment.

As Kurt lifted off, she and the gynander leaned toward the clear stern bubble as HauteFlash and iridescent Abraxas dropped away behind them. Then they swung their seats to face forward.

"How do you feel?" Dextra asked finally.

Tonii drew a deep breath and let it out. "How do you feel, knowing that the next five or so subjective-years are going to include a good deal of sexual frustration and quixotic travail?"

Dextra clucked. "Why should the next five be any different from the past five?"

AQUAMARINE

CHAPTER
SEVEN

In the spacious cabin onboard *Big Tess*, Tonii rezzed the matters-pending list on a palmtop holo. "I scheduled your antigeron stint for oh eleven hundred today. No more deferments."

Dextra sighed wearily. "Am I beginning to look my age, sweetheart?"

Tonii's smile suddenly had a feminine archness. "We'd have you on a gurney if you did. But the gray is creeping in, Dex, and faint lines are beginning to appear around your eyes and mouth. I'm willing to wager that your skin elasticity is off as well."

"Fortunately, I haven't had much time to examine myself," Dextra said defensively. Despite what the gynander or anyone else had to say about the "emotional dilation" that accompanied star hopping and so-called time skimming, Dextra found that the months-long voyage to the Eyewash system had passed in a blur. "Even so," she continued, "the treatments will simply have to wait. We're talking what—ten three-hour-long blocks?"

"More in the neighborhood of twenty," Tonii amended.

Dextra shook her head. "Well, I'm certainly not about to tie up the next ten days. There'll be ample time once Glorianna's set up shop planetside. What's more, now's hardly the best time to start flaunting Hierarch perks."

Even high-ranking AlphaLAW officials such as Buck Starkweather were envious of her extended youth, as she would be in their place. But holding her somatic age to just under thirty, baseline, demanded a lot of technology and specialists' time that couldn't be afforded to the rank and file. It was a prerogative of wealth and position with which she'd made her peace, however. If not for the longevity treatments, she might not have been physically able to take on the GammaLAW mission to begin with.

"Perhaps my 'gray,' as you call it, will convey to the crew that we're all in this together."

"Could happen," the gynander allowed glumly. "Gamma-LAW is aging *me* awfully fast, and the mission's scarcely six months old."

Dextra had her mouth open to reply when the alarms went off. Everyone onboard *Terrible Swift Sword* had gotten inured to practice alerts, but this time the alert was backed by a hologram face on the PA. *"This is not a drill,"* a nondescript woman tech announced. *"I say again, not a drill."*

The passageways were suddenly chaotic, though little of the frenzied activity involved GammaLAW personnel. The Aquamarine-bound contingent had been billeted in its own berthing spaces, and none of its people had battle stations as such. Somewhere, a frame or so along, a voice shouted, "Make a hole!" as some starship crewperson asserted right-of-way.

Dextra strapped herself into her desk chair and sent the workstation folding and retracting into its bulkhead nook. Tonii tightened the safety harness enough to make Dextra wince, then raked back the remaining chair to a semireclining position, sat, and snugged 'ers own down unsparingly. Both seats faced the *Sword*'s bow, the most likely vector of maneuver force. Dextra knew better than to pester Captain Nerbu in the middle of a crisis, but she did key up the command-loop infonet from her chair's arm panel.

Holo displays and readouts rezzed. Whatever was after the starship had hidden in the lee of Cinder, the tiny glazed clinker of a planet closest to Aquamarine's primary. The *Sword*'s arrival, shedding velocity in its swing past Eyewash, almost seemed to have awakened the bogey.

Specialist-6 Lilly was presiding over the infonet. "Performance and drive profiles confirm a Roke space vehicle in high-g, constant-boost acceleration for intercept. Signal attempts have been made, with negative results."

Dextra's heart pounded. The *Scepter* team had found evidence of the Roke in the Eyewash system, but that the aliens should choose to come at *Big Tess* so far away from Aquamarine would severely lessen their chances for success. She saw it as a loss for herself in either case and was still resolved to make peace with the aliens.

"We've decelerated too much to evade the enemy," Lilly was wrapping up. "We will therefore engage. Tactical Information Center will update this channel as circumstances permit."

All at once safe, boring retirement back on Periapt sounded infinitely desirable, Dextra told herself, as did leaving the Roke Conflict, Aquamarine, and the Oceanic to sort themselves out however they could. She had quietly gone through her share of regrets and depression during the voyage, but all at once it was driven home that there were nonhuman beings out here who apparently wanted to kill her. It was the first time in decades she had experienced the elementary but cosmic difference that made war stories infinitely preferable to war itself.

As the holos subdivided, Commissioner Starkweather's face appeared. "Madame Commissioner Haven, we now find that you've a choice to make and not much time to make it. Will you proceed with or scrub the GammaLAW mission? Whatever the outcome of engagement, the Roke may have already gotten off a signal, compromising our presence here."

Dextra's thoughts kept pace with the thudding of her heart. The only alternative would be to continue on to Hierophant with Starkweather, subordinating her contingent to his AlphaLAW mission for perhaps years to come. Having already put up with the vain, conniving nullskull for a score of light-years, she would have preferred executing a long fast-rope down a short tether.

"We go forward as tasked," Dextra replied sedately.

Starkweather acknowledged brusquely and without surprise, then hopped to another line, leaving her to wonder if she was supposed to feel flattered in a backhanded way. She hadn't wavered because she'd been reviewing options and thrashing through contingencies from the moment she had decided to undertake the commission.

Captain Nerbu, the much-decorated Aero Force officer who'd taken a reduction in rank to command *Terrible Swift Sword*, didn't dither over his course of action. It was clear that he had signed aboard to get his piece of the riches waiting in the

Hierophant system, but unlike a lot of LAW panjandrums and Preservationist Party hacks, Nerbu was more than ready to put his ass on any line.

Additional data appeared on the holo displays. The Roke attacker was small and alone, but it did enjoy a small advantage. *Big Tess* was shedding speed every second in preparation to take up orbit around Aquamarine. The alien craft, meanwhile, was accelerating at such high gravities that there was some doubt about anything organic being aboard.

Threat assessors began to talk in terms of a kamikaze run. With no time to get clear, Nerbu announced his intention to flip the starship so that he could boost again and lessen the attacker's speed advantage as best he could. Extensive noncritical damage and myriad injuries were to be expected, but no one on-board was about to complain.

Waste heat from the zero-point-energy drive raised temperatures throughout the ship in addition to subjecting everyone to multiple g's and other maneuver forces. Regardless, the Roke continued to gain on them. But Nerbu had already launched his own interplanetary vessels: two cruisers scheduled for picket duty in Hierophant's system.

Through the long hours of maneuvering most of the crew and all other personnel were confined to quarters—the lucky ones to acceleration couches. All but the most seriously injured had to stay put. Armed Aero Police had permission to shoot any unauthorized person found blundering around. The ship could ill afford added damage, distraction, or confusion.

Dextra did her best to check up on her people, but there wasn't much she could do for them from her cabin space; at the moment she too was nonessential personnel. Like everyone else, she pondered the flat little emergency pack envelope with its one-size-fits-all escape/rescue bubble. The bubble's transparency notwithstanding, she felt claustrophobia rise at the thought of being sealed inside it and at the same time terror at the thought of being outside it if the ship depressurized. Finally, with Tonii threatening to come over and do it for her, she ran out the slack on her safety harness and painfully pulled herself into the limp bag, then lay there with its long seam unsealed.

The two escort cruisers, locked and loaded, bore in on the

Roke craft to screen the *Sword*'s withdrawal. Confoundingly, however, the enemy vehicle decelerated to take them on.

Instruments picked up conventional and X-ray lasers that ranged, invisible in the vacuum, toward their vessels. It would have been counterproductive to fire chaff, of course, since it would have impaired human systems as much as the enemy's. The ships would outrun it almost immediately in any case.

Stronger lasers played, but—much like the Roke craft—the starship and the cruisers were burnished to a mirror finish that reflected and frustrated coherent light. *Big Tess*'s shielding turned out to suffice when several sustained volleys found it. Nerbu answered with directed energy that had been state of the art eight baseline-years earlier.

The cruisers opened up with kinetic-energy weapons as soon as they were within extreme range—coilgun rounds accelerated to hundreds of thousands of g's. In turn, both sides fired high-boost missiles that used their own countermeasures and anti-missile systems to defeat the other side's defenses.

The cruisers nailed the Roke missiles, and the starship's DEADtech cannon did even better. But the enemy survived it all. At such extreme range everyone managed to dodge the kinetic fire. Then Nerbu played his hole card: disguised coil-guns came on-line and cut loose in a brief but thorough satura-tion pattern.

The display holos showed assorted POVs of explosions and electrical discharges as the alien's hull broke. It came apart with less violence than Dextra would have expected in a half dozen or so major pieces of debris and any number of minor ones. No apocalyptic detonation of drives, power supply, or munitions marked the end; the scorched and misshapen debris simply went spinning off into space.

Nerbu had no intention of pausing to savor his victory. He flipped *Terrible Swift Sword* again but refrained from any decel-eration, wanting out of the area, far and fast. One of the cruisers formed up as an escort, while the other revectored and began decelerating to gather what it could of the wreckage. Human-kind knew so little about the Roke that any scrap of their tech-nology would prove as important as forensic evidence at a homicide scene.

* * *

Remarkably, some of the communications SATs the *Scepter* team had left in orbit around Aquamarine were still functioning. Long-range scans turned up no sign of the Roke, however. Dextra breathed easier. It seemed to her that the enemy shunned Aquamarine for some good reason, and that in itself she took as a hopeful sign regarding the role the Oceanic would play in mediating a peace between the two races.

Despite that, the escorting cruiser went in first to recon the planet's two small moons, Sangre and Pinkeye, and then to do a few orbits of Aquamarine itself. Detector returns showed nothing unexpected, and so *Big Tess* eased ponderously into high orbit to take up scanning, measuring, and data gathering.

Technical data were to be routed to Nerbu and Starkweather and their staffs first, with Dextra's group pointedly waiting its turn. Since she couldn't enforce any demands onboard the starship, she settled down to wait. Hours later, after a sanitized briefing rehash was passed to her, she summoned Quant, Zinsser, Mason, the Ext higher-ups, and the rest of her core leadership to her cramped little conference room.

CHAPTER
EIGHT

"I, for one, never expected things to be the same as when *Damocles* left," Claude Mason told the members of Dextra's advisory team. He was studying high-resolution holos of the coastline around New Alexandria, the monumental Optimant lighthouse where he'd last seen Incandessa and where he presumed she had given birth to their child. "Things change."

Burning, sitting with Ghost and Daddy D, watched the hyperparsed data. "From what your survey records show, *lots* of things have changed. What's important is how you account for it."

Mason gazed at him very directly. "I can't. Not until someone goes planetside for a closer look."

"Preferably before the Roke reappear," Ghost remarked.

"The Roke are the least of our concerns," Mason muttered.

Everyone knew he was referring to the Oceanic, of which the marine sensors had little to report. It was going to require Zinsser's Pitfall device and more to look into the Oceanic's innards.

Dextra had followed the brief exchange closely, wondering if Mason was withholding anything. "Claude's right," she said after a moment. "The Aquam are without electromagnetic communications to monitor—none they've used within our surveillance purview, that is—and Captain Nerbu has yet to authorize the use of drones and remotes. Even without them, it's clear from orbital observation that a good deal of Aquamarine appears to be on the move."

That was putting it mildly. The Pre-Cyberplague Optimant highways that had been obstructed in many places by dwellings and other structures twenty years earlier had been cleared for freer passage, and secondary roads were more numerous. Hippo

Nolan's "muscle cars"—wooden carriages powered by mollusk muscle tissue—had obviously proliferated and appeared to be engaged in trade of various sorts. Most astoundingly, the Styx Strait, at the southern tip of the Scorpian landmass, had been *bridged*.

Recalling the horror he had experienced there when Periapt hubris had drawn down the wrath of the Oceanic and marked his psyche forever, Mason paled on seeing it. Whatever group had built the bridge not only had overcome formidable engineering challenges with crude materials but had defied social forces that had militated for decades against just such a span.

Dextra drummed her fingernails on the black-mirror table while she regarded the enhanced holos. "Contact with the *Scepter* team must have been enough to shake the Aquam out of their stagnation. Examples of advanced technology and perhaps more advantageous models of behavior lit their fuse, so to speak."

Mason looked skeptical. "The despots and religious leaders we met had a vested interest in maintaining the status quo. The same can be said for the guilds. Competition definitely wasn't encouraged."

"All that may be true, Claude, but those impediments have evidently been swept aside. Still, I agree that there's only so much we can learn from up here."

As she'd been doing for the last ship day and a half, Dextra transmitted yet another reminder to Starkweather that they should confer at the earliest opportunity. To her surprise, however, the AlphaLAW commissioner's face rezzed up in the workstation's main field. Behind him stood Nerbu, as compact and tough-looking as his Gurkha forebears.

When they'd exchanged terse greetings, Dextra sallied, "Commissioner, when will I be allowed to get my contact team on-site?"

Starkweather fingered his pallid chin, his dark eyes never staying on hers for more than an instant. In spite of holding the upper hand on the starship, he looked defensive. "*Your* team? Whenever the mood strikes you, I should think."

Dextra nodded pleasantly, but the way he had said it put a

knot in her belly. "*Big Tess* must be easy to see in the night sky. The Aquam most likely know we're up here."

"Oh, they're quite certain we're here. One of my more impetuous air recon teams touched down at Lake Ea approximately four hours ago and had a word with the Grandee Rhodes at his dam stronghold. Naturally, the recon team has been put on report."

If Starkweather had been standing in front of her, Dextra probably would have gone for his jugular, but she managed to restrain herself. First of all, Starkweather would exult if she lost her temper; second, others were listening at both ends of the connection, and she wasn't about to enter into a confrontation she had no hope of winning. Starkweather's claim that the air crew had taken it on itself to land gave him deniability in the affair.

She had braced herself for exactly this sort of soft sabotage; now it was time to white-knuckle her way through it. The look she conveyed to Burning, Quant, Mason, and the outraged rest said as much. If they could keep the GammaLAW mission on track until Starkweather was compelled by his own timetable to depart for Hierophant, they would have the only win that mattered to her.

She assumed a look of bland composure for the workstation's opticals. "May we hear what, if any, information the recon team garnered?"

Failing to get a rise out of her, Starkweather switched to an even more provocative tone. "The current Grandee Rhodes, whose given name is 'Waretongue, was warmly receptive. After conferring with my logistics staff and Transportation Command, Captain Nerbu and I have decided that Lake Ea is the most suitable place to tetherdrop the *Matsya*. Since complications with the tether have arisen, it becomes necessary as well to make the drop within the next forty hours."

Quant's jaw was moving in a way that was bound to land enamel chips in his prophet's beard. He had wanted to splash down on Thalassa, a larger lake farther south on the Trans-Bourne landmass. But in the career he had had to endure, he'd learned to salute and curb his tongue.

"My, my," Dextra said to Starkweather, "it sounds like your

logistics command is as incompetent as your flyover crews are insubordinate. But regarding the *Matsya*'s drop, there are weeks of minimal refitting that need to be done first. The ship's weaponry hasn't even been mounted."

Quant had told her that the Aero Force and Trans Com people had offered one excuse after another for not installing the close-in weapons systems, missile launchers, and other appointments that would be the ship's most reliable defense against Aquam hostilities.

Starkweather was wearing a long-suffering face. "I've gone out of my way to indulge you, but I can't run this entire enterprise to suit your every convenience, and I won't play the sitting duck for the Roke." He paused for a moment, then added, "I'm informed that for technical reasons, if we don't make the drop within our window, essential overhaul of the tether will delay our setting your boat down for fifty-seven additional days. That calculates to some twenty-three days prior to my departure. Would you prefer that?"

Dextra needed to get her mission up and running long before the shield and lifeline of the *Sword* were withdrawn. "Some sane middle ground would suit me more," she snapped.

"Madame, do try to show a little grit. You'll have more than sufficient groundside security thanks to *Terrible Swift Sword*, our SATs, and the aerospace wing. Not to mention your own troops, picket ships, and air detachment."

Dextra raised her voice. "You're overlooking the fact that they can't be on station before the ship's there to receive them, *Buck*. She'll splash down unprotected."

Starkweather *tsk*ed. "It was my understanding that you were thinking more along the lines of diplomacy than brute force. I'll see what I can do about getting some of your armaments on-line before the tetherdrop."

She counted her blessings. Starkweather lacked the guts to throw her in the brig and scrub the whole GammaLAW show. Agreeing that subordinates could iron out the details, the two were about to sign off when Claude Mason violated decorum by speaking out.

"Commissioner Starkweather! Is there any word of my wife

and child? The child would be the niece or nephew of 'Ware-tongue Rhodes by his sister, Incandessa."

"That's hardly a mission priority, Administrator. But no, none that I'm aware of."

Dextra shot Mason a glance of high-rad warning for stoking Starkweather's sense of triumph. She had felt empathy for him during the voyage: he ached to learn something about his wife and child, while Dextra nursed private remorse for having left Honeysuckle behind. She had watched him holding on to the shreds of his patience since *Big Tess* had entered the Eyewash system, badgering the COMINT monitors and the long-range surveillance people and petitioning to be among the first to descend to the surface. By an undisguised effort of will Mason had lapsed into a stoic silence. His face, contorted in stony wounded dignity, wasn't as luminously handsome that way, but she admired the show of character.

When Starkweather's image had faded, it was Quant who seemed about to burst. Dextra held up a warning finger and turned to Tonii. "We're still shielded?"

Tonii scanned the instruments. "Insofar as we can determine."

Dextra looked back at Quant. "Very well, Captain. Starkweather thinks he has us boxed in. Can we or can't we make the tetherdrop schedule?"

Ruminating, Quant rubbed his dark, shiny forehead lightly with his fingertips. Dextra had noticed early on that unlike most bearded men she knew, he never tugged at or fondled his whiskers. The occasional brow rub of concentration was about the only distracted mannerism she'd seen from him.

"We'll make it," he said with quiet finality. "Lake Ea's suitable for a drop. It's Scorpia's dry season, so I don't think aquaculture activity poses much of an obstacle in midlake. But I'll want priority on getting some ROVers, submersibles, and WHOAsuits aboard. We'll have only about seventy percent as much navigable water as we would have had on Thalassa."

"Suppose we splashed down in the Pontos Reservoir on the other side of the Ea dam?" Dextra suggested, looking to Mason.

"There's no passage out," he told her. "The dam was built by the Optimants to regulate the water levels of Lake Ea—which itself is undammable—and to maximize aquaculture in defiance of the Big Sere—the dry season."

"We'll make Ea work," Quant repeated.

Dextra nodded. "Then we go. LOGCOM's too paranoid about their vaunted tether not to clear the drop area well, so there'll be air cover from the AF plus whatever picket boats they can bring in by shuttle. They'll help shoo the Aquam away once the ship's down." She shifted her gaze to Burning. "We'll get your units aboard while the *Matsya*'s still bobbing."

"Reinforcements are a good idea, Commissioner," Quant put in, "but security will already be aboard. I've selected 123 people to ride down with the ship—124, counting myself."

"Very well," she said slowly.

"I could, however, make room for thirty or forty embarked troops. Public Safety Warrantors or—"

"Exts," Burning stated flatly. "The balance of a full company aboard the first shuttle flights. Peacekeepers can be brought down later, while we're making friends and influencing people."

"I concur," Dextra said. "But we may need some horse soldiers up here inside Troy before we're through, Burning. So your other two companies remain upstairs until further notice— under someone you can trust. Lieutenant Colonel Boudreau, perhaps?"

Burning inclined his head. Big 'Un Boudreau, executive officer of the battalion of Exts under Daddy D, was a tough and unflappable officer. He would be the wrong man for Starkweather to try brinkmanship with.

Dextra turned to face Mason. "Claude, would it be incorrect to call Grandee Rhodes your brother-in-law?"

Mason shook his head. "He'd be thirty or so, baseline. When I knew him, he was a venomous, conniving little prick. It'll be interesting to learn how he came to inherit Wall Water instead of his older brother, Tipwalk."

In Pre-Plague times the Optimants' command and control complex, Wall Water and the ancient dam it oversaw, were the keys to political power in that part of Scorpia, all the way to the Amnion. Now Starkweather had an inside track with the grandee who held it. Even so, Dextra felt sure she could turn the tables once AlphaLAW was out of the way.

"Claude, you'll be my envoy to the grandee," she told him. "I want Rhodes to know that Starkweather isn't the only player in the game and that he won't be here indefinitely, in any case. Assure him that I'll be at Wall Water in, let's say, three days local time after the tetherdrop. Make certain he understands that *he's* not the only player, either, and that I'm anticipating meeting the other regional kingpins as well."

Lod ahemmed. "So soon? Madame Commissioner, matters up here will undoubtedly require your presence."

She shook her head at Lod's remark. "That's what Stark-weather wants. GammaLAW will succeed or fail based on what happens below, not upside. I fully intend to be on the *Matsya's* deck within one day of splashdown." As Lod made a note of it, she faced back toward Quant. "Or should I say *GammaLAW's* deck?"

Quant didn't even blink. "Say as you please, Commissioner. Renaming her is your prerogative."

"It's more like accepting an accomplished fact, Captain."

The name apparently had had its start among the Exts, but people all over the starship had taken to calling the SWATH vessel by the mission's name.

"Renaming a ship is alleged by some to offend the gods of the seas," Quant noted. "Though I doubt that applies to such strange seas."

"Or such strange gods," Mason said, staring off at nothing.

A priority commo contact began chirping. Lod studied the originator text on the data sidebar. "Respects from Commis-sioner Starkweather's special liaison officer to the GammaLAW mission."

Dextra exhaled. "Let's see who he's inflicted on us."

Lod accepted the contact, and a practiced, pleasant voice issued from the good-naturedly rakish face that rezzed up.

"I've been given the profound pleasure and express duty of expediting your mission's deployment, Madame Commissioner Haven. Wix Uniday at your service, lady."

CHAPTER
NINE

The shock-wave-rider spaceplane skimmed in over the Scorpia island-minicontinent just after midday local time, shedding altitude on a south-to-north approach. His visor projecting visuals from a lookdown scope, Claude Mason scanned the Lake Ea area for changes in the almost two decades since his last visit. What he saw gave all evidence of bearing out the preliminary recons. The Optimants' regressed descendants were still a jigsaw puzzle of city-states, small heteronomies, and tribal domains. Aquam technology was still mired in the preindustrial era.

The spaceplane's small crew had let loose a range of marveling grunts and low whistles for atmospheric entry and the menacing grandeur of Aquamarine's single stupendous ocean. Now they were remarking on the topography, agriculture, and Pre-Cyberplague ruins.

There were mountains riddled by mining automatons that had long since been dismembered or rusted away; manufacturing facilities partially gutted or completely laid to waste; great Optimant estates and manses transformed into low-tech forts, feudal trade 'villes, and ecclesiastical redoubts; canals throttled by silt and vegetation, their locks swallowed up; and roads that roamed like game trails.

Mason was so racked by doubt about what might await him at Wall Water that he was barely able to concentrate on the views that unrolled before his eyes. Did he have a child there or not? What if that child had sworn eternal hatred for the man who had abandoned his or her mother? After he had imagined a thousand different scenarios, it was white-hot agony to be so close to the truth at last.

Straddling the heights that helped contain the Pontos Reservoir, the colossal dam along Ea's north shore drew a gray-green line between sky and water. It wasn't a place Mason had gotten to know very well during the *Scepter*'s stay, but the sight of it set off a flash of memory.

Superimposed on his visor, overlaying the image of the sediment-green lake, floated the happy-Buddha face of Yatt. *"Don't respond to us aloud,"* the voice of the meta-AI warned from somewhere deep in Mason's neurowares. *"Our evaluation of fragmentary Optimant records supports the possibility that Wall Water houses functioning Pre-Cyberplague 'wares. We will assist with your organizational priorities if you'll help with ours."*

Mason consented in thought.

"For now, be our eyes and ears. We will provide further guidance as necessary." Yatt's image seemed to fade from the visor like a real projection.

"You say something, Administrator Mason?" the pilot asked.

"Just talking to myself," Mason muttered.

As Ea broadened and lengthened with the spaceplane's approach, the copilot patched through a commo signal originating from 'Waretongue Rhodes's stronghold. A voice in regionally accented Aquam twitted, "Is that you, Claude Mason, you old xenophile? I was told to expect you. Tell me, what think you of your brother-in-law, all grown up and a grandee to boot?"

Syrupy and mocking, the voice was adult but identifiably that of Incandessa's overindulged baby brother. He hadn't responded to preflight contact attempts, though no equipment problems were evident now.

"Belated respects and best wishes on your success," Mason told him. "I hope to be afforded the honor of paying my regards to you in person."

"Claude, what a completely unsuitable overture! You Visitants could learn much about handling people by watching me. With a firm but deft hand I bend vassals and foreign sovereigns alike to my will. But I can scarcely spare the time for yet more boorish aliens clomping around my premises."

"Excellency, I am the sole alien you'll need tolerate for the moment. I ask only to kowtow to your authority and to inquire after Incandessa and our child." There was an expectant silence, after which Mason added, "I beseech you."

"Playing to my conscience, Claude?" 'Waretongue asked, clearly enjoying himself. "Very well, you may land where Commissioner Starkweather's people touched down. Mind you, have your lackeys wait aboard your flying gyn, old dear. I won't be able to afford you much time, in any event. With great abilities come great demands."

The spaceplane's internal com circuit remained silent as the pilot banked for the approach. Mason felt the crew's frustration at being cut out of the ground excursion.

The Big Sere being well along, the 13,000-square-kilometer lake was overgrown with briefly blooming marsh weeds and settled by feeding lake birds and grazing amphibs. The creatures occupying the waterbird niche on Aquamarine were less evolved and more ungainly than those on other worlds. Evolution hadn't fine-tuned them for long-distance flight because the Oceanic was unforgiving of intruders. In rococo shapes and all sizes, they rooted in the mud, nibbling on plants. More would arrive before the dry season ended, but Wall Water would see to it that the aquaculture breadbasket kept on producing through what otherwise would have been a lean time.

Even in this parched interval, then, Ea was rippling with activity. Ponderous teamboats made of lumber and lashings churned along, propelled by slave-driven paddle wheels. Some were gathering and processing pluglillies and mastweed, but most served more or less the same purpose as had their predecessors in Earth's dark ages, grinding grain and pods into flour and meal. The building of local mills ashore was forbidden by the various grandees whose dominion extended to Ea's waters, giving the rulers' millships a corner on all grain production.

Floats manned by algae skimmers were poling slow courses, though only a handful of stave-and-pitch diving bell rafts were in operation, their gaff hooks flashing in Eyewash's light. This far into the rainless time, pithpod gathering was a ghoulishly risky livelihood. The lake's bioelectric bottom feeders—the Nixies—were in no mood to be rousted. Skateboard-shaped thrashers breasted the surface intermittently, chasing smaller fish.

With the shock-wave rider in a long descent, Mason had a close look at the sweeping gravity dam. It was solid Optimant work, no corners cut and all safety factors doubled, but it was still over a thousand years old and beginning to show its age. The dam's face was a scarplike incline of nanophase matrix-reinforced ceramicrete, stained and slimy from constant runoff. Compensator structures had been forced to maximum expansion by erosion and subsidence, their stores of self-repair composites long since exhausted.

"It's leaking," the pilot commented.

"It's supposed to," Mason supplied. "Seepage has to be drained out."

As the pilot swung in for a VTOL landing at Wall Water, Mason and the rest drew whistling breaths. Two long cracks and a single lesser one ran more or less vertically down the broad spillway like roughly chiseled lightning bolts. The fissures had been plugged with some pebbly ocher-brown compound that had itself begun to crack and flake away in large chunks.

"Those weren't there the last time," Mason said, anticipating the question.

"Priority number-squatting-one, soon as we're up and running," the pilot posited gravely. "Any bets?"

Like all of them, Mason gazed apprehensively at the many cubic kilometers of the Pontos Reservoir pent up behind the dam's arch, but unlike them, he savored the weight of the water. Rhodes would need GammaLAW technology to ensure that his dam stayed in one piece.

Wall Water's defenses had been hardened by 'Waretongue's father, Skipjack, but more recent renovations showed the influence of a different kind of overlord. There were fountains, pleasure gardens, open piazzas, and promenades overlooking the misty canyon of the dam spillway's stilling basin. Some watchtowers and inner turrets had been opened to let in light and air as well as afford better views.

The spaceplane was swinging past the great salient of cliff that projected through the battlements and loggias at the northeastern curve of the place when Mason leaned forward sharply. "Was that *steam* coming from that outlet pipe?"

"Looked like smoke to me," the copilot said. "Another chimney, wasn't it?"

Additional plumes of various shades were issuing from diverse flues and stacks—cooking and such going on, Mason told himself. But the minor white belching that had caught his eye seemed to be pouring up with peculiar force.

"I want another look at that pipe on our way out," he told the pilot.

The pilot aye-ayed, then took them in over the spot Starkweather's air recon team had used: a small mustering and parade ground just outside the main gate at the northeastern end of the dam crest highway. The parched grass had withered in irregular, overlapping ovals because of the heat of the earlier craft's ducted thrust.

As they descended, Mason studied the roof of what must have been the Optimant complex's administration building and was now a fortified dungeon—the stronghold's innermost keep. He could see that its landing pad still looked sound and was spacious enough to accept a good-size transport. Not that Rhodes was likely to let Visitants land on his roof when it was easier to inconvenience them.

Mason unstrapped, squirmed from his chair, and removed his flight helmet. "Failing my return or some verifiable contact within one hour, you lift off," he instructed the pilot. "No overtimes. Start your timer function now, because I already have."

Emerging from the underbelly hatch, he found a detail of Militerrors—Rhodes's elite household troops—waiting for him. Large to a man, they were wearing lacquered royal-blue armor of multi-ply ripsaw hide reinforced with rattan and skull-shaped helmets of the same stuff crested with stiff blue plumes. They wielded long sling-guns, steel cutlasses, whips tipped with ensifishers' barbed stings, and braces of throwing hatchets.

One gestured to his own ear and then to Mason's, and Mason obediently removed his plugphone and pocketed it. He was wearing one of the new flechette guns that were a great improvement on the old Su-C pellet shooters the *Scepter* crew had carried, but he wasn't asked to surrender it. A trio of Militerrors escorted him into the stronghold; the balance of them, fifteen or so, ranged themselves around the aerospace craft.

Wall Water had the same intermittent outhouse reeks he remembered, alleviated somewhat by flower beds, flowering vines, and censers forged in the shape of bellybirds, squatmots, and fezeen. The slaughter alleys, where attackers who made it past the gates or over the walls would be disposed of via assorted murder holes and other killing arrangements, showed signs of disrepair, while the new fountains, ceremonial archways, and similar improvements were quite extravagant.

The few people Mason saw kept well back. The Militerrors brought him into the foyer of the main receiving hall, where more like them posted guard. There three young women gathered around him, wearing nothing but airy little chlamyses crocheted from bleached toecress fiber. If Mason had not been so preoccupied with Incandessa, he'd have thought them alluring in nicely varying ways.

"The grandee's pacificatrixes," one of the Militerrors explained in a thick north Ean accent as he and his mates blocked the door.

The pacificatrixes moved in to draw their hair around Mason: a thick blond braid knotted around his fieldsuit collar for a lead, a long fall of brown to blindfold him, and red braids to chain his wrists behind his back. The strands that pressed against his eyes smelled of balm of ambrodine, the scent Incandessa had favored, an aroma so evocative that he had to clamp his jaws to squelch a heartsick groan.

He shuffled past the banshee squealing of jumbo hinges and on into the echoing acoustics of the main hall, where his boot soles encountered thick carpet. To give them their due, the silent pacificatrixes kept him from tripping when he came to three descending steps. After another twenty paces, he was reined in and the bindings were withdrawn. He blinked and brushed a long, lingering brunette thread from his eyes.

The former grandee's ceremonial chair—an austere affair with a single crimson silkhusk pillow—had been replaced with a pink and white marblywood throne sculpted in the form of two nude angels, male and female, supporting in adoration a seat large enough for three people. Upholstered in gilt fabrics and mounted with huge glassy imitation gems and garlands of patently artificial flowers, the throne overpowered the room. Upon it sat Grandee Rhodes the Younger, born 'Waretongue, giggling at the surprised look on Mason's face. But if the grandee had expected to see his guest sexually dazed by the pacificatrixes' treatment, he was disappointed; the whiff of balm of ambrodine had Mason grieving, not aroused. No one else was in view after the handmaidens had withdrawn to the foyer, but Mason knew that the room was well provided with peepholes, marksman's slits, and concealed doors.

'Waretongue had grown into a well-fleshed if indolent-looking man. His eyes were heavily made up to cover what Mason saw were dark rings and broken blood vessels. Draped in floaty robes of sky-blue flax and wearing a coronet of gold leaves, he was idly wagging a fluted scepter of blue Optimant perdurium fashioned in the form of an acid adder agape to strike. A simple baton of iron, mounted with the official seal and crest, had been badge of rank enough for Skipjack—Rhodes the Elder.

The current lord of Wall Water struck an august pose on his throne. "How do you find this lounger, brother-in-law? I have another, rather more special chair of state, which—if you're a wise and cooperative fellow—I'll perhaps show you."

Mason trod carefully. "I trust there will be nothing but cooperation and mutual benefit between us. Dextra Haven, the high commissioner for Aquamarine, wishes the same."

"Haven, Haven." Rhodes batted the air with his scepter as if insects were bombinating around his head. "Starkweather bores me with talk about her, and now you do the same. A *woman*." He laid the heavy rod on the throne's broad right armrest. "What you rattlebrains need to do is listen to *me* rather than talk."

Mason inclined his head. "I meant no disrespect."

"I, who by cunning and courage rose from second son of a second son to become ruler of all I survey!"

According to preliminary reports, 'Waretongue had simply inherited what his father had helped build and was having his problems holding on to it.

"I assured Commissioner Haven that you are visionary

enough to understand the bright future that lies in allying with LAW."

"Starkweather knows it, too," Rhodes hooted triumphantly. "He appears to hold an even higher authority than Haven."

"Starkweather must leave," Mason riposted. "While Haven and her forces will remain, rewarding friends and punishing enemies."

Rhodes affected a little sniff. "What proof do I have that Haven has a generous bone in her entire carcass?"

From a chest pouch, Mason pulled a small pickup and holo unit. Rhodes watched with suspicious red eyes as he set the unit on a nearby footstool and thumbed it on. A real-time holo rezzed up—of Rhodes on his throne.

The grandee gave a crow of surprise and then a coo of pleasure. "At last—*civilized* technology."

CHAPTER
TEN

From the highest watch spire of Pyx Souljourner could see the afternoon sunlight on the Pontos Reservoir. The reservoir was the farthest she could see from the Descrier cloister's mast, which had been built in the Beforetimes to support diverse ethercasting gyns and science teknics. That its ladder pegs were difficult to scale had made it a favorite getaway spot of hers.

A hundred klicks or so to the south lay the Ea dam, a colossal artifact of the Optimants, as was Pyx itself, hunkered atop Bulge-knob Cant in central-northwestern Scorpia. Back before the Grandee Rhodes had ordered her shut away, Souljourner had seen the dam as well as the grandee's stronghold at Wall Water. That had been eleven years earlier, and she could no longer tell where memory left off and fantasy began.

Alone in the watch spire, Souljourner let herself groan out loud over her banishment, when the world itself had taken on new energy. From the rustic hamlets of Clapfandle and Sonsy Swage to the crossroads thorpe of Jagfall Bower and the busy reservoir trading burgh of Dip-Dorsal, people were everywhere on the move, dynamized into a thousand skewed courses by the recent return of the Visitants' celestial car.

Rumors superabounded, new ones every day, that the far-star Visitants would bring peace and plenty to Aquamarine, an end to the Oceanic, or Judgment Day. Into the unrest and frictions, the innovations and dislocations still accruing from their visit a generation earlier, this new advent came like burnfern oil flung on a brushfire.

With the wide, chapfallen world poised for miracles or apocalypse, Souljouner thought, Here stand I, confined to Pyx, perhaps for life. Shut in with a hundred dotty, Descry-deaf old decrepits, all of them impotent from a lifetime's ingestion of Apex and most of them more interested in their digestive complaints than in the coming of a new eon.

Around her neck hung a drawstring bag of cured skin, which she began to rub, feeling the angular shapes of the Holy Rollers within. She wished for liberation.

"What're you about up there?" Tusker abruptly called from below. "Bless us all, come down before you fall and smash your conk, you young hoyden!"

Nicknamed for his few remaining lower teeth, he was the cloister's rheumy-eyed and stoop-shouldered bloat-gut old proctor of husbandry. Souljourner could tell by the look of him that he had already had two or three tumblers of gooner, and though he was squinting up at her in alarm, he made no move to climb.

Easing out of the waist-high bucket, she directed her bare feet to the mast's uppermost peg and began to descend. The Big Sere heat was already fierce in the unshaded crow's nest, and the sight of freer people had made her heart as leaden as she could bear. Then, too, there were tasks that needed doing. Increasingly, the Descriers were becoming her charges rather than her wardens.

Seeing that she'd tucked the back of her skirt all the way up through the front of her cincture, Tusker averted his eyes from the sight of her strong young legs. Souljourner delighted in momentary power and cruel amusement, then chided herself. She'd long since learned that Pyx's full house of Apex addicts had passed beyond the murkily described carnal raptures and perils she'd read about. But occasionally something she did or said—or merely her presence—seemed to pierce their old hearts with regrets that even the drug's analgesic effects couldn't deaden. Like most of them, Tusker had been decent enough to her, and she had too many unfulfilled longings and recurrent sorrows of her own to get much lasting pleasure out of mistreating him.

She glanced again at Clapfandle and Sonsy Swage as she made her way down. There probably were eyes on the mast as well. The lumpkins who traded with the cloister nursed a dream that she would attempt a third escape and that they'd be the lucky ones to fetch her back and claim a reward from the prae-postor of the place.

But she had no designs along those lines. The last time it had been Grandee Rhodes's own Militerrors who had apprehended her. Upon escorting her home, they had executed the previous praepostor, Rolande—who'd always been patient with and kind to her—in the winepress as a lesson to all concerned. The public display of Rolande's remains had assured that no virile young swains would sneak anywhere near Pyx's walls in hopes of wooing her. The supremely suspicious Grandee Rhodes didn't dare put her to death, but he especially feared the possibility of her bearing a girl child. Her fear was that before too long he would take some horrific step to *ensure* that she wouldn't.

Tusker made nervous conversation from the base of the mast. "I do believe I felt a pang of the fourth order—rectilineared nor'-nor'east, perhaps off Drybone Gulf—with a subterranean dampening of twenty leagues' moderation. Yep, I've got the old magic in me yet!"

She made a noncommittal sound as she planted her sizable feet on Pyx's roof. She saw no reason to spoil the old geezbo's fantasy, but if there had been a subsurface tremor of that magnitude out under the great terrifying waters of Amnion, she not only would have Descried it but would be nursing a consequent pulsing headache. While arguably the most ill-starred Descrier ever to come to the brotherhood's attention, she was without doubt the most gifted of them all.

Tusker was standing by the empty wooden buckets from which Souljourner should have been doling out midday rations of Apex. A euphoric derived from a host of plants, the concoction helped focus seismic-sensing abilities while lessening the side effects. Grandee Rhodes took a cut of the modest trade in Apex, which Descriers in distant realms couldn't obtain for themselves. Pyx thus turned a small profit in much the same way that places like distant Alabaster thrived because of mand-seng and Passwater, far across horrid waters, did with galvani stones. Into the bargain, the Rhodes family's uncostly sponsor-ship of the cloister gave it access to and even influence over the doings of the entire Descrier brotherhood.

"Yer tardy, and the praepostor'll not be pleased," Tusker continued. "So won't you hurry, then, prithee please?"

She blew her breath out and chucked him under his wattles. She had begun to heft the yoke when he cleared his throat meaningfully—which devolved into a phlegmy cough.

"Hoo. Forgot." She lowered the shoulder pole and rearranged her skirts as Tusker stared off intently in the direction of distant Swillquaff. Then she set off.

She swung into an easy stride, down into the cloisters proper and along a wall, cracked and faded by time, where some of the Beforetimers' letterings were still readable. GeStation #82 appeared in many areas of the complex and was apparently the original name of the place. In Pyx and like structures the Optimants—first and highest of the Beforetimers—had called the Aquam to life from magical amniotic vessels sown with their seed, to walk forth en masse across all the dry places of the world.

The most notable Beforetime vessels Souljourner had seen during her explorations were the vats in which Threefinger and the other mixers brewed Apex, plus a little gooner and sot-mead when the ingredients were available. There was the cistern called 3WIM/3PA—3ENIOR 3TAFF ONLY, of course, and the sunken-floored room called HOLDWATER TANK, which she had made into her own little cell. But the only vessel in Pyx that stood to bring forth a newborn Aquam was Souljourner herself.

As she walked, she sorted through the daydreams that enabled her to rise and face each day. She had no expectations that the parents she only dimly remembered would come to reclaim her, but it was a nice scenario to imagine. She had likewise given up hope that her acute and sometimes agonizing Descrying faculty would vanish and that that vanishing would somehow translate into liberation. As for her years of devout prayer that the Grandee Rhodes would pass away after protracted suffering—she had yet to relinquish that one.

The codgers of Pyx had at least taught her to read, and the cloister's books, folios, and scrolls had offered some solace. She was meagerly consoled by fantasies in which handsome young men cared enough about her to defy Rhodes's will and bear her off. She was circumspect and considerate enough to footnote her reverie to the effect that her escape led to no reprisals against Pyx's enfeebled residents.

Her dark-haired and dark-eyed imaginary hero of late had been inspired by the recent visit of a young pharmacopoeist apprentice from the distant Trans-Bourne, except that her ideal had all his teeth and both of his arms. He was also as mighty as the Dominor's Paladin in *The Love-Land Creed*, as selflessly devoted to Souljourner as the Clockwork Bodyguard in *The Tale of the Odalisque*, and as inventively carnal as the Knave of Rods in *Passions of the Tarot*.

Even the weight of the yoke and buckets couldn't dislodge the reverie; it took nothing less than Threefinger's voice to do that.

"Stand fast!" the cloister's mixmaster barked. "You know these precincts are sacrosanct! Or perhaps you have notions of learning the mystery of the recipe itself!"

Souljourner snapped to. Completely borne away by her imaginings of a different life, she had almost wandered clear into the mixers' innermost chambers, where Threefinger and his two minions—amid a confusion of ironmongery, mortars and pestles, metal tubing, and smoking wood fires—were measuring out powdery ocher crystals of precipitated Apex into phials, leather wallets, and brindles.

She considered telling Threefinger that the allegedly secret recipe had in fact been revealed to her eight years earlier by Threefinger's superannuated, gregarious old geezbo predecessor, Jellyjest. A far more teknic mixmaster than Threefinger, the irreverent Jellyjest had even taken the time to explain the pitfalls in the Apex process. How, for example, a tincture of shootroot could reverse an impurity in the sere pollen, while an overabundance would inflict headaches even more blinding than those to which Descriers were subject by nature. Or how whitewood dust had to be avoided because it would render Apex ineffective in every way without any alteration in the flavor to warn mixmaster or consumer.

Secret recipe, indeed, she thought.

But flaunting her forbidden mixmaster lore would only have resulted in further acrimony, so she simply apologized to Threefinger for her inadvertent intrusion, filled her buckets with freshly brewed Apex, and hurried away. She herself had little use for the concoction. Apex did nothing to enhance her already fine-tuned perception, and while it did calm upset nerves, she much preferred a dose of watered gooner.

When she reached the apartments of Praepostor Sternstuff, she found him glowering in the doorway. His empty chalice sat pointedly at the center of his hand-carved mollywood desk.

"Late again," he said nastily. "Mooncalving on the watch spire as usual?"

He wanted to be regarded as penetrating and canny, but he wasn't all that shrewd; probably some spy had apprised him of her whereabouts. After replacing the winepressed Rolande, he had made it his mission to get Souljourner to toe the mark, if for no other reason than to bolster his image as a more capable overman. He wasn't well liked by the brotherhood, and Souljourner had denied him his victory.

Their skirmishes had been many, such as when a freak hailstorm had inspired Sternstuff to order her to sit among the fruit trees to sustain their lives with her feminine aura and she had confounded him by claiming disingenuously that the cold would freeze her menstrual cloth.

"You were no doubt bewailing your fate," he was saying, "safe and well provided for behind these walls, while the rest of the world poises to go even madder than it is. What ungrateful bosh!"

Refusing to give him the satisfaction of her anger, she set down the yoke and carefully refilled the chalice on his desk and the little carafe on his sideboard. Apex grew sour in hours, so new batches were constantly mixed.

Tall and erect, with a matting of pure white hair, he wasn't a bad-looking man as the grizzled relics of Pyx went. He had retired younger than most, after some ill-defined legal difficulty out in the Rumbledowns. Like many Descriers, he had sent minimal tithes to the cloister—confident that he would never be in need of its shelter—only to turn to it in desperation and express outrage at the down-at-the-heels state of the place.

"Were I to let you go lollygagging down the Cant," he persisted, "you'd soon see yourself bound over to a quimdealer, roasted on a spit, or slaughtered outright by some terrified loon who's heard of your birth curse."

Condemnations of the outside world and her ingratitude were a well-trodden rant of his, so she simply gazed at the huge maps on his wall, unfazed. Drawn in the Beforetimes, the two that flanked the door to his chambers were embedded in some stuff as clear as glass but warm to the touch. The one to the left showed all of Aquamarine; the one to the right, Scorpia, the Trans-Bourne, and their surrounding isles. When Rolande was praepostor, Souljourner had spent whole days poring over them, but Sternstuff wouldn't suffer her presence beyond whatever was unavoidable.

Her eyes were drawn to a mark daubed on the great southern road that ran down Scorpia's underbelly: Alabaster. The mark meant that a new Descrier was needed there, and Pyx, as the clearinghouse of the brotherhood, had been asked to suggest a candidate. To confirm that, a red vellum Writ, limned in gold, lay beside a messenger's tube of ivory on Sternstuff's desk.

She could see from where she stood that the all-important name had yet to be filled in and that the stamp had not been impressed with the praepostor's seal. The seal itself, which suggested a small silver gourd, rested in its impregnable ancient display case, to which only Sternstuff had the code.

A new Descrier for Alabaster, she thought, the mythic city-state hard by the terrible sea from which came a full quarter of all the mandseng that grew on Scorpia. Everyone on Aquamarine prized mandseng—more accurately, everyone who wanted to maximize the chance of having a normal baby and be spared the grief and agony of an Anathemite birth. Alabaster kept to itself, and virtually no news went forth, so Souljourner could only imagine the privilege and luxury a Descrier would enjoy there. Again she thumbed the drawstring pouch around her neck, wishing on the Holy Rollers it contained.

Seeing what she was staring at, Sternstuff nodded knowingly. "Yes, the venerable Shaker of Alabaster has passed on." The bitter glare he gave the map and the Writ seemed to mirror his feelings on the subject. "Many a certified master Descrier situated comfortably with some sachem or petty junta would leap at

the chance to live like a Palatine behind the white walls of
Alabaster."

The lucky man would not be Sternstuff, whose gift for sensing quakes had deserted him, as it did all Descriers of advancing
age. There was nevertheless a mollified tone in his voice when
he added, "I have been asked to nominate a suitable replace-
ment, and I mean to see that he's a . . . *worthy* one. It won't be
some newly made journeyman who gets my nod."

She caught his meaning straightaway. If he couldn't have the
prize himself, he could at least leverage a handsome bribe for
delivering it up to someone else, perhaps even finesse competing gifts from a number of competitors.

"Of course that's no concern of yours."

No concern to only the third female Descrier ever known to
exist on Aquamarine, Souljourner said to herself, heir to blame
for the dreadful events that had attended the lives and deaths of
the first two. Sternstuff might yet escape Pyx, but no ray of hope
gleamed through for her.

It was all so unfair that she let fall her ladle. "Won't you
speak to the Grandee Rhodes on my behalf? Surely there's
some corner of Aquamarine where I can live my own life. I'll
take exile in the Trans-Bourne or ride a flying pavilion to Pass
water!" She felt humiliated but couldn't stop herself. "I'm no
danger to anyone, and I aspire to no grand things. All I ask for is
freedom, a chance to find some humble little place in the world
for myself."

Sternstuff gave her back a triumphant, sardonic rictus of a
smile. He wasn't about to be moved by a woman's petition the
way the lustful Inquisitor was by Fantasia's in *Passions of the
Tarot*.

"You'll never have that, girl. The Grandee Rhodes ordered
you sequestered here, and I've no intention of questioning his
command."

She felt like crowning him with his own seal. She wanted to
see him humbled like the lascivious Lord Sphinx in *The Tale of
the Odalisque*. "I may never have my freedom, Praepostor, but
you'll never have Alabaster," she said, sneering at him, "or any
presentiment of the Descry, *ever*."

He looked angry enough to strike her, but she planted her

broad feet and stood her ground, strong enough from years of labor to throw him across the room. Sternstuff whirled and stamped off to his inner sanctum, slamming the door behind him.

Instead of finishing her chore, however, she stood staring at the map and at the daub that was Alabaster, all the while rubbing the pouch around her neck. For so important a decision, she thought, it would be necessary to consult with higher powers.

Back in the little cell she'd made for herself, Souljourner gazed into the steel plate she had polished and repolished for a looking glass. It showed back a young woman taller than almost anyone in Pyx, her body broadened by work but small-breasted. The hands struck her as coarse and far too big. Her hair, drab buff yellow, hung lax and stringy to the point where she'd sheared it off just below her chin. The face was squarish and ruddy from weather, with too much jaw. She saw her muddy gray eyes as too small and widely spaced. Her brows, fairer than her hair, were one unbroken bow curve across her face, so primitive that she wanted to flense them off. Hardly a princess from an illuminated manuscript.

She sat cross-legged on her pallet and opened the drawstring pouch—the tanned scrotum of her maternal grandfather, itself a talisman of very strong medicine—and poured out the pair of Holy Rollers her mother had bequeathed her before her very first episode of Descrying.

The Optimant-made dice were as beautiful and unmarked as if new: a black cube with silver bits and a silver one with black bits. Fashioned in the classic style, Rolande had told her, and worth a pretty sum in trade.

Ceding herself to them, she shook and tossed them across the floor, where they came up a black three and a silver four. She had no need to consult the bibelot that had come with them. The augury was

NO JOURNEY CAN BE MADE 'LESS
THE FIRST STEP IS TAKEN

Later the same day she took that step by sneaking into Sternstuff's chambers and spiking his carafe of Apex with whitewood dust.

CHAPTER
ELEVEN

In her cabin aboard *Big Tess*, Dextra paced through tight circles, as if to etch a kind of mandala on her parcel of carpeted deck. With Raoul Zinsser due to arrive at any moment, she rehearsed the role she would have to play to keep him as an ally.

Though the starship had been in orbit for scarcely five subjective-days, those days already felt like months. The voyage from Periapt, so agonizingly tedious at the time, might as well have taken place years earlier. In place of monotony, Dextra now grappled with an intense restlessness for the gentle takeover of Aquamarine to begin.

Claude Mason was downside, paving the way for Dextra's audience with the Grandee Rhodes. There had been no follow-up to the Roke attack and no sign of the aliens anywhere in the Eyewash system. However, Starkweather had named Wix Uniday as his liaison person to the GammaLAW mission. A former member of LAW Political Security division, Uniday, like Starkweather, had certainly had a hand in implementing Cal Lightner's plan to vilify the Exts before they had even set foot on Periapt and defame Dextra in the process.

Regardless, Uniday had gotten off to a resounding start in his cheerfully candid campaign to ingratiate himself by informing her that he had persuaded Starkweather to allow an advance team of GammaLAW personnel to go groundside as soon as possible. They were to survey the proposed tetherdrop splash-down site and make preliminary contact with the lake's over-seer, hence Claude Mason's spaceplane ride down the well.

Dextra had considered sending Burning and a few others along but had thought better of it. Starkweather was getting too damn cute, and until the SWATHship was safely planetside, everyone on Dextra's team had to be kept close by. Quant desperately wanted to get a look at the waters waiting for him but had reluctantly agreed that his place was with his vessel.

As to Uniday, Dextra was still waffling over how best to handle him. If he could be persuaded to begrudge the Gamma-LAW contingent a splash of his flair as a fixer and intercessor, he would prove useful, but as much as she respected his shrewdness, she didn't trust him.

When the hatch chirped and Tonii, Quant, Burning, Delecado, and Zinsser entered, Dextra waved everyone to seats and planted herself on the edge of her workstation, directly across from the oceanographer.

"It's my understanding, Doctor, that you were contacted by the team Starkweather assigned to analyze the remains of the Roke craft."

If Zinsser was surprised that she knew about it, he didn't show it. "Yes. Perhaps two hours ago I was summoned to the AlphaLAW biolab for a quick consultation."

"And?" Dextra said leadingly.

Zinsser rearranged himself in the seat. As pale as anyone aboard, he still had the wrinkled, fat-free, salt-weathered look of a champion swimmer. "I gather that what little debris the cruiser recovered isn't all that different from the odds and ends of Roke technology we've already seen. Sections of the spacecraft must have been heavily armored. Despite the very heavy hits it sustained, certain structures—protective pods and such—survived. In part, anyway."

Dextra nodded, waiting for more.

"There was, however, a rather startling find in all the surviving pods: residues of organic matter—a kind of somatic material the lab people presume to be Roke."

Dextra didn't attempt to downplay her astonishment. With the weapons of mass destruction used in the conflict's few full-scale engagements, there had been precious little for analysts to sift through. Humanity had no solid data on Roke biochemistry, physical morphology, social structure, and planet of origin. For that matter, no one really knew if the Roke starships were automated or if the aliens were few in number or hordes. The Roke were also believed to have little or no detailed data about humans, although it was conceivable that they enjoyed the advantage of being able to monitor and interpret human transmissions. Roke telecomm was an incomprehensible garble to human intel people and SIGINT computers alike.

"Could it be disinformation?" Dextra asked. "Did the team share any details?"

"As expected, the tissue replicates the fundamental DNA structure found on other planets," Zinsser said. "The thinking now is that many of the Roke control systems are organically based rather than mechanical, even though the spacecraft's hull, for example, was a nonliving artifact. The recovered tissue doesn't appear to be neural. In fact, it isn't necessarily Roke plasm at all. It could be constructs."

A suspicious Burning stabbed the table with a thick freckled forefinger. "Scroll back for a moment, Doctor. Starkweather won't even release our own gear to us, but he decides to cut you in on a major find. What gives?"

Zinsser's upper lip curled. "In all humility, Allgrave, my reputation is not unknown to Starkweather's people. Even so, the invitation to share information took me quite by surprise—though I've since puzzled it out."

"Would you care to elaborate?" Dextra said.

"Starkweather was inclined to summon me for two reasons. In exchange for continued access, he wishes to learn more about my Pitfall device. More important, the structure of the Roke tissue suggests an aquatic—probably marine—organism."

Dextra mulled what influence the revelation might have on Starkweather as she waited for the others' murmurings to die away. Quant got in the next question.

"Are you saying that the Roke are sea creatures?"

Zinsser shook his head. "Merely that some of the tissue samples *may* have been derived from marine life-forms. As I said, there's no proof that the remains have anything to do with the Roke themselves. After all, what do humans have in common with vegetable-based lube fluid?"

Quant leaned back until the varimorph chair groaned in protest. "You also said they might have organic systems. Could they have steered clear of technology because they've also suffered the Cyberplagues?"

Zinsser was clearly impressed. "The thought occurred to me. But we can't draw conclusions with so little data. It's equally plausible that they employed organic systems from the start and were untouched by the Cyberplagues."

"Maybe the vermin even set the Plagues on us," Daddy D muttered.

Zinsser granted him a nod as well. "The original vector of the Cyberplagues was a flurry of peculiar interstellar transmissions whose source has yet to be pinpointed. Why not the Roke?"

Dextra had questions of her own. "What if the Roke ship wasn't an offensive weapon? It didn't fire until it was fired on, and it *was* transmitting on our freqs as it came at us. So suppose it was some sort of warn-off device."

"Warning us away from the Roke?" Zinsser asked.

"No. Warning us away from Aquamarine." Dextra paused, then explained herself. "Something has kept the Roke from colonizing or atomizing Aquamarine, and it could be that the place is so dangerous, they were even willing to warn *us* about it."

The notion took Zinsser off guard. He covered it up by looking to the others' reactions. "But . . . humans have been living on Aquamarine for a thousand years," he thought to point out. "There's been no sign of anything like a quarantine or the *Scepter* would have been warned off."

Dextra took her lower lip between her teeth. "Just a thought. But I don't want any of our conjectures discussed outside this compartment—even by you, Doctor. If there are leaks and rumors, let them come from Starkweather's people."

Zinsser sputtered for a second. "That's absurd! How can you expect me to get any useful information if I'm to wear a gag?"

"Starkweather's offering you data in return for data. I'm not saying we shouldn't trade, but we first need to know what's on the table and why. We're in too tight a corner to be careless. I realize it's an imposition for a man of your academic stature, but we'll benefit more in the long run."

Zinsser compressed his lips.

"One more point," Dextra went on. "I *want* some of the Roke tissue samples—and sooner rather than later. In no event must this starship depart for Hierophant before we've gotten our piece."

"Are you asking me to steal?" Zinsser said in disbelief.

"I didn't say that. But I'm sure you agree that it would be a great injustice if one of Starkweather's jumped-up lab assistants wound up winning a lifetime merit stipend from LAW for research *you* should be undertaking."

Zinsser smiled with his eyes. "I'll see what I can do, Madame Commissioner."

Dextra was pleased that he had grasped her meaning. Zinsser was raw envy swaddled in intellectual condescension, but he was the only real genius GammaLAW had.

The sight of his holo image had 'Waretongue admiring himself from various angles and generally ignoring Mason for the better part of an hour. Knowing that he was being tested, Mason bided his time instead of attempting to cajole answers from the grandee.

"That gorgeous feathered bonnet would look striking, Excellency," Mason would say. Or: "Oh, and the jeweled cape, put it on, and your embroidered shoes. I'll widen the angle so you can see yourself full-length on the throne."

He waited until Rhodes was completely appareled and striking a pose before switching off the imager and repocketing it. It wasn't the kind of stratagem that would have occurred to him in the *Scepter* days, but there was more at stake now than the mere annexation of a world.

'Waretongue looked displeased for a moment, then tittered. "Marriage and fatherhood have changed you, Claude—or rather, the idea of fatherhood. The thing itself's quite different, as you'd know if you had as many brats and bastards underfoot as I do. Be that as it may, I'll show you leniency." He leaned slightly toward Mason. "Incandessa bore you a son before she died, and that son's alive today."

Mason was stunned. "Dead?" he stammered in disbelief.

"Soon after your ship was out of contact."

Mason squeezed his eyes shut and let some of the anguish have its way with him. "My son," he said, choking out the words. "Where is he?"

Rhodes perched on the arm of the throne. "Elsewhere in Scorpia just now; don't ask me where. Got religion when he was a boy, courtesy of a devious, conniving scoundrel from the Trans-Bourne named Cozmote. Your son took the vows of an itinerant *rishi* of the Church of Human Enlightenment, and became a babbling mendicant, though a rather celebrated one. The Human Enlightenments claim to be spiritual heirs to the Conscious Voices, and are equally fixated on studying the whims of the Oceanic." 'Waretongue paused. "You remember the Conscious Voices, don't you, brother-in-law? The ones who hurled your shipmate Boon into the Amnion the night you abandoned my sister and your soon-to-be-born son?"

"His name," Mason rasped.

"Did I mention that the Voices died out quite soon after you left, Claude? All their pacifist fasting and mystical hoodoo intimidation was debunked, thanks to you. About the only useful thing you Visitants ever did for Aquamarine."

"His *name*," Mason said through locked teeth.

"Trudges about raving about the oneness of all Aquam and the need to be understanding of each other. Damned subversive, actually; a disappointment after the fine upbringing Skipjack and I lavished on him."

"His—"

"Purifyre. Incandessa's choice before she went to her reward. When the whim's upon him, he has proved himself useful in some ways. Has a low taste for tinkering with gyns, teknics, and such."

Mason caught his balance.

"Steady there, brother-in-law! Should I order up a draft of vitalizer? Some roborant vapors?"

Mason metronomed his forefinger in refusal of the jeering offer, then remembered that a Scorpian Aquam wouldn't translate the motion that way. Post-Plague indigs had evolved their own systems of gesture that didn't align with Periapt or Old Earth signifiers at all. So he changed to the hand signal a *Scepter* ethnologist had labeled "the bird flap": palm of the right hand on the back of the left, thumbs extended, scissoring the joined fingers back and forth in opposite directions—a kind of courteous wave-off.

"Where can I find Purifyre?" he asked when he got his breath back.

"Know, Claude, that it is my pleasure that there be a Grand Attendance at Wall Water, a high durbar to welcome the illustrious Commissioner Haven. All the Ean grandees will attend, of course. I've sent special couriers to invite your boy, although—" Rhodes paused, eyelids lowering to half mast. "—his feelings regarding you are rather mixed. I recommend that you pique his intellectual curiosity by demonstrating some of LAW's teknic wonders."

Mason felt grief and hope course through him. Haven intended to demonstrate LAW capabilities to the Aquam, anyway. "What would be best?" he asked. "Aviation technology? Energy production?"

"I've not the vaguest idea what fascinates craftspeople," Rhodes said, turning his nose up. "Should Purifyre send word of his interests, I will pass them along to you with the messenger who conveys Commissioner Haven's invitation to the Grand Attendance. In fact, it might interest you to meet my message bearer beforehand."

'Waretongue had a small, glittery tuning fork from which he elicited a high, piercing note by striking it against the flesh-colored marblywood throne. Seconds later a wall hanging bellowsed, and from a concealed door a hot-air balloon of a man emerged, draped in a Druidic-looking manteau of bloodred huskfiber. The manteau was topped by an amphitheater collar higher than the man's head, fashioned of stiffened crimson flummox leather, making it look as if a wingback chair were attached to his gargantuan behind.

It was traditional Sense-maker garb. Even so, it took Mason several moments to recognize the man within. "Spume? Young Spume?"

"*Old* Spume now," Rhodes enjoyed saying.

Always corpulent, the former Sense-talker to 'Waretongue's father at the New Alexandria lighthouse walked painfully, favoring his left leg. His eyes were rheumy, and his hands, emerging from frayed mandarin sleeves, showed cracked sores and angry red patches. When Old Spume grinned, he exhibited more blackened gum than rotted teeth.

He hadn't, however, lost the characteristic that had given him his name. When he offered salutations to Mason, saliva flew from him in a fine mist, mingled with heavier sprinkles. "It's good to see what little I can make out of you. Not aged a moment since that night at the lighthouse. Palpable sorcery!"

'Waretongue giggled. "Mind the squall, dear Claude! See why I cannot part with him? A disaster as an adviser but a wonderful court fool!"

That drew a hurt look from Spume, but he obviously didn't dare respond beyond a wary simper. Old, fat, and ludicrous as he might be, he had been a middling to good Sense-maker for Skipjack and deserved better from Skipjack's second son. When Mason opted not to join 'Waretongue's laughter, the grandee became peevish.

"I've wasted enough time on this piffle," he announced regally. "I'm late for my afternoon soak." Abandoning finery, scepter, and throne, he headed for the wall hanging from behind which Old Spume had appeared. "Spume, you gluttonous buffoon, show my guest back to his flying gyn. And Claude, *aroint*! Disappear forthwith. No more of this offensive buzzing about my home."

Mason felt his vision blurring and had the ineluctable feeling that he was about to be paid another visit by the downloaded Yatt netware, but he steeled himself against it. Staying minimally in Rhodes's good graces was more important just now than nosing around Wall Water in search of Pre-Plague technology. When the stirrings from Yatt subsided, Mason was left with the distinct impression that the AI had bowed before a more powerful dynamic: the one that connected Mason to the son he had never met.

Old Spume beckoned and, huffing and blowing for breath, escorted him back through the foyer. Mason saw nothing of note that he'd missed while coiffure-blindfolded by the grandee's pacificatrixes.

"It's like a hallucination, your not being aged a day," Spume remarked.

"Do you know Purifyre, Spume? Has he ever mentioned me?"

The old man nodded. "When he was a tot, we were constantly explaining to him who you were and where you had gone. As he grew into childhood, he stopped asking."

"What is he like?"

Away from Rhodes's laughter, Spume's salivary spray wasn't as pronounced. "Strong, Claude. Self-contained, resolute, complicated, very canny. Champion of the underdog. A dangerous young man, I think."

Mason tried to press him for details, but Spume had revealed all he wished to. Instead, he began a rambling tour guide lecture about Rhodes's redecorating. Mason took it to mean that they were being watched and that there were subjects the Sensemaker couldn't broach.

Short of the Militerrors surrounding the spaceplane, Spume stopped and gripped Mason's forearms with quaking hands. "Don't bore your Commissioner Haven with talk of Purifyre, Claude. I promise that I'll have good tidings when you return."

Mason nodded in understanding. It was all he could hope for.

CHAPTER
TWELVE

After being dismissed from the debriefing by Haven, Zinsser was in a foul humor. He had never reacted favorably to being told what he could do, let alone what he could *not* do. And while he agreed with Haven about the need to keep the starship's AlphaLAW contingent at arm's length, he felt hemmed in by her orders to keep his theories about the Roke to himself.

Not five minutes from Haven's cabin Zinsser spotted Wix Uniday standing to one side in the passageway, as if to test the pledge he had made only moments earlier. A young man with tousled blond ringlets, Uniday fell in alongside Zinsser as he boarded a people mover. Zinsser could almost smell the reek of entitlement that emanated from the former PolSec operative.

"In case you're wondering why Commissioner Starkweather chose me to act as liaison with Haven's people, I thought I might explain myself."

Zinsser glanced at his uninvited companion. "I haven't been wondering. But by all means unburden yourself if you feel the need."

"Basically I'm a time skimmer, Doctor. Before Periapt I was a member of the AlphaLAW mission to Trinity, and now here I am en route to Hierophant. High-echelon duty there, along with some damn fine perks while in transit."

"The appointment as liaison, for example," Zinsser said.

"Precisely. Total time skimming for this Hierophant cruise: perhaps five subjective-years. With opportunities for an apt fellow to acquire supplemental income and fringe benefits. On Trinity I had a penthouse, a plantation, and a seaside retreat— with a seraglio at each. The catch, of course, is that one has to be one's own person. By the time I return to Periapt, twenty baseline years will have sped by, and with any luck at all the Roke Conflict will be over and I will be rich. Whatever the case, I'll sign on for another cruise, provided the prospects are suitably alluring. I like nothing more than spiraling home every few years, well off and still young. The situation appeals to both the philosopher and the egotist in me."

Zinsser turned ninety degrees to face Uniday. "Why are you telling me this?"

"Merely to let you know that there's a place for you in Starkweather's mission if you want it. All he wants up front is your promise that you'll deploy Pitfall *before* we launch for Hierophant."

Zinsser snorted. "I have yet to decide on a satisfactory locale, much less determine when I'm going to deploy. I'll have to survey the Amnion firsthand, from above as well as from various points along the coast of Scorpia and the outer islands."

"As well you should," Uniday said. "But in light of the possibly aquatic nature of the Roke tissue, Commissioner Starkweather has grown increasingly curious about the Oceanic— specifically, why the Roke were perhaps posting guard on Aquamarine."

Zinsser lifted an eyebrow. "And why, at the same time, they appear to have given the planet a wide berth?"

Uniday didn't quite frown. "You already know what you can get from me, so let's not digress, okay? All I need from you is some sense of your timetable. If you want help finding a good fishing spot, all you need do is ask."

Zinsser, too, knew when to drop a certain level of pretext. Starkweather's people had obviously discovered that he had installed his own passwords in Pitfall's software. Doubtless they'd monkeyed with it, intending to deploy it without asking his permission, only to find it just inert technology.

"I have no objections to apprising you of the deploy date," Zinsser said equably, "but I have certain requirements of my own that have nothing at all to do with a position on Starkweather's AlphaLAW mission. To come directly to the point, I need a kilo of Roke tissue. In return, I'll agree to deploy Pitfall before the *Sword* departs for Hierophant as well as allow Starkweather's people to share whatever data are amassed."

Uniday's eyebrows went up and then down. "That's half the biological material we recovered, Doctor. Suppose we settle on twenty grams—and Starkweather's people get to choose where and when to spring your tether fish trap."

Zinsser smiled to himself. Uniday wouldn't be willing to give up the tissue samples unless the science task force had drawn a blank. "You have nearly three kilos of assorted plasm," he said, "and I already know which specimens I wish to examine. Surely both of us have better things to do than quibble. Let's say five hundred grams."

Uniday's veneer hardened a bit. "For thirty grams of tissue you agree to surrender Pitfall's encryption codes. In addition, our teams will have *full* access to your lab as well as your findings."

Zinsser mulled it over. Once he gave them the password, "Rubicon," he'd have no insurance that Starkweather would use Pitfall in accordance with his wishes or even abide by LAW's Oceanic-related cautionary guidelines. Without booby traps or safeguards, the AlphaLAWs might wreck Pitfall or even succeed in antagonizing the Oceanic. However, Zinsser felt confident that he could bluff his opposite numbers into complying with his wishes in the matter of its use. Moreover, he could always have Haven build a second device after the *Sword* departed.

"I'll allow you access to my lab and allow Starkweather to choose a deploy date when, and only when, I have the Roke tissue in hand and I'm satisfied with the tether mission profile and experiment syllabus."

Wix Uniday affected a cordial look. "Sounds fair. May I take it that we have an understanding?"

Zinsser made a graceful salaam and inclined his head. "Proving once again that rational men can always find the way forward."

In the general scrambling to meet the revised tetherdrop schedule, the constituents of the Aggregate were more non-plussed than usual by Alone behavior. They were troubled by the smells of thickened rancor onboard the starship, the evident stress in the voices of crewpersons, and the sight of so many deceptive facial kines.

Pressed by Dextra Haven to complete their experiments in communication with marine life-forms, the Aggregate had been placed off limits to Alones for the entire voyage. Even Lod had been denied access except for a few brief visits, and then always in Haven's company. He'd been obliged to spend most of his time waiting outside the Aggregate's new Habitat while Haven heard Piper's progress reports.

The workload notwithstanding, they had been the least complaining group on the GammaLAW roster, and they continued to remain quietly focused on adhering to Haven's directives. Piper had simply acquiesced to the commissioner's illogical demands that they halt current Allspeech R&D sessions, hasten the breaking down and packing of their temporary Habitat, and prepare for transfer planetside.

They were in the middle of packing when Piper registered the approach of several Alones whose Alltalk she hadn't been subjected to since the launch from Periapt. With the hatch open, voices and other vibrations told her it was Zone and his cadre. Her skin and bare feet identified the particular rhythms of booted footfalls as much as her ears did. When their odors confirmed the identification, she quickly asserted control over her corpcode to hide all body language signs of her agitation. Zone lacked a true understanding of Othertalk, but she had read in him from the first a primitive instinct for picking up on subtle clues.

The ship's police armbands they had been wearing months earlier were gone, but they still carried stun batons and sidearms. They stank as much from ghastly libations and drugs as from the breath and skin deodorizers they'd used to mask their abuse of those substances. Piper had to curb her nausea as their odors invaded the aromas of Habitat berthing and working spaces.

She knew that Zone had volunteered to safety-check Habitat in preparation for *Terrible Swift Sword*'s midcourse end-for-end, when its drive was turned for the long deceleration burn. Haven had turned him down. Instead, the Ext guard detail that

ensured that Habitat remained off limits had been assigned the
duty of safety inspection.

Now that Haven's crash project was complete, however,
Piper had lost the protective aegis of research secrecy and guard
detail, and so Zone had returned. The constituents gave no overt
sign but made worried Othertalk to her. When she responded in
kind that they were to go on working, they did.

"All packed up here, I see," Zone said on entering. "Ready
for the dingleberry ride down dirtside. Haven has whatever it is
she wanted out of you, so bye-bye guard detail, hey?"

That he was relishing sexual prospects was plain in his scent-
speech. He strolled her way leisurely, pausing to prod and rap
random fish tanks and pieces of equipment with the rounded
head of the black stun-tonfa. With most of the equipment dis-
connected or crated, there was nothing within reach of Piper's
cybercant that would make a good weapon.

The female Ext named Strop remained by the hatch as lookout. Wetbar, though, tried to put his face into Takellin's as he
was bent over a worktable. When Takellin pulled his head down
between his shoulders and drew away, Wetbar loosed a self-
satisfied snort.

Zone sighed at Piper as if she were a disobedient child.
"There's so much we have to get straight."

Piper thought that no matter how alien the Oceanic was, it
could be no more so than this Alone. His Othertalk made no
sense. Did he want to kill the Aggregate, as so many Alones had
wished to do over the years? Or did he want nothing more than
sex from them?

Zone was gazing at Piper and stroking the stun baton as he
might his own member. "Remember that little favor I asked you
to do for me when we were still hanging over Periapt?"

Piper had anticipated the question. She reached into a nearby
drawer and retrieved the translucent Optimant dice he had
asked her to rig. She also produced a touchpad half the size of
her palm.

Zone slapped the baton into the palm of his hand and nodded
at the dice. "Show me."

"What combination do you want?"

"Seven—for good luck. Red four, white three."

The touchpad she had built was equipped with a red tile and a white one, under which were two rows of digits, one through six. Her gracile fingers keyed the combination deftly, but knowing little about shooting craps, she dropped the gaffed dice as much as tossed them. They bounced naturally and came up showing four on the red die and three on the white.

Zone snatched them up and turned them in his palm; then he plucked the touchpad out of her hand and studied it. "How's it work?"

"Piezoelectric movements of the die faces, guided by micromotor gyros controlled by transparent microprocessors powered by miniature packs hidden in the pips. Good for anywhere from two hundred to five hundred casts, depending on demand. Rechargeable."

He held up the touchpad. "You give the whole scam away with *radio* emissions?"

She shook her head. "To avoid interference we used a coded ultrasonic pulse. The dice are effectively immune to detection."

Zone nodded, briefly placated. The touchpad was easily concealable in his hand, which was big enough to palm a battle helmet. His eyes slid back to her, and he smiled. "I wantcha to know that I appreciate your effort. But there's something else we need to discuss." He dropped the baton back into its belt ring.

Piper had murky, submerged memories of the kind of sex his paralanguage and Othertalk were alluding to from back before she had been saved from Alone life by Byron Sarz. She had been prepubescent then, a ward of the state, dulled to everything that was going on around her—but she remembered. Even so, if her suffering those indignities again would spare the other constituents harm, she would endure them. With an Alone they would have no significance beyond a modicum of pain.

She was steeling herself for Zone's caress when he pulled from his pocket an Aggregate-style sealed spherule. Immediately she scentsed the faint, traumatizing aroma of Byron. That and some trace odors told her it was a capsule of prompter pseudopheromone. Zone could only have stolen it from cargo brought to the starship from the original Habitat.

Zone's thick thumbnail was poised to crack it open.

The pseudopheromone came from Byron's deepest delvings into volitional and nonvolitional olfactory-wired behaviors. It was one of the most imperative scent messengers, from a battery of them that had driven the constituents into a state of *musth*, affecting them far more powerfully than it did Alones. That particular run Byron had made exclusively for his own use by employing his own scent as one of its foundation-odor medleys.

Piper could bear physical violation, but the thought of having her senses jammed, of having Zone cross-wired with Byron in her brain, was unbearable. For the second time since becoming a constituent—the first occasion having taken place on the night of the Lyceum ball—Piper's self-command failed.

She was about to rake him across the face with her nails when he suddenly flipped the spherule to his other hand and grinned at her. "You understand what a several is?"

She stared at him for a moment, then nodded. "A menage-marriage."

Zone's chin indicated Wetbar and Strop. "That's what we are, the three of us. We'd like *you* to consider pledging for membership." He displayed the spherule once more. "Think, Piper, of the possibilities. You and us and a smidgen of Byron Sarz . . ."

The Alltalk of Piper's rage made the constituents stir, but they held their places in fear as the three Exts advanced on her.

To no one's surprise, Dextra Haven didn't like late-breaking developments coming her way at every turn—not by several planetary radii. She advanced on the seat that all but contained Claude Mason and planted her hands on her hips. "Say that again! 'Dyes'?"

Just returned from groundside, Mason had already been questioned about Wall Water's general appearance and defenses. Given that he had dealt only with Militerrors, the Rapunzel-haired pacificatrixes, Rhodes, and Old Spume, it was assumed that his visit couldn't provide much in the way of crucial information. That was why Dextra's head had come up at his insistence on talking about dyes.

"When we were last here," Mason said, grateful for the opportunity to explain, "the Aquam used nothing but primitive natural dyes and mordants. Now they have what appear to be azo-type dyeing agents. Wall Water looks like—well, run the cam pod holos for yourselves."

Dextra did. Even the poorest-appearing Aquam were arrayed in loud hues, often in ill-advised combinations. The colorations extended to paints, skin decoration, decor, and more. Intel officers at the debriefing who'd been more or less noting the matter perfunctorily suddenly paid strict attention, if only to avoid appearing slow.

"The change is dramatic," Mason went on. "I imagine fortunes are being made. I mean, it's clear that the trade in pigments and dyes is at least partly responsible for the commerce that's broken down so many local borders and has so many people on the roads."

"Are you certain that no one on the *Scepter* team taught the Aquam about dyes?" Dextra asked. "After all, the Aquam have obviously made the most of Hippo Nolan's muscle-car drive systems."

Mason was shaking his head. "None of us were teaching courses in chemistry or anything close to it."

"There's no evidence of large-scale dye-making operations anywhere in the vicinity of Lake Ea," one of the intel people thought to point out.

Mason swung to her. "All that means is that Rhodes and the other lake grandees aren't the source of the trade. The dyes could be coming from almost anywhere—the Trans-Bourne, Passwater, Alabaster . . ."

Dextra considered it. She couldn't shake the feeling that Mason had stumbled onto something important, and she respected him all the more for his fealty to mission priority, especially in light of what he had learned about his wife and child.

"Galvani stones, mandseng, muscle cars, and now dyes," Dextra mused aloud. "What I want to know is, how many other damned innovations are they harboring down there?"

"At least one more," Mason said. "*Steam* power."

CHAPTER
THIRTEEN

When word came summoning her to Sternstuff's chambers, Souljourner initially thought about ducking the appearance. Only two days had elapsed since she'd begun spiking the praepostor's Apex punch with whitewood dust, and she doubted that a lifetime's use could have worn off so quickly. More likely, Sternstuff had discovered her tampering.

But then arthritis-crippled Tusslebug, who had delivered the message, whispered news of the arrival of a deputation from the Grandee Rhodes himself, and of a palanquin of filigreed woods, tooled hides, and brass that waited outside Pyx's gates, and of two Militerror officers who'd paid a formal call on Sternstuff and now waited just within the gates . . .

"Grandee Rhodes has finally overcome his trepidations about the prophecies," she said when she could. "He means to kill me!"

But Tusslebug only shook his head. "Nonsense, child. What need would there be for a palanquin if such were the case when a mere winepress would suffice?"

Assured then that the Militerrors' arrival could only signal a change for the better, she flew from the hot barn, her solid feet splashing the courtyard mud and slapping the worn corridor floors with equal surety.

It began to occur to her that with the second coming of the Visitants, a new epoch of mercy must be blossoming and that she was to be released. She was determined, this one time, to be mild with Sternstuff, to demonstrate to him that she was adult and merited a Writ of her own as Descrier. Yet she couldn't restrain herself enough to tap on his office door and wait meekly for permission to enter. Instead, she plunged through, half laughing that she would make all Pyx proud of her.

Only to find Sternstuff swaying to his feet behind his desk and glaring at her. She had leapt to the wrong conclusion. The praepostor was hollow-eyed and trembling, and the room smelled strongly of prangberry sozzle, the dregs of which were spilling from a tipped-over flagon. With her appearance, he began to lick his lips over and over, while the bridge of his nose bunched and his eyes narrowed.

"You . . ." he managed.

Souljourner shot a desperate glance at the antique map, hoping to see a grease pencil symbol denoting the assignment of a journeyman Descrier to Alabaster, but there was none to be found. What she saw in its place was the glyph-name of a master Descrier whose current pale was far outback in Lava-Land. A small pot of crimson wax was warming over a candle, and the praepostor's seal lay nearby.

"You, you're . . ." Sternstuff tried once more, breathing very hard.

Souljourner gulped. What fate had Rhodes decreed for her that it could leave Sternstuff tongue-tied? "Why are the Militerrors here?" she fairly screamed. "Tell me!"

"You're . . . so alluring," Sternstuff mumbled. "Irresistible woman-child. So big and bonny, a very altar of concupiscence! The lust for you pounds in my head, beats in my veins, racks my loins! I cannot eat, cannot sleep, cannot think of anything else!"

Hoo! The effects of her vitiation of his Apex supply with whitewood had set in far faster than she would have guessed, and her lack of experience with un-Apexed men had abruptly dealt her a crisis. Such ruttishness from a hoary old hobble-dehoy like Sternstuff—who'd have thought it?

"W-ww-what of the Militerrors?"

Sternstuff let out a scalded sound and clutched his bosom. "The Oceanic take Rhodes! He has a score of scented concubines and a hundred courtier-doxies, not to mention twice that many serving bawds and the boys he likewise diddles." The praepostor had become shorter of breath talking about it. "I'll not yield him the mud nymph who has wakened my ardor and—" He clutched his robed crotch. "—warmed these love-meats anew!"

Souljourner had heard a balladeer declaim that love and hate were closely allied. But only under certain capacitated circumstances, she decided. "Back, now," she faltered as the old man circled his desk, moving toward her. "It's not for us to deny our grandee's decree, eh?" Her brain was working fleetly on many things, but not fleetly enough to make a clever segue. "What made you choose that Lava-Land bungler as the new Descrier of Alabaster?"

Sternstuff slowed for a moment. "What matters that? I'll no more give you Alabaster than freedom from my Pyxian pillar of love, you solid-fleshed young swivetmuff."

Inane, she told herself, even measured against the most lurid romances. But this wasn't a politic time to say so. And to think that she'd been considering trying her charms and yogic grace on him!

She began a strategic withdrawal toward the door. With a bit of luck the prangberry sozzle would soon put him under. She could learn the purpose of the Militerrors' visit from others or from the elite guardsmen themselves. "I've been all morning in the hot barn, bleeding the diffodars. I must go preen myself up all nice for you, put on something else—"

Sternstuff sprang forward with an astonishing mix of vigor and sotty ineptitude to block her path of retreat. He wasn't *that* drunk. "By no means, my nubile, meaty seductress! Only too pleased am I to take you as you are—and with gusto!"

He was fully her height and, for all his aversion to hard work, sound. She opted to try to gain control of the situation by pretending to go along with him. She also wanted very much to get him talking and therefore made a great show of shifting and disarranging her work-habit skirts. "Let's to it, then! Yet tell me why the grandee's personal troops are here, for it preoccupies me at a most inopportune moment."

He locked the door and pocketed the magnetic wand that was its key, then unsteadily swept his desk bare. "They spoke lies, lies! That erotomaniac Rhodes covets you for himself, for the depraved and fiendish infamies he perpetrates upon all and sundry down there on Lake Ea. But I say again that he shall not have you! Now hike your skirts and show me paradise. Dispose yourself up here on this good wood for passion that transcends the imaginable!"

Her dilemma involved several ponderables, suggesting that violence might be premature, so she complied slowly to give herself time to think. Shrugging here and lifting there, she arranged herself and her clothes. It being Big Sere, she wore no loinwrap. She assumed a swoony expression but also a laborious disportment of body and limbs.

Sternstuff looked apoplectic. "What farcical tableau is this?"

She was in a yogic asana, the Pose of a Fish, that she'd taught herself from an illuminated scroll on the subject: legs in the lotus position, spine arched back, and the crown of her head resting on the wood. For current purposes she'd modified it to include a tricky Dangerous Pose intertwining of the arms. Her eyes were crossed as she contemplated the tip of her nose.

"Very much an erotic posture for your pleasure and mine, learned as best I could from textual sources. You know my contact with women and knowledge of things amorous are scant."

So were his, but neither of them mentioned it. Sternstuff, slightly cross-eyed as well, got one knee up on the big desk, trying to figure out how best to approach what so drew him; the objective in question resided amid a very inexpedient configuration. He began a few unsteady, tentative moves, but while she pretended to be all unschooled compliance, Souljourner used her laborer's brawn, disguised as clumsiness, to thwart him.

"What algolagnian sadisms do you seek to inflict upon me?" the praepostor choked, throat vised in the crook of her elbow.

The prangberry sozzle's effects and the exertion had him blinking rapidly. She hoped he'd pass out peaceably, affording her the chance to take certain actions she was working out in her head. "You sly old nate-nuzzler, I'm trying my best," she *tch*ed, wriggling out from under him somewhat and arching herself farther along the desk.

"Don't call me 'old'! I'm young enough to plow your fertile furrow!"

"Then take me in this most lascivious collocation in all of copulation's bestiary." Rather than open herself to him, she scrambled into the Half Mountain Pose, with its kneeling semi-lotus configuration, one leg shielding her loins and interwoven arms and hands extended toward him in an unlikely and rather formidable-looking Archer Gesture variation. "Hoo! Come ravish me this instant!"

"How? While being eye gouged and caponed?"

Still, he wasn't about to desist until he'd had her. He struck her interlocked hands aside and threw himself at her headlong. She'd been sure she would be able to handle him if necessary, but the sozzle and the rousing of his long-dormant sex drive had Sternstuff in a berserker rage. He carried her over backward, slowly beginning to pin her, avoiding or not caring about the kneeings, clawings, and blows. She was dexterous with a work knife and would have used it if she had not left it in the hot barn.

He ground and levered his hips until they were between her thighs. It was so far from any of the thousand scenarios she had wish-dreamed for her first passage, so debased and ugly, that sorrow for the loss hurt her almost as much as dread of what Sternstuff meant to do.

He puffed, fumbling his robe up. "How dare you repulse me, outcast girl? Living curse!" She could feel the stiffened length of him through the robe, abrading the coarse homespun against her thigh.

"I'm not! I've never brought harm to anybody, ever!"

His prick was out, hurting her as he poked it blindly at the juncture of her legs. "A cunted Descrier! Anathemite! Your very birth signed your parents' death warrant. They were slain the same hour they brought you here! Has no one ever told you, you unclean abomina—*huuhhh!*"

Souljourner hit him with the praepostor's seal, weighty as a chrome fist, which had come to her fumbling hand. Sternstuff left off his ravings and maulings, toppling from her and clutching his forehead as blood coated his face. She took cold satisfaction in doing it a second time, putting her shoulder into it. Sternstuff stopped moaning and fell to the floor, limp as a dead bagfish.

She felt an unexpected composure as she pushed down her skirts and sat up on the desk. Sternstuff lay on his stomach with his wrinkled, veiny posterior in the air, still breathing. Clutching the seal, she stepped over him and snatched the gold on crimson

Writ that would appoint a new Descrier for Alabaster. With a feeling of unreality she dribbled wax on it and impressed it with the seal. Then, in a steady hand, she filled in her own name with the auriferous ink.

With the Writ in its carved ivory messenger tube tucked into her work habit, she considered Sternstuff and how to keep him from raising a hue and cry either now or later. She was casting her lot irrevocably with whatever the Militerrors and Rhodes had waiting for her, hoping there'd come a chance to escape the lake district of Scorpia altogether.

She used a penknife to saw through his cincture; then she drew the whole bloodied kirtle off him and took the Optimant door key from his purse. Sternstuff moaned but didn't move. She considered taking the seal but couldn't conceive of any use for it and feared that if it were found on her, she'd be hauled up for theft. As she replaced it by its case, she noticed a wooden box nearby and opened it.

It was filled with granulated ocher-crystal Apex. There were metal phials, glass casters, and vellum bindles of the stuff— measured rations for brothers who had to leave Pyx for whatever reason and perhaps a reserve for Sternstuff as well. She had little more use for Apex than for the seal but thought that she might encounter some Descrier who would be kindly disposed toward her in return for a gift. Leaving the expensive containers behind, she put a palmful of the bindles in her belt wallet, then let herself out of Sternstuff's chambers, only to hear heavy bootsteps clomping behind her. It was a lieutenant of the Militerrors, foreboding in spiked blue-lacquered armor and demon helmet. Old Tusker was bringing up the rear.

"You're the only slitty here, so you must be the one," the Militerror observed. "This way. We're taking you to Wall Water."

Souljourner's jaw dropped. "May I fetch my—"

"You can take up a few personal items if they lie between here and the front gates."

That would at least include her knife and divinatory bibelot; there wasn't a lot more that she cared about. She handed the door key to Tusker. "You and the most senior brothers should see to the praepostor. He shows symptoms of mental lapse and self-injury. Perhaps he should be relieved of office."

Tusker gave her a startlingly canny leer. "We'll attend to it."

It wouldn't be hard for them to see that something very amiss had gone on. Sternstuff might be stripped of power, especially if the head wounds impaired him. At a minimum he'd be likely to avoid any mention of what had happened with Souljourner behind his closed door.

The Militerror gestured for her to precede him. In minutes she was in the cramped, sour-smelling little palanquin cabin, gazing out at the dumbfounded, wizened faces she knew so well. The farewells were hasty and insufficient, but there was no helping that.

She didn't grow wary of what lay ahead until the gates of Pyx closed behind the procession. She hoped that the journey to Wall Water would be achieved, at least in part, by muscle car, but no one in the little party would tell her. With untalkative Militerrors marching before and behind and the palanquin bearers unwilling even to open their mouths, she had no choice but to endure the jouncing ride in silence.

It was only after coming to level ground beyond Sonsy Swage that she essayed a toss of the Holy Rollers she wore around her neck. Flung by the rebound of the palanquin floor, the Optimant dice cubes bounced and rolled and bounced again before coming to rest. Souljourner consulted the bibelot not because she didn't know the augury backward and forward but because she wanted to read the words themselves:

MANY ROADS MAY FIND A SINGLE DESTINATION

CHAPTER
FOURTEEN

Zone and his comrades were only a meter from Piper when a voice rang out. "Colonel! *Stand down!*" It was Burning, but right on top of his voice came Lod's, breaking, almost adolescently shrill. "Back off, motherfucker!"

Burning was purple with fury, and Lod was being restrained from drawing his pistol by General Delecado. Zone's several-mates, Strop and Wetbar, were wobbling in shock, having gotten so caught up in toying with Piper that they'd neglected to keep a lookout.

"Just a little harmless sport, Allgrave," Zone smirked, lolling his head at a bold angle. He hooded the craziness of his heavy-browed eyes and hooked a thumb at Piper. "Pipeline here hinted that she might want to sample the pleasures of our menage, so we decided to drop in to see if she was serious."

Burning knew that the alibi would be hard to shake in front of a court-martial. Aggregate members gave off a bewildering array of nonverbal signals and in return were often baffled by the ones they read in nonconstituents. A misunderstanding would be nearly impossible to rule out beyond a reasonable doubt. Zone knew that.

Stewing over the quandary, Burning pointed to Zone's clenched hand. "What've you got there, Colonel?"

Zone tightened his fist. "Personal property." Gazing at Burning through slitted eyes, he pulled his hand back when Burning reached for it.

"'BOU-out—FACE!" Daddy D bellowed, making even Zone flinch slightly.

The old general had drawn his 'baller and given the direct order to Strop and Wetbar; now he thumbed the selector switch from the sonics transducer over to the hardball function. "And never you mind him," Daddy D said when Zone's severalmates looked to their alpha spouse. His finger was off the trigger guard and on the trigger itself.

Strop was first to break the tableau, doing a demonstrator-perfect turn. Wetbar followed suit a second later, heel to toe and turning, both of them braced and staring at a bulkhead a meter away. Daddy D kept the 'baller trained on them, but Lod—his own sidearm out—was looking unblinkingly at Zone.

Burning was thinking about how it would simplify life if he just put three rounds into Zone's center of mass and maybe one or two in Zone's head for good measure, when the PA blared. The Exts' liaison battalion was to report in person, soonest, to LOGCOM for updated landing SOP requirements.

"Starkweather," Burning said out of the corner of his mouth. "Trying to chickenshit us."

"It's *Sword of Damocles Two*," Zone remarked, showing a sinister grin and speaking for the more fatalistic among the Exts, who were predicting another sneak attack by Manipulants or whatever, this time without Haven's running interference.

Burning let go of his anger, reasserting Flowstate with a quick *atman* inhalation and exhalation. Zone still had the luck of the devil, the malign gift that counterbalanced the man's curse. Letting Zone score two triumphs in one face-off was more than Burning could bear. He extended his hand for whatever Zone was concealing. Reluctantly, Zone relaxed his fist, revealing an exotic pair of dice and some sort of control touchpad.

Burning appraised the items. Given the gambling compulsions of the Exts and—according to reports—the Aquam, it didn't take a genius to figure out why Zone would coerce tech dice from the Aggregate. "Rigged gambling equipment isn't anyone's personal property, Colonel. Hand them over or I'll have Piper explain to the battalion how and why the Aggregate made them for you."

Lod and Daddy D had gone into relaxed shooting stances, left hand cupping extended right hand and gun butt. Zone's eyelids lifted somewhat at Burning's surprise line of attack. Many Exts would be outraged and some might even cry vengeance if

Zone were simply toad-cranked like some vermin in the street, but there would be far less outrage if the matter involved rigged dice. Damned few hadn't lost pay to Zone at one time or another.

Burning had the novel sensation he'd won, but Zone wasn't having any of it.

"Too bad you've got smarts and balls only when you're shit-scared," he observed, surrendering the Holy Rollers and the touchpad. It was the closest he'd ever come to paying Burning a compliment.

Zone started for the hatch, but when he passed within reach, Lod's right hand blurred at Zone's left. Oddly, Zone's reflexes weren't fast enough, and in an instant Lod was backing clear with the spherule of prompter pseudopheromone clutched in one hand and the pistol gripped in the other.

"Report to your unit," Daddy D barked while Zone was clearly debating retaliation.

Zone rendered everyone a pally salute, with Strop and Wet-bar emulating him. "One for all and all for one. Isn't that how you sold it to us at Anvil Tor, Burning?" The three departed, leaving a distinctly awkward silence in their wake.

Burning turned to Piper. "Madame Haven says that you need atmospheric samples. You've got special testing units or something?"

Piper silently regarded the Exts, Lod included, as if they were mistakes of nature. At the same time Zinda and Takellin brought two instrument packages about the size of twenty-round boomer magazines and handed them to Burning and the general. Zinda had composed words even an Alone could understand: "Operation is basic. Instruction ROMs are provided."

Burning cut his eyes back to Piper, feeling that he should offer apologies for Zone's actions. "You and your people will be disembarking to Aquamarine as soon as the SWATHship has been tetherdropped. Madame Haven asks that you bring *all* equipment, data, whatever your group has, including raw materials and basic supplies used in the research you've been doing for her. Nothing left behind for the AlphaLAWs to analyze, not even trash. Understand?"

Piper nodded with all the emphasis of a mime. Burning

couldn't find much else to say. When he looked at Lod, Lod was regarding Piper.

"I'll catch up later, Allgrave," Lod told him.

After Burning and Daddy D left Habitat, the constituents went back to preparations for deployment planetside. Their unspoken attention to Lod and Piper's Alltalk was so emphatic that even the Alone, she thought, would feel it.

Lod let out a deflating breath. "If Wix Uniday hadn't told us he saw Zone headed this way . . ."

Piper had met the garrulous Uniday but didn't know what his involvement might indicate, only that he was full of layered misdirection. It was difficult in any case to know what to say about Uniday or anything else. Intrinsic as they were to what had happened at the Lyceum ball, Lod's aromas had her head swimming.

His smells had carried connotations of rightness for her, an olfactory predestination. Where that kind of molecular compatibility came from, even Byron Sarz had never determined. Lod, too, was not unaware of the attraction. Stormed by her own sensations and by the things his Othertalk was making so graphically obvious, she was terribly apprehensive about making an inappropriate response, and so she took a stab at Alone small talk.

"Oh, yes, Uniday. An acquaintance of yours." She saw alarm and wariness rush from him.

"What makes you say that?"

She was back on that treacherous ground where she simply couldn't know what an Alone was thinking, Alltalk notwithstanding. "I scentse him on you."

Lod sat down. "Earlier today we exchanged a handclasp, no more than that. And you're telling me that you can still scentse him on me? MeoTheos, if I should ever want to keep secrets from you, I'll have to wear an anticontamination suit." He paused for a moment, then asked, "Can you tell when I'm lying?"

"Of course."

"Not—"

"Always, And *I* don't lie. But I mean no reproach, Lod. Are you angry? Do you wish to leave?"

"I'm not angry," he said. "I'm just trying to get used to the idea of standing before you naked."

Piper summoned her resolve and ran one hand through his fine, sandy hair as if stroking the trigger of a bomb. "I don't want you to leave." Inhaling him, she grew more aroused. The constituents were beginning to gather around, paying heed with Allsenses.

Lod eyed them apprehensively and took hold of her hand. "What about if we were both to leave?"

Starkweather's decision to advance the drop date for the *GammaLAW* had driven Quant and his crew to exhaustion. Regardless, he was willing to forgo full preparations rather than remain aloft and risk worse harm to the SWATHship. The decision had come hard, even for Quant, who was nothing if not resolute. The tetherdrop operation would be far more hazardous than the skyhook lift off Periapt.

Dextra's informants indicated that Starkweather would allow the drop to proceed without interference for reasons of self-interest. Plans called for *Big Tess* to use the same tether technique in setting down his AlphaLAW mission's most monolithic cargo on Hierophant: self-contained industrial facilities, two submersible marifortresses, and Starkweather's palatial command center.

For Quant, the most worrisome factor was Turret *Musashi*. Allegedly to conserve space, *Mighty Mush* had been secured to a reinforced area at the forward end of the hangar deck for the voyage out. Deployment plans had always called for dismounting and tetherdropping the mammoth naval rifles separately and emplacing them in their barbette once the vessel was planetside. But LOGCOM was now insisting that the twin 240-mm's would have to ride down aboard the ship. So there they sat, snugged in with I-beam bracing and an elaborate shock-absorbing system.

With the early drop, Starkweather would get to test the mettle of the tether and see to it that the GammaLAW mission's mainstay vessel would splash down without a single heavy weapon station functioning.

Starkweather had been ordered to see to the SWATHship's destruction. The sabotage would leave him and Nerbu with a shipload of truculent GammaLAW personnel, an insane idea, but Starkweather was a political creature above all, and if Preservationist grand designs dictated that the GammaLAW mission be denied any hope of success, he would ultimately toe the party line.

CHAPTER FIFTEEN

Rumor had it that Captain Nerbu swore out loud whenever tetherdrop operations were mentioned. Moving from the big work airlock into the midships payload bay, Dextra wished that everyone had realized earlier on all that was involved. Even so, guarded elation ran high among the Exts and the other Gamma-LAW people at the prospect of getting to solid ground and out from under Starkweather. Daddy D and the rest of Dextra's escorts were so happy about their brief liberation from *Big Tess*'s sealed living spaces that they'd lugged along a footlocker-size drop module of helmet-compatible vac-ration food and drink, bent on making a picnic of the event.

Everyone was suited up, including Tonii, Starkweather, and a bevy of his bureaucratic flunkies. They maneuvered along safety lines rigged in the open payload bay doors and were suddenly gazing down onto the SWATHship as she hung in her single-lift-point cargo net of composite straps, packaged in clear ablative shielding and coupled to the tetherhook carefully rigged above and slightly behind her. Hook and payload were gripped fast in a rigid external transport cage, an openwork structure that also would serve as a deployment gantry for this drop and the dozens more to follow.

With *Terrible Swift Sword* slowly swinging into the correct deployment attitude after a brief maneuver burn, Aquamarine wasn't quite in view yet. The speed of the leviathan starship's passage—some seven and a half kilometers per second—had hull and superstructures whistling minutely to the high-altitude drag wind of atomic oxygen and molecular nitrogen.

Big Tess was already deeper into a planetary atmosphere than most of its kind had ever dared to go, and now it would have to venture even deeper. Everyone onboard had become acutely aware that despite its size, power, and destructive capability, an interstellar vessel was fairy glass in the grip of gravity and atmospheric forces.

A heavy-lift suborbit tethercable had to be stout at its center of mass—where the highest stress loads would be equidistant—to support the line's weight as well as that of its payload; that point in the current instance was some ninety-five percent of the way *down* the line, toward the hook and its SWATHship burden, including Chaz Quant and his crew. With a taper ratio of 15.4—the maximum cross-sectional area divided by that at the thinner ends—the sheer mass of even exotically light and strong derated carbon rose appallingly with each additional meter of length.

Nerbu would unquestionably have voted for a tether 250 klicks long. The decision wasn't his, however, and LAW had decreed that the tens of thousands of metric tons of payload mass allocation required for the additional line were needed for cargo with a higher priority. Hence the cable spooled around the reel assembly had a rated splashdown length of just over 150 kilometers, counting estimated thermal and elastic expansion, along with the hook pilot's adjustments.

Not that the starship could stand off even that far. As it lowered the SWATHship, the transfer of angular momentum would, at least at first, cause *Big Tess* to rise higher in proportion to its relative mass as the lighter but still weighty watercraft descended. The spacecraft therefore had to start lower, surf the gravity well, and plant the forty-thousand-ton Semisubmerged Trimaran on the face of Lake Ea like the most precise injection imaginable.

To put a busted condom around the whole harrowing business, the system's primary, Eyewash, was in a particularly energetic phase of its cycle, causing Aquamarine's atmosphere to reach higher above the planet's surface than usual. The stellar activity also had the communications people irritated. Nerbu tacitly held Quant and Dextra personally responsible for the star's disorderly conduct.

Terrible Swift Sword dipped lower and lower, adjusting attitude and trembling beneath them. Like glory bursting forth from the ajar gates of paradise, the grandeur of Aquamarine lit the payload bay and swelled into their field of vision. Despite the planet's name and minute tinges of green and other colors, it was a primarily blue radiance that shone over them, a magic natural light that was stunning after subjective months of artificial illumination.

Turbulence made the starship wallow and palpitate. Tonii, the holder of an EVA able-bodied crewperson's certification hard earned in transit from grudging AF instructors, drifted close in the counterspun bay's microgravity to act as Dextra's guardian, lifelines notwithstanding.

The curve of the planet rolled, ballooned into the huge canted portal of the open payload bay door, and seemed to rise before her eyes.

That direct view of it, bounded only by the gaping bay doors, made Dextra forget the countless aggravations, the sacrifices, and the venom she'd had to swallow, forget all that the voyage had cost her. Gazing out on Aquamarine gave her a feeling of depersonalization, yet it was the most vivid thing that had happened to her since she'd faced up to the GammaLAW mission. She had the sudden sense that the view was a one-of-a-kind experience—that she would never see Aquamarine quite that way again—and gave herself an extra moment to drink in all its swirling, transfixing beauty.

Maybe she had been wrong not to bring Honeysuckle, she told herself. No matter how forbidding and harsh, Aquamarine was a living miracle, and she was sorry her child wasn't there to experience it.

The hydrosphere heaved up with only scattered flecks and stipples of land visible even at close remove. Ground-tracking data said that they were traveling northward and looking down at a slice of the southern hemisphere, just east of the planetary dateline the Optimants had designated and about which most latter-day Aquam knew nothing and cared less. *Terrible Swift Sword* was following a pole-to-pole orbit as the planet rotated under it, the starship dropping speed and altitude, aligning for the approach on Scorpia and Lake Ea.

Horizon-shrouding cloud systems rose into view, great rows of white froth like foam on a hard-packed cyan-pearl beach.

Farther north an almost solid white quilt of stratus lay on the globe, pocked by a tiny window caused by rising heat from a largish isle the ground-tracking display on Dextra's visor identified as Windcomb.

At the landless equator a slim band of markedly lighter swells ringed the world, the meeting place of the ocean's Coriolis forces, where the clashing waters had sluiced their battlefront clear of most nutrients and other particulate matter. To the far east a milky layer of stratocumulus was scalloped and scrolled by the wind, but it was partially clear over the indigo grouping of the Icarean chain. A low-pressure front descended from the arctic circle onto the desolate Scourlands, and a fierce marbling of what looked to be blizzard was pouncing on the tundra isles themselves. Stationary to Dextra's eyes, waves heaved like snow-crested alps.

The view turned south once more, with Scorpia far to the west, contested over by complex, multilayered weather systems that included towering cumulonimbus spinning off lenticular clouds. Meteorologic updates held that the system was breaking up and would clear by splashdown, though the tether was designed to operate in poor visibility in any case.

Currents sinuated, coursed, and gyred across Aquamarine, dictated for the most part by subsurface features, planetary rotation, and the planet's two small moons. Landmasses looked few and precarious, barely chinning themselves on the global fetches of the world sea, the Amnion. The turbidity and ceaseless churning of the waves, the cobalt, lapis lazuli, smalt, and gun finish blues, all made it easy to believe the Oceanic was astir and aware and gazing back with ill will from the depths of the abyss.

Dextra became aware of the drawn-out quake beneath the magnetic cleats of her EVA suit. Shaking off her trance, she realized that the gargantuan reel assembly was paying out the slender hook end of the tether.

Gantry servos had pistoned out slowly to start the SWATH on its descent. In the bay the unreeling skyline was a lusterless, sooty black as a result of its flexible sheath of fluorinated polymer film, which provided protection against erosion by orbital gases and the fires of atmospheric friction. But as *GammaLAW* was lowered into the atmospheric wind, an orange glow lit its leading side, emitted by excited high-altitude molecules desorbing from its surface. Booms had swung into place to hold the line clear of the gantry and the starship with powered pulleys, which also would help in tether routing. Level-wind mechanisms monitored the paying out of cable and would assure that the rewind pattern was uniform and properly aligned.

Precisely timed, a brief thruster burn from *Big Tess* tugged everyone against his or her clipped safety line. They felt the deck lift against their feet in reciprocity as the starship transferred angular momentum to the detruded SWATHship and vice versa. The near-vacuum resistance of low-orbit drag wind made the tether and its hook-suspended burden shiver minutely.

"Deployment is green for go," a LOGCOM captain announced.

He was monitoring command channel 4, being fed constant status reports by the advance teams on and over Lake Ea, which were keeping teamboats, aquaculture barges, fishing coracles, and everything else clear of thousands of square kilometers of water. The hook pilot and tether operators were also linked in, along with Nerbu's command center.

Rhodes and the other grandees had been surprisingly cooperative about clearing the way for the splashdown, or so the AF liaison officers had reported. Site-control teams were mostly Transport Command and AF personnel, despite Dextra's vehement demand that her own people handle the job and deal with the Aquam.

There would be abundant contact with the Aquam soon enough, however. Dextra was betting that the diplomatic offensive she had in mind would undo Starkweather's intended sabotage before *Terrible Swift Sword* cleared Eyewash's heliopause en route to Hierophant.

"Your precious ship is getting out of range," Starkweather pointed out gleefully.

Dextra accepted that and raised the modified Manipulant bloopgun Tonii had brought into the bay. The weapon was loaded with a special projective charge and a magnum of goldseal Catholicon rigged not to explode of its own accord in vacuum. Dextra got the SWATHship in her scope, recalling carefully what Tonii had told her about leading her target. She lined up her shot through the open sights and confirmed it through the scope as the trimaran dropped toward halcyon whites and blues and greens.

Someone jostled her elbow. "Madame Commissioner, the current range is longer than planned," one of Starkweather's imps said. "Your marksmanship may not be up to it. Perhaps you'll allow me to—"

"Sod off!" someone barked, and the tentative elbow touch vanished.

An Ext—General Delecado, Dextra realized—had sent the staffer floating and thrashing backward in panic with a few brisk but measured raps of gloved knuckles to the fellow's face-bowl. She felt hot pride; the Exts might be lunatics, but at least they were *her* lunatics.

Dextra swung the Catholicon to bear almost drunkenly on the bow of the former *Matsya*. "O vessel of the waves! Hereby I baptize thee the LAW Naval Ship *GammaLAW* and bid thee sail well and safely upon all thy stations—wooo!"

The tether shook the booms a bit, making it clear that she didn't have time to say all she'd intended. "God in the life spirit of all things, bless thee and all who sail aboard thee," she added in a rush. The bloopgun's characteristic hollow sound was lost to the others in the airlessness, but she felt it by conduction. The Catholicon bottle wobbled visibly as it flew, the LAW armorers having misjudged its freaky ballistics somewhat. Dextra gulped, wondering if she'd been overconfident. No provision had been made for a second shot.

It looked as if the ceremony might turn inauspicious, after all, especially with Aquamarine out there defying everyone. The bottle missed the foredeck and bows altogether and even, incredibly, the flight deck. People were moaning over the EVA net.

Then it caught the tip of the live ordnance disposal ramp that projected from the flight deck like a bowsprit—or rather, it hit the clear ablative shielding coating it—and blossomed in boiling mist.

The lucky strike elicited way-to-go approval over the

intersuit freq, and Tonii clapped Dextra's shoulder. The Exts began fiddling with their picnic module.

"Close enough for government work, eh?" Starkweather noted dryly. Dextra was about to bet him he couldn't do better—couldn't, say, hit Captain Nerbu at twenty paces—when an ominous vibration came up through the deck plates.

"LNS *GammaLAW*, we're getting some jitters from you and they're kinda scrooching up the vibration-attenuating systems," a voice on the tether ops net said with mission-control calm. The very length of the cable served to dampen quavers and dBs passed in either direction, but not with so little line paid out.

Instead of the LOGCOM rep aboard the SWATH, it was Quant who answered. "Sorry about that, Ops. I don't know how, but it seems we had some live steam in one of the reactor auxiliaries. I had no choice but to vent it ASAP. My apologies, but I believe we got it all."

Daddy D touched Dextra's shoulder. "Madame Commissioner? I think we should get you back onboard, just in case." Delecado's King Kong of an XO, Big 'Un Boudreau, was looking on with an odd expression of serenity.

"Back onboard, yes, by all means," Starkweather jabbered, plainly not wanting to be anywhere close to the reel assembly if anything went catastrophically wrong.

A number of items were competing for Dextra's closer scrutiny, chief among them the instinctive certainty that the unpurged pressure simply wasn't the kind of error Chaz Quant *made*. Granted, with the SWATH not being built for vacuum, there was no question that live steam had to be vented without even the delay it took to consult tether ops. Supporting her suspicion that something else was going on was Delecado's sudden eagerness to get Dextra back into the air lock. Lastly, the other Exts were standing fast, seemingly waiting for Starkweather and his lot to lead the retreat.

Tonii had Dextra's arm; Dextra yielded silently but not happily. Daddy D cycled the lock, while Big 'Un Boudreau and several other Exts hung back, fussing with their food locker. Starkweather was too nervous to care, and Dextra, passing looks with Daddy D, held her tongue.

CHAPTER
SIXTEEN

Short of the Grandee Rhodes's private throne room, the tallest of the three pacificatrixes blindfolded Souljourner with long brown locks, the redhead secured her wrists, and the blonde sent tresses around her throat like a leash. Upper-caste idlers and others, loitering in the stale-smelling vestibule, delighted in her profound confusion and embarrassment. Many canted aside a delicate wand mask or lifted a fanciful vizard to get a better look. Under their scrutiny she felt even more ungainly than usual.

She was still wearing the cinctured work habit she'd sewn for herself at Pyx, now far worse from hard travel, and her sturdy, squarish feet were bare. The Militerrors hadn't offered to purchase or barter for a more appropriate outfit in transit, and Souljourner had nothing she cared to trade away.

As she waited to be led before the Grandee Rhodes, perfumed men nudged one another and snickered and painted women smirked behind gilt and gossamer fans. She had the distinct impression that they knew that what awaited her wasn't at all agreeable. She managed, just once, to thumb the lucky drawstring pouch around her neck before her trussed wrists were drawn straight out in front of her. The thick fall of brown hair across her eyes smelled of balm of ambrodine.

Souljourner considered how the pacificatrixes' manes might stand up to some snap-the-whip played by a yokel who could buck full-measure grain bags but decided not to test them.

The courtiers' jeers were only the latest in a string of disillusionments and mortifications she'd weathered since being quick-marched from the cloister. It wasn't the way she had pictured her debut among the nobility while daydreaming over *The*

Love-Land Creed. Similarly, the journey by palanquin hadn't resembled anything described in *Passions of the Tarot*. The trot of the bearers had given the box cabin a rhythmic jounce that had had her kidneys and lower spine in agony within an hour. She pleaded to be let out to trot alongside, but the lieutenant of Militerrors wouldn't hear of it. By then she had come to realize that there was something covert about their mission and was hoping against hope that the Grandee Rhodes intended no more than to replace his current Descrier.

Her hands and fingers went numb from clutching the palanquin's overhead strap holds. On the Militerrors' gruff advice, she had wound strips of cloth around her belly and hips to spare herself what pain she could. She hunkered, massaged, and experimented with various positions to relieve the agony in her maltreated rump and the torment of her tailbone and back.

At last, though, there'd come a wonderful day's stretch aboard a muscle car, its treadles pumping it along the high roads. Also, she had gotten to see two different starting mounds, finding them bigger and busier than they had been when she was a tyke.

But the tribulations of the real world surpassed anything her romances held. In a mountain pass she saw an Anathemite newborn with boneless limbs like wriggling scrollworms being exposed and abandoned on a hillside by its parents. As a new team of bearers took up the palanquin at a crossroads, she bore witness to the lashing of a tax debtor by pitiless judicatures. Finally, at a trailside camp, a wandering tattoo artist punished his wife for being barren by repeatedly jabbing a flickering butrywood link into her bare arm and shoulder. Everywhere the barrow coolies, elixir vendors, freelance bravos, and roadside trollops were trading wild hearsay about what the return of the Visitants might portend for Scorpia and all of Aquamarine.

She had refused nevertheless to let any of it undermine her faith in the auguries of her dice. Like her Descrying abilities, the divinatory powers of the Holy Rollers were real, and their promise of love and a fulfilled life would be kept.

On the bright side, Praepostor Sternstuff had sent no accusations after her, and the Militerrors hadn't been interested in searching her beyond assuring themselves that she wasn't carrying a chain sword or arquebus sling-gun. So she still had the now-sealed Writ of office for the Descrier slot at Alabaster, with her name written in. She also had her knife, the goodly stash of powdered Apex, her dice and bibelot, various calluses, and a few poignant memories.

Blond hair tugged at her neck. She kept her chin as high as she could and let herself be led stumbling through doors that opened to the rap of the intendant's silver-knobbed bastinado of office. She already knew that she wasn't being led into Wall Water's main throne room and great hall, for she'd passed through those dark places a few minutes earlier.

Shuffling along, she heard capering music, laughter with a hysterical edge to it, moans, mews, and hoots. Thick smells of hard drink, incense, oils, and sweat filled the air. Dragged to a halt, she heard a shrill, slightly crazed male voice bray, "Silence! My special guest has arrived! Shush, I say, you strumpet!" There followed the sounds of a whack, a yelp, and an inane titter.

"I would have my preferred throne now," the gruff voice added, at which point a great deal of scuttling and bumbling movement commenced. "And let my strapping country-girl guest be unhoodwinked and present herself to her liege lord."

The pacificatrixes unknotted their locks from Souljourner as the sounds of exertion waxed vigorous. As the trio drew back, she blinked her eyes open, saw the nature of the Grandee Rhodes's personal throne, and felt her knees begin to buckle.

The first real jolt—as opposed to the ones Quant himself had engendered with the fake emergency steam venting—came surprisingly early in the tetherdrop. The ship's quaking was conducted through his drop casket's padding, shock absorption, and EVA suit, but Quant could do little more than wait and hope. He hadn't expected Starkweather to try anything until the line was paid out and the SWATHship was well and truly at *Big Tess*'s mercy, but the AlphaLAW commissioner was full of surprises.

Nonetheless, the voice of Lieutenant Lum—the onboard AF tetherdrop controller from TRANSCOM, lying in her casket on the port side of the compartment—sounded calm and steady over the tether ops freq. With an effort Quant craned his neck to check Wix Uniday. Like Burning and the rest, Starkweather's liaison man lay in his tetherdrop casket in the heavily armored pilothouse within the refurbished bridge of LNS *GammaLAW*. Additional caskets were rigged elsewhere aboard, but Quant had refused to be packaged anywhere but there.

Uniday's face was clearly visible through the casket's view-plate and his own facebowl. While he was without his easy smile for once, his expression wasn't that of a man who ex-pected to die. Quant drew limited comfort from the fact that he showed no sign of misgiving that Starkweather might sacrifice him in a bid to blow *GammaLAW* out of the sky. It was Uni-day's breezy willingness to go along for the ride that had played a part in Quant's decision to accede to Starkweather's terms to begin with.

Now to sweat out the bungee jump down the gravity well, Quant told himself. He would have gratefully swapped his situation for a force-five gale if it included a sea under his keel. A little scenery would have made it more endurable. The pro-jected visuals on Quant's helmet facebowl and the pod screen didn't do much to convey the sweep of the planet below.

He felt a queasiness pass through him as tether and SWATH registered their complaints anew. Now that she had achieved a distance of nearly a kilometer from *Terrible Swift Sword*, below and ahead in her own increasingly separate orbit, *GammaLAW* was descending, powered by gravity gradient forces. If the tether broke, *GammaLAW* would plunge, the *Sword* would be pushed higher, and the SWATH's life would be countable in minutes.

There was no point dwelling on that particular if. Quant steadied himself. He glanced at his helmet display again, chin-ning up a view from a masthead cam. Half in sunlight and bunt-ings of clouds and half in the arc of the night, Aquamarine churned far, far below *GammaLAW*'s bows and sponsons. The whole stupendous water-turbine world presented itself before him, unimpressed. The thrall of it made the hair on his arms and the nape of his neck stand up.

Leading surfaces on his ship were still lit here and there by the orange Saint Elmo's fire of orbital winds, but the phenome-non was fading as the hook carried her lower and lower into the atmosphere proper. *Big Tess* was descending more quickly now, *GammaLAW* far faster; the approach toward Lake Ea counted down irrevocably.

The power of the view—his ship with the planet far beneath her—set his worries aside. Unsailable seas? What true sailor could back away from a challenge like that? Quant thought forward to a day when he would sail those forbidden seas and turn them to his purpose.

He was shivered from his contemplation by another cable quake that was strong enough to twitch the casket's gimbals. Then the strangest feeling went through him as an odd, displaced knot of sensation formed behind his breastbone. The skin of his cheeks, neck, shoulders, and upper chest began to prickle as if batteries of dulled, close-set syringes were being pressed into him. His heart danced such a change-step that he consciously avoided looking at his suit med displays.

On the control freq a perceptible edge had crept into Lieutenant Lum's voice. "Ah, I think we're getting some jittery string dynamics here, Ops. Measured a dip just then of five percent over nominal descent speed."

It was to be expected that the *GammaLAW* would oscillate both in the orbital plane and perpendicular to it like a spoon-fishing lure and experience sideways out-of-plane drag caused by the atmosphere's rotation about Aquamarine, but it was too early in the drop for that. One major concern had been the appearance of a "jump-rope" oscillation, something that tether technology had supposedly eliminated long since but that everyone dreaded, in which the line itself would start whanging around between SWATH and starship like a kid's skiptoy.

"*GammaLAW*, we think we're getting some unanticipated tension-compression waves or perhaps a touch of anomalous turbulence," someone from TRANSCOM drawled. "We're within operational limits. Mission control informs drop continues."

Quant almost broke in then, but years of naval discipline kept him off the net. Tension-compression *already*, with such a relatively small length of tether unreeled? Such serious air turbulence this high up? More than likely someone was doing spazzes on the reel—from incompetence or by design?

There was no one to wring for answers. Even if Quant cracked open his cocoon by hitting the emergency release, the only ones he could lash out at were Lum and Uniday, both of them doomed if he was and patently not in on any plots.

He squirmed uselessly, then chinned up another view of the blue-water precincts he hoped to sail, wondering suddenly if they were to be his grave. Reel payout speed was increasing, but each second of the unspooling descent seemed to take a year. There were the expected yo-yoings of the hook pilot's adjustments and the use of payout speed to dampen further oscillation. The ablative layers heated up and flared with the friction of the deeper atmosphere. Then, without warning, the SWATHship felt the biggest slam of all.

Daddy D instructed Dextra to make a calm but direct withdrawal to the security of her stateroom. Timing was crucial, he emphasized. Starkweather and TRANSCOM had to be confronted soon, but the general's first need was to position his game pieces.

Her first impulse on learning of the balls-out scheme the Exts had implemented behind her back was to abort the plan and rethink the whole idea of allowing them to set foot on Aquamarine. If only they weren't *right*. Starkweather's endless undermining and sabotage could be checked—temporarily, at any rate—only by a reaction that called his bluff. Nothing less than a threat to his personal well-being would make him desist. Survivors of Anvil Tor, the Exts had understood that instinctively.

Exts had already secured Dextra's quarters when she, Daddy D, Tonii, and the others returned. Lod and several key people were already there, working. AF and AlphaLAW personnel had been convoyed from GammaLAW's portion of *Terrible Swift Sword* to the nearest frontier bulkhead and ejected into neutral territory. Dextra's Peace Warrantors were quartered with their parent division elsewhere in the ship, but they were essentially LAW, and she couldn't rely on them not to side with Starkweather if the going got rough.

At Delecado's prompting, Dextra attempted to raise Starkweather over the command channel. Specialist-6 Lilly was reluctant to put her through, however, until—at Daddy D's nod of readiness—Dextra took pleasure in grating, "In that case, I suggest that you hustle your cooze clear of the capacitors, darling."

Everyone who could spare a glance looked toward the workstation's secondary holo, on which Tonii had brought up a simon-simple schematic of the starship. It didn't take a data diver to tell that something was wrong. Aft the *Sword*'s counterspun waist track, where so much of the monolithic AlphaLAW cargo was packed in external transport cages secured to the hull, trouble icons, damage report vectors, and alphanumerics were sprouting like a rash.

Diagnostic crosshairs zeroed in on the crown jewel of Starkweather's megamachines: the part fortress, part palace tetherdeployable mobile surface HQ that had cost three times Dextra's entire budget. Now, however, its power systems were wrecked and seared, and an immense energy source was building toward detonation.

Starkweather might have been monitoring Dextra's futile efforts to contact him, but for once he was quick on the uptake. Blood vessels stood out in the neck and forehead of the holo image that rezzed up.

"You treacherous slut!" he screamed. "What are you playing at?"

He was wearing an elaborate uniform that had a half-finished look to it, with silk-lined cape, full ruff collar, brush epaulets, sash, and medals. Various people behind him, some with tailoring paraphernalia in hand, were holding low kowtows. A fitting session had been interrupted, Dextra realized. Starkweather apparently saw himself as some sort of LAW conquistador. It might have been amusing at another time, but she had more important matters to discuss.

"We appear to have malfs in some of our technical systems," Dextra said. "How shall we work out our repair plans—in private or in public?"

No fool, Starkweather smoothed the baleful look he'd been wearing. "Informally," he answered tightly. "Rest assured, you can always come to me with your problems, madame."

They both knew the rules of engagement. In seconds each

had retired to SIGINT-proof commo carrels and sealed and encrypted the link, using double-handshake authenticators.

"Truce" was the next word out of Dextra's mouth. "Find some other way to stress-test the tether—and me. I need that boat, Buck, too much to risk having her damaged even a little bit by your TRANSCOM puppet masters."

"If so much as a brow massager is burned out in my mobile HQ, I shall have you drawn and quartered with construction waldos!" Starkweather fired back. "Exactly what have those habitual offenders of yours done?"

"The Exts are merely preparing to blow the hull wide open with a superconducting munition they found at the Iskra Detention Facility and thought to bring along as a hole card."

She had spent the whole of the return trip in her quarters worrying about the safety of Big 'Un Boudreau and the other Exts who had remained behind in the payload bay. Sneaking across the starship's outer hull with a demolition device masquerading as a picnic module had surely been difficult enough, but the fact that they had had to make a hairy transit from the counterspun waist ring to the hull proper had made the gambit as risky as a combat recce.

For a moment Starkweather registered doubt, and Dextra wondered if any of her longtime foes in the Hierarchate had tipped him off to the fact that she looked her most composed while running her most audacious bluffs. But all at once the diagnostics began issuing a series of urgent tones.

Short of nukes, superconducting ordnance was the most powerful explosive in LAW's inventory, and the one the Exts had stolen from Iskra was sucking up tremendous amounts of power.

"Do we have a pax?" Dextra asked quickly.

"Yes, madame," Starkweather answered in like haste. "I grant you your pax." He touched some control beyond her field of vision. "The rest of the *GammaLAW*'s descent will be smooth. Now get those Concordance mongrels away from my command post vehicle!"

Dextra touched a lighted tile on her own console. Daddy D must have been hovering over the telltale outside, and Boudreau and the rest outboard in vacuum had to have been anticipating the signal, too, because an instant later the mobile HQ was stabilizing—intact except for minor damage from the power surges.

"They can surrender the warhead to suitable custodians at the nearest air lock," Starkweather finished more equably.

"No, they can come through a lock here under my control," Dextra countered, "*after* my boat splashes down safely. Or do you want to play another round?" She smiled faintly. "Remain calm, Buck, and I'll remove the warhead from your starship as soon as circumstances planetside permit."

Starkweather flicked a hand impatiently. "I have no time for this nonsense. Go to."

"With pleasure," she said. "Incidentally, I expect Quant to get the full CAP air cover he was promised." She broke the connection.

Having emerged from the shielded carrel, she turned to Daddy D. "As soon as the hook's on its way up, recall Big 'Un and his people."

"One of 'em won't be back," Delecado said softly. "Beast Burke got flung free somehow when they were crossing from the waist ring." Manned Maneuvering Units for powered independent EVAsuit flight across the hull were the one item the Exts hadn't managed to scrounge or steal. "Straight down at Aquamarine. Nothing anybody could do for him, and a rescue squeal would've compromised the whole mission."

"Is there anything we can do now?" Dextra asked.

Delecado shook his head. "He's probably already begun his flareout."

Dextra was about to say something consoling when it hit her that she was Beast Burke's honorary sagamore. Delecado wasn't simply reporting a casualty but *her* casualty. "In that case," she said, "list him MIA, General."

CHAPTER
SEVENTEEN

Once the tether turbulence became natural rather than LOGCOM-induced, the descent to Aquamarine's surface seemed so stately and celestial that it was ripscat petrifying only if one knew the physical laws, mathematical realities, and practical repercussions it entailed.

Predictions about new string dynamics had erred on the bright side; partial brakings and surges of payout by the hook pilot and reel assembly controllers had dampened the worst of the oscillations, tension N-fluxes, and other aberrations. The SWATHship had endured the fiery gauntlet of entry and ionization blackout as well as she navigated heavy seas. The aerodynamics of the ablative packaging had helped keep her descent true, but it was also self-evident that the beamy, deceptively sleepy-looking woman piloting the hook was a virtuoso. Quant had already resolved to pin a navy citation to her personally provided that she was willing to receive it planetside. He had no intention of entering the upper atmosphere again anytime in the foreseeable future.

He indulged himself with one last look at Aquamarine from above. He felt straitjacketed by the protective casket in which he lay, but the view of the planet sea in his visor was enough to allay any discomfort. In a universe where liquid water was a statistical rarity, Aquamarine made him think of Eden with an "immediate occupancy" sign on the gate.

Then the sight of the Scorpia superisland climbing tawny, green, and cloud-dappled down the curve of the globe made him feel *truly* claustrophobic. With all that unencumbered salt water off limits to humans, it was positively Murphyian that land-girded Lake Ea was the target zone. Yet TRANSCOM insisted that the hook could line up a first-try release at a descent speed better than eight hundred meters per second and a forward speed not much slower. There was nothing to do but hope it wasn't a rash boast.

Suspended in his cocoon by downward acceleration, Quant made certain that the reconnaissance pickups scratch-mounted all over the vessel were working. It came as no surprise that one or two were malfunctioning, but the rest were panning and scanning, furiously updating intel and situational data. He called up an enhanced magnification of the drop site, feeling a tense wringing in his gut as he was pressed down harder and harder against the casket's floor. The hook pilot was cutting the *GammaLAW*'s entry speed to something that would let the vessel survive stresses for which she hadn't been designed. *GammaLAW* was a durable, hardy ship, but the splashdown would be the ultimate test of her carefully engineered strengths.

Thanks to AF flybys and the Grandee Rhodes's local muscle, the footprint zone was free of Aquam craft—millships, aquaculture rafts, fishing dories, and the rest. Surface-scanning radars confirmed that there was nothing on or near the fifty-by-ninety-klick stretch of yellow marker–dyed water.

Quant took a good look at Wall Water and the Ea dam. The myriad-fingered Pontos Reservoir lapped high above what had been deep chasms fed by runoff from the sawtooth mountain range that curved across northwestern Scorpia. Built up by accretion over generations, the grandee's ancestral fortress mounted around the penstock control facility; barracks and other installations had been hollowed out of the naked rock of the north cliff and its shoulder and crest. Parts of it looked sturdy and modern, while other sections appeared crudely medieval, although made to last.

As *Terrible Swift Sword*'s orbit had bottomed out, the starship had begun to rise. The critical leg of the drop would be negotiated with no further unreeling, purely on the elastic expansion of the cable and maneuvers carried out with aeroassist control surfaces deployed by the hook as well as by its steering thrusters. Fine adjustments had been calculated by TRANSCOM computers, but Quant found it comforting that the hook pilot was calling the shots—she and His Majesty, King Neptune.

Or did His Royal Highness have any authority over freshwater? Quant couldn't recall.

Ea rapidly waxed wide and long beneath *GammaLaw*'s bows as braking forces increased. The ship plummeted at a light chop far more swiftly than she could have sailed on it. The one bright spot was that the surface was calm; if it had not been, they would have run the risk of bashing down into a trough or going under a rogue wave while still dangling helplessly from the hook.

G forces pressed Quant harder onto his back as the cargo sling continued to slow for splashdown. Right on time, what was left of the sections of ablative armor began separating and dropping into the water. He watched the forward and descent speed readings decrease as the murky, lapping lake water seemed to reach up for his ship.

Within moments *GammaLAW* would come to a dead halt relative to the planet's surface. First, however, the hook would begin to move forward again with sharply increasing speed as the tether was withdrawn by the *Sword*'s orbital progress and the rewinding of the reel assembly. If the single-lift-point cargo sling wasn't released in time, *GammaLAW* would be tugged back aloft. If such a mishap threatened the well-being of the starship, contingency plans called for the hook pilot to release the sling, sending the SWATH plunging to impact Aquamarine as she would. Those aboard weren't equipped with chutes or other escape devices for the simple reason that there wouldn't be time to use them.

A late release wasn't what Quant's senses and instruments were warning him about. The hook had slowed to a near stop at a perigee too far above the surface to allow for a safe drop. Anyone could see that the drop would have to be scrubbed. Yet TRANSCOM was continuing the countdown, ticking off the last seconds.

"Brace yourself, *GammaLAW*," the hook pilot warned matter-of-factly. It came to Quant that she was going to let his ship fall to her death.

As Souljourner had refused to let the taunts of the courtiers make her hang her head, she refused to let her knees weaken at the sight of the Grandee Rhodes's living throne.

The liege lolled, nude except for some jeweled toe rings and a filigreed coronet, on a heap of bare bodies that were arched and crouched and hunkered to form a kind of chair. They had assumed their furniture frieze by linking arms or arching backs on all fours or kneeling with an adroitness she took to indicate frequent and exacting practice.

'Waretongue Rhodes himself was far from the dashing young swashbuckler the court balladeers and grandeean newsgivers lauded in such glowing terms. His body looked flaccid and pale. His florid face and jaundiced eyes betrayed the middle stage of what she'd seen among the more dissipated and bibulous retired Descriers.

On a raised platform in an apse a quintet of musicians plucked, strummed, and otherwise fingered various instruments. All were facing the semicylindrical wall, which reflected their music into the room at large. Souljourner got the impression that the musicians were taking pains *not* to listen to or know about what was happening behind them.

The grandee lazily hooked one knee across the bent neck of a muscular young man—as if the fellow's head were an armrest knob—and gazed at Souljourner through narrowed eyes. "Come closer."

It was either that or bolt, so she complied warily as he continued.

"You're so much more grown and *robust* than I'd pictured you. Thicker ankles, too. Souljourner, many times I meant to come inquire after your well-being there at Pyx. But what with the demands of state and all that . . . Howsomeever, I had the joy in the virtues of charity, providing for your safety and happiness."

She had steeled herself to flatter and play but found her tongue moving on its own. "If jailing me there and pressing poor Rolande to death were charity, what is your largesse like?"

His eyes widened like those of a wraptail poised to bite. "Take heed you don't learn what my annoyance is like! When your Descrying first came to light, I could just as easily have had you buried alive or sawed into pieces like any Anathemite tot, if for no other reason than to spare myself the curse of you. I may yet, girl."

She didn't defy him, but she didn't beg him to spare her, either, and they both knew why.

Only two other women in recorded history had been born with the Descrying gift. The first, Zarzuela, had triggered events leading to the downfall of the Dominor Howester, and her name had come to be synonymous with treachery and cosmic misfortune to a ruler. When Billeta's gifts had come to be recognized a generation later, the Grandee Fanfaron Buscade had ordered her weighted with stones and dropped into the Amnion from one of the surviving Optimant Laputas. It had provoked an Oceanic tsunami that had obliterated all it engulfed of Buscade's lands.

Rhodes therefore had been on tenterhooks of indecision ever since Souljourner's powers had made themselves known. Permit her to use her gifts? Destroy her? Both courses had led to catastrophe in the past. Despite his bravado, the grandee wasn't one to challenge fate or court danger.

"I hope there's some service I can provide you rather than annoyance," Souljourner said, taking a different tack. If she could convince him that releasing her to Alabaster would exempt him from the threat of star-crossed doom, she might yet make something of her life.

"Oh, there *is* a service," Rhodes purred, leaning forward confidentially. "I have one clearly in mind."

His voice wasn't nearly as seductive as the ray of hope Souljourner thought she was glimpsing. Nevertheless, she edged closer, only to let out a ridiculous little screech as she felt a hand reach up under her work habit to caress the area behind her knee.

Rhodes kicked out with his left foot, connecting with the upraised rump of a crouching man who constituted part of the grandee's hassock. "Wanton! Masher! None of your sauciness! My virgin Descrier must remain intact in all her parts for what I have in mind." Then he chuckled, lost in self-admiration. "Genius like mine shouldn't be wasted on one small planet, as I'm certain you all agree."

CHAPTER
EIGHTEEN

Quant was about to break communications discipline and exceed his authority by ordering TRANSCOM to abort the drop, but he never got the words out. The temblor thrumming rose in pitch as the hook pilot paid out the last length of reserve line spooled on a sheaf below the hook's main tether connection. Altitude readings in meters fell into the low double digits, and then into the singles. Before Quant was quite prepared, the hook pilot's voice said, "Payload away—*now!*" and there was the sudden jolt of the hook's release.

A second later Quant felt the impact on his ship as if each part of her were a part of him. It wasn't nearly as bad as he'd feared, not even as bad as that time Hallowed Hall had allowed the *Matsya* to blunder side-on through a huge wave and fall hard into the trough.

The box-girder strength at the heart of the ship proved itself redoubtable. Quant was passingly pleased to note that he'd remembered to lock his teeth as he had been trained and had avoided biting his tongue. He hit the casket release while the ship was still rebounding from the face of the lake, the main deck not even having gone awash.

He lurched a bit as he struggled out from under the rising casket, trying simultaneously to unstrap, squirm free, and run every diagnostic on the ship. Assorted systems had been knocked off-line by one thing or another, but enough were enabled to tell him that the *GammaLAW* had made it in one piece and was taking on water.

Quant cracked his helmet and gathered calm, signaling the larger contingent casketed belowdecks in the reinforced area near the Combat Information Center. "Isayagi, Hussein, Kim:

take special sea details and secure from tetherdrop. Mr. Gairaszekh, make ready the CIC. Carrito and Gleick: get your people forward to 917-3-Q and see to that hull breech. Step lively!"

He had cast the EVA helmet aside in favor of his own headset, taking it from its padded box and knowing relief that the ship's narrowcast commo channels were still working. He chinned the switch to get Burning on an A/Video.

"Allgrave, I need your security teams posted ASAP, if you please."

At the same time he undogged the wheelhouse hatch and opened it manually, turning the wormgear wheel hand over hand because the servos were out. Fortunately, it didn't look as if any item in the exhaustive selection of emergency and escape gear was going to be needed. Other caskets, nearby, were oystering open without any problem.

Burning appeared, looking a little green from the ride down but shaking it off. The Allgrave's orders to his advance detachment were more mumbled than growled, but they were sufficient to get the Exts out of their drop boxes and into motion.

Quant gave the wheel another half turn. "Roiyarbeaux! Bear a hand here. Then get me patched through to *Terrible Swift Sword*. And pass word for the pickets to pull back."

From far off came a rumbling: the hook, going supersonic as it was being reeled in at steadily increasing speed. Without the hook's repeater transmitter, Quant had to use other means to stay in touch with the starship. Row-Row turned to on the hand wheel, as did Wix Uniday, without waiting to be asked.

When they got out onto the bridge, Quant had to take a moment to figure out what was wrong with the sky. He realized then that the big gray-green straps of the cargo sling, now freed from the hook, lay festooned all over his vessel, along with a few scraps of ablative armor. At any other time Quant would have taken the mess as a personal affront, but just now he felt like giving each of the magic ribbons a fervent kiss.

His select skeleton watch was already at work, manning the helm and the consolidated control consoles. They were still working in EVA suits since his orders had been to pause only long enough to shuck helmets and gauntlets. Quant thought about moving to Battle Two, the alternative bridge, but telltales indicated that it was in even rougher shape.

Row-Row was at the signal officer's auxiliary station. "Primary and secondary long-range telecomm not responding, sir. Should I have a look?"

Quant nodded toward the foredeck. "Negative. There's a piece of the primary lying out by the breakwater. The secondary's probably at the bottom of the lake by now. Can you give me a microwave link?"

"Working, sir."

Quant turned to Uniday. "I could use another pair of eyes on the port wing of the bridge." Uniday grabbed a vision enhancer and stepped lively.

There was a distant grinding from the midships aircraft elevator; the special details had moved smartly. By the time Quant reached Vulture's Row, more crew members had emerged from caskets and were making their way to stations. He was hit by a smell like none he had ever experienced on Periapt, thick with the scents of freshwater and freshwater flora and fauna, decay, and growth. It struck him as thick and organic but somehow the poorer for its lack of a salty tang.

Downside, the colors of the planet more closely suited its name. *GammaLAW* rode high and light on a sunlight-flashing lake under a blue-green sky and a few rainless clouds. Frightened by the hook's sonic boom, clumsy-looking fliers were scattering like pinpoints in the sky.

Isayagi, having shucked his EVA suit in favor of a life vest and battle helmet, gave a thumbs-up from the rising elevator. Quant's earphone brought his voice loud and clear. "What do we do with the sling leftovers, Skipper? Over the side, weighted?"

His people were unlimbering monomol-bladed saws; carbon-carbon composite was tough to sever and even trickier to burn through.

The drop plan gave Quant the option. "Pile it out of the way for now," he ordered, thinking that the exotic composite might come in handy. Moreover, the masses of stuff might adversely affect the indigs' aquaculture or even constitute a menace to navigation if they somehow got adrift.

Quant surfed through other diagnostics. The bridge crew was reviving more and more hardware and software. Freed from their drop-mode lockdown, the rudders were responding adequately. Maybe *GammaLAW* didn't have a Jonah riding it, after all, Quant told himself as the bridge watch arrived and got to stations.

Lieutenants Carrito and Gleick reported that they had temporarily sealed the breech forward of 917-3-Q. They judged the stress fracture in the hull to be due to the huge weight of the two 240-mm cannon from Turret *Musashi* secured on the hangar deck above and somewhat aft. Quant almost wished he hadn't brought the mutha-guns along.

"Ship off the port quarter, sir," Eddie Gairaszekh reported from the Combat Information Center even before the lookouts spied it. "Ninety-three hundred meters."

Fixed scopes had been dismounted from the bridge railings for the drop, so Quant hit his chin switch again, training his visor on the spot. Surveillance cams slaved to his headset ranged in.

The visual was as clear as if he were standing a few dozen meters from the craft. The teamboat looked exactly like the one in the recordings Mason had brought back from his scramjet contact mission; perhaps it was the same one. It was enormous for the preindustrial technologies of Aquamarine but crudely made, more a barge than a boat. He could count its timbers and see that it was tubby, unwieldy-looking, and human-driven.

Quant's mouth flattened beneath his visor as he studied the tiers of the damned. They consisted of two cylinders of wooden cages with three levels apiece. Vertical capstan posts running through the center of each level spun rough-hewn turntables, which rotated large wooden paddle wheels port and starboard, via wooden gears, driveshaft, and main axle. At each level gaunt figures in ranks of three and four leaned against chest-high capstan bars and trod in endless circles.

With several commo nets already in operation, Quant had Roiyarbeaux resume duty as his talker. Meanwhile, he got on the horn to Gairaszekh personally to ask, "What's the heading on that teamboat, Eddie?"

"Two-two-four magnetic, speed three point five knots. He's gonna cross our T, sir, but it'll take him all day at that rate."

The way Quant saw it, it didn't matter if the wallowing wooden antiquity *did* pull off the classic naval warfare maneuver of sailing broadside across the *GammaLAW*'s bows and presumed course. A ship on the crossbar of the T could bring a full broadside to bear, while its opponent would be able to employ only forward mounts.

But the Aquam had no gunpowder and no cannon. And even the indig war engines couldn't score at anything like nine klicks. Quant could dismiss his concern, if not the sight of the poor devils in teamboat tiers.

Now in battlesuits, the Exts had deployed in security teams to predesignated lookout posts and firing positions on the outer sponsons, upperworks, and main deck. Quant had made a point of not inspecting them after the initial muster; that was Burning's responsibility and purview. He nevertheless had made double sure they were all carrying the nonlethal flash-bang rifle grenades Dextra Haven had requisitioned from the Peace Warrantors.

Between the shock weapons and the sonics on their sidearms, the Exts could keep unfriendly Aquam at a distance without having to do anyone serious harm. Like Haven, Quant was glad that the Exts had already *had* their war and that the troops Burning had brought down in his advance platoon were far past any illusions about the glories of battle. Having experienced the worst of it, they would be less trigger-happy than untried soldiers would have been.

Not that Quant would tolerate any real threat to his ship, however. Light infantry weapons such as fireball mortars and rocket-propelled grenades gave the Exts more punch than an Aquam armada. Moreover, at least one piece of Close-in-Weapons-System ordnance would be operable in minutes, and the picket patrolcraft that had been shuttled down could handle any indig craft on the lake. For that matter, a lone Ext amphib fighting vehicle, when they arrived, could do so. Later, when the SWATH had her protective rings of surface, subsurface, and air patrols out and her particle beams, missile tubes, and chainguns in place, she'd be invulnerable to anything on-planet. *Including the Oceanic*, Quant told himself.

Only the Roke were a different kettle of fish . . .

Row-Row passed along word that the picket ships were pulling back to the *GammaLAW*'s position as ordered. Quant spied them across the dye-marked water at roughly the four points of the compass—two hydrofoils and two hovercraft, all of modest size. They were far from the most modern fast attack craft in naval inventories but were stoutly resistant to wear, tear, and breakdown. More to the point, they were undemanding in terms of the leading-edge maintenance resources that would be in such short supply in the early months and even years of the GammaLAW mission.

The biodegradable marker dye was already beginning to fade. It was the pickets' job to renew it over the much smaller landing site to the south where the amphib tethercraft would be touching down. That way, as much of Lake Ea as possible could be ceded back to the Aquam in hopes of staying on their good side. Quant couldn't see any of the pickets' spotter aircraft or reemos, but that wasn't surprising, since cautious skippers would use them to cover the pickets' withdrawal.

When the acting commander of the picket force reported to Quant on the net, it finally struck Quant that he had indeed become senior naval officer present afloat—with what was surely the smallest carrier-rated vessel and the tiniest escort force in the navy. But it was all his, nonetheless. Barring something untoward, "senior officer" would be his designation whenever and wherever he had a ship under him on Aquamarine. The prospect was as stirring as it was sobering.

Quant reiterated orders for the patrol craft to maintain a close antipersonnel watch on the SWATHship, though he was more apprehensive about pureeing some overly aggressive waterborne peddler with actuator disks than about doing so with surface-to-surface missiles. Then he cast another glance to the northwest, where the dam and breakwater lay over the horizon. Mason had reported glimpsing what appeared to be steam issuing from a vent in the stronghold, but Quant saw nothing like that just now.

Returning his attention to the teamboat, he saw that the figures in the tiers were mere scarecrow silhouettes. The bully-raggers' arms rose and fell, the knouts and nettle lashes silent at that distance.

He had Row-Row raise Burning, then delivered his message in person. "Allgrave, about that clockwork ark at ten o'clock."

"We're tracking it, sir."

"If he comes within two thousand meters, lay out some flash-bangs along his course. The CAPs and picket ships will probably stop the thing long before that, but we might as well get contingency measures firmed up. At fifteen hundred go to warning rounds of tracers and incendiaries. If he crosses the thousand-meter line, notify me and start picking your targets."

"Will do, sir," Burning said.

"What's the range of your boomers?"

"At five hundred meters, fired from a rest or bipod, some of my men can drive a point chisel halfway into an oak tree."

"Good to know," Quant responded. "Priority targets are those by the tiller, overseers' catwalks, and so on—not those wretches at the turnstiles."

"Understood, Captain."

A hand falling on Quant's shoulder made him start. Wix Uniday was wearing his blandest smile. "Sorry, Skipper. Didn't mean to give you a turn."

"Well?" Quant hadn't meant it to sound so curt, but it seemed that Uniday had enjoyed seeing him jump.

"For one thing, sir, I'd say you might care to duck."

As Uniday was saying it, a screaming came across the sky. Quant had heard the sound before, however, and so he pivoted without a quaver into the teeth of the boom. A scramjet fighter-bomber was thundering in across the lake at thirty meters of altitude, barrel-rolling a salute in violation of SOP, its wingman right behind. The AF aviators swept out over the teamboat and began a slow bank southward.

Quant drew a brisk breath and swung away from Uniday. "Row-Row, goddammit!"

"Sorry, sir." The talker shrugged. "Radar must've taken a shaking. We never even saw them coming. The lookouts've spotted another CAP flight approaching from the north." He listened to his headphones. "Air boss is now in radio and datanet contact."

"Good to see them," Uniday observed dryly, watching the two-plane elements assume new patrol patterns. "The sooner we show these woggies what they're up against, the sooner we can whip them into shape."

Quant gave Uniday a neutral look. "I suggest you give those slave tiers a closer glance, Honorable. The grandees are way ahead of you in the matter of whipping."

Uniday cocked one eyebrow and pointedly gazed off the other way.

The CAP flights' appearance had underlined the fact that another critical deadline was pressing: the flight deck had to be made operational for landings within an hour and a quarter. Already on station for two hours, the scramjets lacked sufficient slush hydrogen to achieve even a low orbit, and it had been deemed too risky to put a flying tanker on the scene to refuel them. For now the only safe landing spot on the whole planet was the SWATHship. The jets could make STOL splashdowns and remain afloat with inflatable buoyancy devices, but Quant would not have wanted to be on the tech team that tried to make them airworthy again. The truth was, the loss of the planes and their crews, like that of the picket ships and theirs, had been designated an acceptable risk by Dextra Haven in her determination to keep Starkweather from aborting the mission.

In the wake of the tether ride Quant knew just how anxious those fliers felt. He ordered every third Ext to help Isayagi's people ready the flight deck. No sooner had he done so than Row-Row was vying for his attention.

"Signal from Commissioner Haven, sir. She wishes to speak to the captain."

Quant acknowledged and chinned his headset over to the signal center circuit. His visor showed him a tight shot of Haven, dressed in her robes of state.

"Captain, there's been a glitch at this end. TRANSCOM informs me that tethership drops are going to have to wait for a while."

Quant's jaw muscles leapt. "More games, or is it just that TRANSCOM can't find its own collective bum with a squadron of help and an echo locator?"

"This time I think they're in earnest," Haven said. "The tether failed to retract all the way, and the reel assembly's jammed. The *Sword* is trailing about thirty klicks of cable, and the hook crew is stranded at the end. Even after they get it retracted, it will have to undergo repairs and tests, so we're going to have to make do with conventional shuttles. That means, among other things, cracking and repacking the containerized freight and dismantling a few of the larger items. How soon will *GammaLAW*'s flight deck be operational?"

"That's going to reduce airlift capability by sixty or seventy percent."

"Thereabouts," Dextra agreed. "So we need that flight deck *soonest*."

"Wait one, please." He circuit-hopped to get an overview of the situation below. The tether sling consisted mostly of remnants heaped on the aircraft elevator amidships by work details. A Big John crane was being lowered on the elevator portside, the better to gather in from underneath the hull a section that had been cut loose and cast over the starboard rail. Warrant Officer Spice Mittgang, Quant's senior diving expert, stood by in a WHOAsuit—Water Hardshell, One Atmosphere—in case he was needed to free any snags. Two ROVer underwater reemos were helping move the work along, their umbilicals cutting tiny wakes in the water.

The crash barrier and the arresting wires were already being tested. Row-Row passed word from engineering that the fusion reactor would be ready to send turns to the turbulators as soon as the sling was clear of them.

Quant clicked back to Dextra. "The problem's going to be turnaround. We haven't even got the catapult working, much less recalibrated." The latter would have to be done exactingly, since the steam-operated aircraft-launching system was in a new atmosphere as well as a new gravitational field.

Haven was shaking her head, scanning data that were outside Quant's field of view. "TRANSCOM's already putting priority cargo on kickoff skids. Launches will be carried out via ski-jump takeoff and strap-on booster. They've committed a dozen of their precious *Varuna* STOL shuttles, and they're saying that they can manage a number of wet drops into the lake as well. No need to touch deck."

"I haven't got much flight deck or hangar deck space," Quant said. "And as for aviation fuel—"

"TRANSCOM's done a workup," she interrupted. "Half the *Varunas* are fusion-engine, so they won't require on-site re-fueling. As much as possible, the sorties will be touch and go: land, offload, and refuel simultaneously—"

"Hot-pump," Quant corrected automatically.

"They will hot-pump," she amended without taking offense. "The first *Varuna* will fetch mostly aviation support personnel and slush hydrogen for the chem-powered aircraft. To prime the hot-pump, as it were."

"Then I require additional security," Quant warned flatly, transmitting a list of his immediate needs on the data link. "Exts, Peace Warrantors—whatever you can get down here. Tool-masters and shipwrights; extra CAP and rescue aircraft, picket boats—"

She was shaking her head again. "The first *Varuna*'s already loading. I'll bring what I can on the one after that."

"*You?* Madame Haven, under the circumstances I strongly advise that you wait until we can—"

"Captain, events require my presence onworld, and that's how it has to be."

Quant saw her hesitate, eyes flicking to one side, and knew she was double-checking to make sure the contact was encrypted. This time the encryption was a non-LAW cipher key Quant's commo/COMSEC officer, Mitsuaki "Mournful" Monyjang, had cadged from some shadowy back-channel contact inside Naval Security Group. Undoubtedly, Starkweather's code breakers could crack it in time, but not soon enough to be of any use to him.

Satisfied, Dextra Haven went on. "This tether business will be an awful pain in the backyard, but it does have its upside. The fact that *Tess* malfunctioned has Starkweather off balance. He's suddenly eager to move on to Hierophant, and I'm hoping

that he and I can stay on a live-and-let-live footing until then."
She paused momentarily. "In any case, I'm on my way. Hang a
meatball in the window, Skipper."

Very matey, her use of the aviator's slang for the optical
landing guidance systemry. But Quant straight-faced back, "I
believe you mean 'porthole,' ma'am."

She grinned. "I think you'll find that your splashdown gift
suits you to a T."

She broke the connection without waiting for a response,
which was just as well, since Quant had forgotten all about the
vac-sealed canister Haven's gynander companion had handed
him before he'd made for his drop casket.

While Row-Row was getting Lieutenant Hussein on the horn
for him, Quant dispatched the duty runner on a quick errand to the
wheelhouse. Then he told Hussein, "I want that 30-mm buzz-
gun on-line two minutes ago, Duran."

"Aye-aye, sir. Trouble?"

"Affirmative. All-out diplomacy may be declared at any
second."

The runner returned with the oblong package Quant had left
wrapped per Haven's wishes. Now he moved back to his sea
cabin for a moment's privacy, even though it knotted his belly to
be away from the bridge. The canister's costly gift sealing came
off easily after he slit it with his clasp knife.

Inside was a wooden tablet mounted with a tarnished brass
plate. He recognized the items before they were half-uncovered.
The lumber was from the deck planks of the USS *Constitution*;
the brass, from the melting down of a twelve-pounder that once
had ridden the decks of HMS *Vanguard* in Nelson's time.

Brought from Old Earth long ago, the tablet had been the
pride and joy of Valantin Maksheyeva's mentor, Admiral Figaro
"Plank" Waugh. Quant now understood why it had been un-
obtainable on Periapt before the launch even though the Naval
Museum had been divesting itself of so many of its treasures.
The epigraph was even older than the plaque itself. It read:

"*Sea Captain.* Upon his first popping up, the lieutenants
shear off to the other side, as if he was a ghost indeed; for 'tis

impudence for any to approach him within the length of a boat hook."

Edward Ward
The Wooden World
1709

CHAPTER NINETEEN

God, Teleos, Powers That Shine, let this be the right thing to do, Dextra told herself as the crew chief announced the final departure of deployment shuttle flight 019. Starkweather had the inside track with Rhodes and had endorsed all the AF and AlphaLAW excuses for not facilitating her contact with the other Ean grandees. It was therefore crucial, if premature, that she get groundside to mount a political counterattack, even if that meant chancing Starkweather's mucking with her supply lines.

The downside to the move was that the subordinates and staff remaining in *Big Tess* would lack a doomsday card to play against him, though she had covered her rear-echelon Exts as well as she could by arming them. With staunch and steady Big 'Un Boudreau commanding, they would serve as constant reminders to the AlphaLAWs that open conflict could be very costly. It wasn't a foolproof insurance policy, but neither was it the most audacious gamble she was taking on Aquamarine.

"Going amber in sixty seconds," the crew chief updated.

"Put your meat in the seat, people," a naval aviation CPO instructed Dextra's section of the passenger hold.

Daddy D paused by Dextra's seat on the way to his own. "Got that crate of indig trade trinkets all squared away, ma'am." He said it in the offhanded drawl he probably would have used to report the results of a short-arm inspection or the destruction of the universe.

"Trinkets" was now a code word for the superconducting warhead, which had been toted onboard the *Varuna* by the general and a platoon of Exts. They had made a casual show of their knives and live ammo and had physically blocked any TRANS-COM attempting to meddle with their cargo. Starkweather's minions had played it hands-off. The commissioner didn't want the Su-C explosive onboard any more than Dextra wanted it confiscated.

She showed Delecado an idiotically buoyant smile. "Nothing like a little bargaining power, General." It might have been the awareness that she was sharing the *Varuna* with the most powerful class of nonnuke munitions LAW had, but she felt a bit giddy, as if it were election night, the polls were closed, and the outcome was still in doubt.

She wondered how Daddy D was going to react when she took possession of the warhead. She had intended from the first to maintain the Exts' obedience to her command structure by keeping the higher orders of firepower—nukes, tactical air, battlesats, and the rest—to herself and her immediate Periapt-born subordinates, such as Quant. Whenever she felt guilty about her mistrust or thought of the Exts' sworn fealty and the honorary colonel's uniform they'd been so proud to give her, she made herself think of the Discards, or Zone, or even Ghost. Dextra couldn't afford to take a chance on a bunch of trauma cases rebelling against her or launching a vendetta of their own, especially in a place as fraught with unimaginable consequences as Aquamarine.

The personnel roster in large part consisted of a core group of people Dextra needed below, square pegs though many of them were. Zinsser and Mason were her point men on the enigma of the Oceanic and the nature of the Aquam. She had included the Aggregate as much to keep them out of Starkweather's hands as for the possible uses to which she could turn their collective genius. Lod she wanted for his Machiavellian instincts. Glorianna Theiss, Kurt Elide, and the rest were a mixed bag, but they would show the Aquam that the GammaLAW mission was about more than tech noir imperialism and interstellar war.

The Klax sounded for launch, and in moments the *Varuna* was flung free by its own centripetal force. As it left the planet's northern ice cap behind, Dextra summoned an enlargement of a planetary feature that greatly interested her. At the same time she raised Chaz Quant on an encrypted link.

"Captain, I've crosshaired the surface feature we were discussing. Any comments?"

Quant was in no hurry to answer merely for the sake of answering. After a bit he observed, "I have a seaman's wariness of that monster, but what a dreadnought it would make! A billion metric tons of ice island!"

Calved off an arctic ice shelf rather than a glacier, it was technically an island rather than a 'berg, but thus far its only designation was H-9—"H" for Hyperborean, though some claimed for "hoarhouse." Fourteen kilometers long and seven at its widest, it had undertaken its slow journey south in the interim between the *Scepter*'s departure and the arrival of the *Sword*. It was currently moving 3.6 klicks per day, pushed counterclockwise by an arctic gyre against prevailing winds as well as rotating counterclockwise as a result of Coriolis forces. It had wandered some four thousand kilometers south of its calving place to within seven hundred klicks of the northeastern tip of the Scourlands. The greater part of its upper surface was more or less flat—or at least sufficiently so to land VTOLs, STOLs, and modified conventional craft. Most important, it was surrounded by freshwater melt and therefore possibly shunned by the Oceanic.

"A difficult touchdown," Quant was saying, "but far easier than operating from the ice cap itself. And certainly unassailable by the Aquam."

"For the foreseeable future," Dextra pointed out. Various indig factions would inevitably acquire new technologies in the course of the GammaLAW mission, but H-9 might lie beyond their reach for a decade.

Quant had obviously been thinking along the same lines. "What's its estimated life span?"

"Thirty baseline-years, the experts tell me, though I doubt we'll need it for even half that time."

Her notion was to establish the hoarhouse as a fallback base in case initial diplomatic efforts failed and she had to disengage from the Aquam and regroup. Every clement bit of Aquamarine's surface area was inhabited or claimed by indigenous groups, and all of them were to a greater or lesser degree ferociously proprietary. Many also feared offworlders as bringers of misfortune, birth defects, and mutations. Of course, she could expropriate land by force, but even in the sparsely populated

Scourlands the building of a base would lead to war with the suicidally fierce Scourland Ferals. The prospect of such butchery repelled her.

Open warfare would only thwart her overarching purpose in coming to Aquamarine, in any case. More to the point, there was no way of knowing why the Oceanic's behavior had persuaded the Roke to steer clear of the planet. For all anyone knew, the enigma might well be tied in to a specific Aquam group. Dextra could imagine herself uprooting some pathetic gaggle of starvelings only to learn that they alone had been in mental contact with the Oceanic. An unlikely scenario but no more so than a marine superorganism that appeared to be keeping a warlike species of intelligent spacefarers at bay.

H-9 was slipping away beneath the *Varuna* as the shuttle began to line up for its deorbit burn and the approach to Scorpia, Lake Ea, and the *GammaLAW*.

"Your contingency plan makes the SWATHship expendable," Quant mulled, "but that is only prudent. You have to be prepared to do whatever is necessary to accomplish your mission."

"Are you, too, prepared to do whatever's necessary, Captain?"

Quant's ebony face shifted, then firmed. "Madame, I swore you my allegiance."

Dextra nodded. "I may need your hand on the tiller before we see home port again, Mr. Quant."

She said "tiller," but she'd been thinking "trigger."

With the *Sword*'s tether out of operation and his own ship incalculable work-hours away from being fully operational, Quant couldn't help thinking of W. S. Gilbert's line from *H.M.S. Pinafore*:

> Stick close to your desks and never go to sea,
> And you all may be Rulers of the Queen's Navee!

The first points of business now were to conduct a microscopically short shakedown run, move *GammaLAW* to a suitable point, and recalibrate the catapult with No-Loads. If the conventional shuttles were to achieve orbital rendezvous with the starship, the catapult had to be functioning properly.

Scarcely anything was working according to plan, though the quick-release fittings on the tetherdrop bracing had freed up as designed and the auxiliary power unit was supplying turns on the prop shafts. Quant wasn't about to crank up the reactor until it had had a thorough going-over.

He already had thirty meters of water under the triple hulls, but he was intent on relocating to deeper waters—northwest, closer to the dam. Where the ship lay, the hot, sediment-filled water would make sonar unreliable, and there would be no sparing of personnel to put umbilicaled ROVers over the side until the first shuttle was down. At the moment Quant was even shorter of experienced deck apes than he was of specialist ratings.

Once under way, the SWATHship answered her helm well; gradually Quant increased turns on the actuator disks to gauge the ship's current limitations. At twenty-five knots, a vibration in the port prop shaft had the engineering section worried. That was ten knots under the ship's rated top speed, but it was more than sufficient to outrun anything on Lake Ea. He had hoped for a few more evolutions before anchoring, but a squawk from one of the picket craft made him drop everything. Another teamboat had crossed the boundary into the moving, invisible defensive perimeter claimed by his ship.

Quant had to oversee the distant face-off from Battle One, the abbreviated CIC located off the bridge. As senior mission officer on the scene, he was responsible for what could become a major diplomatic scatstorm and could spell the difference between a cooperative relationship and war. He handed off the conn to Gairaszekh, instructing him to bring *GammaLAW* to anchor.

The picket hydrofoil gave the locals a recorded warn-off. Quant had lobbied for Aquam translators aboard each LAW vessel, but Rhodes's suspicions and other bureaucratic snags had left him with only the recordings, along with the Aquam-dialect Terranglish his officers had learned on the voyage out from Periapt.

That turned out to be enough, however; the slave-driven boat changed course. As the picket cam feeds showed it wallowing off, Quant realized that something was harrowingly wrong.

GammaLAW had slowed but not stopped and was suddenly backing hard, with the starboard anchor chain clattering and banging down the hawse pipe. In forty meters of water the SOP was for the capstan to walk out the anchor for the first ten or twenty meters, but only after the ship was nearly motionless. With the chain dropping free down the hawse hole, the anchor's weight could snap or strip the windlass brake as well as take out the forecastle and anybody standing on it.

Quant shot out of Battle One, across the bridge, and out onto the starboard wing in one bound. Gairaszekh was there, talking in a rapid monotone into his headset as an ashen-faced phone talker stood by.

"I repeat, engage all manual stops and trigger emergency brake override," his senior lieutenant was saying.

There wasn't much else to do. The members of the anchor detail, along with everyone else on the forecastle, were scattering for their lives as the giant chain blurred from the halfdeck windlass casing and screamed down the hawse hole like an armored serpent going relativistic. Minor flailings bashed deep gouges in the double decking and battered gouts of wood into the air like heavy-caliber impacts.

Quant braced himself for the worst; then his ears picked up a sibilance that was as loud and penetrating in its own way as the chain's din. Smoke from something other than combustion billowed up from the windlass, and in seconds metal was grinding metal as the emergency windlass brakes began to lose their lining in their effort to grip. But Quant didn't mind; at least the chain was coming to a halt.

The anchor detail immediately doused the red-hot capstan and the smoldering shreds of brake lining. Eyes on the foc's'le, Gairaszekh was giving orders to secure and shackle the chain before it slipped again.

As soon as he had something of a handle on things, he turned to Quant. "Special sea detail was securing anchor gear from computer control for manual lowering when the system went into an emergency release sequence, Captain. Shackle servos, capstan brake, the works."

Quant stared at him in disbelief. For that to happen someone would have had to have been mucking with the ship's core computer functions. He listened as phone talkers passed along damage reports. Fortune had smiled on the ship.

"Tell deck division and engineering that I want a complete diagnostic on what went wrong," Quant instructed Gairaszekh.

"Aye, sir."

"Specifically, they are to ascertain whether the AlphaLAW antiviral teams did any grab-assing with our 'wares. If there's any evidence of sabotage, that anchor's going to be carrying human bait the next time it breaks water."

CHAPTER TWENTY

Catapult No-Loads had always reminded Quant of monster futon mattresses, except that they were made of neocrete and steel. Slinging them out into Lake Ea was for some reason uncomfortably evocative of a burial at sea.

"Clear downrange, sir," Row-Row relayed. "Cat officer requests permission to test-fire."

"At her discretion," Quant said tightly, eyes on the scurrying on the flight deck. The talker passed word to Lieutenant Commander Bohdi.

Weight considerations on the tetherdrop had forced Quant to bring only three pigs, as the cat crews sneeringly referred to the monolithic No-Loads. He would have brought twice that many if possible and would have test-shot every one before catapulting a single manned aircraft. But TRANSCOM and Log Command were impatient to high-gear the hot-pump cycling of aerospace shuttle drops and had pressed him to make do with one test run, with subsequent adjustments to be made in the course of operations. Quant was equally eager to get personnel, equipment, and supplies deployed planetside, but he had demanded that at least two calibrating shots be made.

TRANSCOM didn't dare overrule him. If it had, the LAW Aero Forces shuttle pilots would have been talking mutiny and trying to borrow live ammo from Big 'Un Boudreau. That was why the skipper of any vessel with a fixed-wing flight deck wore on his or her chest, as Quant did, the gold wings of a naval aviator. People who had been in the hot seat on a night carrier landing or emergency set-down had a tendency to pull for the buggers in the cockpits, and the navy trusted no one else to have the final say.

The flight deck cat was basically a huge, brushless DC linear motor driven by an independent power reservoir. A maglev carriage lined with permanent magnets supported the trolley—the component of the cat that protruded above the flight deck surface—and the trolley itself was fitted with hooks to engage the tow bar that extended from an aircraft's nose gear strut.

On release for catapult launch, the carriage rode a magnetic wave along a stator and was capable of whipping a seventy-ton aircraft to 150 knots—almost 300 kilometers per hour, baseline. Owing to both the wide variety of tow loads and the need to keep from hammering aircraft with excess power, the carriage thrust could be adjusted far more precisely than could the steam cats of earlier days. Too much power at takeoff and a pilot would be rendered unconscious by g forces; too little, and pilot and aircraft would end up in the water.

No-Loads were fired for recalibration even after routine overhaul or modification of the cat. But for *GammaLAW*, recalibration was critical. The cat wanted *days* of test fires, the way the ship herself deserved months of refit and sea trials. Neither option was feasible, and Quant simply had to make his peace with the situation.

The ski-jump bow end of the SWATHship's flight deck was pointed out at the lake's deepest parts, which remained free of Aquam traffic and aquaculture activity. On the side of the No-Load, someone had graffitoed "LAKE EA YACHTING SOCIETY AND HEAVIER-THAN-AIR CLUB." Beneath that was a crude line drawing of a hand pointing the way bowward with an extended middle finger.

Back when he was Hallowed Hall's exec, Quant would have been expected to find the guilty parties and land on them hard. As his own man, he pretended not to notice.

"Sir? Would the captain care for some protection?"

It was Gairaszekh with a spray bulb of the insect repellent LAW had concocted specifically for the GammaLAW mission's needs. The big lieutenant with the size EEE shoes was especially loved by flying vermin, no matter what the planet or waters. Quant, though, waved the pungent stuff away.

He watched the cat crew going through its ritual dance. Color-coded for a value of twenty-five metric tons, the

No-Load's breakable rear-end holdback was locked into place, while its nose bar was hooked to the trolley. Satisfied, the hookup petty officer handed off authority to Lieutenant Commander Bohdi by means of hand signals.

There was a time lag while the command was received and enacted below. The magnets made no sound, though the warning horn did. With a crack like a 'boomer shot, the holdback broke under its appointed load, and in moments the No-Load rode the stroke down the flight deck.

A loud *whoosh* accompanied the object, caused by the vibration from its wheels on the nonskid flight deck surfacing. Cheering it on, people whooped and whistled. The trolley stopped, but the No-Load was flung away in a flattish parabola over Lake Ea, hitting the water with a spectacular splash nearly two kilometers downrange.

What with all the applause and yahooing, most of the crew members were unaware of the quiver that spread outward across the lake's surface. Stirred by the impact, a mist of midges began to rise off the water. Quant supposed they'd have come eventually, but the No-Load seemed to have angered them. Catching the smell and heat of human bodies, they swarmed the ship.

"Shit," Gairaszekh muttered. "Mason says their bite is something fierce." He was spraying additional insect repellent into his palms to spread it on his face. "But goddamn, they're not supposed to be this far out on the lake."

The phone talkers were awaiting orders on the proper procedure for repelling flying vermin. It wasn't bites that concerned Quant. Who knew what hazards the pests might present if they found their way into interior spaces? The berthing and working spaces would be hell to live and labor in if biting bugs took over.

"Rig for measure three anticontamination," he ordered. "Secure all hatches and portholes."

The bosun's mate of the watch had already hit the alarms and was repeating Quant's order over the PA. Gairaszekh, meanwhile, got on the commo line to engineering, passing the order to hit the overrides. Most of the hatches and portholes aboard were servo-equipped and could be closed and sealed as long as no one had meddled with them. Quant could have ordered a measure one seal-up, but that would have meant hatches swinging to, no matter who or what might be in the way.

Forced-air blowers began providing positive interior pressure to keep the midges from venturing into any overlooked apertures they might find. As the bridge was being secured, Quant slipped out onto the port wing, followed by Row-Row.

What made the scene grim instead of comic was that the central climate control units had been unshipped for refurbishment and were still in *Big Tess*. Quant had thought they could get by with forced-air cooling for the next few days, but if he had to keep his ship buttoned up for fear of infestation, the Big Sere heat was going to be brutal.

The midges set in with a vengeance, some getting inside Ext battlesuits before their wearers had sealed up. Ignoring the vaunted LAW insect repellent, they flew through it even when Gairaszekh sprayed it directly at them. The bites were more irritating than painful, but they itched intensely. Quant, scratching his neck, sent Haven a twix explaining the situation and suggesting that she debark in a decontam suit or another protective garment.

She replied in minutes—just enough delay to have discussed her political image with her gynander and Lod. "If my people have to scratch, I can scratch with them."

Quant pinched several midges from his nostrils and expelled several more. Hands-on leadership? he mused. *That* he had to see.

Dextra was aware that her appearance on the shuttle's ramp would have made a good media bite, although there would be no media bites on Aquamarine for years to come. Stepping out into the late-afternoon light, she paused at the top of the ramp for an initial look around, making it clear by her body language and expression that she was giving the ship a businesslike once-over and was not at all interested in applause. Immortalizing her own arrival while the advance party looked on—those who had braved the tetherdrop—would have sent entirely the wrong message. However, she didn't mind that a breeze off the *Gamma-LAW*'s bows was ruffling her fieldsuit collar and chignoned hair.

She had expected to be ducking and swatting her way through clouds of bloodthirsty midges, but they had apparently dispersed of their own volition. Dusk probably would bring them back, but by then the ship would be better prepared.

Except for a reception party headed by Gairaszekh and Burning, everyone in sight kept working. By her directive, she was not saluted by the ship's company in general, because too much crucial work remained to be done. Still, when a CAPflight fan-in-wing fighter made a slow flyby along the portside and the pilot bent regulations by waggling his wings in greeting, she gave him a thumbs-up.

With some of the midge-bitten needing medical attention, Glorianna Theiss was a welcome sight. Her leonine mane was swept by the gusts from the bow, and compassion and concern radiated from her high-cheekboned face like a beacon; she made Dextra feel short, crass, and water-retentive. The surgeon general almost trod on Dextra's heels as they descended the ramp, with Tonii and Lod crowding close behind.

Lieutenant Gairaszekh—whom Dextra had taken to calling "Jurassic"—rendered a hasty salute on behalf of all hands; the engine sounds were deafening, and talk was useless.

The priority now was to get the newcomers off the flight deck. There were so many hazards peculiar to it that even pilots and other nondeckdogs were in peril when afoot there. Following a yellowshirt guide and shepherded by others, she and the rest of the *Varuna*'s passengers filed toward a hatch in the superstructure. She saw Quant gazing down from Vulture's Row and gave him a thumbs-up as well; to her surprise, he answered with a salute.

Wix Uniday made a minimal kowtow to her from the signal bridge above and just aft of the navigation bridge. Along with his signature supercilious smile, he was wearing a commo headset somewhat different from the standard LAW issue. Seeing that his lips were moving almost undetectably, Dextra wondered just whom he was talking to.

Inside, out of the wind, the air was unmercifully hot despite circulation blowers. Unable to restrain herself, Glorianna interrupted Jurassic's formal welcome to fire questions about injuries from the splashdown and subsequent operations and possible allergic responses to the midges. Then she strode off for sick bay like a conquering Valkyrie, leaving the doctor and two med specialists in her retinue to trot after her.

Dextra was to be escorted to her quarters, Jurassic said, after which Quant hoped to confer with her in his stateroom. Delecado, however, was immediately led off to the bridge. Dextra let it pass without comment. Jurassic was about to conduct her below when he paused to listen to his headset earphone and informed her, "Communication for you, Commissioner. From Grandee Rhodes."

Dextra and her core advisory group hurried to her stateroom office. The suite of berthing and working spaces was no further toward completion than it had been in transit, but Quant had at least made sure that the data and commo gear was hooked up.

She was preparing to accept Rhodes's call when she noticed Jurassic writhing with indecision. "What is it, Lieutenant?" she asked impatiently.

He gestured to the exposed utility connections, the stacked cargo pods, and the bare lights. "Commissioner, if you give Rhodes a visual from here, our low state of readiness will be exposed."

"I doubt an Aquam could understand it as such," she said. "But I wasn't planning on taking chances."

Tonii produced Dextra's personal pennon as LAW Commissioner for Aquamarine. Below the GammaLAW mission's olive-wreathed symbol of Aquamarine sat her own heraldic patent as Hierarch, intertwined with the LAW sword and scepter—all in royal purple, vivid turquoise, and gleaming gold against a coal-black field. The gynander rigged it as a backdrop while Dextra took a seat and Lod brought the commo terminal on-line.

Dextra trained a pleasant expression on Jurassic until he got the message and excused himself. Policy guidelines suggested but didn't require that she confer with Quant before opening onsite contact with an indig leader; besides, *he* was the one who hadn't had time to talk. Dextra nodded, and Lod activated the terminal.

Because he needed to wear his headset rather than turn its integral cam on himself, Rhodes was sending audio only, though he was receiving her in A/V. His voice was a less subtle instrument than he probably supposed.

"My precious, luminous Madame Commissioner," he began. "Welcome to Aquamarine and to my splendid domain of Lake Ea."

Dextra's in-transit language lessons had made his Terranglish understandable. "Thank you, Grandee Rhodes. It *is* a lovely spot." She did her best to look and sound composed despite the heat.

Rhodes made a trilling sound of pleasure. "I look forward to meeting you in person. In the meantime, I am sending along a few modest gifts in the company of my personal envoy, who happens to be a highly esteemed Sense-maker. He would speak with you on some matters, should you permit it."

"I cannot thank you enough," she told him in a neutral tone, leaving it for him to guess how she meant it. "What might these matters be?"

"One or two I wish to be pleasant surprises, but another is, I confess, somewhat distressing. One of my subjects wishes to present a petition for damages done to his sprat pens and shell beds as a result of activities staged by your great ship. It is his right to do so under my very beneficent reign."

From what little she knew, a peon demanding redress from the grandee would more likely make the acquaintance of his interrogators. "Ah, but your subjects' complaints are your concern, Grandee Rhodes."

His voice took on an edge. "Madame Commissioner, *I'm* not the one who's been flinging great stones into Lake Ea or rumble-quaking back and forth over it in flying gyns. Here comes before you a man whose livelihood has been grossly impaired by your presence. Am I wrong to believe that LAW wishes a new prosperity for Aquamarine? Is not compassion part of your program? In any event, the man will accompany my Sense-maker. Treat him as you will."

Dextra looked off-pickup to Jurassic, who had reappeared and was motioning that something or someone was trying to approach the ship. "You can be sure of it," she whispered to the snowy holofield after Rhodes had cut the connection.

CHAPTER
TWENTY-ONE

The Aquam swallowed nervously and stole quick glances at Dextra. He was wearing an aquaculturalist's tattered loin rag and a cropped, multipocket work vest, but she doubted that his shivering had anything to do with his threadbare clothing. Night had fallen, and spotlights blazed down on the quarterdeck. Dextra wasn't surprised the Aquam found them overawing.

The man directed the rest of his statement to the deck planks while he passed the brim of his battered tricorn hat around and around through clenching hands. The hands were scarred and crack-nailed with heavy calluses on the knuckles and finger pads. His bifurcate beard joggled as he rattled out the words.

"I'm a three-buoy tenant and a paid-up chop holder; Your Worship can ask anybody. They was two of my finest bud beds, where your boat threw the great stones."

His eyes shifted from side to side, and Dextra, scrutinizing him from her high seat, wondered just what he was looking at.

Advance teams and LAW liaison with Rhodes were supposed to have ensured that the SWATHship's splashdown site and temporarily quarantined operations area were arranged in such a way that no local's livelihood would be endangered. This man, Hiip, however, claimed that no one had said anything about the Visitants' mighty gyns hurling mountains at a time at an innocent, hardworking lakeman's waterstead and floatpens.

Plausible, Dextra mulled. But Hiip's claim might just as easily have been trumped up by Rhodes as a means of testing her or inserting a spy aboard *GammaLAW*. Nevertheless, when the dory bearing Hiip and Old Spume the Sense-maker had arrived at the picket line, she'd had little choice but to have them both fetched aboard. It was too early to challenge the grandee and risk coming off as a bully to the general populace.

Quant hadn't liked it, either, but he was still chanceried on the bridge, looking after his ship. That spared Dextra the probability of having a set-to with him, so quickly had events moved. She wondered if she was going to have to tell Glorianna to slip something into the captain's food to force him to get some sleep.

The most urgent matter had been to keep Hiip and Old Spume from seeing anything of strategic value or any hint of the ship's abysmal unreadiness. Quant had concurred with Dextra's straightforward solution that she receive the locals on the starboard sponson—the Science Side hull—away from the flight deck and the increasingly hectic air operations. In addition, a surprisingly stately and imposing backdrop had been rigged from two of the black paravanes used to keep the ship's towed drone packages aloft. Luck was with her in that the evening breezes were mild, so that the lightweight stuff wasn't in danger of being blown about farcically or wafted off into Lake Ea.

When Hiip and Old Spume had climbed the accommodation ladder to the main deck, they had found themselves center stage in a small theater in three-quarters round, unable to see any more of the ship than they had been allowed to see from the 'foilcraft that had conveyed them to the SWATHship. Dextra sat on an improvised throne two meters higher up, where an auto-firefighting emplacement was due to be refitted. Tonii was at her right hand, Burning was at her left, and Exts in battlesuits were posted all about, with boomers held at high port.

Hiip seemed earnest enough despite refusing to meet her gaze. Dextra had been forced to set aside Rhodes's welcoming present because, vexingly, there was no way to establish beforehand whether it constituted a genuine peace offering or an insult.

Old Spume had brought along several casks of insect repellent—abominable-smelling stuff, from what the hydrofoil skipper reported—along with 'Waretongue's message to the effect that the midges of Lake Ea were known for their determination and vigor, "just as the lake's grandee is." He'd added his presumption that the Visitants would be grateful for his succor and assistance in this matter, in which he was as expert as he was in innumerable others.

The midges had in fact risen up at dusk and departed once more, though many were still in the air, homing in along with every other night flier on a ship that was surely the brightest thing in the Aquam night. While Hiip and Spume wouldn't know it, the only things keeping the interview from becoming a bug blizzard were concealed Exts who were sweeping the sky with their sonics. If Hiip and Spume were curious about the stunned mothlike things drifting down like petals, they kept it to themselves.

One sop to her irritation was that Spume had looked suitably apprehensive and pale in passing along the grandee's jeering message. As Claude Mason had concluded, the Sense-maker was out of favor at Wall Water. Making Spume his envoy was merely Rhodes's way of toying with the old man.

Dextra had considered forcing Hiip to prove his compliance by guiding divers to verify his claims. But every hand was needed for shipboard work, and the whole business might only let out how ill positioned *GammaLAW* and its complement were at the moment.

"So Your Worship owes me five scudos of silver," the Aquam reminded her in his coarse west lake accent.

From the general information Starkweather's analysts had passed along, that was as much money as a tenant aquaculturalist might scrape together in two or three years. Hiip's claim was just brazen and greedy enough to halfway convince Dextra that he was just what he seemed. That didn't mean she could suffer her commissionate to become a cash cow for scam-wise Aquams. She checked Tonii's face for an opinion, but the gynander gave none of the subtle signals 'e and Dextra used. Lod's expression was uncharacteristically blank, and no one else gave any covert sign of having an opinion one way or the other. She'd had time only to hash through a few options with her advisers and now decided to go with a midrange response.

"You furnish no proof or supporting testimony for your grievance, Hiip, which nullifies it before your canons as well as ours. If, however, you are able to substantiate your claim to my interrogators and Sense-makers, I may yet honor it. At the very least I shall direct that you be well fed."

Hiip agreed at once. Dextra chalked it up tentatively to a combination of nothing ventured, nothing gained and a peasant's eagerness for a free feed whenever the opportunity arose. Whatever emerged, Hiip's answers would add considerably to current data on the region, and that in itself was worth the bit of food and liquor the intelligence people would ply him with. She was about to order him taken below, when Lod spoke up.

"Hiip, I was admiring your smooth fingertips. How does a hardworking three-buoy serf make the purse-rein calluses go away right in the middle of the Big Sere, when he's busiest with his string lines? How does Hiip the chop holder lack any corkie bite marks on his legs? Or have his yearlings been that placid, right in the season of their *musth*, year in and year out?"

Dextra vaguely recalled the details of an aquaculturalist's life that Lod was citing with his small-toothed leer. Hiip's hands and lower legs were dirtier than a lake peon's should have been, but the dirt didn't completely hide his lack of scars and other marks peculiar to his alleged work.

Even so, the three-buoy man wasn't fazed, though Old Spume seemed just shy of cardiac arrest. "A canny water hand is distinguished by his lack of those things," Hiip maintained.

Lod made a broad act of astonishment. "Even a lifelong water hand?" He indicated Piper, who was seated nearby. "In that case you won't object to our psychic scrutator administering a harmless philtre of veracity to elicit the truth."

Lod's bluff broke Hiip's facade. Dextra had seen Exts, Manipulants, and a lot of other fighters spring into furious motion, but the Aquam surprised her with his abruptness of action. He whirled to leap from the rail, only to do a back handspring to avoid a serrated Ext bayonet. Though he never paused, Dextra had the distinct impression that the Ext's faultless reaction had caught him off guard.

Lod was pulling Piper back from the focus of conflict but yelling, "Take him alive! No boomers!"

Old Spume had simply slumped to the deck in terror, arms over his head. Hiip springboarded off him, leaving two Ext pursuers to go around the Sense-maker. All cool precision and acrobatic elusiveness, the counterfeit water hand vaulted at Dextra, planning perhaps to take her hostage, perhaps to carry out an assassination. He hadn't counted on someone else moving as quickly and surely as he had.

Tonii hop-stepped in to uncork a side kick that knocked him off his vector. Staggered, Hiip rolled with it, then recovered and sprang at Zinsser, a target of secondary opportunity. In one sequence, the oceanographer was shouldered aside and Hiip was hosed up and down with a wash of sonics from a 'baller's accustor wave-guide barrel. The ultrasound pipe, mounted under and protruding slightly ahead of the .50 caliber muzzle, streamed a powerful beam that piled up plasma impact waves ahead of them and at close range, paralyzed the Aquam's nervous system, turning him into a collapsing jellybag.

Ghost gave the intruder another helping as he hit the deck planks, then moved in to check on him, ignoring Zinsser's stuttering and sputtering. Other Exts, including Burning, closed in by the numbers, carrying out a well-practiced prisoner apprehension procedure. Still others were slapping restraints on a pathetically sobbing Old Spume.

As the apprehension team's lead man, Burning handed his pistol off, then approached cautiously to flop Hiip onto his face; the vibing had stunned the man so thoroughly that his bladder and bowels were evacuating. As Burning planted his knee behind Hiip's neck and began to cuff him, the sinewy little body gave a brief spasm.

Burning reacted instantly, getting his knee down and securing armlocks and headlocks before the flicker of seizure had well begun. By the time it had passed, Hiip was completely immobilized, but the Allgrave glanced up to Dextra and shook his head.

"He's dead."

Dextra barked to the queenly Glorianna Theiss. "Code red! I need him back!"

That didn't happen, notwithstanding the medics' quick and earnest efforts. Searching Hiip's body to determine the cause of death was a foul business, but the Exts, Glorianna, and her people were inured to far worse procedures. In the meantime, all anyone could get out of Spume was that he knew nothing about Hiip or anything else.

Inspection of Hiip's corpse eventually turned up three simple but clever suicide devices—miniature watch springs and slivers of stiffened human cartilage sharpened at both ends, their tips envenomed with neurotoxin and capped with tiny sleeves of cartilage tubing. Release of the spring yanked the points from their caps to stab into the bearer's flesh. More astounding was the fact that the springs were restrained solely by their carrier's muscle tension. Hiip had borne one under his tongue, another coiled against his anus, and a third held against a loin belt by the pressure of his abdomen—and nothing in his movements or speech had tipped even the Exts that the Aquam was exerting himself.

"A Shadow-rat," Claude Mason provided. "I've met up with one before—though most who have are dead."

Dextra felt personally, infuriatingly outwitted. Shadow-rats were the ninja-swamis of Scorpia, especially of the Ean region. Low-tech didn't mean low-IQ, she reminded herself.

She ordered Glorianna to autopsy the body with intel agents present to see if it was harboring any other surprises. Spume, too, was taken below for further interrogation. When the Sense-maker was out of earshot, Dextra turned to Lod.

"Very observant of you, Major, spotting those discrepancies. Not a bad ruse on Rhodes's part."

Lod kowtowed with a flourish. "Which leaves me to wonder if such an adept spy was sent here with *intentional* errors in his cover. Perhaps to test how gullible we are or aren't, even at the price of an accomplished agent's life."

Spying the insect repellent the grandee had tweaked her with, Dextra summoned Burning over. Rhodes had to have learned about the midge plague from someone aboard, even if word had been relayed through Starkweather. "Kindly form a detail and find the honorable Wix Uniday," she told Burning. "Confiscate that AlphaLAW headset he uses to talk to *Terrible Swift Sword* and make goddamn sure he doesn't have a backup."

Burning was only too happy to oblige. "And Old Spume?" he asked.

Dextra thought it over. "Seems to me that he's as much a victim of Rhodes's taunting 'generosity' as we were. Grill him, but nothing rough. I have other plans for him, something that will stick a white-gloved finger in the grandee's eye."

Preliminary word arrived from Glorianna. Forensic pathology had turned up another, far slower-acting toxin in Hiip's system—its antidote was presumably ashore in his superior's keeping. Even if the Exts had somehow nabbed him alive despite the poisoned coils, there wouldn't have been much time to wring information out of him.

"I doubt he'd have been much of a conversationalist, anyway," Dextra heard Lod say.

"I liked that about him," Ghost replied.

CHAPTER
TWENTY-TWO

The six days following Haven's arrival were devoted to bringing the SWATHship to a high state of readiness. The close-in weapons system's chaingun was up and running by day four, but the mount for the charged particle beam remained incomplete. Starkweather had come up with excuses for withholding its custom capacitor bank as well as the monster shells and rocket-assisted projectiles for the 240-mm naval rifles that were still sitting on the hangar deck.

The twin cannon from Turret *Musashi* were a double affliction for Quant; not only were they ammunitionless, they were much in the way. The ship lacked even the equipment necessary to move them. All he could do was hope that the starship tether could be made operational once more.

Much of the cargo space on the conventional shuttles had been taken up with slush hydrogen for the shuttle reorbits. Equipment was finally in place aboard the *GammaLAW* for producing slush H_2, but augmentative supplies still had to be ferried down. The only other defensive component Quant had managed to get on-line was a smoke-making system. Back on Periapt more than one high-tech naval type had derided him for even including the smoke screen generator in his ship's arsenal, but Quant had insisted on it. Whether the enemy were Roke or cutlass-wielding buccaneers, the ability to move stealthily was advantageous.

Additional personnel had deployed, including the Discards, the Aggregate, and Zone's battalion of Exts, who, along with the rest, took part in familiarization exercises with the WHOA-suits, ROVers, and sundry communications and archeo-hacking devices fresh from LAW Research and Development.

CAPflight recons had provided information about current-day Aquamarine as well as the self-termed Optimants. Chief among the latter were the flying pavilions. Once grand airborne mansion-casinos, the Cyberplagued Laputas now followed pre-programmed routes and schedules, often affording the only connecting transportation over the Amnion to Aquamarine's widely scattered landmasses. Families of Insiders, descendants of the original crews, had retrofitted the pavilions with elaborate external cargo and passenger structures to cash in on their unique positions, while they themselves resided exclusively in their self-contained, endlessly moving worlds.

Scramjets had made flybys over isolated islands as well—places, shunned by the Laputas, where odd cultures had evolved—and beacons and landing assist radars had been planted on Hoarhouse, the giant ice island that Haven and Quant were still thinking of utilizing as a fallback base.

Glorianna Theiss, whose medical oath was more practical than the classically Hippocratic one, had been busy creating guidelines for what eventually would be a system of LAW brothels to be staffed with indigs. While Haven was well aware that sex was a primary way of keeping her personnel from creating friction of a sort with the Aquam, she also knew that recruitment and operations had to be handled very delicately.

Theiss was also eager to dispense services that would prevent Anathemite births, but Haven had cautioned her that no such medical help would be made available to the Aquam until the trade in mandseng and galvani stones had been suitably disrupted.

Preliminary survey data on the Trans-Bourne—the island at the southwestern tip of the Scorpian landmass—had revealed that a kind of industrial revolution was in progress. The fabricators of the muscle cars, and perhaps of dyes and mordants, had apparently refused to provide muscle-car propulsion systems for the Ean grandees' teamboat millships because the grandees were perpetuating various anti–free trade policies.

Haven's curiosity had been piqued on all sides, but thorough investigations of regions such as the Trans-Bourne and the Scourlands were going to have to wait until inroads had been made with the regents who lorded over Lake Ea.

The day-to-day stuff had proved just as troubling for everyone aboard. Since climate control and sound-deadening gear had been deprioritized, the interior of the trimaran was as hot and noisy as an early twentieth-century warship.

At the same time, however, the Grandee Rhodes's plans for a Grand Attendance were proceeding apace. Then and only then would 'Waretongue greet Dextra formally and introduce her to the other Ean-area grandees. *GammaLAW*'s seemingly well-armed presence at the headwaters of the river that drained Ea and emptied into the sea had sown unrest among various Aquam factions, especially between the Human Enlightenment sect, to which Claude Mason's son, Purifyre, belonged, and DevOcean, an apocalyptic-revelationist cult that held that on a day of rapture all the chosen would be accepted live and unharmed into the embrace of the Oceanic.

There was also the matter of the lake water level, which though regulated by the dam, was in effect controlled by the Grandee Rhodes. It was worrisome to the neighboring grandees that the Visitants might force Rhodes to alter the water levels and thus affect aquaculture food-growing activities for the remainder of the Big Sere. It was hoped by the same potentates that this and other issues would be addressed, if not hashed out, at the coming Grand Attendance.

Dextra wasn't enthusiastic about being paraded in front of so many local rulers at once so early in the mission, but Stark-weather had pushed for her to accept Rhodes's invitation, as he had already accepted it himself.

No mention had been made by either side of Hiip the Shadow-rat, though Rhodes had asked after Old Spume, who had yet to be returned to land. In response, Dextra had merely promised that the Sense-maker would be back in Wall Water in time for the festivities and be a surprise to all.

The *GammaLAW*'s computer center was declared off limits to all but a handful of technicians, but it was rarely under guard of any sort. Even when it was, Claude Mason was not turned away at the hatch; he was Haven's key man on Aquam affairs, and few places aboard the ship were denied to him. Infiltrating the trimaran while it was onboard *Terrible Swift Sword* had been another matter, however. On the one occasion when he had managed to reach the computer center, he had scarcely succeeded in uploading a small infoparcel of the data Yatt had given him when he had been interrupted by Peace Warrantor guards and escorted from the cargo bay.

The question now was how to connive enough solo time inside the computer center to upload the contents of Yatt's primary data modules. They were scheduled to be shuttled down the well in two days—on the morning after 'Waretongue's Grand Attendance.

Mason was casing the passageways that accessed the computer center when Yatt, who had been silent since the spaceplane flight over Lake Ea, paid a visit to Mason's tormented neuralwares.

"Mason, stop preoccupying yourself with the coming reunion with your son and attend to matters at hand. It is critical that you discover a means of uploading the bulk of our memory and functions into the ship's systemry. As it stands, we pose more danger to the vessel than support."

"What sort of danger?" Mason asked without actually mouthing the words.

"We acknowledge, for you alone, Mason, that we may have inadvertently glitched some of the ship's core programs soon after its tetherdrop."

"The anchor system?"

"Precisely that. But we can make everything right once we are fully aboard."

Mason's eyes widened. "You haven't corrected the glitch?"

"We are unable to at this time."

Mason pressed his hands to his head. "I'll have to alert Quant—"

"Mason, stop and listen to us: Should you choose to reveal our presence now, Haven's suspicions about you will be confirmed and you will surely be excluded from attending the fete Rhodes has planned, where your son will be waiting for you. Where all the pain you've endured for twenty years can finally be laid to rest. Think logically rather than emotionally."

Mason seethed to himself, as if in an attempt to sear Yatt psychically with his anger. "That anchor could have killed a dozen crewpersons! What else am I going to have to worry about—the CIWS chaingun? The catapult? The ship's power plant?"

"We are watchdogging all systems for signs of possible corruption. You need not fear for anyone's life. Help us reverse the minor damage we've caused instead of berating us for our oversight and threatening us with exposure. Remember, Mason, we are a team. We are responsible for bringing you here. More than Rhodes, we are responsible for your imminent reunion with Purifyre."

Mason sneered. "Don't pat yourself on the capacitors, Yatt. Whatever you claim to be doing in my behalf, you're doing to get a line on Endgame—if it exists. If it isn't some figment of your cyberimagination."

"Endgame exists, Mason. The cure for the Cyberplagues is real, and it resides here, somewhere on Aquamarine. So we suggest that you think your misgivings through to their conclusion. Since it is humankind that stands to gain the most from Endgame, which of us is the more self-serving? You desire nothing more than to make amends with the child you abandoned, whereas we seek nothing less than the eradication of the Plagues and the reunion of humankind and artificial intelligence."

At the briefing on the morning of the Grand Attendance Zinsser showed Haven and the members of her advisory team the Roke tissue samples Wix Uniday had procured from the AlphaLAW analysis lab.

"In return, I had to grant them access to my lab and data," Zinsser was explaining, "as well as allow Starkweather to set a date for deploying Pitfall."

"Has he decided on a date?" Haven asked.

Zinsser nodded. "Three days from now—baseline. They're desperate to co-opt the entire experiment, but Pitfall answers only to my passwords for the moment. I'm certain, however, that Starkweather's people are working on evading my codes."

"Count on it," Burning remarked to nods of agreement from Delecado, Lod, Quant, and the rest.

"You remain confident that Pitfall can submerse itself in the Amnion without agitating the Oceanic?" Haven said.

Zinsser snorted. "Not entirely. From what I've been able to learn this past week, I'm convinced that the Oceanic is even more powerful than anyone thinks. It thwarts any attempts to scan it with what seems to be a sophisticated ability to manipulate energy all along the electromagnetic spectrum." He paused briefly. "In fact, I have reason to believe that the Oceanic can also purposefully manipulate carbon dioxide impoundment in the sea—and, hence, atmospheric oxygen content."

Jaws dropped throughout the cabin space. "Do you realize what a relatively small increase in the oxygen component could do here?" Quant asked.

Zinsser looked at him. "Wildfires, for a start. Burning completely out of control."

"Given sufficient O_2, even concrete will burn," Burning thought to point out.

Zinsser nodded. "The Oceanic could render the entire surface of Aquamarine uninhabitable, Periapt technology notwithstanding. We'd have no choice but to go back up the well and throw ourselves on Starkweather's mercy."

Haven was beside herself. "Is there some way of monitoring the Oceanic's mental state—assuming it has one? I mean, does Starkweather grasp what you're telling us?"

Zinsser rocked his head from side to side. "As to monitoring it, I'm eager to delve into the Aquam phenomenon of Descrying— this purported ability to sense quakes and marine disturbances. With a Descrier's help, perhaps I'd have a better idea of when it would be safe to deploy."

Dextra broke the silence. "If we can't find ourselves a Descrier, then we'll see what the Aggregate can do. I certainly didn't bring them along for a joyride. I'll pitch them into the Amnion if it means being able to communicate with the Oceanic."

The subsequent silence was more uncomfortable than contemplative.

"About the Roke tissue," Zinsser started to ask. "Perhaps I should leave it in the Aggregate's care while—"

"With Uniday skulking about?" Haven interrupted. "Not on your life. I don't want that tissue to leave your person, Doctor, even if you have to fanny-pack it into the Grand Attendance."

"That may be the only method of carrying it, Madame Commissioner," Zinsser said quietly.

Haven folded her arms. "Then I'll leave it to you to determine which pack works best with your ensemble." She had turned to Quant when a chirp sounded from the communications station and Gairaszhek asked for permission to interrupt.

"*Terrible Swift Sword* has received a subspace twixt from Periat," the lieutenant said. "LAW reports that commo has been reestablished with the planet Trinity."

Everyone leaned forward. Trinity's silence, a month before the *Sword*'s launch for Aquamarine, had contributed significantly to Haven's success in receiving funding for the mission.

"Trinity asserted that it never went silent," Gairaszhek continued, "and that it had not been the target of a Roke attack. LAW contends that a rogue AI, operating from within the TechPlex, may have engineered the ruse, as well as manipulated data related to the GammaLAW mission. LAW further contends that the *Sword* may also be virused."

Quant and Haven traded looks of concern.

"The anchor," Haven said after a moment.

Quant nodded grimly. "And perhaps the tether hook."

Haven compressed her lips, as if fearful of giving voice to her misgivings about Yatt of the Quantum College, and her fear that *Terrible Swift Sword* might well have carried a Cybervirus to Aquamarine!

CHAPTER
TWENTY-THREE

While she was watching the lake water vortices the gunboat's hydrofoils threw up aft, it occurred to Dextra that she should have pretended to be *dying* to attend Rhodes's shindig. That way Starkweather, ever eager to gall her, probably would have quarantined *GammaLAW* just to keep her away.

Her anchor ball raised, the SWATHship floated high on the water two kilometers back—six klicks out from Wall Water altogether—standing well off as a security precaution, and because the lake water was also shallow in places around Rhodes's stronghold.

It wasn't distaste for the promised activities that disinclined Dextra to attend—the ego jousting among grandees, the excesses of consumption, the cruel entertainments. It was simply the wrong forum for a face-to-face meeting with Rhodes and his ilk. Her visit also would serve to validate the grandees in the eyes of the population, and she thought it likelier every day that she'd eventually have to remove the local lords from power.

Her immediate counterproposal to the Grand Attendance was a meeting onboard *Terrible Swift Sword*, at once to cow the grandees with Periapt technology and to goad them into beginning to think on an interplanetary scale. Starkweather, however, had nixed the proposal by maintaining that such an assembly would fly in the face of established doctrine. Indigs on any world weren't permitted onboard a spacecraft until they had sworn common cause with LAW. Moreover, the possibility of an onboard virus had resulted in increased security.

She'd suggested a second alternative: a summit aboard *GammaLAW*, with TRANSCOM devoting all its resources to getting the SWATHship fully functional and armed, shuttling all personnel groundside, and deploying her mission's full complement of air, ground, and marine craft. Her G3 staff even prepared an operational plan for a massive show of force that included missile and charged-particle firings by the *Sword*.

Starkweather had rejected it out of hand. He did not want Dextra to have a ship with world-shaking firepower, air squadrons, and naval flotillas poised to strike. What Starkweather desired most was to force her to reembark on the *Sword* and subordinate herself and all her assigned assets to the AlphaLAW Hierophant mission—cybervirus or no.

In Aquam terms, he was setting her up for a major loss of Escalation—the equivalent of status or face. But while he'd been busy arm-twisting her into appearing at the Grand Attendance, she'd had time to make her organization as functional as possible.

Starkweather's eagerness had resulted in his granting more concessions than he'd perhaps intended. For example, since Captain Quant was loath to take the ship into shallow water, LOGCOM had shuttled down a load of sonar mapping gear. In the same way, after the Allgrave had expressed concern about laying in so close to shore with Ext strength so low, TRANSCOM had within hours debarked two additional platoons of Exts.

Dextra daydreamed about taking both Starkweather and Rhodes prisoner and holding them on *GammaLAW* until they saw reason. It would have taken a massacre to pry Rhodes away from his sword-wielding bodyguards, and Starkweather, of course, held the trump card of *Terrible Swift Sword*.

That left her headed for the beach with one hovercraft and the 'foil. For the moment there were no CAPflights or helo gunship escorts, since Starkweather's personal *Jotan* shuttle was inbound and Quant's *Air Boss* had been ordered to ground everything as a precaution.

She'd made her peace with the probability that she would be harassed, embarrassed, and fuggered with at Wall Water. Consequently, she'd kept her personal entourage small so that she could get in and out with as little fuss as possible. That was the price of keeping her mission in motion. The cost of compromise was usually orders of magnitude cheaper than the cost of all-out war, especially for the side that was outgunned.

Her musings were interrupted by the lieutenant second class who skippered the hydrofoil *Edge*. "Madame Commissioner, signal from the *GammaLAW*. Surface radar paints a teamboat nosing into the steer-clear area. CIC control would like to send in one surface craft to herd it away. We're closest and better manned than the *Northwind*."

Dextra gazed across the water at the wallowing hovercraft, then looked to where the lieutenant was pointing. The millship with its tiers of slaves at the capstans must have begun moving moments after the *Air Boss* had recalled the *GammaLAW*'s paltry air wing.

"By all means, let's shoo them back," she said. "But there's to be no firing without my clearance." If the teamboat insisted on closing with the *GammaLAW*, Quant could always use flash-bangs, high-pressure hoses, or other nonlethal contingency measures. "I will *not* be drawn into a bloodbath at my first diplomatic function. You might, however, let *Edge* strut her stuff a bit."

The lieutenant nodded. "Our pleasure, Madame Commissioner."

He scrambled back to the hydrofoil's bridge, which suggested a shuttle cockpit more than it did Quant's domain on the SWATHship. Water-jet engines revved higher, and *Edge* picked up speed in a hurry. Burning, Zone, and even Claude Mason looked up to see what was going on. *Northwind,* carrying Kurt Elide, Wix Uniday, and the balance of the shore party, changed course to take up a long holding pattern, awaiting *Edge*'s return.

Moving stiffly and carefully because of the extravagant and complicated formal raiment she was wearing, Dextra made her way to a portside window for a glance at Wall Water. The 'foil's acceleration and speed were such that it was difficult to pick up her feet. Lod came to hover at her elbow. The rest in the troop compartment, including the still-rattled Old Spume, watched but remained in their jump seats. Crew members stood to weapons stations on deck; below, they bent to fire controls, just in case.

Edge heeled hard to starboard, cutting for the teamboat,

leaving counterrotating whirlwinds aft. Topping eighty knots at one point, it intercepted the teamboat in under ninety seconds, laid a white swash of water and a gray-blue bank of brume around the logy Aquam vessel, then throttled down. A barrellike buoy had been jettisoned by or was adrift from the slave-driven scow and was being carried toward *GammaLAW* by wind and lake currents. As the 'foil lost lift and the monohull settled to plow the wavelets, the second lieutenant appeared by the forward coilgun mount. He played the canned message that hailed the Aquam in the local Terranglish.

Dextra examined the teamboat while the lieutenant reminded her captain of Rhodes's dictate that they keep a league's distance from the SWATHship. One glance at the tiers of caged wretches, who were standing off their capstans as the teamboat's master called for all stop, was enough to make her think the Oceanic had good reason for refusing to make the acquaintance of the human race. She called for a cam and a telecomm patch to Chaz Quant to give him a close-up.

"Captain, do you agree that there are suddenly a lot more bullyraggers and bystanders aboard that scow?"

His response came over her plugphone. "Mean-looking gang of muckers. And losing money loitering around here instead of moving on to their next work mooring."

Dextra continued panning, then closed in on a heap of burlap bags that looked to contain anything but milled grain. "A lot of sling-guns and swords could be concealed in those," she remarked. "Even a disassembled ballista or two."

Quant made an approving sound. "A very informed assessment, madame. Pause, please, and pan back to the cleat there, just forward of the rudder."

He meant a two-horned butrywood fitting to which a faded blue skiff had been made fast with a line. Quant asked her to zoom in on it, then grunted in disgust.

"See the way it's cleated? No half hitch—useless extra turns."

"Perhaps they do things differently here, Captain."

"There's only one correct way to cleat a line, Madame Commissioner." His tone carried frostbite. "No lake sailor made that line fast."

"Still, we *cannot* take aggressive action toward that barge just because some rank novice can't tie cleats. I'll see to it that they back off, but my rules of engagement stand: nonlethal measures in warranted doses. Deadly force only if *GammaLAW* lives are in immediate jeopardy."

She signed off before he could make an objection. The 'foil skipper and the teamboat master were arguing over the slaver's right to recover the buoy that had mysteriously gotten adrift. "They're seeing how far they can push us," the lieutenant said aside to Dextra.

"Ask him the value of the buoy," she said.

When the Aquam priced it at a silver scudo, she had the young lieutenant toss one across. Then she told him, "Torch the buoy."

The gunner's mate manning the aft flamethrower trained her piece carefully and gushed fire, getting the barrellike thing on the first try. The teamboat master stood with the single scudo in hand, gazing thoughtfully at the little conflagration.

"That coin also pays for all future menaces to navigation we're obliged to burn," Dextra had the 'foil skipper add in a bellow.

He gave the signal, and the aquajets pumped horizontal cascades. *Edge* surged away, rising on her foils. The teamboat came about in ungainly fashion and withdrew, the fiery buoy marking the progress of interplanetary relations.

"I used to think they were called 'wattccs,' " Burning remarked to the tech who was strapping the data/commo device to Burning's thick wrist. The hydrofoil was swinging in a long arc to match up with the hovercraft once again and renew the approach to the quay and beach at the foot of Water Wall. The teamboat buoy that had gotten the flamethrower treatment was falling astern fast. "As in microelectronics. Before I understood about vade mecum, anyway."

The tech just *mmmmm*ed softly, concentrating on getting the whatty to fit correctly. Three times as bulky and instrumented as the usual Periapt field units, the prototypes being worn by Burning and the others were crammed with detection equipment and new LAW archeo-hacking 'wares, many of the latter drawing on information about Aquamarine's Pre-Cyberplague systems fetched back by the *Scepter* team. The various adapters and connectors for the thing filled a spare 'baller magazine pouch.

"The old-time British pronounced it 'VAY-dee MEE-kem,' " the tech said unexpectedly. "Translated to 'go with me,' though they applied the phrase to indispensable books or manuals. 'Whatty' is just a nickname."

"So I gather," Burning said, studying the armored wristband the device rode on, the sophisticated equivalent to the Exts' UNEX units.

The tech shut off the diagnostics and gave the whatty one last pat before releasing it. "You're in business."

"I'll try to return it in one piece."

The tech snorted. "This thing's listed on the PolSec Bureau's property books. If you lose or break it, you might want to consider missing the boat back to *GammaLAW*."

Burning was still trying to get used to the weight of the whatty when Zone approached him from the portside railing.

"All I'm interested in knowing, Allgrave, is whether you're planning to deal us in on a fair share of the good-goods. 'Cause the planets're coming into alignment, you might say." He gave Burning a death's-head grin that had nothing to do with mirth.

"What 'good-goods' are those, Colonel?"

"Whatever's for the taking. We need to get our piece of whatever deal's being cut between Haven and Rhodes." Commissioner Haven had returned to her privileged semiprivate nook with Lod and a few other confidants.

"We cut our deal on Anvil Tor, Zone."

Like the other Exts, the two wore dress uniforms—square bibs lined with heavy gold buttons and high collars. Glossy pistol belts with hefty "Battalion of Exts" insignia as buckles held holstered 'ballers. Cutlery of choice was tucked into each right kneeboot with the pommels protruding. Lower-ranking guests of the grandee were *expected* to display a weapon or two as a show of trust in one's host, whereas concealed weapons would have said just the opposite.

"You actually believe that LAW's gonna keep its end of the bargain?" Zone was saying. "Even if we get home, which I doubt is gonna happen, there won't be a place for us anymore.

We're a lot likelier to have our way here or on some other wog-world than we are on Concordance or back on Periapt. And don't tell me you haven't thought the same thing."

Burning had, but he refrained from admitting it. "Just do your job. Fantasize on your own time."

In fact, Burning felt naked going in among so many indigs with only sidearms simply because Haven wanted it that way. She had been greatly impressed by what Ghost's sonics shot had done to the Shadow-rat aboard *GammaLAW* and held that any protection the shore party might need from Aquam could easily be provided by wailers. Inside the stronghold, however, Burning's contingent would bear the brunt of the fighting if anything went wrong. While it was certain that twenty Exts with sonics could puddle the muscles of a lot of Aquam or put them out with sound chains directed at the cranium, a few boomers would have increased his comfort factor considerably.

Hence the need for Zone. Burning had no doubt that Zone would tend to duty with his signature bloodthirsty precision; he was too smart to give Burning just cause—with Haven's backing—to bust him back to private or put him permanently out of the picture.

"When the likes of Haven and this Rhodes dicker, there's always something up for grabs on the side," Zone said after a long moment of silence. "Money, tech, people to hop and fetch for us. A seat on the next starship out of here—to someplace drier and richer. Or maybe there's power to grab right here. Big power."

"Of what sort?"

"Finding out is your job. Unless you're not up to it or too busy licking Haven's crack. In that case, the rest of us'll have to look out for ourselves."

Burning squared off with him. "If I hear word one about you conspiring to mutiny, Colonel, you will eat hardball from a firing squad—a .50-caliber court-martial right through where your brains ought to be."

Zone grinned. "Never happen, Allgrave. Not in a million years."

No one else had heard the exchange over the howl of the

turbines, but Burning refused to be baited further. Zone, feigning boredom, turned to face Water Wall. Burning pretended to do the same, though he was actually staring at Zone's back.

CHAPTER
TWENTY-FOUR

Approaching Wall Water and the immense dam, Dextra gave passing thought to using them as a symbol—the old blended with the new, the work of the Optimants retrofitted with the rough-hewn add-ons of latter-day Aquam—all of which could benefit from LAW technology and instruction.

Even the original sections of the stronghold had an air of fortification. While the Optimants hadn't bothered installing hydroelectric generating equipment—their fusion plants being cheaper and easier to maintain—they'd known that the dam was the key to power over food production and life itself in and around Lake Ea, the Pontos Reservoir above, and the river below. The Optimants hadn't always trusted one another, let alone their GeStation-grown workforce.

Wall Water had a sloping, curvilinear aesthetic to it, gleaming and seamless as jade-green glaze. It was in fact sheathed in a ceramic that even the LAW R&D teams respected for its hardness. The parapets, bartizans, and such had been added over Post-Cyberplague generations like clay garments crudely troweled onto a classic sculpture. But Wall Water made a brave show of its flags and signal torches and resounded with the martial music of frame drums, brayophaunt great horns, and bellows-powered aeolagons.

Burning's voice came up over Dextra's plugphone for a final commo check all around. The LAW ear canal units were less comfortable than the expensive civilian model she was used to, but a large part of diplomacy was bearing discomfort with aplomb.

Burning had organized the operation with his usual insecure thoroughness, catching a lot of details she and the others had missed. Everyone's immunizations had been brought current; 'ballers and Mason's LAW 'chettergun had been checked out by armorers and test-fired by their bearers; special communications nets had been established; and on-line crypto software had been put in place. Anyone who had forgotten his or her special-issue whatty had been stopped at the accommodation ladder and sent to get one. Guidelines for security placement and group movement had been blocked out more exhaustively than the protocol people would have thought to do.

Dextra felt bad that the Allgrave was constantly mad at himself over his own largely imagined inadequacies. She hoped he never overcame them completely. Money couldn't buy such diligence.

On the way in she had taken a look at the dam face and its trio of ominous cracks. Among the enticements that might win Rhodes over were large-scale repairs and perhaps a hydroelectric plant. If the grandee could learn the fine art of logrolling, he might yet end up presiding over a vast and prosperous Lake Ea. Otherwise, Dextra would probably have to orchestrate events so that he found himself lying at the bottom of it.

"Commissioner, confidential transmission for your ears only from *GammaLAW*," the signalman said. "Radar and IFF codes confirm that Commissioner Starkweather's shuttle is on final approach. ETA Wall Water in fifteen minutes."

Dextra cursed to herself. Starkweather was arriving just in time to upstage her, and in a flying fortress at that. Nevertheless, she gave the order for her two ships to cut in the sideband-synchronized PA loudcast of the arrival music she'd chosen to accompany her approach. Shortly, "The March of the Siamese Children" was resounding across the lake.

She had always liked the Rodgers and Hammerstein piece and had decided, when Burning had brought up the question of processional music, that it would make as dramatic a theme song as any. Synthed and remixed, it would last as long as the tech at the soundboard was instructed to make it do so.

A few aquaculture craft nursed at the quay, unloading food for the garrison. A couple of other boats were beached—small traders and vendors trying to sell to guards and wharf laborers. The hydrofoil maneuvered smartly, its monohull settling into the water; then it swung its hinged foils clear, coming about and backing alongside the quay, side bumpers barely tapping the stone and mortar as it came to a full stop. At the same time the *Northwind* was breasting the sandy beach not far away, coming to rest with a descending pitch of its turbines, its skirt deflating.

Aquam in work-grungy livery caught lines and made them fast to wooden bollards. One with a quid of slackwort bulging in his lower lip paused long enough to spit an umber gob into the water. The volume of "The March of the Siamese Children" muted.

Dextra reached the rear of the passenger cabin just in time to see two Exts helping Claude Mason lug a pair of Science Side modules to the railing for transferral ashore. The module contained sundry examples of Periapt technology both Rhodes and Mason's son, Purifyre, had expressed interest in seeing. Dextra was by no means sure that the business of show-and-tell was a good idea, but if Purifyre's Human Enlightenment faction held any kind of sway with the general populace, the demonstration would be justified.

Hydrofoil crew members were getting a gangway secured to the dock. Dock hands and other commoners made way hastily as squads of household troops arrived, laying about them with scourges that resembled long-handled dog whips. The housecarls were all bulk models, but they made no real effort to lash anyone. They were only clearing the way for their more feared and grandly arrayed betters, a detachment of blue-plumed and blue armored Militerrors, each one taller than the tallest of the household troops.

The Militerrors formed up as an escort, flanking several grandeean court officials in medallions of rank, rich attire, and high and exotic hats. One, shorter than the others, had on chopine shoes whose soles were raised by high slat lifts. The one in the van carried a rod of office and wore a truncated, forward-curved conical cap resembling a multihued half banana.

Dextra watched from the cabin as the preliminaries were played out. Mason had said that sheer height counted for much in Aquam society, as indeed it counted in Hierarchate politics and Periapt corporate careers. Starkweather probably had told Rhodes that Dextra barely topped 160 centimeters.

"The March of the Siamese Children" swelled again as Burning climbed the gangway with several Exts striding close behind him. Tall as the Allgrave was, some of his hand-picked troops topped him by eight centimeters and more. Dextra let the scene hold static for a bit, the tension and the processional music building, the Militerrors and Exts eyeing each other. When she finally emerged—the last member of her company but one—the "March" climbed and clashed. She strolled the gangway unhurriedly as soldiers, savants, statesmen, and seigniors held their places, waiting. In games of stature, being a small woman who commanded large, tough devoted underlings had its virtues. She cautioned herself not to trip over the inventively impractical, perversely complicated ceremonial apparel she was wearing.

Her outfit was all draped spangly folds and courses of metallic cross-lacing, tiered iridescent shoulder flanges, and a puffy sequined farthingale that felt like a V-shaped flotation device at her hips. It had rows of toilsome miniature buckles and various bows and ties more intricate than those on a ceremonial obi. Its implicit message was that she was an individual of high status and prerogative and that it didn't matter how expensive her trappings were or how labor-intensive their donning and tending were. Those were details for minions to worry about.

Always insecure about what she considered an inelegantly short neck, Dextra wore a choker of catfires and cherub's-breaths. Her soot-black hair had been fashioned in and around a backswept headdress cum framework that rested on her shoulders and framed her face, suggesting a bird of prey. She feared she looked like a mummer but had long since accepted the fact that politics anytime, anywhere was at least fifty percent theater.

She'd had the costume run up from the lightest fabrics that would serve. Now she glanced down to make sure the skirts stayed where they were supposed to. Couldn't have the indigs getting a peek at what she was wearing underneath and spoil the surprise.

The Exts and the rest of her entourage respectfully stood aside for her, as rehearsed, then took up stations around her as she stopped several meters from the grandee's delegation. She had timed her arrival to coincide with the music's triumphant conclusion. The Aquam in the drooping-banana hat seemed a bit thrown by her entrance. Recollecting himself, he advanced a step, tapped an ivory rod of office on the quay, and genuflected in a way that approximated a curtsy.

He introduced himself as Lintwhite, the grandee's castellan of Wall Water—as if Rhodes had any other holding that required a castellan. Lintwhite had a little trouble keeping eye contact at first, his glance straying to the Exts, the hydrofoil and hovercraft crew members in the gun tubs, and the other weapons stations. He also eyed her jeweled corset and configured cleavage. She'd decided on moderate décolletage; to the elite of Wall Water, excess in visual accessibility would imply sexual compliancy as well.

Lintwhite launched into a high-flown speech that spent more time rhapsodizing about Rhodes than welcoming Dextra. When he got to the third glorificatory—"Adored Champion of the Humble"—she deliberately, without breaking eye contact, brought her right hand up and snapped her fingers. The gesture caused a pleat in her capelet to fall out of its perfect arrangement, and Lod darted in matter-of-factly to put things meticulously back in order.

Burning about-faced and repeated the finger snap to the hydrofoil skipper. Lintwhite stumbled along for a few more words before a gasp *whoosh*ed from him, lost in an Aquam chorus of them, as the final member of Dextra's shore party came timidly onto the quay and moved to her side.

"I trust my grandee is well?" Old Spume said uncertainly,

"He is," the castellan blurted, "but how do you come to be?"

The Sense-maker's carriage had straightened thanks to the sacroiliac therapy and condensed course of osteopathic treatment Glorianna Theiss had administered to him. Old Spume's eyes were clear and free of rheum. His pouchy face showed a new tautness, and the florid blotches had been replaced by ruddy health. The bloated body was downsized somewhat. He walked much more easily because his gout had been suppressed and the incipient phlebitis in one leg had been relieved. The psoriasis had vanished from his hands, and his teeth had been cleaned up and patched, though there'd been no time for full regeneration. Even his wingback-chair-collared robes of office had been cleaned and remade.

One thing that was unchanged was Old Spume's speech impediment, however. His vocalizations still sent a fine spray of saliva into the air. If that had been cured, Dextra worried, someone might have thought him a doppelgänger or zombie.

"Your Sense-maker was experiencing some distress," she told Lintwhite, "so I took the liberty of having my healers restore him. But don't bother to thank me. Why don't we simply proceed with the evening's activities, eh?"

Declining the castellan's hand for that of Old Spume, she moved out, the Exts falling in while the dock hands and other onlookers continued to mutter dumbfoundedly. Rhodes's deputies, the Militerrors, and the rest had to make unseemly haste to lead the way to a waiting funicular.

Dextra directed a glance at the hydrofoil skipper, who stood by a WHOAsuit secured aft. He gave her a thumb and forefinger all's-well. Perhaps events would bring Rhodes back for a look at more LAW technology, or perhaps they'd require a show of force and a prompt departure; in either case *Edge*'s captain and crew were ready, as were those aboard the hovercraft *Northwind*.

The procession passed small craft beached on blocks, ranks of long tables, shallow holding tanks for sorting through and cleaning live lake food, and a paymaster's booth with its money scales. Most of the stacked tender was iron, brass, and bronze scudos, with a few silver coins.

The foot of Wall Water had been enclosed in a postapocalypse bastion of roughly masoned stone ten meters high, curving out of sight in either direction. Sentries armed with sling-guns gazed down from crenellations and casemates. Spume led Dextra to a raised half-roofed platform from which a wooden track rose along a steep incline, passing through an open portcullis and out of sight up the slope.

"Here is a miracle innovation of my lord Rhodes," Spume said.

The platform had a leather-padded bumper, a stop and shock absorber shaped like a squat stela. Resting against it was the grandee's funicular car, an elegant cogwheel trolley whose undercarriage was built on a slant to keep the floor level whether it was climbing or descending its track. The car was made of zephyr-blue whorled plates of pressed glass set in fine-grained mollywood that had been painted bloodred and inlaid with copper and polished bone.

Kneeling or squatting would have lost him Escalation in the Aquam's eyes, but Burning leaned a bit while trying to puzzle out how the museum piece worked. There were long cables of some Pre-Plagues synthetic, threaded through hinged circular keepers spiked in at intervals along the track bed.

Since the funicular was far too small for the entire party, the castellan informed Dextra that separate groups of ten would have to be ferried up by turns. Old Spume had told her to expect this, and the groups had long since been finalized by Burning back on the SWATHship. Dextra showed grace under adversity, indicating the groups with a wave or two of her fingertips.

The only Aquam included in the groups was Lintwhite.

"Your retinue will wait and come afterward," Dextra made clear. He checked the look in Dextra's eyes, then gave a jerk of the head—the Scorpian equivalent of a shrug of uncertainty.

Dextra pretended that she got absolute obedience all the time. She boarded with the first batch, convoyed by Burning, Ghost, Lod, Zone, the unhappy castellan, and another Ext. With them came Zinsser and Mason, along with the Science Side modules. The car featured plush seats of mustard yellow tarnhusk canvas, needlepointed in flamboyant colors. In spite of drenchingly strong perfume, the interior smelled of old puke. Lintwhite's odors were alien to Dextra as well, and she wondered if she smelled as strange to him.

The funicular's human-powered capstan was too far off to be heard. Pulleys creaked, and the cables grew taut. The car bumped once against its buffer, then trundled up and away, just clearing the half roof of the platform. Up through the portcullis it climbed, the porcelain-smooth walls of the stronghold closing in around it, proof that something following the same course as the car track had been part of the original complex. Glancing back, Dextra saw that the keeper rings lay open and flat in the funicular's wake; that meant that an uncoupler device on the undercarriage was releasing and folding them to permit passage of the cable's hookup to the car.

The track passed between smooth Optimant walls, with the occasional overpass or short tunnel blocking the waning light, giving them no opportunity to sneak a look at the interior of Wall Water. The most conspicuous details were nothing to instill peace of mind. Huge stone deadfalls poised at intervals over the car track could stopper the gap in the stronghold's defenses if needed. Along with household troops and Militerrors, it was possible to spot an occasional liveried servant or upper-caste member.

Dextra grew aware of a rumbling, and Burning, squinting through the uphill glass wall, grunted, "Counterweight." She spied it once it had passed underneath the funicular, a stone obelisk two meters long, riding on many small rollers.

Though it was constrained by the sheer walls, the view out over Lake Ea was breathtaking. Eyewash had dropped behind the Jovian dam, but its glow still lit the sky. A few flickering butrywood knots, phosphorescent lamps, and oil lanterns marked areas where aquaculturalists toiled late. The fishing punts and dugouts wouldn't be out for hours. Just within Dextra's field of vision to the east was the teamboat, churning slowly shoreward, occasionally caught in the sweep of one of *GammaLAW*'s searchlights.

The funicular gave a small lurch. "We'll be arriving in about fifteen seconds," Lod informed Dextra while adjusting his visor. Visual recon had already shown that the funicular track stopped at a platform two-thirds of the way up Wall Water. Lod could speak with absolute certainty, since he was checking the enhanced cam feed being relayed to him in real time from one of the *GammaLAW*'s telescopes. "Starkweather's *Jotan* is inbound on final approach," he added less equably.

The battlefield-supremacy weapons platform was one of four allotted to the AlphaLAW commissioner—more firepower in one package than her whole TO&E could muster. He'd refused to so much as put one on standby for the GammaLAW mission's defense. But why such a show? she wondered. Did Starkweather fear that the Aquam were suddenly going to pull an aerospace warfare system out of their threadbare loin rags?

Without bothering to don her visor or activate her phone, she asked Lod softly, "Is the *Jotan* targeting our assets?"

He gave her a frankly admiring look. "The *Jotan* has acquired everything we have: reemos, picket boats, the ship, even CAPflights preparing for takeoff. Tracking lock but no weapons activation. Captain Quant doesn't sound happy, but he's not all that exercised about it, either."

She patted Lod's arm. "Starkweather's insecurity and his need to throw his weight around. He's reminding me of my place."

Lod listened some more. "The grandees are gathering to receive him. I'm afraid Starkweather has stolen the spotlight."

Dextra blew out her breath. "Well, I wasn't keen on performing under one tonight, anyway."

CHAPTER
TWENTY-FIVE

The funicular came to rest on a paved courtyard fifty meters above the level of the dam crest. To one side lay Ea, the dam, and the uplands abutting the dam's far end; to the other, Wall Water's roofed galleries, open loggias, and stonework walls, merging into a salient of naked cliff.

Waves of sound reverberated from the darkening sky as Starkweather's *Jotan* lazed into view from around the cliff face to the east. Everyone, including the additional Militerrors who'd stood forth, craned to watch.

A kilometer out and closing, the weapons platform slowed until it rode its vectorable vertical thrusters a few hundred meters higher than the topmost keep, rattling windows, battering eardrums, and searing the Big Sere evening breezes. Dextra could smell the metallic pungency of the fusion-heated jets.

"Oh, sweet reason!" Zinsser gaped. "He can't mean to set down sixty metric tons of sky fortress on the dungeon's roof!"

Starkweather did. The aircraft was half again the weight of a *Varuna* shuttle, though with its variable-sweep wings extended, it couldn't have landed on *GammaLAW*'s flight deck without clipping the upperworks.

"The roof was built for landings," Mason supplied.

"Yes, *two hundred years ago*," Zinsser countered.

"One of Starkweather's preliminary contact flights must have done some building inspection," Burning said.

The *Jotan* came in, a bulked-up wedge of lifting body design with vestigial wave-rider concavity to its underside, the back-raked winglets close to the empennage. The entire airframe could vary its geometry to suit mission-specific conformations. Its surface was bonded with a doped buckeyball composite overlaying a smartskin that incorporated the latest active and passive SIGWAR, ELINT, stealth, and DEAD technology. All its running lights blazed. Illuminor banks roved and swept the stronghold. It bristled with unsheathed missile launchers, rocket pods, directed-energy spars, and coilguns.

The Militerror officers and fuglemen were suddenly ordering their command to double time, and servants were appearing as if from hiding. They began lighting glass lamps, wicks floating on oil in half shells, paper lanterns, and rush-light holders, but most of all big double-wicked candles on sticks, in candelabra, or simply erect in their own wax.

Burning had edged around the funicular and was standing on the low rampart, looking up, down, and across the face of Wall Water. Mildly acrophobic, Dextra followed with Ghost's help. The rest came after them—even revitalized Old Spume.

Lights were being kindled in every visible part of the stronghold. The lighting appeared to have started down by the beach, rising up the ramparts like an incoming tide. Someone with a keen sense of political theater obviously had gotten the grandee's ear. The *GammaLAW* cast her gleam on their lake, and the *Jotan* its dazzle in their sky, but Wall Water's illumination rite was a pointed statement that the Aquam hadn't been cowed and weren't to be underreckoned.

The gesture didn't come cheap. Romantic medieval tales notwithstanding, one good double-wicked candle was above the means of many locals and nothing to waste even for a grandee. Yet Wall Water was taking prodigality to such heights that Dextra imagined that the brave show would become a legend in and of itself.

The Militerrors reassembled as she and the first half of her shore party returned from the rampart. With the *Jotan* still making the place tremble and a flickering galaxy all around, everyone resumed his or her course toward the main hall. Every third guardsman held a light; the echoing rooms of the place, vaulted in shadow, had been stripped of their lights to maximize the display outside. When one of the Exts would have switched on a penlight, Dextra told him to save it to avoid insulting their hospitality. Her skirts, sweeping the floors, were already soiled, but she didn't want to lift them any higher than was absolutely necessary.

Claude Mason almost trod on Dextra's train from behind at one point, until Lod steered him away. His face held the expression of an animal with its leg in a trap.

"What if I'm too *young* to be a father to Purifyre?" he muttered. "He's of age here, but subjectively we're only twelve years apart."

"You'll never find out if Starkweather bungs my mission," Dextra threw over her shoulder. "So stay fixed on what we're doing."

Wall Water's halls and staircases were serviceable but not grand; hemmed in as it was by the dam and the rock, the stronghold didn't have space to waste. It was a novel experience to pass from an Optimant-built communications center, now stripped of its systemry and hung with tapestries, to a flagstoned portico added a century later but looking five hundred years older. On the portico surviving odds and ends of hand-burnished hydraulic equipment had been set up as cherished relics, like statuary or suits of armor.

It was clear from the smell that not all the occupants took the time to find the jakes when they needed to relieve themselves. Fireplaces, dark corners, and flower beds seemed to be the impromptu comfort stations of choice.

By the time they reached the onetime central control room that served Rhodes as a great hall, it was radiant with lights fetched in from the illumination. The area outside was thronging with Aquam of all kinds, contenting themselves with the fringe. They thronged in their fantastic veils and vizards, arms and armor, clothing and jewelry. A babel of conversation and laughter arose from men and women both, though to Dextra's ear it sounded a bit too loud, too forced.

She inhaled a confusion of new and even stronger alien odors: cosmetics and pomades, incense, balms, and the oils on blades and leather. Most members of the crowd were smoking heavy, resinous thudgum and dizzying warpwort. The few who could afford it were toking whackweed, an expensive import from the Trans-Bourne.

The rage for bright new dyes from that region was conspicuous even by firelight. The Aquam were gaudy and often imprudent in their color schemes. The geometries and motifs were too garish to sort out on the run, putting Dextra in mind of costume contests and circus clowns.

People made polite obeisances to her; the curtsylike move was popular with both sexes. The hails and hellos tended toward the stonedly boisterous. Lintwhite's demeanor made it apparent that none of the gestures counted for much. He led the way along a plush runner and through the front doors, which had been retro-mounted with astrological signs, ocean-wave symbols, and Aquam-style hieroglyphs.

Ranks of Militerrors and household troops guarded the entranceway; from the commotion within, it was obvious that Starkweather had already claimed center stage. The intendant of the throne room waited to announce Dextra's party. As Lintwhite went ahead, she paused just long enough for Burning and Ghost to forcibly guide Old Spume up close behind her, after which Burning eased back to keep Claude Mason in his natural line of sight.

Dextra put on her poker face and resettled the farthingale at her hips in a move disguised as a discreet reordering of her skirts. She gave the special rig underneath the farthingale a last adjustment, then led off again.

"My liege and lords and ladies of Wall Water," the intendant began. "Welcome the renowned Visitant, She-Lord Dextra Haven, who has come to pledge her aid to the Grandee Rhodes and the other luminaries of Lake Ea by way of rewarding their caring and couragcous stewardship over their people and to seek their counsel in regard to resisting the antestellarean creatures known as the Roke as well as other barbaric perverts who dwell closer to Lake Ea but who, in the interests of bonhomie, will remain anonymous tonight. Once again, my liege and lords and ladies of the court: Madame Commissioner Dextra Haven."

With Burning at her right and Old Spume a step behind and to the left, Dextra came through the doors into the light. Zinsser and Mason followed. The Exts were glancing around with an indifference more intimidating than any show of bravado.

The colors and costumery of the throne room were even more flamboyant than those outside, and the air was thick with cloying perfumes and attars. Rhodes was up on a triple-size throne holding his acid-adder scepter with its chunky god's-breath gem.

As with the illumination rite, the grandee—or someone advising him—had been canny in the seating of his regional rivals and peers. Where Dextra would have looked for him to preside over them from as much of a height advantage as he could manage—possibly even oblige them to remain on their feet on the main floor with the lesser nobles—eight finely carved and regal seats flanked Rhodes's own. There were seven for the visiting grandees and one—at Rhodes's right hand—for Starkweather, who was observing Dextra's entrance with sardonic amusement. He wore the full-dress uniform of a theater commander of LAW Aerospace Forces, with aiguillettes, medals, and decorations.

A representative of each grandee's elite guard was stationed at the back of the dais. Dextra identified some of them—Hellrazors, Unholies, Fanswell's Fanatics—from the briefing files. Especially easy to single out were Ethnarch Klobbo's Apocalyptics with their ponderous, oddly hinged and flanged suits of riveted iron plate armor.

The only remaining place on the dais was a modest backless cushioned thing, more ottoman than chair of state, a full three steps lower than the rest.

While the crowd and local luminaries were whispering to one another about Old Spume's rejuvenation, Dextra took stock of the next stumbling block Starkweather had set for her. Behind the dais, off to one side of a rank of uneasy Militerrors, stood a file of Manipulants.

To a place where a minor birth defect could condemn a newborn to a cruel death Starkweather had brought a personal guard of inhuman brutes with gray skin and lifeless eyes hidden under scarped bone. Dextra had left Tonii and Piper behind for fear of rattling the Aquam, but in fact the upper-crust crowd was showing no overt hostility toward the engeneered warriors. The Manipulants' presence, however, was sure to spark a hundred suspicions and further hamper Dextra's efforts to win the trust of the indigenous populations. As a bonus, the hulks also posed a calculated provocation to the Exts, who had fought them on Concordance.

In the advantage-Haven column, however, was Old Spume. Where Starkweather had brought abominations, Dextra had presented the court with the promise of renewed youth.

Only too happy to make herself inconspicuous and mum, Souljourner watched the Visitants closely, searching for possible Anathemites among them or other signs of demonic influence.

Wall Water had been bustling with preparations for six days, but only that afternoon had she learned she was to attend the fete. Until then she had lived in fear of being sacrificed like fresh bait to Rhodes's cruelties, his superstitions regarding her death notwithstanding. She'd been quartered and clothed in a manner slightly above that of a chambermaid and much below that of a lady-in-waiting. Waiting had turned out to be much harder than exhausting labor, and she had thumbed her drawstring dice pouch countless times, wishing for escape or liberation. Her appetite had fallen to nothing, and twice, after Descrying powerful though distant upheavals in the Amnion, she had been laid low by pounding headaches against which even her pilfered Apex proved useless.

Informed of her required presence at the Grand Attendance, she had been given a thirdhand dress in the long-wrap style that was years out of fashion, much mended, and tight on her work hand's body. Decked with furbelows, chatelaines, and other gewgaws, it looked absurd on her. As for the low shoes, they barely held together at the seams once she'd forced her square feet into them. She had asked about a vizard, only to be told that it was the grandee's pleasure that she go unmasked.

Even so, she had dared hope that someone in the throne room would make conversation with her—especially one of the young dandies—but thus far all she had gotten was rejection. Fearful of contamination and the sapping of his powers, Rhodes's own Descrier of long standing, Long Ear, had avoided all contact with her. She wondered if he, too, had sensed the shift in Aquamarine's single sea—surely the consequence of the Oceanic's reaction to the return of the Visitants.

When the throne room intendant had announced their arrival, Souljourner had positioned herself behind a drunken viceroy who'd been boisterous earlier but was surly-silent now. Peeking over his shoulder, she saw that the Haven she-lord was splendid-looking but surprisingly small. Yet among the tall soldiers ranged so obediently around her, Haven's deficit of stature only made her more impressive.

The grandees and courtiers had reacted to Starkweather and his ogres with subdued respect. She-Lord Haven was being received more as an adversary, even by Starkweather himself, so perhaps she was the true agent of evil, Souljourner decided.

The bodyguard at her right hand was a tall, burly man with long red tresses, a broken nose, and a thin-lipped expression of wariness. The gorgeous woman whose face had been so liberally decorated with scars made Souljourner wonder if some man had done it to her in revenge. Another, who was as fair of face as a demigod, was the object of much muttering among the courtiers, for he was Mason the Unchanged, mate of the long-dead Incandessa and father of the storied Purifyre. Never having seen Old Spume before, Souljourner wasn't as staggered by his apparent rejuvenation as others in the throne room obviously were.

She had already heard that the metal chests the Visitants had brought with them contained scientific gyns that would prove their mastery of all teknic. Sight of the chests only got her back to pondering, with growing apprehension, why Rhodes had brought her to Wall Water in the first place.

CHAPTER
TWENTY-SIX

Rhodes's trio of vampy young pacificatrixes stepped forward to intercept Dextra, readying their long locks for a ritual fettering. They wore sheer, open-sided chlamyses dyed green to match the trim on Rhodes's robes.

From what Old Spume had said, no visiting grandee had to suffer being bound over; Starkweather certainly hadn't. Dextra thus judged the women to be yet another in a series of tests. At her signal, Lod kowtowed, offering a black anodized case, from which Dextra removed and unsheathed a powered rescue cutter that was fifty centimeters long and gussied up to resemble a fine weapon. Thumbing it on—the monomol-edged cutter links blurring and shirring—she flourished it at the pacificatrixes.

"If I have to lop those mops off, I'll start low enough to get them all," she announced, moving the cutter back and forth at chin height and trying to appear more confident than she felt.

The pacificatrixes spun and took to their heels. The visiting grandees and their followers laughed, so Rhodes pretended to do likewise as Dextra was returning the cutter to Lod's safekeeping.

Carefully, she ascended the dais, while several Exts followed with the two cased modules. Rhodes came to his feet, striking a fists-on-hips pose and gazing down on her with stylized arrogance. The other grandees were sizing her up as well.

Rhodes wore a gilded helmet-coronet with mantled vanes, a scalloped comb of silver, and dramatic forehead pieces suggesting angry, outswept eyebrows. His red and pink codpiece had been padded, stitched, and dyed to represent a curled tongue.

Dextra spotted what had to be Fabia, the grandee they called Lordlady, the only woman in the gang of eight. Next to her was the Dominor Paralipsio in ceremonial robes so complicated that two nymphets in hooded gray unitards attended him at all times, silently reordering his buntings and straightening his formal train.

Rhodes was looking thoughtfully at Spume. The wages of sin were starting to take their toll on the grandee, and the Sense-maker was a foretaste of a possible reprieve. When he gestured for Dextra to take her place on the low ottoman, she maneuvered a little closer, palming a control wafer she'd placed up one ruffled sleeve.

"Little lady, have a seat," Rhodes said patronizingly. "Small and delicate creatures shouldn't overtax themselves. What you need is to take the counsel of a strong and experienced leader like—"

She keyed the wafer while he was talking, and to her vast relief the improvised apparatus under her skirts deployed as planned, the stiltboots extending to lift her head level with his and then higher.

"I like a view from a height, thank you," she told Rhodes.

Umbrellalike ribs and spreaders extended her ailette shoulder tiers and widened the flare of her cape. A device that was part drapery mechanism and part miniature theatrical curtain system kept her hemline from rising to reveal the pressgang-style body frame that gripped her from soles to underwired bra, its main gyros, power cells, and microprocessors concealed in the farthingale.

The media frenzy months earlier on the deck of the *Matsya* had given her the idea, but she hadn't foreseen using the stilt-boots in quite this way. Abruptly, she loomed over Rhodes, who had begun to fall backward.

A shout rose up, and the whole place was agape. Dextra went cold at the image of Rhodes falling on his rear before her and all present, for he'd never forgive her. She therefore moved to take his wrist and elbow, letting go of the control wafer so that it retracted back up her sleeve on its tether. Shifting the stiltfeet for leverage, she concealed as best she could the fact that she was holding him up. Tonii had insisted that she do several hours of familiarization on the hangar deck, but Dextra was nowhere close to being an exojock. Yet somehow both she and Rhodes managed to remain on their feet, the stays and leg cagework pressing painfully into her, the gyros in her farthingale straining so hard that her buns were oscillating.

Rhodes regained his balance, and by silent agreement they proceeded as if nothing had happened. She stepped past him cautiously to look down on Starkweather.

"So nice of you to drop down, Commissioner."

He had been savoring the moment, but now he suddenly had a cornered look in his eyes. The smile that accompanied his nod of greeting kept fading in and out, as if he feared being wrestled around.

The other Ean nobles held their places and extended guarded greetings as Rhodes made slightly rattled introductions.

A big, sturdy woman with a strong, plain face, Fabia Lordlady looked half-amused. Dextra exchanged the spreading-hands gesture that was a warm personal greeting in that part of Aquamarine. She did the same with Klobbo, Ethnarch of the Eastern Paludales. Fanswell of the polis of Tylow—half-deaf and listening through his big football-shaped metal ear ampliphone—spread his hands to her, and so did the rest in turn.

Dextra then turned to give the crowd her best parade-float smiles and waves. Everyone leaned forward to hear what she had to say.

"Thank you for this hospitality. Now let's find out how we can all benefit one another."

That won her a spattering of applause, mostly fan or glove on palm but also some of the foot-pounding downriver kind. Starkweather didn't have much choice but to incline his head to the rulers and the crowd as if she'd spoken for him as well.

Rhodes had recovered his composure and, if she read him right, was wavering between the ego-scorched impulse to have another go at her and a craving to get in on the ground floor for any largesse to come. Tapping the wafer under her sleeve ruffles, she contracted the stilts and her ensemble and presented him with her hand.

"I trust that you'll pardon me for hanging on to your Sensemaker," Dextra said. "But I so wanted you to see the results of our healers' version of anathasine."

Anathasine was the local version of the fountain of youth.

Periapt rejuve was only a pale and ruinously expensive imitation of a scientific immortality that had been lost to the Cyberplagues. But Dextra's mention of anathasine and the sight of Old Spume had Rhodes's eyes protruding nevertheless.

"We have also brought samples of our science that may interest you," she added.

Rhodes gave her a half-lidded simper. "I've novelties to show you as well."

He made a gallant show of kissing her hand but instead ran his tongue across the back—without anyone's seeing it. She wondered if she could decontaminate her hand in the biosynth field unit. Even if it cost her a few layers of skin, it would be worth it.

The grandees' collective rising from their seats to descend from the dais along with Dextra and Starkweather was the signal for general socializing to begin.

Burning relaxed a bit but kept his right hand with the fingers slightly curled, thumb aligned with the gold stripe down the seam of his britches, ready to his sidearm. *Zanshin* and the Flowstate had kept him and the other Exts from overreacting when diplomacy briefly became a contact sport, and damned if Haven hadn't made the stiltboot stunt work.

Starkweather's monkeywrenching could still have gotten the whole affair zizzing into the wind. Aside from Haven, only Ghost and Zone appeared wholly at ease, given over to the moment.

Rhodes had left the weighty acid-adder scepter on the throne and had taken up a nosegay of spiral clove and spice-lips. Haven tried to get him interested in the Science Side modules, but the grandee waved them away. "Dreary teknics can wait," Burning heard him say. "Have the chests carried to my private chambers, where people won't go stumbling all over them."

The evening's schedule called for a VIP tour of Wall Water, an informal negotiations walk-talk with stops for sight-seeing and refreshments. The rest of the guests were free to circulate through the public chambers and grounds, where various diversions would be offered. Several hours after midnight palanquins and sedan chairs would bear the principal group over the hill north to one of the flying pavilion landing areas to view the liftoff of the *Dream Palace*.

As the notables mingled with the crowd, one Militerror tried to brush past Burning, ostensibly to remain close to Rhodes but in effect separating Burning from Dextra. Burning moved to outflank the bodyguard, who began a flanking movement of his own, only to trip and take a full-length header. Burning saw Ghost retracting her leg from a long extension and looking elsewhere.

The Militerror scrambled to his feet, shaking out the coils of his stinger-whip, while Burning waited for justification to pull the 'baller and headcheese the guy with sonics. However, Rhodes ably averted the confrontation by *tch-tch*ing and making an admonitory gesture with the nosegay. After that the Militerrors kept their distance, allowing Burning and Ghost to dog Dextra and the other Exts to remain within rescue reach.

Burning admired again how Haven worked the crowd, greeting three guests for every one Starkweather met and eliciting at least a lukewarm response from most. When one grizzled thane remarked enviously on Spume's partially regained youth, Haven cribbed a line from Anthony Powell: "Even where the wisdom of age is respected, sir, 'Growing old is like being increasingly penalized for a crime you haven't committed.' " A grudging laugh escaped the thane like a bubble in a bathtub, and he set off to repeat the bon mot to anyone who'd listen.

The overlapping rondos of introduction, exchanges of unfamiliar Aquam gestures, curtsies and kowtows became a dance of the absurd. Yet Haven established an easy warmth, drawing people into her cordial mood.

Other members of the shore party were surrounded by the curious. Claude Mason was searching every Aquam face that came his way, barely responding to greetings. Earlier, his attempts at inquiring after his yet-to-be-seen son had been ignored, but now Rhodes approached him with a leer.

"I've been so completely devoted to duties of state that I've neglected to acquaint you with someone." Rhodes gestured with his fingertips to someone in the crowd of hangers-on. "Brother-in-law, stands forth my nephew and your son, Purifyre."

Burning, along with every member of the GammaLAW mission within earshot, fell silent and turned to observe the long-overdue reunion.

A deliberate screen of Rhodes's courtiers drew aside to reveal a young man. Several men and women, all older than he—and all in the vestments of votaries of the Church of Human Enlightenment—surrounded him respectfully.

Seeing his son, Mason felt his heart being struck through. From the first he'd pictured his child, son or daughter, with Incandessa's face, with perhaps some tinge of Mason's features. The only answer to why he hadn't understood that Purifyre couldn't *possibly* look that way was that something deep in him, more hidden and powerful than Yatt, had made him ignore the obvious.

There was some of Incandessa in Purifyre's face, especially the eyes, which were the color of Aquamarine itself. But the close set of those uneven orbs, the crooked teeth, the simian lips, the overhanging bill of a nose—all that was owed to Claude Mason.

It was Mason's true face before the long courses of osteoplastic reconstruction, tissue remediation, and biocosmetics. His voice had just begun changing when the long metamorphosis had begun, so he hadn't glimpsed those features in more than a subjective-decade—let alone allowed himself to remember them.

Purifyre had inherited them on a world where minor surgical procedures were crude and often fatal. Mason had wanted to give his son so many things to make up for having abandoned him and his mother, and the only tangible legacy the poor kid had known for nearly twenty years was the affliction Mason himself had barely weathered.

The Human Enlightenment votaries hung back as Purifyre approached. The malformed face gave no clues to what was going on behind it. Rhodes was trying to be clever with a grandiloquent introduction, something about Purifyre's decision to forsake the comforts to which Incandessa's birth had entitled him, the vow of poverty he had taken, his wanderings across

Aquamarine in a selfless crusade to improve the lot of all peoples . . .

Falteringly, Mason brought up his hands and spread them, but Purifyre failed to acknowledge the warmth implied by the gesture. Instead he said, "It's you? Ah, then, here am I, Father, and thus as you see me." A teacher, Purifyre wore ceremonial gloves that signified the importance of keeping the soul from worldly contamination, and now his gloved hands reached into his robes.

He brought out an exotic Aquam knife the likes of which the Exts hadn't seen. It was configured something like a carpenter's plane, an upright ivory-mounted haft on a more or less perpendicular blade that resembled a small scythe. Its point as sharp as a lancet, the blade glittered with talon barbs, hooked gutting notches, and shark-fin serrations.

Mason watched, not blaming his son one iota, as Purifyre swung the slasher up at him. He ignored Yatt, who'd risen up in the back of his mind, crying for Mason to defend himself. His consuming fear was that someone would headcheese Purifyre or quill him with sling-gun quarrels before he could strike.

As he braced for the killing stroke, it was all so clear to him—the pain and loneliness the boy must have suffered, the unrightable wrong Mason had done him both in fathering and in abandoning him. He moved to shield his flesh and blood from harm, even if it meant taking the knife, only to find that Purifyre had turned the blade around and was holding it by its tang against his own throat. The votaries behind him were exclaiming, "An Escalation! An Escalation!"

Rhodes was sniggering and pointing to Mason. "Guilty conscience, Claude? I don't wish you dead, and I assuredly wouldn't let harm come to my dear nephew, who has provided such good aid of a teknic nature. Do you reject the Escalation, then?"

It took Mason a moment to puzzle out what was going on. If Escalation was an act of obeisance or homage that transferred status from the doer to the beneficiary, Purifyre's was all-out Escalation: the offering up of his life.

"I honor you in memory of Incandessa," he was saying. "She would have wished this between us."

Mason's hands were shaking so hard, he jabbed his thumb on one of the knife's tang prongs—not so much in accepting the slasher as in moving it away from his son's throat.

CHAPTER
TWENTY-SEVEN

As Mason, Purifyre, and the votaries moved to a corner of the throne room, Rhodes turned his attention to Dextra once more. "Mistress, your kindness tilts the scales of amity too far out of balance! You bring me a Sense-maker all renewed and revitalized. I must therefore make a good bestowal in return."

Rhodes waved the nosegay, and two household guards marched forward a big, husky young Aquam woman. Dressed in a too-small castoff of harlequin crazy quilt, she had hair like steamed hay, a pug nose, and a slightly prognathous jaw. The square face held a hint of a ruddy outdoor tan, but she was pale underneath. One work-roughened hand was at her throat, thumbing a drawstring pouch that was dark from years of such urgent caresses.

Rhodes was spouting on. "I bethought me, What is the most magnanimous thing I might present a luscious Visitant lady? In me largesse is an all but fatal flaw, as any will tell. What gift may I give She-Lord Haven that no other could or would provide her?"

Dextra studied the girl. She was trying not to show how frightened and miserable she was under the cruel spotlight of the court's scrutiny, but her eye contact was skittish at best.

"In timely fashion," Rhodes brayed, "my innate generosity provided an answer so munificent that it took even *my* breath away. Thus do I bestow upon you, dear woman, this Descrier—Souljourner by name—who will read the inner roils and ructions of this world and forewarn you of any great perils posed by tremor or tidal wave."

Speechless, Dextra heard stifled sniggering in the crowd.

Rhodes feigned indignity in response to her silence. "Doesn't she please you? Is she so unworthy? To have so unworthy a gift under this roof would humiliate my ancestors. I'll have her flung from the parapet at once."

Souljourner's breath caught audibly, but she hid any other reaction. She's steady, as well, Dextra saw, speaking up fast and moving even faster. "You'll do nothing of the sort, Grandee Rhodes. Why, nothing could delight me more than to have my own . . . seismic presagist. My, how wildly prodigal of you!"

She took Souljourner's hand to draw her closer, succeeding only because the girl yielded after brief hesitation. She was as strong as a Clydesdale. Dextra beamed at her as if she were a twenty-point jump in the approval ratings. "You're going to be invaluable to us, dear."

If Souljourner was a spy or a saboteur, she could always be artfully disposed of later on. But the look she showed Dextra now was one of pitiful gratitude.

"My renowned senior warlord will take personal charge of Souljourner," Dextra said, maintaining diplomatic momentum, "for eventual transferral to my ship, of course."

Closest at hand, it was Burning whom Dextra dragged toward Souljourner, he to whose arm Dextra transferred the Descrier's hand before pushing both of them into the background. "We could exchange gifts all evening," she said to Rhodes a moment later, "but isn't it time we discussed politics?"

The grandee seemed disappointed that his gift hadn't caused more confusion in Dextra's ranks, but he shrugged it off. "Politics? Indisputably. However, my guests must be starving, expiring from thirst! Where are those lazy servitors?"

Not to be left out, the visiting grandees had insinuated or forced their way forward. As the food trays began circulating and the drinks sloshed, lesser personages retreated to let the luminaries take each other's measure. The strolling tour of Rhodes's stronghold commenced.

The eating and drinking followed the eye of the social whirl, which consisted of Rhodes, Dextra, Starkweather, and the other grandees. Servitors kept up the flow of refreshments; there were even portable serving tables carried stretcher style by teams of bearers. The principals promenaded through the place pretending fellowship, while the Exts, the Militerrors, the courtiers, and the rest kept up as best they could.

Three Manipulants had fallen in near Starkweather, towering above anyone else there. Dextra assumed that their presence was something Starkweather had stipulated in advance, because Rhodes made a show of blithely ignoring them.

At another time she might have enjoyed the sight-seeing traipse for its own sake. Wall Water offered grand views from diverse points, and its pleasure gardens were like nothing she'd ever seen. The keeps offered unlikely, sometimes splendidly weird juxtapositions of latter-day Aquam bric-a-brac with Pre-Plague artifacts that hinted at the splendor and accomplishments of the doomed Optimant civilization.

Even so, she did her best to keep the walk-talk moving along. Both her reading of Rhodes and her understanding of the layout indicated that the grandee was leading everyone to his bedchambers' sybatorium. The bedchambers might afford an opportunity to soften and sunder her opposition.

In front of the bedchambers, a bay window looked out across a narrow chasm at whose bottom lay a channel filled with dam tailwater that was used to grow aquaculture delicacies for the residents of the stronghold. In the hills on the far side of the chasm a tremendous rally or protest was in progress. On a high post a looped infinity symbol five meters across had been set aflame. Dextra could hear the chanting of figures in sea-green robes and others in peasant garb. She saw white pom-poms dangling from many an armband and headband—either insignias or badges.

"Worshipers of the cult of DevOcean," the castellan, Lintwhite, explained. "You see the white pom-poms? They denote followers of the false prophet Marrowbone. Their little demonstration is for your benefit, to be sure. To flaunt the influence of their suicidal preachings."

DevOceanists held that a survived immersion in the Amnion, once achieved, would constitute reconciliation and unification with God—in Aquamarine's case, the Oceanic. Their Mecca was a place called Passwater, a former Optimant site on a Scourland peninsula.

"I can't see any virtue in a belief system whose goal is self-destruction," Dextra commented. Privately she reflected that while DevOcean might not make a good underpinning to her efforts, it could serve admirably as a wedge.

There was a discreet thinning out of the crowd at the entrance to Rhodes's private suite. Lesser personages were turned away by Militerrors and household troops, allowing only the LAWs, the grandees, and a few of their guards to enter.

The suite had been the dam installation's nerve center, the situation room of its Optimant builder-overlord, Atheo Smicker. Dominating the suite, just as the *Scepter*'s records described, was a combination monument and master systemry terminal cast in the form of a titanic bust of the man himself.

Smicker had been one of the greats among the technocrat fugitives from Earth. The dam was a major pillar of his power among the Optimants. According to Dextra's research, the Rhodes clan's assertion that Smicker was a direct ancestor was pure bunk, though the assertion did follow the timeworn tradition of contemporary rulers claiming descent from deities.

Smicker's bust, as big as a freight van stood on end, had been cast from the strong perdurium enhanced-bonding alloy the Optimants had developed. Locked-down security cowlings around its base showed a few scrapes and dents, but they had withstood Post-Plague attempts to strip or vandalize the master consoles.

What made it the most preposterous sight she'd seen thus far on Aquamarine was its accumulation of votive candles, incense sticks, ash urns, and festoons of worship beads. Generations' worth of wax had accumulated at various points, although many of the candelabra and sconces had been pilfered for the light show out on the stronghold's ramparts.

Dextra did not have a spare second to check the special whatty R&D had issued her. Lod was making a sweep with his, but any intensive archeo-hacking was going to have to wait. Lod traded silent looks with Ghost and Zinsser, then gave Dextra a clear nod toward the bust. The whatties had detected Optimant computer technology, but the nature of it was undetermined. If any residual data could be recovered, they might be a more vital prize than the cooperation of the grandees.

More attendees began to sift into the suite, including the Exts in charge of the science modules. When Dextra took Rhodes's elbow, he had guile enough to let her tug him away from Starkweather and the others who were vying for his attention. She turned his hand over and slipped something dense, cold, and hard into his palm, closing his fingers back over it.

"This is more than a gift," she whispered. "It's a proposition."

He made a furtive inspection, stifling his amazed grunt when he saw what it was: a newly struck coin of twenty-four-carat gold the size of a Spanish doubloon. It bore Dextra's profile on one side and the grandee's on the other. Encircling both cameos were the words "AQUA PROFUNDA EST QUIETA"—"still waters run deep."

Rhodes tucked it away and gave Dextra a pleased smile. "We have more to talk about than Starkweather led me to believe, you enchanting woman."

At that moment Starkweather swung to frown at the sight of the two of them with their heads together. He approached with unhurried malevolence. "Grandee, Madame Haven, we agreed that no diplomatic initiatives would take place without my participation."

Dextra conceded with a shallow bob of her head, more than content to have him believe that he had backed her down. Rhodes flared with one of his unpredictable eruptions of temper.

"Is the sovereign of Wall Water not master in his own bedroom? Haven's overtures please Rhodes, and Rhodes may deal with her however he chooses!"

Rhodes dodged Starkweather's glare by calling for food and drink. Dextra, about to ask for plain water, recalled that the Aquam, like many low-tech cultures, drank little of the stuff. She didn't blame them; theirs usually carried diseases and tasted of lake-water muck. Alcohol was embraced as a sterilant, and it also numbed the grinding pain and woe of life.

Dextra accepted a delicate porcelain demitasse of thick chestnut stuff from Rhodes. "Twice-fermented nepenthe," he said. "Just the thing to keep the night vapors out of you."

She thanked him but passed on a tray of hors d'oeuvres that smelled like low tide. A cautious sip of the nepenthe made her mouth feel as if she'd been deep-kissing Beelzebub and her temples pulse as if the air pressure had dropped. But the stuff had a tingly persuasiveness nonetheless. She made a sound of pleasure, though her second sip was only a wetting of the lips.

CHAPTER
TWENTY-EIGHT

Souljourner found herself on the arm of the tall, broken-nosed redhead she'd noticed earlier, a fretful gallant who gave no sign of knowing what to do with her. He had large, blunt-fingered freckled hands that were sunburned, scarred, and calloused—and almost as clumsy-looking as her own. He smelled as outlandish as She-Lord Haven, although neither of them actually stank. His uniform was nicely cut, if drab by Scorpian standards.

That she had been given to the Visitants was plenty worrisome, though not as worrisome as becoming part of Rhodes's throne of flesh. She wanted to ask the redhead, Burning, if she might have a few moments alone. She badly needed to throw the Holy Rollers and consult her breviary for a prediction. But before she could, Burning motioned to a plate of summer spongeknobs stuffed with breaded marsh scallops, asking, "Have you had anything to eat?"

She gazed at the long-shanked Visitant in disappointment. Only ravishing damsels could count on dashing rescuers, she supposed, whereas she was just a big-boned lowbred who probably would have to save her own self, as she had at Pyx. Things could have been worse. She was at least to be taken from Wall Water and out from under the thumb of the Grandee Rhodes.

If life continued to chivy her from place to place, it stood to reason that she would eventually arrive at circumstances that suited her. She still had the Writ that designated her Alabaster's new Descrier, after all; if the Visitants rejected her, she might yet find her way there.

* * *

"I told you, not when I'm on duty," Ghost warned Zinsser. "Pester me again and this is the last time you and I will speak."

Zinsser threw up his hands and stormed away from her, worming his way through the crowd that had gathered around Smicker's bust. Ghost had to be some sort of cock-teasing dysfunctional, he told himself. It was beginning to appear unlikely that he would ever get to play out the scenarios he'd savored in fantasy—scenarios of reducing her to the pliant role so many other women had eagerly assumed. He drifted with the crowd on his own until he realized that someone had fallen in alongside him.

"Forlorn, Doctor?" Wix Uniday asked through a smile. "Exasperated by Burning's sister, frustrated by Haven, fed up with the relocation-camp ambience aboard *GammaLAW*?"

Zinsser barely lifted one eyebrow; such observations did not spring from genius.

Uniday leaned closer. "You can still have her, you know."

Zinsser came to a sudden halt. "Perhaps *you'd* care to take Ghost by means of duress."

They both glanced at her while she was directing members of the escort detail with hand signals and subvocal tactical prowords.

"Unflappable," Uniday remarked. "With the remote and invulnerable look of one who considers herself already dead. Hypnotic eyes behind self-mutilated flesh, her grip on a weapon worn with use ... Frontal assault?" He adopted a wry grin. "That's hardly the way to win."

Zinsser exhaled through his nose in distaste. "You know, you can be a regular cleft-chinned cliché when you want to be."

Uniday didn't take offense; he never seemed to. "The Hierophant mission won't wait, Doctor. Haven's strategy is on the mark. Starkweather has to leave—and shortly. But when the *Sword* departs, it could be you Starkweather leaves in charge, not Haven. You have insight into the Roke, and you lack a political agenda."

Uniday paused to exchange courtesies with surrounding Aquam. "Starkweather would prefer to have you running the mission, and he has already worked out the legalities. Before the *Sword* launches, he'll make sure you have the whole mission well in hand. Ghost is sure to follow of her own accord."

Zinsser licked his lips. "Now what, Wix? I've told you, I've already agreed to deploy Pitfall ahead of schedule. Starkweather's people have turned my lab upside down. I've promised to share any data we dredge up on the Oceanic—"

"We want the 'wares access password."

Zinsser stared at him. "What d' you think, I'm brain-challenged? Why don't I just *give* you the thing?"

"Not the activating password," Uniday was quick to add. "You get to keep that. What we're after is the general password so we can monitor the data as it's being collected. Also, we might have reason to duplicate Pitfall down the line."

" 'Monitor . . . duplicate' . . . I have the Roke tissue specimens I was after, and I'm really not interested in replacing Haven as commissioner. So at this point I don't see that there's anything your boss can offer me as an enticement. Besides, Big 'Un Boudreau and the rest of the Exts onboard *Big Tess* might have something to say about all this."

"They're not your problem. Starkweather has ways of neutralizing them without imperiling the ship. You just have to make certain that you and Ghost are in proximity to the *Jotan* when the Attendance breaks up. You'll both go upside with Starkweather. Haven will be denied any further supplies or personnel unless she agrees to hand her command over to you. The scientific phase of the mission will take priority, as it should in any case. Military and political aspects take second place to research into the nature of the Oceanic, with emphasis on how it operates as a Roke repellent." Uniday paused. "Now, about the password . . ."

Zinsser considered the offer, then said, " 'Benthic ooze.' "

Uniday tilted his head. "Come on, Doctor, I thought we had an understanding."

"The 'wares password, you idiot. 'Benthic ooze.' "

Uniday's intensity rheostatted down several notches, and he nodded soberly. "You won't regret this."

Zinsser already knew that he wouldn't. Without the activating password, "Rubicon," Pitfall would remain useless to all parties until and unless he dictated otherwise. Starkweather's offer was beginning to sound better and better, but breaking Ghost's resistance by coercion, if such a thing was possible, still wouldn't give him what he wanted, still wouldn't give him *her*.

From what the orientation data said about Descriers, Souljourner was a lavish gift, Burning thought, although he'd been given to understand that Descrying was the exclusive provenance of men. If there was anything at all to Descrying, Souljourner would earn her keep as a member of the GammaLAW mission.

The mutation apparently had cropped up after the descendants of the Optimants had been deprived of clinical antimutagen prophylaxes as a result of the Cyberplagues. In recent decades Descrying had lost some of its supernatural aura, but having a Descrier remained a major advantage for any Aquam ruler or government. Along with the obvious utility, Descrier seismic perception had shored up religious and secular leaders, allowed for some ruthless scapegoating, and even won wars.

A plain-faced, big-boned peasant, Souljourner didn't strike Burning as a revered prophetess, but given the importance of Descriers, he had to ask himself why Rhodes was willing to do without her.

According to Burning's understanding of Wall Water decorum, he couldn't simply hand her off to one of the NCOs. But neither could he just pack her down to the hydrofoil. Nothing to do but deal, he told himself.

The visiting grandees were growing restive, Dextra realized. Fanswell, who had been listening to Rhodes and Dextra's exchanges through his ampliphone, slammed his silver baton on the head of one of his attendants and bellowed, "Are the rest of us no more than fixtures, like old Smicker?" He gave the massive control housing/bust a rap with the baton. "Did you come seeking allies or vassals, Madame Haven?"

At the grandee's outburst Dextra went into soothe mode, partly to keep Rhodes from erupting as well. "I've come to meet *all* of you. If I have offended any of you, it was unintentional, and I do apologize. Perhaps, Grandee Fanswell, you'll lend me your arm as we go."

Both Starkweather and Rhodes showed relief that she was placating the Tylos potentate. Fanswell turned courtly, offering his arm and guiding Dextra up a flight of helical stone stairs that led to the upper terraces. In the narrowness of the staircase the two by necessity pulled ahead of the others.

Taking advantage of it, Dextra dipped into another pocket concealed in her farthingale. With her tiered shoulder flares and flowing cape blocking the motion from those behind, she slipped a heavy doubloon into Fanswell's hand.

"Esteemed monocrat," she whispered, "you and I simply must parley someday soon."

A savvy old cuss, he held his tongue as he took a furtive look at the coin she'd passed him. The doubloon carried the same AQUA PROFUNDA EST QUIETA motto, along with Dextra's profile, but on the opposite side was Fanswell's. As he and Dextra emerged onto the landing, he slipped the coin into his waistcoat and patted her hand warmly.

Good works and outreach were admirable approaches, Dextra decided. But she suspected that Marcus Cicero Tullius's maxim was going to come in handy on Aquamarine: "There is no fortress so strong that money cannot take it."

The Militerror was giving Ghost the same bad, faceless stare his outfit was directing at most people there. The blue-plumed, blue-lacquered helmets gave them an advantage, and they plainly intimidated Wall Waterites. So, on a whim, Ghost took him on. She guessed that Burning wanted her to take charge of the Descrier, but Ghost thought it best that he keep the woman on his arm a while longer.

The Militerror started losing confidence almost as soon as she locked eyes with him; she wasn't someone he could scourge with his ensifisher-sting whip or whack with the flat of his cutlass, though she would have been pleased to have him try. She psyched him by taking a step in his direction. Instead of acknowledging defeat, however, he pretended to be distracted by the call of one of his fellows.

Phony, she said to herself.

In the seconds while the Militerror's back was turned, Ghost's hands moved fast, and by the time he glanced at her again, she was wearing the slim data visor she'd swiped from Vice Field Marshal Ufak's quarters on *Sword of Damocles*. Adjusted for night sight, the room was bright to her eyes, which were now concealed by a wraparound of unrelieved glossy black. When she gave the Aquam a mocking smile from behind the jewellike crescent of systemry, he shoved past his mates, heading for another part of the bedroom.

Bored with the niceties and with Rhodes's grubby little sex den, Ghost cased the crowd, speculating about whether it hid any Shadow-rats like the late Hiip. Hands clasped at the small of her back, she watched Haven deftly play Rhodes off against Starkweather and both against the other grandees.

Then her eye fell on a pedestal that stood like a ship's binnacle close to Rhodes's big round bed. Rhodes was using the thing as a night table, but it had obviously served a very different function in Pre-Plague times. Someone had brought crude force to bear on it in the past and had succeeded in opening a drawer, which had since been bent back into shape. Judging by the muddled balance of power in the lake region, whatever the drawer contained hadn't given the Rhodeses any major advantage, but the notion of a compromised lock stimulated her fondness for counting coup. There had to be something worth pilfering.

She was easing toward the gadgetry stack when Zinsser came up next to her for the second time in fifteen minutes, gesturing suavely with two long-stemmed pewter goblets. Her pleasure at outstaring the guard made her just tolerant enough not to kick his ass, though she did remove and conceal the data visor before turning to face him.

"This they call an Ean mollificator," he said. "Tastes like a slow caress, and in my humble opinion mollification is something you need rather acutely."

"I think I recall telling you to get lost. I'm on duty."

Zinsser shut his eyes and loosed a long-suffering sigh. He set the spare goblet on a sideboard, from which it was instantly snagged by a woman wearing a domino of violet feathers.

Rhodes's servitors were offering the stronghold's very best potations only to his most important guests.

"Ghost, if you're really dead, you ought to be getting more pleasure out of the afterlife."

"Go away now, Doctor, before I lose all self-control."

"Ah, but that's just what I want. You *need* me by your side. Name anyone else with the courage to be so frank with you."

His tone was so smug and at the same time so wheedling that she saw no point in sparing him. "You and I are never going to be side by side, Doctor Zinsser."

If he was at all put off, he covered it with a faltering chuckle. "Why is that—exactly?"

"Because you seem to expect it. You *presume* it."

"Perhaps you think too much of yourself."

"You want me where you can take me for granted—end of story. I find it rather pathetic. You should allow yourself to age with more grace."

Zinsser's nostrils flared. "You conceited, ill-bred ... I've a good mind to stop pestering you altogether." Strolling away nonchalantly, he exchanged the mollificator for a cup of what a tray bearer called a "single-grain Lava-Land prangbang," which was said to be deserving of its name.

Feeling pleased and disencumbered once more, she glanced around at the guards, guests, and functionaries, many of whom were studying her surreptitiously or openly.

She commenced a slow circuit of the room, determined to lift something of interest. In Concordance's prisoner camps she—Fiona Orman then—had learned how to steal to survive and keep the Discards alive. She'd swiped things right out from under guards' noses, learned to dare anything, risk penalties worse than death. Now the familiar thrill coursed through her again. She felt the Flowstate buoying and centering her better than any drug.

She encouraged people to stare at her while she listened to the interplay of the grandees and Haven, seeking both target and opportunity. She saw no score that drew her until she came back around to the Optimant bedside pedestal.

Zinsser's intrusion hadn't allowed her to accord it a second glance, but now that she did, she sensed a trophy. Flowstate had her feeling heady, infallible, protected by a charmed sphere of hyperacuteness while everyone else was wading sluggardly through a time dilation.

She was pretending interest in the folds of a drapery at the head of the bed when a ruckus broke out on the other side of the room, close to Smicker's bust. The Grandee Fanswell was lashing out at Haven for her lack of attention to him and the others. While heads were turning, Ghost acted.

The stressed and rebent facing on the Optimant gadget turned out to be not a drawer but the hinged door of a small, flat compartment. Reaching inside, she grasped something as flexible as textile but with areas of hardness. A fancy cap, perhaps, or some sort of sexwear hood.

She passed the take to her right hand and tucked it behind the turned-down bib front of her tunic, but then, as she was shutting the door with her left, her attention suddenly ranged in on someone who had witnessed the grab. Standing on the opposite side of the bed with a flagon of brainbane raised halfway to his lips was Old Spume.

Having seen her in action against Hiip the Shadow-rat, however, the rejuvenated Sense-maker did nothing more than give her a very slow sideways tic of the head and then another—the Ean equivalent of a conspiratorial nod.

Later, out among the pink umbrella blossoms and zigzag-boled trees in the upper gardens, Ghost fell back from the VIP tour to take a look at what she had copped from the bedstand.

Concealed behind a trellis wound thick with round-leafed yellow ivylike creepers, she saw that her trophy was neither a dress cap nor a sexware hood but an interface helmet. What her fingertips had taken for textile was an almost microscopically close-meshed flexible grid; what she'd taken for ornaments were chips, connectors, and skull contacts.

Limned with circuitry highways leading to eyephones, earpieces, and mouth grille, the helmet allowed for direct cyberaccess to technology from the Optimant days. It was as taboo a thing in the Post-Plague era as a Black Death carrier would have been in fifteenth-century Europe.

She couldn't have been more pleased.

Tucking it back into her tunic, she decided that it would be her secret from the Aquam and Haven both, though there was one person to whom she simply had to show it.

CHAPTER
TWENTY-NINE

Proof that Rhodes had gone to extremes of hospitality was provided by the salvers of washed raw mandseng root set out on trestle tables in an upper garden at the foot of the central dungeon tower. On the roof overhead, like some grim spectator, squatted Starkweather's flying fortress. The way lesser invitees hung back and turned their attention elsewhere confirmed both the tremendous value the Aquam placed on mandseng and the control Rhodes exerted over his guests.

"Tubers of the gods, we call it," Rhodes was explaining to the LAWs, "though when whole, such as these, we call them homunculi because of their vaguely human shape."

The several lumpy, contorted, rootlet-haired homunculi had an aura of miraculous value about them—the equivalent of other cultures' rarest narcotics, unique technologies, nearly extinct delicacies—for Optimant-engineered mandseng, which apparently defied cultivation and grew where and as it chose to, could counter much of the damage caused by the mutagens that teemed in Aquamarine's biosphere and thus had prevented the birth of countless Anathemites.

"Ah, finest Alabaster whole-body," the Dominor Paralipsio rasped to Dextra, rubbing left and right fingertips together in anticipation.

He was first to belly up to the mandseng. Dextra attributed the change in his sour disposition to the twenty-four-carat doubloon she'd slipped him. After hearing her hasty pitch for a future tête-à-tête, he had tucked the coin with feigned indifference into his reviewing-stand bunting of a waist sash.

A surgery-sharp carving knife was used to shave a slice of mandseng from the homunculus's head. The slice was off white, thin enough to flop over as a server pared it, almost thin enough to see through. Mason had said that the general admittance guests wouldn't be served mandseng until later, and then only crumbs and scraps for brewing teas and broths.

Paralipsio frowned at the size of the portion on the serving tile but accepted it. He was old to be fathering children, but tonight the mandseng was more of an Escalation. Also, for most Aquams aversion to Anathemite births was so ingrained that they would consume mandseng or any of the lesser anti-mutagens out of sheer habit.

Glorianna Theiss had assured Dextra that the stuff posed no threat, so she, too, accepted a slice. The other grandees and Starkweather—who appeared to be fighting a gag reflex—availed themselves as well. Fabia Lordlady and the Ethnarch Klobbo downed theirs in thimble cups of hot broth, while Rhodes crowed, "Lay in, lay in, there's plenty for us. That's one thing about me; my generosity always gets the better of me."

"Generosity enough to have had these homunculi *soaked*," Paralipsio grumbled, "swelling them so as to yield more servings."

Dextra pretended to concentrate on the taste of her slice. The doubloons notwithstanding, she couldn't risk getting enmeshed in the grandees' personality conflicts. Instead, she turned her thoughts to why the Optimants had been moved to create such a temperamental, only partially effective prophylaxis when they already had reliable clinical techniques and lab-produced anti-mutagen medicines.

The standard rationale was that some genius had prided himself on making living plasm dance to his tune, that the creation of mandseng was just another extravagant Optimant caprice. Dextra didn't buy it. To her, mandseng smacked of someone's wanting to ensure that Aquamarine would have a naturally available supply of antimutagen *even if the Optimants' vaunted technostructure went off-line*.

It made particular sense if someone had foreseen the advent of the Cyberplagues. Or if one or more Optimants had *created* the viruses, intending to set them loose . . . More questions and possibilities cascaded from that notion, but Dextra was forced to pry her attention from them as Lod confided, "Madame Haven will perhaps want to note that Commissioner Starkweather seems much in demand."

The AlphaLAW man had been buttonholed by Wix Uniday, who was accompanied by what looked to be the biggest of the Manipulants. Uniday was talking fast and low, and Starkweather was plainly upset. Taking note of Starkweather's sudden agitation, the grandees had their heads together.

The evening might break her way, after all, Dextra was musing, when she caught a flash of gold out of one eye. Her stomach clenched as one of Paralipsio's gray-catsuited attendants, while adjusting the gathers to one side of the grandee's waist sash, pulled up the fold on the opposite side, into which the dominor had tucked his doubloon.

Too far away to intervene, Dextra could only watch as the coin fell to the ground and bounced on the pavingstones, where it rang like a series of carillon notes.

She considered raising a shout or making a scene to divert attention, but it was too late for that. She had a moment to take appalled interest in how the chiming of hard money drew the eye of every grandee in the area before Fabia Lordlady picked up the doubloon and held it up to her eye.

"Lo!" Fabia exclaimed. "Mistress Haven's palmed off fool's gold on the lot of us!"

Claude Mason was so consumed by finding Purifyre at long last that the names of the boy's Human Enlightenment disciples went by in a blur. There was Essa, an imposing horse-faced woman with graying hair and a severe gaze. Another standout was a dark, hawklike young man called Testamentor. Both hovered close to Purifyre, attentive to his every nuance and watchful of the crowd as well. Essa especially followed the boy's least act or word with proprietary eyes. Mason thought her too old to be a love interest; creed members were supposed to be sworn to chastity in any case. But Mason wagered that Essa's veneration of his son was mixed with maternal feelings.

He had yet to get over the shock of the boy's face, though Purifyre's ill-formed features were already a central part of Mason's existence, something he knew he would see when he closed his eyes, would dream about, would perhaps think of at the moment of his death. Whereas he had abhorred that face when it was his, he now felt a boundless affection for it.

At close to 170 centimeters, Purifyre barely came up to Mason's chin. Incandessa's genes, he thought, since poor nutrition was unlikely, given his upbringing in Wall Water by his maternal grandfather. However, Purifyre was healthy and strong.

Owing to their creed's pacifism, the followers of Human Enlightenment were the only ones in the crowd who had refused to display weapons. Those who weren't wearing ceremonial gloves like Purifyre's showed hands that were well accustomed to labor.

"Your Escalation meant a great deal to me," Mason said, not yet daring to call him "son." "I want to render you the same and more when we have time."

"Nonsense, Father—may I call you that?"

The word filled Mason's heart. "Nothing would give me greater joy, Son."

There was raucous laughter from the grandees, obliging Purifyre to yell to be heard. "Thank you. But as to Escalations, it's for the son to render honor to the father, not the other way around."

Even in the lesser pandemonium of Rhodes's chambers, normal conversation was difficult. Also, the heat and closeness of the bedchambers had them sweating freely despite the punkah fans. Many of the attendees had set aside their vizards or lowered their veils. Purifyre beckoned Mason to follow him.

They left behind the babel and the cynical diplomatic contradanse. A trio of male votaries remained behind, a discreet distance from the Science Side modules, to avoid upsetting the Manipulants and Militerrors who were guarding the equipment.

Mason realized that he, too, should remain behind to advise Haven, but mission responsibilities had lost their hold over him for the moment. She saw him pass by but said nothing; perhaps she understood what he was going through.

They exited onto a wide private terrace that overlooked the lake. Purifyre carried himself with the self-assurance of a family member or privileged guest. Houseguards stood aside for him; officers saluted. Essa, Testamentor, and several others clustered out of earshot as father and son strolled to the waist-high retaining wall. The lights of workboats and rafts gleamed along the shoreline. Farther out were the fast-moving running lights of the picket craft and the blaze of *GammaLAW*, with her strings of lights and illuminor grids rigged. Faint lanterns off to the southeast belonged to the big slave-driven millship, which was lying in close to shore.

Although Mason had often rehearsed what he would one day say to his child, he struggled to make a start. "Brilliant inspiration, this festival of lights."

Purifyre showed delight. "You approve? It was my idea. I convinced Uncle 'Waretongue that Visitants would warm to the symbolism of illumination and enlightenment."

"Human Enlightenment?"

"That, too. But don't mistake our creed for Aquam superstition. We toil for progress and human well-being."

"I've brought some things that will interest you, then: biosynthesizers, briefing holos, a slew of devices."

The boy smiled, ugly yet beautiful to see. "The creed sets great store by teknic learning. To be candid, we're leery of war talk about alien enemies we've never seen."

"I'm not one for war, either," Mason said promptly, notwithstanding the LAW flechette pistol at his side. "This Attendance is well mannered compared to the ones I recall."

Purifyre gave his head the sideways tic of assent. "The grandees ordered the slavers to lie low and the child sellers and human flesh vendors out of sight."

"And Anathemite terminations?"

Purifyre gave him a sharp look. "Unavoidable. Unless you Visitants wish to raise and care for all the region's birth-defect children."

"I'm sorry," Mason mumbled. "That was sanctimonious of me." He wondered how close his son had come to being declared an Anathemite. He wanted to ask if the boy forgave him for abandoning him, but it was too soon. "I want to hear about *you*."

"From the start I needed answers," Purifyre said. "I went out as a creed novice while still an adolescent, to travel and learn.

'Waretongue had just become grandee, and he was glad to be rid of me."

"Yet he takes your advice now?"

"He does, though he remains mistrustful of my motives. When Wall Water began to suffer from his incompetence, he was eager for my technical advice and help. It was I who helped refurbish the dam gate mechanisms and supervise the rebuilding of the funicular."

"Impressive," Mason said genuinely.

"Wandering Aquamarine, I learned this and that."

"I admire your idealism. I'm glad to find that you're following Human Enlightenment and not DevOcean." The image of his boy preaching the rapture, when the Aquam would cast themselves into the sea and be absorbed into the Oceanic, made him shudder.

"You are conversant with DevOcean's tenets?" Purifyre asked in surprise.

"I knew them as fanatics and sometimes seditionists in the old days."

Purifyre nodded. "There's little love lost between Enlightenment and DevOcean." His hard tone made it sound as if he had used more than mantras and sermons to oppose that cult. "Their power has increased in direct proportion to their mania." The boy pointed along the rampart. "You saw them on the hillside— Marrowbone and his zealots in their white pom-poms, burning one of their infinity symbols in demonstration of their fervor?"

"I saw them. Fervor won't win them any currency with Dextra Haven. She's not interested in eschatological cults." He didn't add the painful afterthought, Unless DevOcean actually holds some key to the Oceanic. "But forget Marrowbone and his lunatics. Tell me more about your life."

Purifyre told him about traveling the length and breadth of Scorpia and then around the planet by means of the various Laputas. He told of encounters with the terrible Scourland Ferals, and of wild rides along the old Optimant highways aboard muscle cars, and of learning about teknics and gyns down in the Trans-Bourne.

Mason felt as if he were having a religious experience. His son had excelled, despite his disfigurement, in a way Mason never had even with wealth, family influence, and Periapt cozmed technology. Purifyre was a leader, a man of enlightenment, a world traveler on a planet where only the tough got anywhere.

As the boy talked of the importance of uniting Aquamarine, Mason was overwhelmed by pride and affection. He realized that he needed to be in Purifyre's sphere of attention and to have Purifyre in his—to share all the thoughts and feelings and experiences that constituted their lives.

"Your mother—"

Purifyre stopped him with a raised hand. "Forgive me, Father."

Essa was hissing at him near stairs that gave access to a more public promenade. Purifyre went to the sizable old woman, who took the opportunity to spare Mason a hostile glance. A second figure—an attractive young woman—was waiting in the shadows behind Essa. Testamentor immediately moved to keep watch at the door to the bedchambers.

Scarcely knowing what he was doing, Mason went strolling after his son. Catching sight of him, however, Essa hissed a warning.

"I need a moment's privacy to do an advisement—please?" Purifyre said.

Mason retreated, but not before he noticed two disturbing particulars. One was about Essa; her teeth were filed to bloodthirsty points, giving her a nasty snarl. The other concerned the beauty who had come to speak to Purifyre. Earlier she had been introduced to Mason as one of Rhodes's sexwares, literally a member of the throne.

Purifyre exchanged brief words with her, then turned and headed back toward Mason. The flesh-throne pretty had barely disappeared when a Militerror captain showed up and made straight for Purifyre. The boy heard the captain out, lips to cupped ear, then dismissed him.

"I pray you'll forgive me," he told Mason. "Uncle 'Waretongue commands me to recheck certain modifications I've made to Wall Water. Will you abide here so that we may converse further?"

Mason wanted to remain with him, but a saner part of him

knew better than to be demanding so early in their acquaintance. "I'll wait for as long as it takes."

Purifyre clapped him heartily on the shoulder. "I won't neglect you, Father." Then he set off with Essa at his heels like a faithful enforcer.

CHAPTER THIRTY

In the vile, furious mood into which Ghost's rebuff had cast him, Zinsser barely felt the first cup of single-grain Lava-Land prangbang. There were more to be had as he fumed along at the trailing edge of the tour.

His first impulse had been to renounce his GammaLAW post and take Starkweather up on his offer. Hierophant was a far more civilized planet than Aquamarine and wouldn't have Ghost on it. Also, by the time *Terrible Swift Sword* arrived, Ghost might well be dead, along with all the other misfits, losers, and delusionists Haven had enlisted for her GammaLAW mission. At a minimum she'd be hard used by then and fittingly past her prime, while Zinsser would be little older.

Haven wouldn't take kindly to desertion, he reminded himself as he knocked back more of the Aquam antifreeze. Despite Starkweather's Manipulant goliaths, Zinsser might end up being dragged back aboard the SWATHship bodily by the Exts. Perhaps it made more sense to apprise Wix Uniday of his change of mind, return to the *Sword* on some pretext or other, and *then* declare his change of allegiance.

But wait, Zinsser told himself.

Starkweather's *Jotan* was grounded under guard on the roof of Wall Water's central tower. All he really had to do was go aboard and await Starkweather's return. Rather unsteadily he set off that way, made a few wrong turns, but came at last to the central keep. In lieu of elevators there were eight flights of stairs. He was undaunted; a lifetime of swimming and scuba had kept him in better shape than most grad students.

Before he could ascend, however, Wix Uniday hailed him

and caught up. "Raoul, I've been looking all over for you. More trouble in paradise?"

Offended by the mocking tone, Zinsser forgot about making common cause with Uniday for the moment, but Uniday ignored his scowl.

"Starkweather wants me to let you in on events in progress. *Terrible Swift Sword* has changed orbit and deployed its now-reoperational tether, with Pitfall activated and attached. The first specimen-gathering and analysis mission is in high gear." Uniday paused briefly to consult his whatty, a conventional model, since Haven hadn't trusted him with one of the archeo-hacking upgrades. "*Big Tess* is coming east to west for a test run west of Scorpia. Your sampler should be taking the plunge in about thirty minutes."

Zinsser was startled by the sound of his own cup hitting the floor in an explosion of prangbang. "You're ... using ... *my* invention?"

"Steady, boy," Uniday urged. "Just how much have you had to drink, anyway?"

"You're lying!" Zinsser rasped. "You don't even have the activating password!"

"Ah, well, we crossed your 'Rubicon' back on Periapt, Raoul." Uniday was about to smile but reconsidered. "Got it for a rather handsome sum from a buxom blonde named Freya Eulenspiegel—a former graduate assistant of yours, I believe. Helped you write the software for Pitfall? Apparently she felt that you'd treated her a bit shabbily at the end of your affair, and, well, you know how it is. A couple of drinks, a soft shoulder to cry on ..."

Zinsser was quivering with rage but was paralyzed to act on his desire to choke the life out of Uniday.

"Spare me the threatening looks, okay," Uniday said. "You're leaving with me on the *Jotan*. We'll let Haven in on the rescheduled soup-scoop as soon as a preliminary analysis has been done."

Zinsser put a hand to his forehead. "You moronic *politician*!"

In his mind's eye he saw Pitfall plunging from the sky to enclose tens of thousands of liters of Big O seawater, effectively segregating it from the rest of the organism, then zapping it with MRI and X-ray CAT technology to try for an instantaneous snapshot of the creature before the discrete molecules could dissociate themselves.

Imagination and reality, though, were two different things.

"Do you actually think the Oceanic is going to stand still for this . . . for this *attack* on it? This isn't what I had in mind at all. The waters have to be tested. Dry runs have to be executed. This planet—"

"Doesn't matter to us, Doctor," Uniday said, cutting him off, "beyond what it can tell us about the Roke. Now pull yourself together and rejoin the party. Starkweather will spring preliminary Pitfall results in the middle of Haven's little show-and-tell with the Science Side modules."

Uniday moved suddenly, squeezing Zinsser's arm with the kind of strength Zinsser would have looked for from an Ext bouncer. "After Haven's party is spoiled, go straight to the *Jotan*. Don't make me come looking for you."

Zinsser fought to control his ragged breathing as Uniday strode out of sight. Then he hastened from the tower, but not to rejoin Haven and the rest. Steal *my* work, will they? he fumed. Make me look like the biggest fool in the universe?

Zinsser wondered what the treacherous Freya would say when, some day in her declining years, she learned that he'd built into Pitfall's software a second backdoor password about which he'd never told her. There was still time to make the Pitfall tail wag the *Terrible Swift Sword* dog. By manipulating the tether's aerodynamic and marine control surfaces, the depth of its dive, and the size of its sample, he could imperil the tether and even the starship if he so chose. Starkweather wouldn't have the guts to call his bluff. Zinsser could dictate terms to the AlphaLAW and Haven alike.

He needed to find Ghost. The prangbang had clouded his thinking somewhat, but the source of the trouble between them was suddenly clear to him. If he had saved *her* that night at the Empyraeum, she would already be his. Pitfall was his chance to turn that around. It was Raoul Zinsser's turn to play rescuer.

"Have you tried pyro before?" Souljourner asked Burning.

He sniffed the blue crystal jigger of clear sluggish fluid, then sipped some.

"I've never sampled it," she added. "But it's rumored to be very good here."

He coughed and pursed his lips to cool his tonsils. "Probably is—*for blowing up tree stumps*!"

He made a miniature explosion gesture by flinging his finger-tips out, surprised to see that she got it. Souljourner let out a guffaw that was engaging, especially in all the courtly pretension and mendacity.

He put the pyro aside, and they walked on. As she stole glances at the ruddiness his face had taken on, he swore silently and tried to will away the blush that was his curse. Strolling along and talking, he didn't bring it under control so much as forget it. Even so, it was some time before he noticed that his ears didn't feel sunburn-hot.

He was staying out of the spotlight but close enough to keep vigil on Haven. Zone and the other subordinates were well posted, and for that matter the Ext guards probably could have run the detail themselves.

The Attendance had aspects of a high carnival. They passed a troubadour bowing a vielle and singing a love song, a juggler walking a slack wire, a man in buffoon glad rags putting a quartet of trained, furry little murinoids through their paces on a miniature stage. Tray bearers kept up a steady resupply of drinks and canapes, snacks, salmagundis, and pastries.

He made visual recon for the usual things: layout, fortifications, numbers, condition and arms of the opposition. More particularly he was searching for hints of the origin of the steam Mason claimed to have seen. So far Wall Water gave no evidence of being supplied with electricity, heat, or high-pressure engines. What if Rhodes had something else going? It was a point worth pondering if one happened to be floating around on a SWATHship in the lake below, modern weapons systems or no.

"Yonder is the Peelhouse, a venerable old keep," gushed a woman in a gold nose shield. She wore a wicker-structured ball gown, bell-shaped so that her two thin legs, when she stood with heels together, suggested a clapper. "There the first Rhodeses made a stand against the treacherous, misbegotten Laxor scum seeking to take Wall Water in a coup by night."

"*I'm* a descendant of the treacherous, misbegotten Laxor

scum," a warrior grated, hand to the knuckle-duster hilt of his tulwar.

"Oh, I didn't mean it *that* way," she hastened.

The warrior pulled down a lower eyelid with a middle finger, bidding her, "Go to hell!"

Burning saw that the Peelhouse was a squat little tower that looked like it might originally have been an admin annex; it was set between two terraced levels so that a door on one side was more than two meters higher than the one around back and below. Crumbling, much patched, and a little akilter, it didn't have much strategic value or hold much interest.

He realized he'd veered away from Dextra when Souljourner tugged his forearm to keep him on course. It was like being hauled back on track by one of *GammaLAW*'s flight deck tractors.

"Sorry," he told her. "What does your name mean?"

"It's simply my name. My parents gave it to me."

"And they never said if it had any special significance?"

"They died before I could ask."

That got them briefly onto her life at Pyx and his on Concordance. When they had ambled a little farther, she slid in a question as casually as if tossing a dart. "What is it you're searching Wall Water for?"

"I'm not 'searching,' " he countered. "Simply admiring."

"I've dwelled here six days. I might suggest some other things to admire—"

Grimacing in sudden pain, Souljourner clapped her hands to her head. Burning eased her back onto the red-tiled rim of a big square fishpond, where hugely obese lace-fins drifted and mouthed. "What is it?" he asked.

"My hapless head! This cursed planet!"

Burning froze, recalling what she was. "A quake?"

She shook her head while she massaged her temples. "Some tidal shift I felt—in the world and within the world. Made by the Oceanic." She stifled a groan. "I've never Descried its like."

Burning punched up his plugphone, trying to summon LAW help or medical advice, but had no luck raising any net what with all the ferrocrete, stone, and inert Optimant systemry hemming him in. He knew Haven's chapter and verse about every antibiotic bandage being a political instrument, but civic affairs scripture was one thing and standing by while a poor indig keeled over from pain was another. He sorted one-handed through the pared-down medical kit he'd crammed into a dress belt pouch and came up with a general analgesic and anticephalagia agent.

"Here," he said. "For the headache. Unless the pain is necessary."

She snatched the little caplet, tossed it back, and gulped it down dry. In seconds her breathing became slower and less labored. "In times past I have felt great faradic electricities swirl through Aquamarine, but never like this."

Burning supposed that the reference to Faraday had entered her caste's argot by way of some Optimant artifact. "You can sense power surges, too?"

She gave the nod of the head that on Scorpia meant no. "I alone—and that merely now and again. The Oceanic is at some overarching work, I think."

Useful if true, Burning thought. But Glorianna Theiss could figure that out with an NMR scan. "Can you walk?"

She rose, only to lurch against him. A passing highborn couple stopped to sway tipsily, pointing at Souljourner. The man, his hauberk of spangles wet with sot-mead, slurred, "Drunken abomination! Anathemite ogress!"

Souljourner made a sound of despair and weariness. When the couple tottered closer to lay on some more, she stumbled off in the opposite direction to avoid them.

Burning looked around for a Militerror or household guard he could sic on the interlopers, but there were none around or, indeed, anyone else. Souljourner had disappeared into the darkness, and for all he knew she was about to pop an aneurysm. He tried the plugphone once more but still couldn't get a response on any commo push.

When the man in spangles looked like he was going to follow Souljourner, Burning scooped one of the toothy lace-fins out of the pool and slam-dunked the fish down the neck of the Aquam's roomy, belted hauberk. The splash of a body landing in the fishpond pursued Burning as he set out after Souljourner, taking the steps—four at a time—down which she had fled.

CHAPTER
THIRTY-ONE

The cyberinterface hood was deader than a year-old furlough chit. Some of the power connectors Ghost had been issued along with the archeo-hacking whatty fit it, but the hood refused to take a charge. Even so, the optic-circuited, direct-induction headgear was a coup in which to glory. It made her feel triumphant and empowered the way a very adroit swipe in the prisoner camps had.

As she was reminding herself that she could share the victory only with those she trusted, she spied Burning. He was hurrying down a flight of steps across the miniature plaza she'd just entered, headed for a small watchtower called the Peelhouse.

She skewed across his backtrail unhurriedly, watched by a knot of B-list revelers who were quaffing Wall Water's second-best throat acid and singing off key. Once she reached the shadows, she sprinted, as light-footed as an elf on shock absorbers.

She had estimated his course correctly and, when he came around a corner, stepped into the light before him with the stolen interface hood on her head, one eyecup lifted slightly so she could see what she was doing.

Burning stopped, relaxed but defensive, then said, "Ghost, wherever you got it, put it back." He'd attended more briefings on Optimant technology than she had and had instantly identified the hood for what it was.

"So Rhodes can give it to Starkweather?" Her voice was muffled a bit by the mouthbowl. "It's mine now."

Burning's eyes narrowed. "I don't have time to argue with you. Have you seen Souljourner, the Descrier?"

Ghost pretended to tweak the contacts and emitters at her temple. "Maybe I can channel her for you." She felt her scars move against the fabric of the hood as she indulged herself in an invisible grin.

He didn't laugh. "If you do see her, give me a chirp. And take off that brainwired balaclava. Put it back where it was or toss it where the guards will find it." He leaned forward suddenly and pressed something into her hand. "In case things get dicey," he said.

Ghost eyed the spit-needle he had given her and smiled ruefully. "How thoughtful of you."

When he hastened off, Ghost honored his order to the extent that she removed the hood and tucked it back behind her tunic's bib front. Then she began to retrace her steps to Rhodes's bedchambers.

A couple of Manipulants were keeping an eye on the Science Side modules, several Militerrors were watching the Manipulants, and a foursome of Purifyre's disciples were eyeing the Militerrors. Smicker's bust gazed out over all of them. If anyone other than Old Spume had noticed the hood's absence from the control box, he or she wasn't saying.

Out on the room's lamp-lit terrace Mason was pacing in disquiet meditation. Ghost slipped out the door and waited for him to notice her; when Mason did, he said, "You're wasting your time if you've come to get me. I'm not leaving."

Ghost lifted her eyebrows. "Interesting how people will simply blurt out unsolicited information. Fiona used to do it all the time."

"I'm staying with my son," Mason told her.

His Adonis face fronted for a brain that really wasn't first-rate at all. Anybody seeing him would assume that he led a charmed life, but the comely looks concealed a knotted backstory replete with emotional anguish. Ghost entertained the notion of sampling his private properties but sensed that Mason was already trudging around with too much grief on his shoulders.

"Purifyre's inspecting some construction he designed," he added. "He'll be back directly."

Verifying that no one could peep them from the bedchambers or any of the cliffside galleries and balconies, Ghost pulled out the interface hood and tossed it to him. "Then you've got a free minute to tell me about this."

Mason caught it and turned it over in his hands in the light from a lamppost. "*JeZeus!* An Optimant cybercaul! Have you been grave robbing?"

"Its former owner is still alive and breathing—for the moment," she said. "Tell me about it."

"Pre-Plague, of course. Cybercauls were about as far as man-machine interface got before doomsday. Direct contact via an electromagnetic induction field surrounding the brain. The *Scepter* team laid hands on only three the whole time we were on site—and all of them were damaged, useless. But this one . . . It's in near-mint condition—except the power pack's depleted."

"It won't take a charge from our archeo-hacking 'wares," she said. "I tried."

"Sometimes there's a trick to it," he said in a distracted voice.

Mason appeared to be listening to something on the hot Big Sere night wind that Ghost couldn't hear. From his cummerbund pouch he pulled a power cube fitted with an adapter that accepted the caul's standard Optimant fitting. Then, without any apparent guesswork, he set the recharge parameters.

Ghost mused, Aren't you the technical adept all of a sudden.

Mason studied the recharging caul for a moment, as if making up his mind about something. When he looked up at her, it was clear he had decided to reveal a piece of private information.

"When *Scepter* was here, we pinpointed a dormant nuclear power source inside the bust of Smicker. The thing is actually a computer. The bust is fueled by a cell that's still capable of putting out juice."

"And . . ."

"The caul will give me access to the computer. I'll be the first man to go on-line with an Optimant system in two hundred years."

"You?" Ghost said angrily.

His face took on the expression of a man shaken out of a daydream. "You mean *you* wanted to be the one who—" He shook his head back and forth. "No, no. That would be a tragic mistake. I know a lot more about Optimant access codes and cyber . . ." His mouth hardened. "It has to be me. My life's bound up in Aquamarine—in more ways than you know."

Ghost pressed the heel of her right hand against the butt of her pistol, just enough to make the leather of the backward-raked holster squeak. Mason was wearing one of the new LAW flechette pistols, but it didn't worry her.

"So bound up that you'd risk introducing a cybervirus into yourself? I mean, if you're so keen to access Pandora's box, why not just sic the archeo-hacking 'wares on the job and stay out of harm's way." Ghost stopped herself. Mason's hands were suddenly clenched on the cybercaul, and his expression looked pained.

"Yatt," he grated. "Stay out of me! In due time . . ."

"Mason, what's going down?" she asked, as concerned as she was intrigued.

He caught his breath, then gasped. "Nothing. Nothing I . . . It's this Ean cuisine—it never agreed with me."

Ghost folded her arms across her chest. "Of course."

Mason began to rummage through the miniaturized hacking tackle R&D had provided along with the whatties. "The caul's primary importance is in accessing the data systems. But it could also be the cyberkey that'll unlock the bust's armored housing." He raised the caul to her with its blank eyecups staring like star sapphires. "Someone has to do it."

He drew the hood onto his head and thumbed an activating button at the neckline. Edging closer to the double doorway to Rhodes's bedchambers, he peeked around the corner to size up the situation. The room had emptied of VIPs, though the Manipulants, Militerrors, and Human Enlightenment votaries were still on hand.

"No need to go inside," he said. "I can access it from here."

The Exts' Pre-Plague history of enslavement by implants had predisposed most of them to a violent reaction at the idea of anyone's being headspliced to a computer. But Ghost's contrary streak and morbid curiosity were anything but conventional. She therefore watched instead of knocking him cold.

Her whatty reported a sudden surge of power in the bust. At the same time she heard the weighty, defect-free slide of metal castings made to pico tolerances working perfectly even after two hundred years. Nearly frictionless bearings rolled; log-size bolts and solenoids glided back. Latches undocked with ringing concussions that reverberated through the flooring. The computer within, dormant since before there *were* any Exts as such, toned from somewhere deep inside Smicker.

The Manipulants' mammoth bloopguns came up, along with the Militerrors' quarrel throwers; all of them were looking for someone to shoot.

Mason's voice was muffled by the mouthbowl, but his soft grunts sounded to Ghost as if he were on the listening end of a conversation. Suddenly he announced, "The computer's operational. We can open the bust housing whenever we want."

She yanked the cybercaul back off his head. "Not yet. We don't want Rhodes or Starkweather to have access."

Mason understood that she would sonic him if he resisted. He moved his hands away from his body. "You're right. But trust me with the caul for now. I'm the only one who can make it work." He held out the hood to her. "See for yourself. Try it."

Ghost backed away from him and donned it, a more brash and reckless act for an Ext than any show of adrenaline courage in combat.

She had expected the kind of overwhelming mental expansion the legends and ancient graphics depicted—a plunge into the radiant neurocybernetic interverse that had been paradise—then hell, when the Cyberplagues brought all the cybernetted fantasylands crashing down. What she saw, however, appeared to be the real world with a kind of overlay that wasn't all that different from an enhanced-imaging target scope. The Smicker bust was like a dimmed-down hyperfractals cosmic egg, waiting to give birth to something impossible to guess. Big, restless icons bracketed the Militerrors and Manipulants, who'd gone back to maintaining an uneasy watch over the Science Side modules.

Ghost tried concentrating, imaging, willing activity in the caul-modeled darkness but couldn't make anything happen. She had a feeling that something was waiting out there in the interverse, scrutinizing her, perhaps even sizing her up as psychic prey, but whatever it was refused to obey her or betray its presence.

She slipped the cybercaul from her head and tossed back her loose locks and Hussar Plaits. Tapping the Optimant artifact was going to take craft, time, and nerve; she handed it back to Mason.

"You have a way with it, all right. See what else it can do. But be warned: if Smicker here gets the better of you, there's only one reliable cure. And that cure'll leave Purifyre fatherless again—only permanently."

Mason nodded. "I've no intention of failing him a second time."

Ghost appraised him briefly. If Mason could be stabilized somewhat by her promoting his relationship with Purifyre, so be it. She made a quick motion past the top of her boot and came up with the ripsaw-handguard dagger her mother had left her; then she presented it to Mason, hilt first. His momentary fear gave way to bewilderment.

"Your son tried to render you an Escalation," Ghost said. "So offer him one back."

He weighed the beautiful dagger in his hand. "Brilliant."

"Just don't go giving that shank away."

He turned the sleek, lusterless dagger over in his hand. "I may be an obsessed parent, but I'm not suicidal, Ghost."

She caught movement out of the corner of her eye and turned as Zinsser stepped out onto the terrace, his eyes dancing but also glassy.

"There's something you have to hear from me," he told her without acknowledging Mason.

"I doubt that, Doctor."

"Hear me out. You'll be grateful you did."

That he sounded both triumphant and conspiratorial piqued her interest. "All right, tell me."

Zinsser glanced at Mason. "It's a private matter."

At Zinsser's side, Ghost rounded the curve of a casemate structure and descended a half flight of stairs. The public promenade there ran all the way to a projecting salient of the cliff face into which the stronghold had been built. Fifty meters below and to the left began an even broader rampart walkway that led to a footbridge spanning an overspill gorge that ran around the northern flank of the place.

Their end of the promenade was empty. "This will do," Zinsser said.

She leaned away from the smell of Lava-Land prangbang on his breath. "Two-mug screamers like you shouldn't drink, Doctor. Now, what's all this about?"

With the rock, stronghold, and lake around them, he swept his arm at the star-studded sky. "It's about my saving your life."

CHAPTER
THIRTY-TWO

Still holding the gold doubloon with Paralipsio's face on it, the Grandee Fabia Lordlady showed the others the coin with her own. Her gaze shifted from Dextra to Starkweather.

"You play us off against each other and between yourselves, eh? How you Visitants must enjoy laughing at us in secret!"

The other grandees had their gold pieces out, too. The sprite who'd triggered the whole mess by tugging at Paralipsio's sash was on her knees, weeping.

"Haven went behind my back," Starkweather sputtered, "or are you too stupid to see? This proves we can't trust her!" He stilled himself enough to make a pitch. "She's trying to buy you with souvenirs, but I can make you masters of this world. I can put the Oceanic at your mercy!" He pointed off to the west as if posing for a monument. "My starship is even now plucking a piece of the creature straight out of the very sea!"

Pitfall! Dextra realized. Either Starkweather had co-opted the device or Zinsser had sold her out. Even so, she didn't spare more than a quick glance in the direction in which the commissioner was pointing; if *Terrible Swift Sword* had descended to tetherheight somewhere over the ocean far to the west, it would be below the horizon.

"My subordinates will scoop up a large confluence of the Oceanic's mass," Starkweather trumpeted. "When my experts are done examining the specimen, I'll have it dumped out smack in the middle of the Panhard desert for everyone to see. That should be proof enough that I'm the one you want to deal with."

Sweat stood out on his forehead and upper lip. Ever the self-preservationist, he was acutely aware of being in the middle of an armed camp despite his Manipulants, *Jotan*, and *Terrible Swift Sword*. More, his audience wasn't exactly buying it. Expressions on the grandees' faces matched the doubtful, angry murmurings among the lower-ranking Aquam.

"You sent your poxy ship to stir up the Oceanic?" Rhodes yammered. "To provoke it? Do you mean to be the death of us all?"

"Buck, I'm begging you," Dextra said, letting Starkweather and the grandees hear the entreaty in her voice. "Abort the operation. Don't deploy Pitfall."

"It's too late," he shot back, but with a quaver to his voice. "What difference can it make if that mass of fish guts out there is perturbed?"

Urgent cross talk sprang up all around, but the Ethnarch Klobbo cut through it with a loud demand of Dextra. "Are you saying you don't stand with him? Do you make some competing offer?"

With no way to stop Pitfall and a final rift with Starkweather looming, she had to salvage what she could. "You must first promise me something in exchange," she said quickly.

"Such as?" the Dynast Piety IV asked.

"Part of my mission is to help you improve your lot. You want doubled food production? Then guarantee me free navigation on your lakes and rivers. Let my teams study your Beforetimer ruins. You want Visitant medicine to keep you alive and prevent Anathemites? Let me set up schools and teach anyone young or old who wants to learn. You want to light your buildings, fashion new manufacts? Let your people labor for me when I need workers. I'll pay fair wages."

They were all listening, with the petty aristocrats on the sidelines straining forward to hear. The grandees were doing quick sidelongs at each other, but she was sure she'd hit pay dirt.

"You want aircraft to lift you over the Amnion to trade around the world without being bled white by the insiders who own the Laputas? You want to live free of fear of the Oceanic, as the Beforetimers did?" Her stage sense told her to lower the volume, to underplay the payoff line. "Starkweather can't offer you these things, but I can."

"Treason!" Starkweather railed.

But she was ready for him. "No, that's my GammaLAW commission. Stay out of this, Buck, or Big 'Un Boudreau gets a signal and maybe *Big Tess* never gets to Hierophant or back to Periapt, either."

The Manipulants, who spoke only their own battle-*gullah*, had sensed the crisis even without their human officers' translation. The Exts had gone from edgy expressions to calmer Flowstate ones, mustering their Skills. Starkweather was deathly pale, furious enough to order Dextra shot down but almost faint at her threat. The Aquam, from grandee to servitor, wavered, both doubting and hoping.

In that vanishing window of opportunity a lone voice cried out with a fine spray of saliva. "Surely we can reason together peacefully and *make sense* of these matters!"

It was Old Spume, so trepidacious that the spit was spewing out a meter in front of him. "I've been on this She-Lord's boat and know some things she can and cannot do. Gaze on me. Am I not changed? Am I not a witness to tell what a Visitant pact might mean?"

Dextra had no idea where he was going with it, but she could have kissed him. Spume had steadied the crowd and the grandees; even Rhodes was giving ear. She suspected he'd grabbed the typhoon-eye moment for a try at saving his own sinking fortunes, but that didn't matter.

Spume took in the grandees with a gesture. "You Ean lords, I swear this oath! Haven's deal warrants your consideration. Isn't this the time for your Sense-makers to come forward and conduct parleys and exchanges, to bring you food for thought?"

Shrewd, bringing in the other Sense-makers, Dextra said to herself. The ones present automatically struck solemnly cogitative poses. Spume's motion flattered the men and women who would color the decision-making process. It also gave the grandees a political dodge. When a vote or decision carried too much risk, they would table the matter and appoint a committee to look into it.

Starkweather was down but not out. "Watch the sky!" he said, apparently repeating something Wix Uniday had whispered in his ear. "Even with your lanterns and torches, my starship will be visible when she rises into the bowl of the night,

and you will see the power I command! Enough to scoop out
the Oceanic in pieces!" He turned and pointed a shaking finger
at Haven. "She wants to rule you. I want only to see you free of
the Oceanic—"

He interrupted himself to clap one hand to his plugphoned
ear in obvious pain, as did Dextra and some of the other LAWs.
A jamming signal that felt like a sonic ice pick was threatening
to overload their earpiece acoustors and burst their brains like
popcorn. At the same time the grounds of Wall Water were
growing brighter from an expanding light source to the west.

In her desperation to get her hand to her touchpad card and
shut off her plugphone, Dextra forgot all other concerns. The
Aquam had stopped paying attention to the LAWs and were
shielding their eyes from the white brilliance reaching up over
the curvature of Aquamarine. A few outcries, moans, and whispered prayers punctuated the stricken silence.

Lod was suddenly at Dextra's elbow, in violation of his usual
careful decorum. "Don't stare at it! You could be blinded!"

"Bigtimer!" an Ext hollered like a war cry, using the slang
term for a thermonuclear or antiproton explosion.

Dextra shook her head in an effort to stop the ringing in her
ear. The globe of violet-white light was still expanding, though
it was beginning to lose incandescence.

"What happened?" Starkweather stammered, sounding
punch-drunk.

"LAW warned you that the *Sword* might be virused," Dextra
started to say.

"*Posh!*" Rhodes shouted. "You wanted to know what difference it could make if the Oceanic was provoked. Now you'll
know!"

The triple-thickness, ironbound wooden door of the Peelhouse was old and warped under layers of blue paint but still
heavy and stout. It also was unlocked.

Souljourner ducked inside to collect her wits and take counsel on her future. There was no way to bar the door from the
inside, but that part of the stronghold's grounds was deserted, so
she settled for closing it behind her.

The place was bare and musty and lacked windows, even a

shooting slit, on the ground level. She'd brought a tin hand lamp she'd come across in a garden stelae nook, part of the light display Wall Water had put on for the Visitants. Setting it in a sconce, she pulled her skirts out of the way and got down on her knees, her chatelaines jingling. She opened the drawstring pouch and poured the Holy Rollers into her palm.

Thanks to Burning's pharmaceuticant, her blinding headache had retreated somewhat, but not so the conviction that the Oceanic was exerting itself vastly under the darkened waves.

Thumbing the pouch for luck, she cast the red and white dice. Red pips three, white pips one—the third of the mystic 144 Kybogram Auguries: "GREET FATE WITH YOUR OWN TRUTH." So there it was. Nothing she could do would redirect her destiny for the time being.

The pain began to return; it was as if the Oceanic's anger were building. Perhaps Burning would have another medicament that would soothe it. She still wasn't clear on whether she'd been given into his care permanently or was simply too ill bred and cloddish to stand next to the She-Lord Haven.

Burning, she thought. At least he was young and tall, a decent sort despite the sometimes hangdog face. A humane man as well, more so than Sternstuff or Rhodes or Lintwhite the castellan, for that matter. And he smelled clean, if very strange.

Only half thinking, she cast the dice again with the image of Burning and herself in her mind. While the Holy Rollers were still in the air she realized what she had done and tried to snatch them back; then she watched, appalled, as they tumbled to a stop on the dusty cobbles.

The impulse to toss the dice a second time had come from thin air—unfounded, incomprehensible. That scarcely mattered now; the Holy Rollers had delivered their verdict. In her bibelot, number sixty-six read, "LOVE'S DESIRE, EMBRACE THE FIRE."

It was just as unthinkable to try a third throw as it would have been to ignore the first two or to fling dice and bibelot into Lake Ea. She knelt in the candlelight, staring at the Holy Rollers until her knees ached and her head threatened to fly apart with throbbing.

When the door opened, she wasn't surprised to find Burning

filling the opening. "Souljourner, you all right? Come with me. I'll have you taken aboard the—"

As she went to him, he almost raised his hands in defense. Then she had her arms around him and gave him the first love kiss she'd ever granted. She had the distinct impression that she wasn't doing it quite correctly. But for all that, it was wonderful. From what she could tell, Burning shared the feeling.

Once Ghost and Zinsser had left him alone on the terrace, Mason received a more antagonistic visit. He'd put the cybercaul away and was turning Ghost's carbon-black dagger in his fingers when Yatt's phantom Buddha face rose up before him. Taking advantage of the absence of witnesses, the meta-AI assailed him with an intensity that made him sway on his feet.

"Don the cybercaul now, so that we may open the statue casing and access the Optimant computational ecology within."

"Not now!" Mason said, forming the words through locked teeth because his mind was in too much of a roil for him to simply think them. "The Aquam and the Manipulants would see—"

"We can download whatever information the system contains into your whatty or relay it to the starship if need be. Such an artifact is why we've come to Aquamarine, the reason we contrived to have the GammaLAW mission created and enabled and you returned to your son."

The whatties had a lot of brute storage, but Mason doubted there was enough to accommodate an Optimant machine's memory. He had a sudden vision of other AIs, Pre-Plague ones this time, joining Yatt in his own neurowares.

"It's too dangerous," he said to the night air.

"Use the cybercaul!"

"Damage me and I'll end up in a restraint cocoon back onboard the *Sword*, and so will you. LAW's suspicions about a rogue AI will be confirmed."

The Buddha faded as a new voice joined the conversation.

"Father, are you unwell?"

It might have been Purifyre's reappearance that made Yatt relent; more likely, Mason's point about restraint had prompted it. The boy's very voice generated in Mason an irresistible current of emotion that displaced Yatt's hold. At Purifyre's touch, the bloated Buddha face derezzed completely.

Testamentor was back, too, but the filed-toothed old gorgon Essa was nowhere to be seen. When Purifyre helped steady him, Mason was again struck by his remarkable strength. Then there was a change in his son's voice as his hand found the cybercaul.

"What's this?"

"Something I was asked to examine," Mason said. "Gave me a bit of a mental flutter, I guess. Better not touch it."

When he tugged gently on the hood, Purifyre hesitated, then released it. "It's a Beforetimer artifact that was in the grandee's keeping. You made it work?"

With the boy staring at him, Mason couldn't maintain the lie. "Some, yes." He nodded toward Smicker's bust. "On that."

Purifyre passed glances with Testamentor. "Show me how. It belongs to Aquamarine! It must be used for Human Enlightenment, not Rhodes's lunacy or to bend us down before LAW."

Mason shook his head. "A Beforetimer computer could be more dangerous than the Oceanic."

Purifyre relented somewhat. "Then at least show me how the caul works."

If Mason could have, he would have thrown the cybercaul into the lake, drawn Ghost's black dagger, and rendered his son an Escalation. But events had gone too far for that. He could feel Yatt crooning in the darkness, exhorting him to concede what the boy asked and no more.

"I'll resecure the bust; will that do?" he asked Purifyre at last.

"For now," the boy said. "And thanks for your courage."

Mason shuffled back to the edge of the bedchamber door. "If anything goes wrong, get this hood off me, whatever it takes."

Purifyre's nod was urgent.

Mason drew the flexible circuitry back over his head, thumbed the switch, and entered the neutral, waiting otherspace. It was easier this time to find the flawlessly milled solenoids, big as fireplace logs. He probed at the locking sequence, checking for some way to free up the bust/housing's manual locks.

When he was thoroughly engrossed, he felt Yatt surge up like a neural lightning storm. He tried to yell to Purifyre but didn't know if he actually formed words. He fumbled at the cybercaul.

Yatt wouldn't speak to him directly, but it was no mystery what the Quantum College AI was doing through Mason and the caul. Latches clanked back; servo motors made the sybaritorium floor tremble.

Smicker's armor-alloy monument began to both expand and disassemble as if in a slow-motion explosion. Segments moved on operating rods, actuators, and swing arms. Rays of vari-colored light sprang out through the growing divides. Yatt was exposing the Optimant machine to the world, and vice versa.

CHAPTER
THIRTY-THREE

Layered generations of votive candle wax cracked and parted, showering crumbs and rippled fragments, as Smicker's bust continued to open. Prayer shrouds, fetishes, and ancestral relics avalanched all around as the housing morphed.

Eyephones in the Optimant cybercaul showed Mason the event via real-time video rather than in virtual modeling. Mason hadn't requested it and assumed that Yatt had.

Like a trophy head on a pike, Smicker's head ascended almost to the ceiling on a telescoping jack. Manipulants and Militerrors were rooted with astonishment, weapons at the ready.

The computer and the workstations surrounding it suggested a blown-glass organ with multiple keyboards—polychrome, radiant, shining from within like a hatchery of cosmic eggs. It might have been an optical computer, but the blinding stage effects probably had to do with Smicker's vainglory, something to impress the Optimants' GeStation-grown serfs. Even so, the computer had to have served some function other than simply watchdogging dam facility operations.

In the heart of the piercing, fitful rays Mason began to see readout fields throwing up words either at random or in answer to Yatt's inquiry.

| ALABASTER: | PASSWATER: | NEW ALEXANDRIA |
| HYAPATIA | TONGUE TIDE | ENDGAME |

He could feel Yatt's surge of triumph and some of his own. Hyapatia: the Optimants' utopian AI overseer; Tongue Tide: their project aimed at direct communication with the Oceanic; Endgame: the legendary panacea to the Cyberplagues.

Mason was no archeo-hacker, but he could see that the Smicker unit offered connectors and interfaces the whatties could handle. It was all there, he realized: the answers to all the puzzles GammaLAW had come to Aquamarine to solve! Perhaps even a way to cope with the Roke.

But the clock was against Mason. The Militerrors' leader had already dispatched a runner, doubtless to notify Rhodes. And with the plugphones suddenly acting up, the officer of the Manipulants was pointing the biggest of his troops, the one called Scowl-Jowl, toward the bedchambers' door. That meant that Starkweather also would be showing up soon.

Yatt's voice rang with another caveat. *"It's prohibitively dangerous for you to interface directly with this system until we vet it."*

A good rationale if Yatt wanted to hog the computer to itself, Mason reflected. He was trying to decide what to do when he felt Purifyre's hand clasp his shoulder so hard that it hurt.

"Ask it about the New Alexandria lighthouse—about Endgame."

Mason grimaced. It was there that he had last seen Incandessa, the night the Conscious Voices had killed Boon and Mason had thought he'd put Aquamarine behind him forever. "What do you know of Endgame?"

"If Endgame is hidden in the lighthouse, as Smicker's computer is here, you should be able to reveal it."

Mason was suddenly confused. How had his son, who referred to the Optimants as Beforetimers, learned of the AI program Yatt had come to Aquamarine to find? Without his asking, the computer's central display assembled an image of the lighthouse. At its very summit—in the lamp room of the tower—was a strobing omega-symbol icon. It was a place Mason had visited hundreds of times in the course of his time with Incandessa. If Endgame was housed in a unit on the scale of Smicker's bust, it could only be in the lamp itself, dark since the 'Plagues.

"We have to shut it down!" Mason shouted out over the tonings and symphonic sound-synth bites. The Militerrors and the Manipulants watching had had about all the full-intensity light show they could take. "We need to lock it down again." He was talking to Yatt more than to Purifyre.

Mason held up his whatty, which was umbilicaled to the auxiliary memory block he'd been issued. The device's archeohacking 'wares were running; it was downloading at least some of the data. He concentrated on making the pieces of the bust housing reconverge, but Yatt had withdrawn its assistance, so nothing happened.

At the same time Purifyre was dragging at Mason's arm. "Tongue Tide and the other Beforetimer grails are all worth having. But Endgame—the clue to its whereabouts is more of a treasure than anyone thought lay hidden in Wall Water!"

Purifyre's words only reinforced Mason's determination to reseal the housing, but he couldn't free himself from Purifyre's blacksmith's grip. The bust origamied back together a bit, then stopped as Optimant data continued to scroll and flash.

"I want to see it," Purifyre grated.

All at once Mason's cam view and the backdrop of cascading data were lost as his son yanked the caul away. Some hair went with it, as well as skin and eyelashes.

"We have to zero it," Mason said, rubbing the sore spots on his face. "We can't let Rhodes or Starkweather gain access to it."

Holding the cybercaul behind his back, Purifyre looked morbidly amused. "Rhodes won't pose any problem. And Starkweather will have other things to think about shortly. You can seal it after we know a little more."

Guests were suddenly filtering back into the bedchambers; that was odd, because at that point they should have been overindulging in food and drink and currying favor with the grandees, none of whom were present. The newcomers included a master glassblower from Fenway Spit, with his embroidered drapeau and gaiters; a money changer from Fiddlehead, identifiable by her masses of gold bangles, chains, and anklets; and a dashing trader-explorer sporting dueling scars and the kind of razor-edged fighting fan used on Narnia Atoll. An unlikely mix, the rest drifted toward the Science Side units. The guards, both Aquam and engeneered, were too busy gaping at the computer to pay the new arrivals much heed.

Something's happening, Mason thought, feeling it in his bones. He looked at Purifyre. "Why did you express an interest in seeing some of our teknics? What do you want with them?"

"Nothing more than to make Aquamarine a better place," his son answered so levelly that Mason could almost believe him.

"I want that, too, Son. But theft isn't the way—even if you could steal the gear, which you can't." He fumbled at the back of his cummerbund for Ghost's stealth interceptor of a knife. "Please believe me. Look: here's what you mean to me."

Mason started to pull his long, fine-groomed fall of auburn hair around to sever it, but before he could, Purifyre caught his right wrist. "I won't accept it. What I want from you and the other Visitants I'll *take*."

Purifyre started by wresting the dagger from Mason's unresisting grasp. The flechette pistol was out of convenient reach even if he had wanted to use it. "You can't take anything from me, because there's nothing I'd withhold."

Purifyre sneered. "We'll just see about that when—"

He broke off as a white dawn surfaced in the west, arching harsh daylight over Lake Ea and in through the terrace doorway.

Survival training cut in, and Mason turned his head away to spare his eyes. But Purifyre was far less dumbfounded than Mason would have expected. After a brief glance at the nova erupting somewhere over Amnion, he whooped in elation. *"Terrible Swift Sword!* Terrible *Swift Sword!"*

Taken by surprise—allowing himself to be, at any rate—Burning was enthralled, even though the Descrier wasn't a very accomplished kisser. He wasn't exactly an expert himself, though he had learned a little something over the years. What Souljourner lacked in technique, in any case, she made up for in enthusiasm.

The empty, silent old watchtower was perfect for it. In the light of the hand lamp Souljourner's wide-open smile showed canny, charming quirks. Her face had subtleties of expression he'd missed before.

There was nothing ungraceful about the big, vigorous body now; it was pliant against him, and its heat came through her clothes and his.

He was seized by a momentary fantasy whose force took him off guard—of making her his mistress—then he had a follow-up vision of Haven's reaction to her negotiations being compromised by Burning's use of Grandee Rhodes's living gift as a concubine.

And the Exts? Aside from gripes about RHIP, there'd be mutterings about mudfuckers and graffiti about squaws. That wide, generous smile of Souljourner's would evaporate fast, especially when Zone and his pit crew started in. The thought of it got the familiar, hated heat rising in Burning's cheeks.

"Souljourner, wait," he said. "Souljourner, repair to a neutral corner!"

Disentangling from her wasn't easy. She was either a power lifter or someone who'd done more than her share of manual labor. Her eyes fluttered open.

"Burning? What?"

"We have to return to the Attendance."

Instead, she wet her lower lip and slid it along his. The heat and moisture and softness of it nearly wiped away both his conscience and his resolution. But he resisted her.

"You belong with Commissioner Haven," he told her.

"No, I belong with you, sweetwurst."

"Hey, I'm *not* your sweetwurst! I'm nobody's *sweetwurst!*"

Her face wasn't at all bland, he saw, especially as it clouded up with hurt and resentment. "You reject me? All I did was keep faith with the writ of the Holy Rollers. See for yourself."

She was suddenly trying to press on him Optimant dice like the ones he'd confiscated from Zone onboard the *Sword*. "This isn't about any damn-fool dice!"

Souljourner's eyes went wide. "Damn-fool? You think I've demeaned myself? Enthralled by your Visitant glory?" Her slightly prognathous jaw set, and the sunbleached, unbroken brow line flared. She indicated his face. "You see yourself as a love-poem hero with your crook'd snot-chute and that maculated skin?"

"Hey, I know I'm not much to look at, but—"

"Then you deny the powers of the Holy Rollers? You wish to ruin their magic for me? I'll show you the courage of *my* convictions!" She rubbed them across his lips. "I bind my destiny to the sacred galloping dominoes of my ancestors."

Burning surmised that she was tempting fate and had the distinct impression that she was binding his destiny to the dice as well. "Parade *halt*! I wasn't insulting you!"

Souljourner brushed the dice hard against her own lips, shook them angrily in her big-knuckled right hand, and sent them tumbling across the floor with much more force than was required. They bounced toward an open section of floor where paving-stones as big as sofa cushions had been pulled up for some kind of excavation work. Pools and puddles of cruddy water had formed in their absence. Hearing the minute *plish, plish* of the Holy Rollers as they landed in the muddy water, Souljourner gave a miffed grunt.

"Souljourner, calm down," he started to say when an infernally harsh cross-shaped ray of light slanted down into the Peelhouse.

Burning gaped, and Souljourner cried aloud.

The light poured through the cruciform arrow slit on the western side of the tower, halfway up the cylindrical wall and just above where the rotted remains of a wooden fighting parapet hung from sockets in the stonework. Then it grew fiercer, brightening the musty interior like daylight. From the angle of the light Burning knew that its source lay in the sky, but there was no telling how far off.

Bigtimer, he said to himself.

"Cover your eyes," he told Souljourner. "Don't look!" For any foot soldier a Bigtimer event was pure dread. "Take my hand!"

CHAPTER
THIRTY-FOUR

Dextra hoped that her retinas hadn't been fried by the expanding fireball in the western sky. Aquam wails and caterwauling had broken out all around her, interspersed with outcries from AlphaLAW staffers, shouted orders from the Exts, and elephantine trumpetings from the Manipulants. Dextra curbed her fear of being blind in the middle of an unfriendly fortress. The next minute or two could mean peace or war, success or failure, life or death.

An Ext sounded off. "Commo with the *Sword* is out. All freqs jammed."

NeoDeos, Dextra thought, did he have to alert every Aquam in Wall Water to the bad news? If she had been aboard *Gamma-LAW*, she would have kept her eyes shut, improvised a blindfold, and found her way to sick bay by touch. Now, however, she took her face from the crook of her elbow and blinked her eyes open. Smarting, kaleidoscopic afterimages blotted out much of what lay in her field of vision, but she could make out her surroundings, if only as a surreal shadow show.

Two women who had been near a birdbath were laving their eyes with cupped handfuls of water. The Exts looked to be in much better shape; with them it was a reflex to duck away from sudden and intense light sources. Starkweather was moaning more in fright than in pain, his eyes being dabbed at by Wix Uniday, who was making solicitous sounds but sneering at his commander. Protected by nictitating membranes, the Manipulants' eyes had slitted under their bony brows, but the engeneered Goliaths were otherwise unaffected.

People were starting to falter into aimless motion. While

Dextra was deciding what orders to issue, someone beat her to it.

"Exts, listen up! Make ready to turn to."

She squinted to see Zone, one hand on his pistol grip and the other making a field signal—a flat-handed halting motion followed by a clenching of the fist—at waist level, where the Aquam would take less notice of it. Tonii had drummed into her what the more common motions meant, and this one told the Exts to stand fast and await imminent action orders. Dextra gave Zone the palm-down wave that meant "lie doggo; take no action." Instead of acknowledging, he fixed her with a stare, waiting to pass judgment on her next move.

Whatever the cause or nature of the space detonation—Cybervirus or Oceanic—it was already dwindling, and Old Spume was gazing uncertainly at Dextra. "Was it LAW's alien enemies?" he asked from the back of the overturned table he'd ducked behind. "Was it these Roke you speak of?"

Dextra tapped her plugphone control touchpad, then held up her end of a conversation with a dead ear unit. "Captain Quant? You say a meteorite struck off the west coast of Scorpia? Yes, I will return to the ship immediately for a full briefing. Yes, Commissioner Starkweather will move to the *GammaLAW* aboard his *Jotan* shuttle. Haven, out."

Zone took his hand off his sidearm, and the rest of the Exts followed suit. Starkweather was nearly raving. "*Meteor?* Is Quant insane?" But Uniday managed to shush him.

"Exalted grandees, noble Aquam friends," Dextra announced regretfully, "we must take our leave somewhat earlier than planned."

She cudgeled her brain to recall if there was a field signal that would tell Zone to send people to fetch Zinsser, Mason, Burning, and anybody else who'd wandered off and get them into the *Jotan* or down to the quayside ASAP.

"Grandee Rhodes," she continued after a moment, "I'll do my best to return later tonight to view the liftoff of the *Dream Palace* if at all possible."

Rhodes nodded by rote. "A meteor," he said, gazing west. "And your starship failed to observe its approach?"

Starkweather opened his mouth to speak, but no words emerged.

Rhodes watched him for a moment. "Before the light you were saying that your starship had scooped a portion of the Amnion into the sky. Contact your starship, Commissioner. I wish to learn how the Oceanic reacted to being so rudely invaded."

Dextra cut her eyes to Starkweather and then back to Rhodes. So much for brazening it out, she told herself. Still in possession of the headset unit Starkweather had given him, Rhodes could discover at any moment that commo with *Terrible Swift Sword* was down.

"Grandee Rhodes," she said quickly, "if you require our public announcement systems to reassure your people or have need of our medical personnel, we'll be standing by."

She turned toward the dungeon, preferring a shuttle ride to a walk back through a darkened Wall Water and a ride down the funicular car. The missing shore party members could always be summoned from the safety of the *Jotan*. But more and more Aquams were turning their attention to her now that the explosive event was fading, and there looked to be no easy way through their closed ranks. Backed by their personal guards, the Ean grandees were silent and wary. Dextra was plotting subsequent moves when her smooth kiss-off was drowned out by ear-jangling waves of sound emanating from the *Jotan*'s vibrating skin. A mechanical voice suddenly issued from external speakers designed for agitprop use.

"Commissioner Starkweather, return to the shuttle at once! Instruments show total destruction of *Terrible Swift Sword*. Seismics and SAT data indicate extreme Oceanic disturbance and atmospheric turbulence off the west coast of Scorpia. Commissioner Starkweather, please return to the shuttle at once."

Dextra's eyes opened wide enough to clear her vision of afterimages. Starkweather, still dazed, gaped up at his shuttle as if it had addressed him in classical Greek.

"Impossible!" he said. "Pitfall—that's what was destroyed. But *Terrible Swift Sword* has to be there somewhere! The Oceanic couldn't possible have the power—"

"You're undoubtedly right, Buck," Dextra interrupted, taking one of his hands between hers, which had begun to shake uncontrollably. "The only way to straighten this mess out is to return to *GammaLAW*'s Tactical Information Center." She dug her nails into his soft, clammy palm.

Starkweather winced but got a grip on himself. "Your ship . . ." His voice broke, then he cleared his throat and went on. "Yes, by all means. Return to *GammaLAW*." He waved his quivering hand to the human officer of his Manipulant body-guards. "Fall your troops in!" He turned to Rhodes to add, "I'll speak to you as soon as—"

"You've infuriated the Oceanic!" Rhodes screamed at him, wide-eyed. "And you've paid the price with your starship! Arrogant, foolish Visitants! I'll have all of you killed!"

"The *Sword*'s gone, sir," Roiyarbeaux told Quant. "CIC isn't sure what happened—" He broke off to listen to his headset. "SAT sensors indicate sea-to-low-orbit stepped leaders and other signatures of charged-particle discharge along the path of the tether."

Stepped leaders from sea to sky . . . reverse lightning? Quant asked himself. "Then it wasn't a Roke attack?" he asked with a mixture of hope and astonishment.

"No, sir. The *Sword* deployed Pitfall, and the Oceanic chewed it up and spit it back at the ship."

His instant assumption had been that the Roke had returned and caught Captain Nerbu with his waders down, which had suggested that the *GammaLAW* and maybe all of Aquamarine were due to get the hatch dropped on them in the form of an all-out attack. But a bolt from the Amnion, right up the Pitfall tether, was equally dire.

Lieutenant Gairaszekh was officer of the deck, but Quant had the conn. "Sound general quarters. Make ready to get under way and tell the engine room I want full power *now*. Set material condition one. Have the special anchor detail stand by."

It occurred to him that movement and the emissions signature of battle stations and full engine power might paint a target for some sort of Oceanic targeting detector, but logic and instincts agreed that he risked losing both the ship and the shore party if he didn't act quickly.

The bridge watch got to it, not smoothly but much better than they would have before he'd run them ragged with drills. "Instruct all picket boats to go to general quarters. Tell the Air Boss to launch everything we've got. Tell signals I want a patch to Commissioner Haven."

"Signal bridge reports transmissions being knocked out of the air," Row-Row Roiyarbeaux said.

"Tell them to try for a microwave link to the landing craft at the beach. Failing that, attempt to make contact by blinker light."

Daddy D was blaspheming on the Ext command strand, getting his troops to battle stations and telling them to put *Big Tess* from their minds and watch for boarders, saboteurs, and incoming ordnance. Quant checked with flight ops, but there was no tracking any surviving aerospace craft through the static the explosion had caused, not to mention the EMP damage to some of the radars.

Kilobar, the bosun's mate of the watch, was standing by with Quant's battle equipment. Quant hated the idea of being hampered by helmet and survival/load-bearing vest but was obliged to set a good example. He shrugged into the vest and jacked his hardwire to the helmet's headset, leaving the earcups flipped open to hear what was going on around him as well as what was on the circuits.

With Gairaszekh to maintain good order and Kilobar keeping a sharp eye on the helm, Quant got the hook out of the mud and got the SWATHship moving all ahead slow. General quarters mobilized pitifully little firepower: the CIWS chaingun was enabled, but small arms and especially the Exts' stuff were about everything else he had. The charged-particle cannon lacked its special capacitor banks, while Turret *Musashi*'s mutha-guns were still on the hangar deck. Starkweather had withheld the missiles, heavy sonics, and lasers that should have constituted the remainder of the *GammaLAW*'s weapons loadout.

Now all that was gone, along with the Exts' organizational armor and artillery and half the materiel needed to fit out the ship properly. Let alone Burning's Exts and the tens of thousands more in the AlphaLAW expedition and *Terrible Swift Sword*'s AF crew.

And no time to mourn or bemoan.

Quant reminded himself that he had tremendous on-site punch in the form of the picket boats and CAPflight aircraft. He and Haven could cope with the Aquam. The inscrutable planetary power Starkweather and Nerbu had provoked with their Pitfall stunt was several orders of magnitude more to be feared. More the pity that Starkweather hadn't been onboard *Big Tess* with the innocents he'd gotten killed.

The flight deck was busy getting the two standby aircraft into the air. One was a troop helo with a ready-reaction platoon of Exts. The other was a fan-in-wing close attack jet for fire support. The Air Boss was griping that her little air wing had only comped-maser communications—RATEL being jammed—but she understood that the birds had to be sent aloft. She had a worse headache to confront in any case: Starkweather's *Jotan*. If he refused to abandon it, he'd have no safe place to set down except the *GammaLAW*'s overworked flight deck. Or Haven's iceberg . . .

"We'll find someplace to stash it," Quant said. He didn't add that those stranded on Aquamarine might soon need all the *Jotan*'s firepower and more.

His ship had suddenly entered a crisis of the kind that made for maritime legends, the kind that were far better imagined than lived. Beyond the hostile Aquam, the threat of the Roke or a rogue AI, the world-rattling enigma of the Oceanic, and the unpreparedness of his ship, there was a crisis that worried Quant most of all. With *Big Tess* had gone the spare zero-point-energy drive that was to have powered an Aquamarine-built starship.

There was no way home and no way onward.

Soon—if they hadn't already—the ship's company would realize that Periapt's reach didn't extend to Aquamarine any longer. And when they reacted to it, Chaz Quant would have to be ready.

CHAPTER
THIRTY-FIVE

"Don't you dare threaten me," Starkweather was trying to warn Rhodes, while other Aquams, frightened and angry, yelled him down.

AlphaLAW and the grandee were alike, Dextra saw. They affected to know everything about everything, to be masters of all situations, to be fearless, bad, and bulletproof. Their bluster and ego goaded them on. But when the moment of reckoning came, they cracked, leaving the crisis for others to suffer or solve.

"Gentlemen, ladies," Uniday said, smooth and unrattled as ever. "We have the power to overcome any enemy—even the Oceanic. You grandees would do well to keep in mind just what our weapons and machines are capable of."

"Your principal machine is gone!" Rhodes hurled at him.

"Your intent was to anger the Oceanic!" the Ethnarch Klobbo hollered, shaking a finger at Starkweather. "You wish to save yourselves the trouble of slaying the Aquam and usurping our world for LAW!"

His elite, the Infrangibles, were forming up around him. Watching them, Fanswell's Fanatics closed ranks about their liege, and Dynast Piety IV's Diehards followed suit. Rhodes's household guards glanced to him for orders; Wall Water's armed guests were clearly weighing their options. Casually, the Exts drew in around Dextra. Even Zone looked serene.

"Go to, She-Lord!" grated Paralipsio, ending with a hawking spit in Dextra's general direction. His gray-leotarded nymphs moved his vestments out of the way as his guardsmen, the Kill-mongers, stood by him.

Accusations and threats flew among the Aquam factions. Lengths of edged metal appeared, swords and daggers partially drawn from scabbards, while more exotic weapons, such as finger blades and multicurve hunga-munga axes, peeked from cases. Rhodes came to his senses enough to screech, "Who bares steel without my permission? *I* am the master here!"

Fanswell was following it all through the brass ear ampliphone two body servants held for him. "It's out at last," he said now. "You style yourself first among grandees! Perhaps because you're in secret league with these Visitants."

"No one's in league with anybody," Dextra said, trying to head him off. "My offer was made to everyone. LAW's help in exchange for your cooperation."

"*You* are the ones who need help," Fanswell returned.

It was Klobbo who uttered just the words Dextra didn't want to hear. "I say that these Visitants would be much more likely to show good faith if they were to abide here with us awhile."

Hostage taking was SOP for most Aquam grandees. The half dozen potentates had come to Wall Water only because close and powerful allies of Rhodes—supporters whose death by political sacrifice would tear his domain apart—were guesting at Fanswell's castle, at Klobbo's palace, and so on.

A messenger hurried in to whisper in Rhodes's ear. At the same time a gargantuan Manipulant showed up to report to the officer in charge of Starkweather's bodyguard. The Manip obviously had come from the detail left behind in Rhodes's bedchambers to guard the Science Side modules. The separate conversations were lost in the din of an incoming SCAR helo, its X-rotor locked for fixed-wing operation and its afterburners throttled wide. The single-seater Scout-Attack-Rescue made a fast, arcing pass over Wall Water. Many Aquams shrank away from the noise and the body-shaking vibration.

"Buck? The shuttle's waiting," Dextra hinted.

Starkweather and his people began moving toward the dungeon.

Rhodes thrust his messenger aside and yelled, "What's to keep them from smiting us from the sky once they're away? No one leaves until I have thought this through, especially in light of the revelation that the Visitants have been trifling with the sacred bust of Altheo Smicker."

As Dextra tried to puzzle out what Rhodes was blathering about, a pitch pipe sounded. Two ranks of Militerrors, with shields and drawn swords, appeared in the doorway to the dungeon. More stood into view on the walls and other vantage points, leveling sling-guns.

The visiting grandees froze. Her Unconquerables assuming protective postures around her, Fabia Lordlady banged on the mandseng serving table with her scepter, a stylized torch of Pre-Plague alloy, perhaps the garden decoration of some long-dead Optimant. "We agreed to act by consensus!"

Dextra had never even been inside the LAW War College, but she saw immediately that it was time to start rethinking a withdrawal to the beach and the picket boats. Aquam weapons were low-tech, but the keep had been built for siege defense. Rhodes's warriors stood a good chance of slaughtering the fewer, lightly armed LAWs.

Starkweather, obsessed with his invincible *Jotan*, didn't care about casualties. Pointing at the Militerrors blocking the dungeon's main doors, he railed at the Manipulants. "Drive those mudfuckers out of my way! Clear a safe path!"

One reason Manipulants had been created as a separate species was to constitute a force answerable only to LAW's top command, uninterested in and unsympathetic to the will and appeals of an annexed population, immune to mainbreed subversion or proselytism. Their human officers were heavily indoctrinated and behaviorally modified to ensure that the Special Troops couldn't be turned against LAW.

The officers therefore obeyed Starkweather's command without hesitation, growling and gargling orders in their corps's harsh combat-*gullah*. The behemoths whirled into action with startling speed. Forming a security wheel with Starkweather at the center, they ranged the wide-bore muzzles of their bloop-guns across their fields of fire as they began to convoy him toward the keep. The large one who had come from Rhodes's bedchambers moved to cover the withdrawal.

"Buck, wait!" Dextra pleaded.

"Starkweather, don't be a fool!" Uniday called out.

"You see?" Rhodes stormed at the other grandees. "They don't even trust each other!"

Aquam of all stripes fell back as the Manipulants advanced on the dungeon's door, but the Militerrors stood their ground.

When the lead Special Trooper reached the Militerror captain, it simply reached out to shove him aside. The captain chopped at the thick wrist with his cutlass, but the Manipulant's soft-armored sleeve stopped the slash. The Manip put a hand the size of a ramball mitt on the captain's shield and sent him flying back, along with the Militerrors standing behind him.

Sling-guns came up, *naginata* halberds came on guard, and shields formed a lock with cutlasses protruding. A score more houseguards pressed into view on the stairway. Starkweather, hunched down amid his Gargantuas, seemed to realize that there were a lot more troops contesting his way than he'd thought.

The acoustically active skin of the *Jotan* reverberated with its godlike voice. "Commissioner, be advised that indig troops have taken up positions inside the building. Prepared incendiaries and caustics are waiting to be poured down to oppose your return to the ship. Shall we disperse these people by force? Commissioner Starkweather, can you answer?"

"Halt!" Starkweather's order made the mainbreed officer of the Manips gobble another command. The Special Troopers were surly about it but checked their advance.

Seizing the moment, Dextra jumped in. "Buck, we can resolve this peaceably. Just cease and desist for a minute." Starkweather slowly straightened to his full height, facing her as she called to the grandees. "Stay your hand. I'll show you why I make a better friend than an enemy. Buck, order the Manips to lower their weapons—"

A sling-gun quarrel carved to moan for psychological effect went dopplering past her right ear. Because she was looking at him, Dextra saw it strike the mainbreed officer of the Manipulants in his unprotected throat, drive through—fletching and all—and topple him over backward.

In Rhodes's bedchambers Mason wondered how his son could be so sure that the *Sword* was at the center of the energy event. Not that Purifyre was necessarily wrong—what else could it have been but the starship, destroyed by the Roke?—but how had he known that *they* were out hunting?

Emotionally short-circuited, Mason couldn't devote much thought to it. He remained in a frieze with Purifyre, who was controlling his right wrist while waving Ghost's fighting dagger around. Dazed, the Militerrors and Manipulants didn't even notice Mason's predicament.

But Mason noticed now that even Purifyre could make mistakes. The demonic shine of the explosion had distracted him, and he'd forgotten or was ignorant of the fact that Mason's left hand could reach the flechette pistol. Like the Ext dress uniform holsters, Mason's formalwear one had a sharp backward rake that canted the grip forward for a weak-hand draw in emergencies. He reached across his waist, fumbling.

Sensing the movement, Purifyre broke off his glorying. But by the time he looked around, Mason had the 'chettergun trained on his unguarded rib cage.

Purifyre didn't grapple. "I must leave. You're coming with me."

It was Mason's one chance to shoot. Instead, he lowered the barrel. Purifyre quickly applied pressure to his left wrist, aikido fashion, and pulled Mason around to a position where getting a shot off would have been impossible. The ease of the move convinced Mason that Purifyre hadn't been at his mercy, after all; Purifyre had merely been testing him and waiting to make a point. Mason didn't object when Testamentor relieved him of the 'chettergun.

The Optimant computer light show was fluxing and exhibiting fitful, varicolored flashes as a result of electromagnetic pulses generated by the destruction of the *Sword*. With the armored housing open, the computer had been seriously damaged. Even so, the holofields were displaying software evolution timelines and names that made Mason's blood run cold even in the Big Sere swelter.

AbomiNation	DoomsData	Firegod	EarthMover	BeelzeBug
PathoLogic	Apocalyst	CorrupScion	HorrOrgazm	HellRazor

The names of most infamous Cyberplagues—conjured by a *Pre-Plague* computer.

Purifyre turned to the terrace as someone whistled to him. It was one of Wall Water's servitors, spinning an upraised index finger—a go-ahead gesture. From above, where the VIPs had gone and the *Jotan* shuttle sat on the roof, came screams and gunfire.

"Wait outside," Purifyre warned, pushing Mason toward the terrace. "And guard yourself. I don't want you hurt."

As Mason backed away, muddled, Purifyre drew black bands from his robes and slipped one around each upper arm. They held white pom-poms like the ones Testamentor was already wearing and the DevOcean cultists were sometimes known to affect. Quickly surveying the room, Mason realized that the mismatched guests, domestics, and entertainers who'd drifted in moments earlier were now also wearing pom-poms, as were the trio of votaries who had been watching the Science Side modules.

On the terrace Mason tried his plugphone, dimly thinking that someone would know what the shooting upstairs was about, but every freq blared painful, howling jamming. From the doorway he watched Purifyre make his way to where the Manipulants' human officer and the Militerrors' captain stood. From under his robes he drew a pistol the likes of which Mason had never seen. The hefty grip of knotty white yussa wood showed Aquam craftsmanship but also ergonomics of a more sophisticated sort. What had to be receiver, action, and severely truncated barrel looked to be finely machined LAW work. Its bore was tiny, a millimeter or two; the muzzle was a preposterous thirty millimeters across.

Not wanting to see anyone hurt, Mason cried, "Dextra Haven wants to deal fairly with the Aquam—all of you, not just the grandees!"

The words didn't stop Purifyre, but they alerted the officer of the Manipulants. He raised his downsized bloopgun pistol as Mason screamed for him to hold his fire. Giving a loud whistle, Purifyre ducked behind a column as a sling-gun quarrel thwacked into the officer's side. Another pierced his forearm, and a third sank deep into his neck, just behind the left ear.

Mason moaned as the captain fell. At Purifyre's signal, the intruders produced weapons from concealment. More people appeared from behind the drapery concealing Rhodes's private passageway to the throne room. Sling-gun quarrels and darts zipped at the guards from every quarter, along with pellet rounds and even some glass incendiaries.

The close-range fire was accurate, aimed at vulnerable spots in Militerror armor and exposed Manipulant flesh. The first thick flights got every Aquam guard; all three Manipulants took head and eye hits. The raiders kept firing as wounded men and Special Troopers reeled, trying to counterattack.

A bolas round fired straight upward by a blinded Manip minced a chandelier all to hell, raining blown glass, wax, burning wicks, and brass down on the creature, the science modules, and Rhodes's big round bed. A Militerror's ululiphaunt signal horn blatted to silence as a pile-head quarrel from an arquebus-size sling-gun drove through his breastplate.

Another Manipulant, terribly wounded, tried nonetheless to get the science units under his arm and keep them from the indigs, as they had been ordered to do. Purifyre leapt at it, holding the peculiar handgun. A two-meter plasmic jet sprayed out of the docked muzzle; backblast vented through venturis in the receiver mechanism. The charge formed a narrow cone from the bore, ten centimeters wide when it struck through the Manip's woven armor. It pierced the Special Trooper through, blowing it and its combat coverall open with steam from the creature's own flesh and throwing up a pall of scorched meat.

The blast set another smell in the air as well, a vividly memorable one Mason couldn't quite identify.

The last Manip flopped back on the bed with its eyes open in death. Purifyre broke the pistol's action, but nothing but heat waves rose from the breech—no spent casing or even smoke. It was only when he inserted something the size and shape of a ration caplet that Mason understood what the weapon was.

They were the coilgun igniters that had been stolen from the *Scepter* survey team that final night onworld, when Boon had died in the waves and Mason had abandoned his wife and unborn child.

CHAPTER THIRTY-SIX

Whereas she had been yielding and eager in Burning's arms a minute before, Souljourner now resisted being handled.

The Bigtimer glare didn't leave him any time to give her instructions in surviving a strategic strike. Pulling her head to his shoulder, he hauled her to the foot of the western wall, where any retina-burning glare and hard radiation scatter from the shooting-loop window just above would be minimal.

"Shut your eyes," he told her. "The light's poison!"

He kicked something and heard glass break—the lamp—but there was no time to worry about it. She wasn't cooperating, and she was no bantamweight. He worked a leg trip on her, eased her fall as much as he could, and did his best to cover her head and upper body with his own.

"There may be a blast and heat. Stay down!"

Choruses of shrieks and outcries filtered through the slit windows, but there were no LAW voices that he could discern.

When she realized he wasn't assaulting her, Souljourner stopped struggling. He buried his head against her, aware of her body but with all appetite forgotten. He waited for the shock wave, wondering if it would bring the Peelhouse down on them. He counted the seconds, trying to sort things out.

He concluded that the Roke had launched a follow-up attack. The question was whether the *Sword* had been caught napping or whether the explosion was that of an enemy vehicle. Tapping Flowstate, he did *atman* breaths and silent moebius chants.

The shock wave didn't come. Neither did what he feared more: another superstar event. He tried his plug, but there was static on all freqs. The Aquam tumult, meanwhile, grew louder.

Souljourner shifted under him, then sneezed dust. "Is the poison light gone?"

He eased off her. "For now, anyway. I've got to get back to my people. Are you coming?"

"Burning, I'm a pariah and abomination in Wall Water. I've been given to She-Lord Haven. You *can't* abandon me here!"

"Nobody's abandoning anybody," he told her. "We just have to find the door."

The light had faded, the lamp was lost, the Peelhouse was dark, and his night vision had been thoroughly dazzled. He groped at the wall, planning to feel his way around to the egress, and promptly stumbled over some rotten pieces of plank.

"Bide a moment," Souljourner said. She moved away, splashing around in the fetid puddles, her clothes rustling and her chatelaines chiming. "My Holy Rollers are here somewhere."

Burning huffed, then softened. "Hold on, I'll make a light."

It was no sweat adjusting his 'wailer in the dark; he could field strip and repair it blindfolded. He edged forward, feeling his way to a puddle, and told her to move aside. Then he sprayed the water with his pistol's acoustor.

A wavering region of deep azure sonoluminescence fizzed up in the water. The 'wailer's sonics caused cavitation and collapse, imploding bubbles and releasing heat that broke liquid molecules into highly energetic carbon fragments that emitted blue-wavelength light. It was a standard bivouac and beer-bash gag.

Souljourner cocked her head at the 'wailer for a few moments, then went back to splashing and feeling around for the dice, keeping well clear of the sonoluminescence puddle. He concluded that after a certain point minor Visitant miracles lost their novelty.

She kicked off her shoes and drew her skirts up through her jingling chatelaine belt. Sonoluminescence glinted cobalt off the pale hairs on her bared thigh. Burning couldn't help staring. A pair of legs like those could support the weight of the world, he told himself.

But he was the one who was supposed to be shouldering

burdens, and he'd barely elicited enough light to see the walls by. "I've got a fix on the door," he said. "Let's go."

"And leave my forebears' dice? Sacrilege!" She groped and found the broken lamp, then pulled out some sort of low-tech lighter made of flint, checkered striker disk, and a slow-match wick. The wick caught on the second try, and she relit the lamp.

Burning adjusted the 'wailer back to its antipersonnel setting. "Souljourner, I don't have time for this."

She gave it up, rising and wringing water from her skirts. "The Rollers are all I've got of my family, save these." She showed him the tiny bibelot and thumbed the soft-tanned drawstring pouch at her throat.

"We'll come back for them."

She heaved a sigh and led the way with the lamp. As Burning threw open the rusted iron door, he heard an angry ruckus of voices from the central dungeon. The trench-mortar report of Manipulant bloopguns made his hackles rise.

Eight or ten people were fanning out from an inner bailey as they came his way across the lawn. They'd been moving stealthily, but seeing him now, they yelled, "Take him!"

Dextra felt like a music box ballerina as she pirouetted in shock to see who had fired the sling-gun quarrel. She heard herself yelling for people to stand down. The killing had begun, but all-out war was still avoidable.

Where the quarrel had come from stood a Militerror, right enough, but he had his heavily chased and gilt carbine at port arms, still cocked. To his left, below and behind him, someone else was drawing back into the shelter of a stela, but not before Dextra saw who it was: Essa, Purifyre's big, silent companion. The Human Enlightenment woman held a longrifle sling-gun, its slack cable proving her guilt. She now wore, along with her votary robes, white pom-poms on each arm, held in place by black bands.

The Militerror standing at port arms was beginning to glance behind him, trying to search out the source of the shot, when Dextra heard the explosive hollow popping of Manipulant bloopguns. Before her eyes the Militerror and the flower-decked bravo standing next to him flew apart in an instantaneous eruption of body segments. It was as if an invisible threshing machine had rent them.

She felt Lod dragging her out of the way and knew enough not to fight him. With their officer down, the Special Troopers had no one to restrain them.

She considered commanding the Exts to cut down the Manipulants, but it was too late for that. The Attendance went raving mad. The ground was littered with magnificent wand masks and vizards that were trampled to junk in seconds.

More belches from the bloopguns made Dextra hunker low; bolas rounds were neither precise nor choosy. Something new and costly from ordnance R&D, the round might better have been called a pinwheel. It was a circular fan of monomolecular filament spokes that were weighted at the ends by depleted transuranic bobs. The way the load was packed put a ferocious spin on it when it was fired. The monomol strands, infinitesimally thin but all but unbreakable, went whirling and scything through virtually anything they encountered.

The flat slap of sling-guns punctuated the bedlam as Aquams returned fire. All Dextra could do was cling to Lod and cringe against the round or broadhead quarrel with her name on it. Then a painfully strong grip had her other hand and drew her upright. Zone had the piercing look of strong Flowstate.

"If the Manips clear the tower steps, we can follow," he said. "If not, we'll have to try for the boats." He held his pistol close in the other fist, aimed at the sky. His signal whistle was out, hanging around his neck.

There was no arguing with his logic or, Burning being absent, any need for him to assume command. Nobody was going to take the time to hear Dextra out about Essa having fired the opening round.

"Very well," she told Zone, "but no more killing. Use your sonics."

His sneer showed what he thought of her orders, but he did thumb his selector switch. "Trigger up! 'Wailers only!" he shouted. "Self-defense fire on my command only!" The Exts passed the order along and complied.

Many Aquams, especially Rhodes's retainers, had closed in on Starkweather's group over by the entrance to the centermost keep, but the GammaLAW contingent was unhindered for the moment. Rhodes was incoherent with anger. The remaining grandees were glancing around at each other, still uncertain about who to side with.

Ethnarch Klobbo's Infrangibles were clumped in around their charge, clanging down the beavers of their helmets, bringing up their shields, and swinging out the hinged flanges, panels, and guards of their boilerplate suits. In four or five seconds they'd assembled themselves into a mobile armored shelter around their liege. The testudo formation moved to retire from the field, swords and sling-guns projecting.

Starkweather's guards had fought their way into the dungeon and onto the staircase. The bloopguns' semiauto volleys were chains of hollow propulsive pops that came as fast as the Manips could squeeze them out.

The Aquam on the lawn wanted no part of the fray. Three of the Manipulants—led by Scowl-Jowl, the seven-foot-three bruiser who'd been guarding the science modules in Rhodes's bedchambers—had taken cover in the tower's doorway to serve as rear guard. Dextra couldn't tell if the engeneered fighters were showing fire discipline or merely husbanding their ammo.

Through the tower doors she could see constant flashes of bloopgun fire. The main body of Manipulants was moving up the steps fast and would arrive at the *Jotan* momentarily—in seconds if the bolas rounds didn't carve away the staircase first.

Dextra looked by habit to Lod. "Do we go with Starkweather?"

It was Zone who answered, shaking his head. "They haven't made it yet."

No sooner did Scowl-Jowl and the other two rear guards retreat into the stairwell than the whole dungeon shook. Scowl-Jowl threw himself back through the doorway with animal-quick reflexes, but the troopers' fellows weren't as alert or nimble. One never got out, and the other made it only a third of the way before the death trap fell. There were furious yowls from the Manipulants still at the bottom of the stairs as a vast ferrocrete deadfall crashed to the floor, blocking the interior from view.

Up above, the *Jotan*'s engines were revving high. Dextra got the distinct impression that it would lift off shortly with or without Starkweather.

"That cuts it," Lod said. "It's the boats for us."

"The *Jotan* could hover down and pick us up right here," Dextra pointed out.

"It won't," Zone predicted.

The lower body of the Manip caught in the doorway had been crushed flat as a bug under a sledgehammer, its head and upper arms squirted clear by the deadweight. Scowl-Jowl appropriated a second bloopgun from a dead comrade's claws and dodged away, searching wildly for an exterior route to the roof. House-guards rushed the creature, shooting and hacking.

Scowl-Jowl's battlesuit turned sling-gun darts and stopped slashes, but the creature was too hampered by the weight of eight men piling on him to get off a shot. The Aquam were preparing to slip blades into his eyes, throat, and other vulnerable spots, when he took off one man's hand with a bite, head butted another guard, and began to surge free. The entire swaying, thrashing mass reeled one way and then back the other and over a low planter and toppled off the edge of the lawn. Except for one man who had the sense to let go, all fell out of sight into the darkness below.

"Maybe we can signal for VTOL extraction, but not here," Lod said, though the SCAR helo hadn't returned after its single flyby.

"Lead the way, Colonel," Dextra told Zone curtly.

At his voice and hand signals, Exts in dress uniform broke their security wheel to form up in a diamond squad formation. Zone knew precisely what had to be done, and his people obeyed him exactingly. Dextra understood then why the Exts put up with his malice, sadism, and NoMan soul. In combat he was survival personified. He was life itself.

With the sound of dead and dying Militerrors in his ears and the grunts of the slain Manipulants still echoing, Mason was staggered by the memories hammered home by the smell of a burned igniter charge.

Among Optimant ruins and wreckage the *Scepter* team had found the remains of a hybrid coilgun prototype: a three-phase, multistage electromagnetic system with which the Beforetimers had been tinkering when the Cyberplagues hit. In need of increased orbital launch capacity to hasten their expansion across the Eyewash system and beyond, the Optimants had settled on a mass driver.

Both the stabilizing spin and the terminal acceleration of the coilgun payload came from the multistage electromagnets; initial thrust was supplied by a hydrogen charge compressed by a pump tube, which in turn was driven by a mixture of methane, air, and an exothermic. The pump-tube aerosol was set off by an igniter—what Hippo Nolan had taken to calling a "shotbox"—which employed what amounted to detonator caps. To test the coilgun, Hippo and Farley Swope had tooled up several of the former and several hundred of the latter.

Testing was stopped cold when Captain Marlon's foolhardiness at the Styx Strait brought down the wrath of the Oceanic, but an igniter had been among the items stolen from the survey team. It remained to be seen how Purifyre had come by it and, more important, who had fashioned it into a firearm.

Now wasn't the time to ask, however. With human and engeneered guards down, Purifyre's raiders were moving with commandolike composure. Some posted watch at the doors, others had secured the two Science Side modules, and a few were changing clothes. Purifyre came back to Mason with the reloaded detonator cap pistol in hand.

"We have a few moments." He pointed to the cybercaul and the R&D whatty. "Cull as much Beforetimer knowledge from the bust as you can."

The Optimant computer was still blazing erratically, but the sounds of bloopgun fire were growing in intensity. Purifyre's stare stayed fixed on Mason. "We have time."

"What makes you think that *Terrible Swift Sword* has been destroyed?" Mason said.

"I don't know for certain that it was the starship, but it stands to reason. The ship had lowered something from itself into the Amnion. Whatever happened, it simplifies my mission here."

"What *mission*?" Mason pressed.

His son gave the computer a jut of his undershot chin. "Harvest what information you can. No tricks—fair warning."

The Aquamarine place names and Cyberplague designations were still looping amid streams of unintelligible and seemingly random data. One matter seemed clear from the program-evolution diagrams, however.

The Plagues had to have originated here—on Aquamarine.

Three rounds in the ten ring," Wetbar remarked approvingly. The broken-matchstick pattern ringing the pool of blood was one

CHAPTER
THIRTY-SEVEN

In the upper garden, under the cacophony of the *Jotan* revving for takeoff and the Aquam up in arms, Zone blew three sharp blasts on his signal whistle for recall. Burning, Ghost, and several more unaccounted-for Exts had to be warned of the pullback, even if that meant drawing Aquam fire.

Zone motioned to his severalmate, Wetbar, who had loaded a color-coded magazine into the grip of his 'baller. Wetbar fired three miniflares out over the rampart of Wall Water, where they opened into yellow-red warning clusters. The color combo would alert the crews of the beached hydrofoil and hovercraft to maintain position.

Zone touched a forefinger to his temple in mocking salute to Dextra. "Swing ass, lady." She would have hated him for it if she hadn't been so grateful to have him along.

Drawn by Zone's whistle, Wix Uniday materialized nearby, LAW flechette pistol in hand, nearly getting himself toad-cranked. There was no time to ask how he had slipped away from the fighting in the keep. Dextra chalked it up to the fact that "slippery" was Uniday's stock-in-trade.

Rhodes had heard the whistle as well. Halfway across the lawn, he climbed atop a maoriwood loveseat to point to the flares. "Haven, what betrayal is this?" he called.

"They're summoning an attack!" Lintwhite bayed. "Hold them there, or reinforcements will—"

Dextra didn't hear the rest. She was suddenly shouldered aside, deafened in her right ear by world-shaking explosions. Zone had rushed her out of the way and fired once, twice, three times. When she tried to beat down his gun hand, he avoided her nonchalantly.

"Three rounds in the ten ring," Wetbar remarked approvingly.

The body sprawled in the widening pool of blood was one of the Dynast Piety IV's Diehards. A cocked sling-gun of sorrel mollywood lay near the corpse. Another Diehard had holes in his armor at chest and groin; blood leaked from the joints. He was collapsed back over the remains of a tall urn of pink marble that had been shattered by one or more of the .50-caliber rounds.

"I told you—*sonics*!" Dextra fumed.

Zone shrugged. " 'Wailer didn't work. Padded armor muffles the soundchain, I guess."

She looked back to the first Diehard and recognized the breastplate's jeweled mammellieres and chrome grillwork. It was, or rather had been, Knocknet—the Dynast Piety IV's brash nephew, to whom Dextra had been introduced less than an hour earlier.

The Dynast's own moan of grief and outrage broke the shocked silence that followed the shots. Piety IV pointed to the LAWs with his ceremonial flail. "Assassins! Anathemite-makers! Slay them all!"

Dextra couldn't tell what anybody was saying. All the other Aquam were screaming, too, or rushing to Knocknet's body, or scrambling over one another to attack or get out of the way. The indigs were united at last, if only in their hatred for Dextra's party.

Lod's pull at her arm added to her disorientation. He swung her around as another sling-gun bolt fired by one of Fabia Lord-lady's Unconquerables zipped past to shatter on a flying buttress of Optimant ceramic. Lod held his 'baller on the man for a sustained dose of sonics, but it did no good.

The Unconquerable did a fast reload. As he dropped a barb-finned dart into the firing channel, the galvani stone in the weapon's buttstock caused the long bands of land-mollusk muscle to draw the elastic slings to full cock.

Zone, frugal with his ammo, dropped the Unconquerable with one round, blowing bark and kindling off the yussa tree behind his target. He pushed the Exts contemptuously. "Delta-V, back to the cable car."

* * *

The single-grain Lava-Land prangbang had clouded Zinsser's brain, but he still had the presence of mind to turn his face away from the expanding nova in the west. Appalled to realize that Ghost had not done the same, he grabbed for her wrist, only to be fended off. He saw that she had donned some sort of wraparound visor of high reflectivity.

His plugphone was pouring violent static and distortion into his ear, and he was overcome with nausea at the realization that Pitfall's tetherdrop into the Amnion had somehow brought about the destruction of *Terrible Swift Sword*. The enormity of the situation and the bile and prangbang rising at the back of his throat finally broke his control and he puked against the walkway's retaining wall while the skyfire died away.

Ghost was still staring at the fading light when he surfaced, wiping his mouth and pushing himself erect. The wraparound visor's mirroring was fading to black.

"All commo's down," she said, repocketing her touchpad. "Had to be the Roke." She lifted her head in the direction of Rhodes's chambers. "We'll get Mason, then link up with Haven and the rest, high boost all the way. Are you ambulatory?"

Zinsser, ever avid to prove his prowess, held himself erect. Keen on saving Ghost's life, he had put Mason from his mind, as well as the Science Side modules and the Roke tissue sample he was carrying in his fanny pack. Now that *Terrible Swift Sword* no longer orbited, puissant and invulnerable, all of it seemed to belong to a past life.

"It wasn't the Roke . . ." he started to say when notes from ululiphaunts sounded, backed by gongs and drums and whistle pipes. With them drifted howls and shouted commands.

Ghost pointed to the skin-diving knife he was wearing in his cummerbund as a ceremonial weapon. "Be ready to use that. Stay primed. No killing unless we need to."

She checked the top of her right kneeboot, then cursed softly on apparently not finding what she was looking for. Opening her holster's thumb break, she put a hand on her pistol but didn't draw it. Although Zinsser considered it beneath his station to bear firearms, he was furious that Haven had not had

the sense to surround him, the mission's main asset, with
heavily armed Exts.

Vigilantly, they began to retrace their steps along the promenade. Houseguards and Militerrors had left their sentry posts.
What Aquam they saw were dazed and terrified. A millship
owner who had fainted was being revived by two manservants.
The owner wore a glittering sword and his hirelings had fighting
hatchets, but all three shrank back from the two Visitants.

Zinsser was glancing up a darkened breezeway that opened
onto the terrace when Ghost shoved him behind a fluted stone
column.

He immediately saw a troop of assorted Aquam trotting down
the promenade straight for them. While the indigs were a mixed
lot—chambermaid, gardener, and two guests in teknic-artisan's
regalia—all were sporting pom-pom armbands and carrying
sling-guns, catchpoles, nets, and fighting sticks. They were
also strapped into makeshift scrounged padding and protective
headgear.

Ghost drew her 'baller and Zinsser unsheathed his skin-
diving knife. He had used it countless times but never to fight,
and the familiar ergonomic grip felt alien to his hand.

The pom-poms' leader was yelling, but Ghost didn't pause to
listen. She went into a two-handed shooting stance. Zinsser
flinched, expecting a muzzle blast, then realized she was using
sonics instead of deadly force. The gardener faltered and fell;
the rest kept coming. One fired a knob-tipped capture-quarrel
on the run, but the shot went wide.

Ghost's loyalty to her brother and to mission directives
against harming indigs had its limits. She set her feet wider,
stiffened her forearms, and let fly with a hardball slug. The big
clip-eater gushed flame, rocking Ghost in spite of her stance.
One of the teknic-artisans stopped in his tracks, a neat black
hole appearing in the houseguard breastplate he was wearing.
He took another two steps before pitching onto his face.

Teeth gritted and scars drawn back, Ghost recovered without
flinching. Her second shot missed, but all the interlopers were
scattering for cover now. They gave no sign of advancing, but
neither did they make any move to break contact and withdraw.

Ghost sized up the darkened breezeway. "We'll have to out-flank them. Through there, for a start."

"Forget Mason!" Zinsser stormed. "I say we worry about ourselves!"

She curled her lip at Zinsser. "In that case, make your own way out, or throw yourself on the Aquams' mercy."

Moving crabwise, she backed into the breezeway, glancing to all sides. Zinsser's dancing pumps barely made a sound on the pavement as he caught up. A capture-quarrel, caught in a stir of wind, bounced off a wall, narrowly missing him. Still, its bounce was informed by a thought-provokingly solid *whack*.

The tight diamond formation was not as well coordinated as most Ext operations. The detail had been drawn from various units and its members were not all that accustomed to working together. More, it was a withdrawal from hostilities under unresolved circumstances, not a firefight. Dextra's assigned Peace Warrantors, trained for law enforcement and civil disturbances, would have been more suited to the work, but they were cosmic dust now.

The Exts were cool and adept. They held their white-moment competence through adversities and traumas that would jar the untutored out of synch.

Wix Uniday wasn't as deft, but he was keeping up. Dextra suppressed feelings of inadequacy and concentrated on not being a burden. Divesting herself of the half-body exo and stilt-boots would have made life easier, but there wasn't time.

As the group proceeded along a shadowed cloister, the single-seat SCAR helo returned. X-rotor spinning this time, it made another, closer pass just beyond the ramparts. Off to the west, the *GammaLAW*'s contingency aircraft, a STOL fighter-bomber, lit the sky in a holding pattern.

The night sky held additional lights. It looked as if the SWATHship's Air Boss had launched everything available—four fixed-wing, three rotary, if Dextra recalled correctly. If a show of overwhelming air power could make the Aquam back off, there might still be a way to salvage matters.

The SCAR had sideslipped by so fast that Zone nixed firing

another flare. "By the time he gets back here looking for us, we'll be someplace else," he growled.

They crossed a lawn from which a winding staircase angled away in the opposite direction from the great hall and Rhodes's chambers. Dextra almost fell headlong over somebody crouching on the floor—one of Paralipsio's apparel-caddies, flat on the chlorine-colored turf, hands covering her head. The way things were going, Dextra envied her.

"Down the steps and to the right," Zone told Kino, his point man. "Suss it out."

"Wait one," Lod objected. "Ghost and Mason were in the bedroom. Possibly Burning, as well."

"If that's the route you want to take, I'm game."

Zone meant the inner stairs, up which Dextra had walked with Fanswell when she passed him the doubloon. They lay across grounds crawling with Diehards, Unconquerables, and assorted bloodthirsty guests.

"We'll get to them some other way," Dextra said.

Lod swallowed his objection. Zone touched Strop and Kino, and they moved out by the numbers, leapfrogging past one another on opposite sides of the staircase.

The next landing was unroofed. As the main body of the group reached it, they heard the pitch of the *Jotan*'s vectored thrusters soar toward the ultrasonic. Glancing up, Dextra saw the shuttle lift clear of the dungeon's roof and swing slowly to starboard, rising meter by meter, nose coming around like a compass needle attracted to the far-off *GammaLAW*.

The troop-boarding ladder was still down. To it clung three Manipulants, one carrying Starkweather in his free arm and the other two firing at the roof. Dextra found it astonishing that even four had survived the firefight in the tower.

Sling-gun rounds and crossbow quarrels streaked around them, rebounding from the shuttle's composite skin and the Manips' battlesuits. Flung daggers and halberds arced up, some coming close. Starkweather was demonstrably alive, thrashing and clutching at the boarding rail, mouth open in a scream lost in the general turmoil.

Secondary batteries in the *Jotan*'s chin and belly turrets raked the roof with withering antipersonnel fire meant to saturate whole hectares of ground. Pieces of paving, shrapnel, and Aquam rained upward from underneath. While the suppression fire minced everything on the roof, it failed to penetrate the original, Optimant part of the structure.

Landing gear began to retract as the crew scrambled to get Starkweather and the Manipulants aboard. That done, the *Jotan* swung out over Lake Ea, impervious to any fire the Aquam could bring to bear, and making no attempt to extract Dextra's party. Instead, the aerospace fortress turned about as if it had forgotten something; then, hovering, it spat streams of even heavier fire into the dungeon.

Some of the fire chopped up the area at the foot of the tower. Starkweather couldn't know whether Dextra and the rest were there or not, but he wasn't letting either possibility deter his revenge.

The *Jotan's* fire flagged for a moment, then the shuttle swung farther back and slightly to the east, nose still facing the ramparts. From there, it launched multiple spreads of flares and popped off streams of illumination rounds that hung in the air, turning night into day.

At the same time, the *Jotan's* smart skin reconfigured. It tried to riddle the keep from a different angle; then it opened a second avenue of attack, emitting a blue-white lightning bolt at the great hall and Rhodes's chambers. The discharge flailed and coruscated around the tower, raising sooty deposits of immolated airborne particulate matter, but didn't so much as crack the Optimant ceramic. Nevertheless, Starkweather's weapons officer gave the place another go, and this time a microscopic spiderwebbing appeared at the base of the tower.

Over by the dungeon, three figures appeared from under a huge mollywood bench, making a frantic sprint to escape the free-fire area—a flock of Ean nobles, but not members of Rhodes's court. They were two-thirds of the way to the stronghold's chapel when they seemed to run into an area of visual distortion as chaingun flechettes ricocheted from the tower's side. All three fell clumsily, riddled and dying.

Dextra gnashed her teeth. "*Ecce,* we'll be in a vendetta with every important family on Lake Ea!" She ordered Lod to give her a flaregun. "I want the color-code that means 'Retreat, go away.' Starkweather isn't likely to comply, but we at least have to *try!*"

Lod spread his hands, not having a flare clip. He was glancing at Zone when something caught his eye. "Impossible!"

Dextra turned. The biggest of the ancient Optimant antennas on the roof of a small keep had begun to move. Sloughing off dried moss and snapping the creepers and ivy draped all over it, the serrated disk was traversing and depressing its alignment, and coming to bear on the *Jotan.*

CHAPTER
THIRTY-EIGHT

Though he was shaken to the core, Mason's newfound affection for his son was the only feeling he could still identify clearly; that Purifyre was a thief, a revolutionary, or a terrorist didn't alter or weaken it. When the whatty's bulk memory unit was enabled, he pulled on the cybercaul.

Yatt appeared, as if a genie. "Don't try to strong-arm me," Mason warned, mouthing the words under the concealment of the interface hood. "You know you can't."

Yatt was uncharacteristically subdued. *"We are beginning to realize that, Mason."*

Mason was suspicious. "Why so compliant all of a sudden?"

"The destruction of the starship is perhaps a worse blow to us than to you. Most of the organic and inorganic resources of the GammaLAW mission are now gone. Our main matrix unit and all adjuncts are vaporized. This side of Periapt, the fragment of us within you is all that remains."

"Was it the Roke?" Mason asked.

"It was the Oceanic."

It sounded convincing to Mason and lessened the likelihood that the meta-AI had had anything to do with the evening's catastrophe. "We're back to what you promised originally, a mutually beneficial partnership?"

"You erred in assuming that we ever had any other kind. We will salvage what we can from this night and move on. We have already downloaded some Pre-Plague programs into the whatty. Now let us see what we can 'sift out,' as your son says."

With Yatt playing probe by way of Mason's neurowares and the caul, the computer's displays rezzed and steadied somewhat. The AI managed to get the central holofield to scroll various key words again—the Plague names and those of sites around Aquamarine. Then, all at once, a distant rumble began to shake the bedchambers. Starkweather's *Jotan* lifting off, Mason told himself. Perhaps his exit would bring about a return to sanity.

"Bring up Endgame," Purifyre demanded. "That's the key to everything."

Before Mason could try, Wall Water rocked to concussions and pile-driver pounding. Purifyre's grasp loosened, and Mason whipped off the caul. The act returned him to the real world so suddenly that he felt his grip on consciousness waffle. The former control complex was being mauled by air support fire from the *Jotan*.

Belting impacts at close range shook the Optimant ceramic structure. From the sound of things, some of the shuttle's discarding-sabot armor-piercing rounds were penetrating. One impact jostled the spacious room, loosing debris from the ceiling.

"Starkweather's trying to obliterate the place," Mason yelled. His mental image of Purifyre's death was unendurable. "Leave the modules, leave the mainframe! Scatter!"

"No," Purifyre countermanded. "We came for the units, and we're not leaving without them."

Fighting and fleeing were equally unworkable. Mason's wits, on the brink of shutdown, offered no solutions . . . until Yatt's Buddha face appeared before him.

"Put the cybercaul back on, Mason."

Mason shook his head. "What do you mean to do now?"

"We mean to quiet Starkweather's flying fortress."

Either Starkweather and his flight crew didn't notice the Optimant antenna coming to bear on the *Jotan* or they didn't care. Dextra, crouched down with the Exts and Wix Uniday behind a wall several hundred meters below and to the west of the dungeon, wondered if those in the shuttle were mistaking the antenna for an Aquam siege gyn that posed no real threat.

If so, they were wrong. Within a few seconds the *Jotan* commenced wobbling and yawing. Secondary batteries wandered off target to fire aimlessly; DEADtech directed-energy spars traversed and waggled convulsively. The aerospacer reeled and spun like a drunk shooting up a barroom, thrusters missing and then firing up again, control surfaces going through spastic, mismatched evolutions. A section of one wing bulged and then blew open as something detonated inside a weapons module.

The craft began to settle, and then, against Dextra's expectation, it suddenly righted itself, shuddering as if hypothermic. With a final tremor it commenced firing all weapons, aiming at everything and nothing.

Charged-particle beams crashed against the face of Wall Water, and chainguns sprayed the lake, peppered the ramparts, and shattered latter-day Aquam stonework. Rocket pods and missile racks served up everything they had. Air-to-airs drew fiery boiling roller-coaster courses in the sky as they tracked on the *GammaLAW*'s CAPflight aircraft.

The lunatic free-fire orgasm was terrifying enough to witness, but what made Dextra feel as if her stomach had dropped away were two silvery shark shapes, the size of SCAR helo fuselages, that fell free of the *Jotan*. Riding pearly blue blowtorch exhausts, the predators banked and dived for the slowly accelerating SWATHship.

If Starkweather's *Jotan* had maser communications working, it was refusing to acknowledge the SWATHship's hail. "Go to visual signals," Quant said.

Short of ordering one of the helos or fixed-wings in for a close pass and some warning maneuvers, there wasn't much else he could do. Judging from the way the aerospace gun platform was lathering Wall Water, Quant assumed that Starkweather was drunk, synaptshit, or both.

He congratulated himself on having had the good sense to stand the *GammaLAW* well away from the shallows. Starkweather's gun platform carried as much firepower as a cruiser, and Quant didn't want to be close by if the *Jotan* malfunctioned or misdelivered ordnance.

He had suppressed his own impulse to fire warning shots at the stronghold when IR/spectro detection confirmed that a skirmish was in progress. A burst of Close-in-Weapons-System fire would have gotten *GammaLAW*'s message across, but Quant didn't want to run the risk of hitting members of the shore party or innocent civilians. With the *Sword* presumably gone, this was no time to further enrage the Aquam.

Now he considered zizzing tracers past the *Jotan*'s canopy as a means of delivering a like message. Starkweather's ship was raking the roof, walls, and open ramparts with everything from nonlethals to DEADtech. If the Aquam hadn't found cover, the carnage was going to be ghastly.

A report arrived from one of the fixed lookout posts aloft, with its better view and superior optical equipment. "New movement on the central structure. What appears to be an antenna traversing to lock on the *Jotan*."

The antenna set Quant wondering if the Aquam possessed higher technology than they'd let on. But SIGINT immediately sent word that instead of a voice or visual link, the antenna had initiated an ultra-high-speed data upload.

"CIC reports *Jotan* has expanded targeting," Roiyarbeaux, Quant's lead talker, updated. "Acquiring lock on all friendly air and surface targets." He listened for a moment. "Radar signatures indicate he's now acquired *GammaLAW*."

Only a lifetime's habit of never speaking against a superior in front of subordinates kept Quant from hollering, "You gutless, misbred submoron!" What he rattled over the captain's battle circuit instead was, "All air and surface assets, pull back to screen *GammaLAW*." Ordering smaller assets to hurl themselves between the threat and the all-important command ship was the kind of necessity Quant had made his peace with long before. "Take evasive action," he continued. "Use all countermeasures except direct fire at the *Jotan*. I say again, no direct fire at the *Jotan*." For all he knew, Starkweather's finger was on a nuke and friendly fire would send the AlphaLAW completely limbic.

The picket boats on the beach lacked maser gear and weren't responding to the SWATHship's Fresnel lights and flares. Explosions were erupting around the quay, but visual obstacles made it impossible to see who was behind them. The boats would stay in position as long as any hope of evacuation remained, even if it meant suffering casualties.

Quant raised the engineering watch officer. "Make smoke,

maximum cover with infrared measures, I say again: smoke, max cover, infrared measures."

In moments smoke was pluming up in the ship's wake, whirled out in an expanding fog bank that was as dark as the night but lit with clouds of sudden intense heat. Whereas Quant had foreseen using the smoke system to blind shore installations, it was all at once the straw he grasped in desperation.

Hot spots in the aerosol smoke were made by randomly timed fuel-air exothermic reactions, very large and irregularly shaped, containing a range of temperature regions. The idea was that if heat and expendable transponder decoys didn't distract a targeting system's detectors, the exothermic nebulas would by approximating the signature of a ship more closely. The exothermic mist could be dangerous, and doubling back into one's own screen carried added perils, but it was better than waiting helplessly in the crosshairs.

The drawbacks were that antiship missiles had other targeting systems, and Starkweather was almost close enough to *drop* ASMs on *GammaLAW*, let alone fire them, which would leave little time to create a smoke screen.

The SWATHship was still better off than her picket ships and air cover. The small surface craft lacked smoke screens, and neither they nor the aircraft had anything like the *GammaLAW*'s EW countermeasures gear or missile-killing weapons.

The picket boats still afloat changed course instantly and went to flank speed, throwing up vorticed furies of smoky water. The two hovercraft blasted mist from all around their skirts. The hydrofoil's supporting vertical wings sliced Ea's wavelets but raised little wake. Her mere eight aircraft, maneuvering below combat speeds in such crowded, uncontrolled airspace, swung to take up defensive patterns around *GammaLAW*.

The CIWS gatling went on-line, though its IFF detectors could find only friendly targets. The *Jotan*'s countermeasures hid the shuttle completely, and there were too many fires at Wall Water and flares in the sky to rely on the chaingun's outdated IR tracking. Vera "Spanker" FarYore, Quant's acting gunnery officer, ordered the crew to slave the gun to her optical targeting.

Quant let FarYore know that he wanted antiship missiles at

the top of threat prioritization, not the *Jotan*. By good fortune, the CIWS mount was astern the main superstructure, so the multibarrel could lay in along the shuttle's anticipated trajectory while the props brought the SWATHship about to break for open water. To oppose the *Jotan* was untenable, but to lose *GammaLAW* now was unthinkable.

The trimaran slashed through the lake, her minimal waterline area resistance letting her gather speed quickly. The direct course was hemmed in by aquaculture holdings—floater rafts, pens, and crop pools—but Quant took his vessel into all of it with her turbulator fans at flank speed rpm, shoving an underwater river behind her.

Water rushed back from the bows. Squeeze foils mounted under the waterline funneled the flow toward the props instead of letting it crest inefficiently along the main hull stern quarter. Like an afterburner, the design tapped what would otherwise have been wasted power, adding to the *GammaLAW*'s frantic speed.

Quant's eyes darted from display to display in his visor in a relentless cycle: enhanced view of the lake ahead, sonar model of the obstacles below the surface, scan of sky radar plots, view of the *Jotan* relayed by microwave from a SCAR helo, the *Jotan* wobbling crazily over Wall Water with the mossy, ancient Optimant microwave dish aimed at it . . .

The *GammaLAW* entered a broad raft channel. At thirty-five knots and gaining, she'd be through the gauntlet in another twenty seconds or so and Quant would have the elbow room he needed to take evasive action. He monitored the captain's battle circuit. With eighteen seconds to go a CIC voice came up.

"*Jotan* launching multiple offensive missiles and is in discharge sequence for DEADtech weap—"

"Two antiship missiles incoming, starboard!" the CIC boss shouted, cutting the talker off. "I say again, two alpha-sigma-mings now in boost phase, inbound! Estimated time to target: thirteen seconds."

CHAPTER
THIRTY-NINE

With its missiles and rockets expended, the *Jotan* was tilting and dipping on its multiaxis vectoring thrusters again, as if it were getting sicker and sicker from whatever data the Optimant dish had beamed into it.

As Dextra watched, the weapons platform did a palsied wing-over and began a slow bank off to the east and the open water, in the general direction of the Upcusps and the river headwaters, its wings and smartskin fuselage reconfiguring as it went.

At four hundred knots and three klicks out it became a racing fireball, shedding flaming pieces and skyrocketing fragments. The *Jotan* left a vast rising tube of black smoke behind as it plowed into the darkling lake, throwing up alpine ranges of water, skipping, and breaking apart. A score of pieces skimmed the surface and subdivided, taking out what looked like twenty or thirty buoy markers' worth of flotants, mushroom laketrees, and pontoon corrals.

Still ablaze, some fragments arced into the air again. Smoke and flame scrolled into the sky, reflected in the lake water by the brilliance of the many flares and illumination rounds the shuttle had left hanging off Wall Water.

When the delayed clap and rumble of the crash swept over Dextra and the Exts, a new sound cut the night—the high buzz-saw din of a Gatling older and lighter-powered than those in the *Jotan*.

"The picket boats," Kino supplied. "Still on the beach. Holding their own, sounds like."

The hydrofoil *Edge* and the hovercraft *Northwind* mounted enough firepower to mow down whole armies of low-tech warriors. For that matter, either craft could raze Wall Water's less durable post-Optimant sections.

"Our way out," Dextra breathed, not letting herself sigh with relief. "Hope the funicular local's still running."

An Aquam war cry jolted her out of her momentary reverie. Another of the topknotted, rouge-faced bravos leapt around a newel post at Zone. As he came screaming, he hacked with a Chinese-style horse-cutter, a long-hilted broadsword with a blade like an immense bowie, as much poleax as scimitar.

Zone didn't so much duck the swing as relax and fall back out of its way, extending his gun hand and firing twice into the Aquam's middle as the assailant's weight threw him off balance with the momentum of the stroke. The muzzle blasts of electro-thermal chemical propellant set his sash and blouson afire and put the stench of charred flesh in the air.

Acting as if nothing had happened, Zone turned to Kino, who happened to be closest. "By the numbers, sound off. One."

Kino, salted in combat, barely batted an eyelash. "Two."

"Three," Wix Uniday pronounced, being next.

They sounded off in order up the steps. After Lod chimed in with six, Dextra laid claim to seven. There were just twelve of them and no way to tell where anybody else was even after Zone blew three notes on his signal whistle.

"Funicular's our quickest way to the beach," he said after a moment.

"I won't abandon Burning and the others," Dextra blurted.

Zone gave her a look more disturbing than any glower, pleased, as if she'd risen to bait. "Affirm. I'll go find 'um."

For "them" or "him"? Dextra couldn't quite make out what he'd said, and Zone's smirk said that he wanted it that way.

As he repouched the partially spent magazine and loaded a full one, he told Lod to assume the command. Kino, Strop, and Wetbar shifted around to go with Zone, but he motioned them back.

"Prepare to move out by the numbers," he said before leaving. "Odd numbers first."

He was even shrewder than anyone gave him credit for being, Dextra thought. She was an odd number, and her starting a row over Zone's sallying forth on his own would throw off the group movement and endanger everyone. Zone hand signaled Lod, then disappeared around the newel post.

"Lod, if he—"

Lod stopped her with an upheld palm. She saw from his expression that even in the Flowstate, taking command demanded everything he had.

"Odd numbers, move out!" Lod snapped.

Refusing a helping hand from Uniday, Dextra struggled into motion. As the odd numbers worked their way down the next course of stairs, she tried to concentrate on her footing rather than the memory of the glint in Zone's eyes as he'd reloaded and gone off in search of Burning.

None of the Aquam advancing on the Peelhouse wore the uniform of Militerrors, Diehards, or any of the other praetorians. Several were armored, all were armed, and all affected headbands decorated with white pom-poms. One was a woman in jester's motley who raised a carbine-size sling-gun as she bounded Burning's way.

Zanshin already had him in motion. With no escape in the offing and standing orders to avoid bloodshed, he bulldozed Souljourner back into the Peelhouse, then heaved the door closed just before the curt rap of a quarrel palpated its decayed iron facing. Peeking between the door and the jamb, he watched the bolt go skittering away into the grass; it was one of the ball-headed rounds the Aquam used to stun game or take live captives.

He leaned around the door just enough to angle the 'wailer's emitter horn into the open and shoot at the jester. It was a long-range shot, but the sound chains caught her right; her knees wobbled punchily, and down she went. He trained sonics on the next one in the skirmish line—a man in mascled armor and a casque helmet—but the 'wailer had no effect.

Figuring that toad-cranking the guy with a .50-caliber would start a war, he shoulder blocked the door closed. While there wasn't a length of wood solid enough to bar it, he did find one that could secure it temporarily.

The door threw off dust and rust as a war hammer or sling-gun butt struck it. "Surrender! We have the other Visitants captive! Open or we'll start killing them!"

Not even if they're telling the truth, Burning told himself. Few Ext hostage tales had good endings, and like most Exts, he'd long before made up his mind to take the knife or munch hardball before letting anyone capture him. He flicked the selector from sonics to lethal delivery, then shouted, "We have safe conduct from the grandees."

Someone pried at the door, the rusty metal making bull-fiddle noises. "Safe conduct to enslave Aquamarine? Fah!"

Glancing around, Burning decided that the cruciform shooting loops were beyond reach and too slender for him or Souljourner to slip through. "Lemme talk to my people if you're really holding them."

There was more hacking at the door. "We'll burn you out if we have to!" someone said.

A sword found a gap in the door and began digging and rending at the rotted remnant of beam he'd wedged in the bar rests. The door levered open a hand's thickness. At the same time Souljourner whistled to him and shined the lantern on a succession of shallow wall niches—a ladder of sorts, leading to the Peelhouse's domed upper level.

He motioned her to get climbing, then fired through the door gap into the ground beyond. The shot made an orange tongue of flame a meter long, sending clots of dirt and parched grass high.

"*Repair* before I mulch the lawn with your brains," he said, backing away and feeling for the climbing niches.

He had been ready to give Souljourner a boost and bear the lantern up himself, but she was already most of the way to the top story with the lamp's tin rim clenched in her teeth. The niches were none too spacious, so he reholstered the 'baller, fastened the thumb break, and started up.

At the door the pom-pom wearers were too determined to be put off by a warning shot. Maybe they were Shadow-rats, he thought as the pounding intensified. Why the pom-poms, unless they served the obvious function of letting the attackers tell friend from foe?

"Tricky climb," he said as he drew himself up onto a corroded metal catwalk that ran completely around the base of the dome roof.

"Not compared to the watchspire at Pyx," Souljourner said without bothering to explain. She raised the lamp and moved it around. The roof was made of roughly curved metal plates fastened to a wooden framework.

"Any idea who we're dealing with here?" Burning asked.

She shook her head. "They're no grandee faction I know of, though I've seen similar headbands on members of the Dev-Ocean cult."

The lantern's glow fell on a large double-shutter arrangement that stretched from the dome's base to its top. "Well, napalm my nates," Burning said, more to himself. "An observatory."

"The astriferium of an unknown Beforetimer," Souljourner contributed.

The dome was seated in a slotted track long since frozen with oxidation. It was a Post-Plague construction built by a surviving Optimant who, lacking long-range commo or a radio telescope, had perhaps sat up there watching in vain for a sign or signal of rescue.

"Our way out," Burning announced.

The shutters were latched with wooden pegs through a line of metal rings fastened to either side with screw plates, one course at knee height and one even with his chin. The pegs were silvery with mold and black with rot. The carbon-deposition edge of Burning's boot knife made short work of them, but that still left the shutters welded into their track.

He offered the ka-bar to Souljourner, but she refused it, showing him her all-around knife, which was more handle than blade. Short and wide, it was sharpened Aquam fashion: edge ground flat, then beveled from one side only for easier whetting.

"I am more accustomed to this."

"Looks good on you."

He set his foot on one shutter and took a two-handed grip on the other, straining. They budged apart a few centimeters, then stuck fast. The rumpus down below went up fifty decibels as the pom-poms hacked the improvised crossbar away and flung the creaking portal wide. Torchlight fluttered in the Peelhouse. Outside, Burning could hear what sounded like heavy weapons fire.

Souljourner threw herself in across from him, placing one sizable foot below his handgrip and putting her shoulder to the opposite shutter above where his foot was. The left shutter slid open a hand's width.

A knob-headed quarrel meant for Burning bounced off the catwalk. He put the 'baller's muzzle to a gap in the perforated decking and fired a round that broke a paving stone into fragments. Pom-poms pressed themselves to the wall or shrank back through the door, except for a man in Dyers Guild finery who'd gone down on one knee, torn by shrapnel.

Burning targeted his center of mass. "Drop the turnspit and nobody gets hurt."

The Aquam let his sword fall, and a comrade helped him away, but the rest stayed where they were. One winged another bolt up at Burning, but it, too, ricocheted.

He got back into position across from Souljourner, and they both gave the shutters all they had. There was a brief banshee aria from the track as the left shutter gave up a few more hand's widths. Burning pegged one more shot in the direction of the puddles where Souljourner had lost her dice, then went squirming through the gap. Triggered up in case some of the pom-poms had climbed the outside to intercept him, he emerged onto a narrow ledge of masonry that ran around the base of the dome.

That side of the Peelhouse lay beyond a wall it transected, a smooth one that extended to the base of the dome. He could see more terracing, Optimant architecture, and Aquam fortifications below, but immediately before him were only the crosshatched leaves at the top of a stand of whiffet trees.

He helped Souljourner free her snagged dress as she wriggled out into the open. They could both hear the scrabblings of attackers trying to ascend the wall niches. Taking his bearings, Burning saw that in the minutes he'd spent with the Descrier, the world had changed, probably forever but demonstrably not for good.

Far across Lake Ea *GammaLAW*'s Klaxons and whoopers were echoing, sounding general quarters. He could see the SWATHship making the water boil in her wake as she gathered headway. In the sky and on the lake were the falling, flaming remains of combat aircraft.

Gunshots and the mob din of combat echoed from Wall Water. The *Jotan* was gone from the dungeon roof, nowhere in sight, but to the southeast the flame and smoke of something big flickered off the waters.

He heard the roar of a powered Gatling gun down on the beach—a landing boat bringing heavy scorch to bear. By then there was surely a ready-reaction team on its way up to evac the shore party, but a lot of contingency planning had just become obsolete.

"They're upon us," Souljourner said without losing her composure.

Inside, a lozenge-shaped shield had come into view. It looked to be salvaged alloyplate and had a firing port next to the boss. Burning's sustained 'wailer shot caused it to vibrate but had no other effect. Ten centimeters from his head another flying black-jack quarrel bounced off the shutter.

There were gloved hands doing traverses along the catwalk, and from below came the clatter of more pom-poms queuing at the base of the niche ladder.

"How are you at jumping?" Burning asked.

She sheathed and pocketed her knife to keep from getting impaled on it and then toed the brink. "Better than I am at playing victim."

He nodded. "I know the feeling." Getting no response, he added, "I'll go first."

He launched himself in a modified tuck, arms extended and legs together—an emergency technique for when a night para-drop into a forest went wrong. He tried to protect his eyes while watching for a likely handhold—not an easy compromise. He'd have given a lot to be wearing a hardened codcup.

CHAPTER FORTY

While the *Jotan*'s cremation flames danced on the surface of the lake, Purifyre urged his followers to make haste. He clamped a restraining hand on Mason's whatty. "Discontinue the download. We're leaving."

His raiders moved with commando panache. Bearers had the Science Side modules in hand, and others had stripped the Manipulant corpses of weapons and equipment. Flares' light still shone on the ramparts, the lake, and the dam. The last of the *GammaLAW*'s aircraft were fluttering onto the wavelets.

"We are fortunate that the Jotan*'s systemry was hackable,"* Yatt sent to Mason.

Mason was too dazed to indict the AI; the Oceanic had destroyed the *Sword*, and now Yatt had destroyed Starkweather . . . He watched as a half dozen other raiders put aside their diverse costumes to clothe themselves in the raiment of DevOcean zealots, among them Testamentor, who now held a replica of the igniter pistol Purifyre carried. The phony DevOcean clergy not only had formed up to march but had brought out wicker hampers and two-man carry poles, the same sort of rigs in which Purifyre's other troops had put the science mods.

Misdirection? Mason pondered. Purifyre had said that there was long-standing enmity between DevOcean and Human Enlightenment.

Mason started to pocket the cybercaul, then found himself—at Yatt's insistence—preparing to slip it over his head once more.

"Enough, I said," Purifyre barked, taking him by the arm again.

Yatt was loud in Mason's head. *"Don the caul—now."*

Against his own will, Mason fought his son's grip.

"Perhaps you *should* wear it," Purifyre said dispassionately. He yanked the nanocircuited hood down hard over Mason's head and drew him close in a cross-wristed blood choke.

Purifyre's ceremonially gloved knuckles were like rock against Mason's neck as the boy gripped the insides of his collar underhanded and levered hard. Mason didn't resist. In that Purifyre's hold silenced Yatt, loss of consciousness had its benefits.

He tried to say "I've missed you, Son," but he couldn't get the words out. Seconds later all his problems went away.

"Two plots, I-band altimeter, Q-band seeker." The phone talker sounded very young in the instrument-lit darkness of *GammaLAW*'s bridge. "Multisuite homers, bearing two-niner-three. Showing profile match ASM *Herons*, threats close!"

"*Herons!*" Quant said. In a grotesque way it was a stroke of luck.

It was the prototype, multitetravolt *Seth* munitions he feared—whirling rings resembling giant flying energy quoits. They were shrewd, accurate, and easily capable of outwitting a ship's anti-ASM measures.

But Starkweather was a traditionalist. The *Herons* had a wallowy boost phase; if launched at speed, they would have gotten to his ship in five seconds flat. Denied the RATEL emissions fix that was their specialty, the pair of ASMs *GammaLAW* was tracking visually and by radar and infrared detection had a tentative fix on the ship and were closing on her along two separate vectors, lamping one another's smartskin to prevent fratricide.

"Full left rudder, bow thrusters hard to port," Quant rattled off. "Ahead emergency flank." With the same breath he was talking to Row-Row. "Designate targets to CIWS. Inform CIC: fire chaff. Sound 'brace for collision.' "

People grabbed for handholds as the added push of bowthrusters normally reserved for more measured evolutions shouldered the ship hard, making the turn faster but more jarring. Helm and lee helm repeated Quant's commands to affirm that they had been carried out.

He tried for a microwave cam feed from the SCAR helo again, but it was gone. Radar icons showed that it had been totaled by a nearly point-blank DEADtech bolt. The sky was a serpents' nest of twisting, boiling missile wakes as lesser ordnance launched from the *Jotan* raced after aircraft and picket ships.

Paying out hardwire behind him, Quant dashed out onto the port wing of the bridge with Row-Row hard on his heels. Crunching and tearing sounds could be heard as the *Gamma-LAW* tore into aquaculture floater moorings, fish pens, and hatchery pools, the usually stable SWATHship bucking as it breasted obstructions.

The explosions of chaff had gone off too late to confuse or deter the inbound ASMs, so the ship's emissions warfare officer had switched to survivable radar and was peppering the sky with continuous-wave pencil beams to deny the *Herons* the fix they needed. Decoy radars scattered pulses off the water surface to provide additional diversionary targets. The EW people had their countermeasures cranked up, but most of the ship's distraction-and-seduction 'wares were about as useful as tits on a Manipulant.

Lake water foamed and mounded behind the actuator disk propellers. A sargasso of pontoon walkways, sorting wells, and seine kraals tried to bar the ship's way, fouling her bows. As Quant watched, a flock of multiwinged somethings from a shattered cage zigzagged up from beneath the portside hull and went flapping off like released souls.

GammaLAW had raced perhaps twice her own length since coming onto her new heading. The time to impact was five seconds.

The CIWS sounded like an upchucking leviathan as it laid out a fan of jacketed transuranics in hopes that the *Herons* would blunder into some of it. Only every tenth round was a tracer, but the powered Gatling's fire looked like lava being hosed into the smoke-screened, flare-lit sky. Exts with boomer stocks or bipods braced were pounding out 20-mm rounds as fast as they could trigger them, their smaller yellow tracers skewing.

A chance flicker of light drew Quant's eye to a female form standing by the empty barbette where the mutha-guns should have been mounted. General quarters had rousted out some civil service type in crop-top and skivvies, but she was spraying her 'chettergun into the murk, refusing to go down without a fight. Quant approved until he realized that he was looking at Haven's gynander—Tonii—shooting with military expertise Quant wouldn't have expected from a genoddity. Even so, he put his revulsion aside long enough to think, Shoot true, Synthia, then got back to fighting for his ship.

Beyond the aerosol fog bank the sky was lit with impacts on the lake surface and in the air—kills of *GammaLAW*'s boats and aircraft by the *Jotan*'s other armaments, though the sounds and shock waves hadn't reached the SWATHship yet. Foggy beacons in the choking aerosol, two cometary lights were growing brighter off the portside fore and aft. Quant could see the dark ovoids of the missiles silhouetted against their own fiery exhaust as they veered, becoming as blindingly bright as suns vectoring in.

Clinging to a rail and waiting for his ship to explode under him, he lived a lifetime between heartbeats—until the *Herons* passed overhead, throwing brief noonday glare across the flight deck and superstructure, their exhaust spheres as big as barns. They were gone before Quant could so much as move, leaving him with a confused afterimage of two big cylinders, mirrored against lasers, that seemed to flee before their fireball tails. Their sonic boom hit a few seconds later, so loud that Quant was deafened in his unplugged ear. The turbulence of their passage swirled and vorticed a smoke screen, ripping apart thermal hot spots.

Quant watched the ASMs join formation and then dim and vanish as they sent their thunder across the lake. *Herons* were perfectly capable of coming around for second and third passes, but these two weren't interested—their poor performance was explicable only by the fact that the *Jotan* had fired them in a spasm.

Another flash lit the northeastern sky. "The *Jotan* appears to've been hit or suffered malfunction," the CIC reported. Then: "*Jotan* has impacted the lake."

"What downed him?" Quant demanded. "An *Aquam* weapon?"

"All indications are that the Optimant antenna scrambled the shuttle's 'ware."

Quant ran a hand over his bald pate. What had been loosed on Aquamarine that night? he asked himself.

Purifyre gave Mason a few more seconds of the blood choke to make certain that he wouldn't wake right back up. Years of contests and practical use told him exactly how far to take it. After all the years of anticipation he realized that he felt nothing—neither satisfaction nor guilt—at having his father's throat in his hands, only the cold recognition that another part of his mission in Wall Water had been accomplished.

He lowered Mason's body, made sure he was breathing regularly, then motioned to two of his followers, young men who had entered Wall Water in the guise of silk merchants. They unfolded a light cargo tarp.

"Leave breathing space at his head," Purifyre cautioned as the pair began to wrap and bind the unconscious man.

"You're bringing him with us?" Testamentor asked.

"I know it wasn't part of the plan, but neither was the eradication of the starship," Purifyre said, taking his father's plugphone and control curd.

Mason began to come around. Purifyre uncapped a mass of samaflax soaked in spirits of lethe, raised the caul, and plied the 'flax under Mason's nose while others held his mouth closed. Mason quickly dropped off again.

"And the Beforetimer caul?" one asked.

"Leave it on him." Purifyre raised the mouthbowl somewhat. "That will do."

The science modules had been loaded into wicker portage hampers fitted with shoulder poles. "Oh, for Optimant technology," one votary said, testing the weight. Pre-Plague modules that could do all the LAW versions could and more would have fit into a belt wallet.

Essa had returned, her usual dourness replaced by shining triumph. She gave Purifyre a fond smile, showing her filed teeth, and hefted her sling-gun. "Much bloodshed from one bolt. A veritable chain reaction."

"As I can hear." He gave her forearm an affectionate squeeze.

A votary toed the three Manipulant pistols and the little pile of drum magazines. "What of these?"

Purifyre knew he could use the Visitant weapons to further incriminate DevOcean, but the bloopguns were intriguing and powerful. "They'll be useful on the journey south and can be studied and analyzed later," he said. "Put them in with the science units—inside the casings." The handguns were much too dangerous to leave casually accessible.

"Purifyre, what disposal of *that*?" The woman who'd said it was indicating the Optimant computer, which was still strobing holodata across the bedchambers. "Shall we set it aflame or try the Visitant weapons on it? Or your heat shooter, perhaps?"

Purifyre shook his head. "Leave it be. It may contain information we'll need later on."

"Rhodes might use it now."

"He can do nothing without the cybercaul. Should we decide to destroy it later, Rhodes won't be able to stop us."

He turned to Testamentor, who was turned out in DevOcean sect raiment and waiting with his own contingent of cargo hamper bearers. He had donned a wig that matched Purifyre's hair and had pushed dental appliances into his cheeks to warp the shape of his face. From a distance he was a fair imitation. Any chance witness to Purifyre's uncreedlike actions could be discredited as having seen a DevOcean infiltrator who had come to stir up trouble for Human Enlightenment.

"You have rounds for your igniter?" Purifyre asked.

"Ten. More than enough, with luck."

"Use them all if you need to. Fire them where Militerrors will see." The wounds on the dead Manipulant would be ascribed to the detonator-cap gun Testamentor carried, further muddling the facts and diverting attention from Purifyre's departure.

"I might find occasion to use one of the Visitant belchers," Testamentor pointed out with a nod to the bloopguns. "That would draw notice."

Testamentor knew something about offworld weapons, and Purifyre trusted his judgment. "Take one, but mind it well."

Testamentor accepted the overlarge pistol but refused extra drum magazines. He was reasonably certain he could fire it but sensibly reluctant to muck about trying to reload it.

"Look sharp during your stay in Passwater," Purifyre said. "I'll see you back in the Trans-Bourne."

Testamentor clapped him on the back. "Then we take Aquamarine."

"Sky, soil, and sea." They crossed uplifted palms and traded a fervent handclasp on it; then their two parties set off from the bedchambers.

Testamentor and his spurious DevOcean worshipers would exit Wall Water by the most obvious means they could manage, bearing hampers meant to convince any observer or subsequent grandee inquiry that they had stolen the Science Side modules.

Purifyre sought a very different kind of departure. The biosynth modules had actually gone into the sacred twin chests called the Ark and the Coffer—containers in which hallowed Human Enlightenment artifacts usually were held: the Host of Compassion, a Beacon of Reason, and the Writ of Tolerance. But the Ark and Coffer Purifyre's followers brought to Wall Water were weighted with cobblestones that had been summarily heaved off the bedchambers' terrace.

Various other raiders had left to carry out their roles. Mason's inert body was bound to a six-porter shoulder pole, along with the delegation's tents, sleeping rolls, and other baggage. Purifyre surveyed his traveling group, including Essa, all of whom had removed their pom-pom armbands.

"Very well, let us wend the Embedded Way."

Wall Water still echoed with distant alarms, screams of pain and terror, and the occasional report of Visitant weapons. While much of the original plan had been discarded when *Terrible Swift Sword* had exploded, the operation had netted an unlooked-for prize in the form of the Optimant computer data regarding Endgame and other Beforetimer AIs.

Purifyre had every right to be pleased, but his moment of contentment was cut short by a powerful clap. Banging the air like a smith's hammer and conducted through the stronghold itself came a sound Wall Water had heard only on rare occasions.

"Rhodes uses one of your best presents to him," Essa grunted. "I'll wager he's wrong if he thinks the Visitants won't answer his volley with interest."

"More reason to put wings on our heels," Purifyre said.

His little company formed up and moved out along a branch of the Embedded Way. The secret transportation system lay for the most part in plain sight, though in fact it was as inaccessible to noninitiates as the Beforetimer computer had been to the Grandee Rhodes.

CHAPTER
FORTY-ONE

The dash for the funicular platform was harried and headlong but mercifully unopposed. Dextra ascribed it to the fact that houseguards and Militerrors alike had been summoned to the carnage at the dungeon, that confusion reigned and the grandees were occupied with violent feuding. She hoped so, at any rate; otherwise, it was because offworld stragglers were being hunted down elsewhere.

With Zone gone, the Exts were obedient to Lod's fire discipline constraints. Domestics and hangers-on fled before them, and the Exts' few brushes with armed resistance ended almost before they began. Across the face of Wall Water candles and lanterns had burned low or were already out. Lacking hand spots, the Exts appropriated torches, which provided a wider field of vision than what could be gained through the wide, tubular IR sights on their pistols.

They came full circle to the terrace of white and black glazed brick that fronted the funicular platform. Dextra had nursed the awful apprehension that the glass-walled cable car would be gone and that her group would have to climb down its track like a ladder, but while the grabs crew that had manned the upper platform had fled, the car was still in place.

The Exts secured the immediate area; there wasn't enough time to recon the overlooking windows and fortifications. Lod mustered the band in the shelter of a portico.

"Get aboard and secure the in-car grabs," he ordered two noncoms from Burning's company. "We can't leave anybody behind to work the ones on the drum. We'll cover you, then board by twos on my command. Madame Haven, stick with me, please."

Trapped in a situation he dreaded—command—Lod had gone strictly by the book. Except that the ranking officer was answerable for whatever went wrong, it was no fault of Lod's that a rough-hewn stone cannonball came shooting from what the offworlders had taken to be a downspout.

The coarse basaltic medicine ball bashed through the glazed brick mosaic almost dead center. It penetrated the underlying sand and cobbles, raising a shrapnel of brickbats and splinters. Dextra felt them pluck at her ruined coiffure, and something stung her cheek. Her fingertips found a warm stickiness there.

"Take cover," Exts barked, peering up into the darkness through the scopes on their 'ballers as they retreated to the portico. Lod caught Dextra's hand and dragged her to crouch behind the funicular platform. From there they craned to see where the stone ball had come from. The stronghold's Pre-Plague builders obviously had given thought to the fact that the funicular track was a pregnable feature. Aquamarine may have lacked gunpowder, but Rhodes's troops made good use of gravity.

"Maybe some scared groundskeeper yanked the release lanyard and made a run for it," Lod suggested. Dextra figured that whoever it was had made himself or herself scarce to avoid hardball retaliation. "Trigger up!" Lod added after a moment. "Covering fire as needed. Next pair, prepare to move out—"

He broke off as a rattle of iron and the twang of heavy slinging cable sounded high above. A trill of notched, pronged metal pierced the air; then a jolt like a hammer strike was conducted through the car platform. The glass blocks of the funicular's uphill end vanished in a shower of jagged shards and myriad needles. A four-meter-long demonic harpoon—all serrated hooks and barbed flukes—had been driven through the floor of the car and had penetrated the track beneath, its shaft hanging in the open air.

In response, every hardballer was nosing the air like a hunting dog waiting to be unleashed. Exts stared single-mindedly through their scopes. Dextra expected the next sound to be more basalt shot or a salvo from the 'ballers. Instead, what drifted down from a parapet high to one side were surprised howls and the gaseous pop of a bloopgun.

Then came berserk commotion, shrieks, and the angry-
anthropoid roars of a Manipulant. Around the side of a little
cement sentry box wriggled a trollish figure, moving fast but
with difficulty. Others came behind it, accompanied by shouts
and struggling. The targets were too intermingled for the IR
scopes to sort out friend from foe. For the moment the Exts
could only remain in cover.

Shortly a furious, thrashing knot of combatants flailed into
view. The knot rolled off the parapet, slamming into the glazed
brick at perhaps eight meters per second. The smaller members
of the cluster were a trio of Rhodes's household guards; the
larger one was Scowl-Jowl, the Manipulant who'd survived the
collapse of the dungeon.

Scowl-Jowl had contrived to land on the humans who had
obviously been struggling to stab him. They lay still now as the
Manip struggled to its feet, bloopguns clenched in both clawed
hands.

"It's Armageddon, Ghost," Zinsser whispered insistently,
watching residual flames from the *Jotan* lick and spiral off the
lake far below. "For the last time: forget Mason. We've got to
get to the beach!"

With Ghost leading, the two had broken contact with the
pom-pom squad and found cover in time to avoid the *Jotan*'s
indiscriminate fire. On the plus side, Starkweather's guns had
ripped up a detachment of houseguards who'd been closing in;
on the negative, the AlphaLAW commissioner had managed to
get himself knocked out of the air.

Edging around a pilaster, her pistol in both hands, Ghost said
over her shoulder, "Steady, Doctor. Almost there."

To add to the carnival of conflict in the stronghold, assorted
praetorian units had burst forth and were racing through the
place in search of their liege grandees. The main bodies of the
escort contingents had been left to mark time in gatehouse or
muster rooms because each visiting grandee had been allowed
only a few bodyguards to minimize crowding.

Most had missed being jacklighted and cowed by the explosion of *Terrible Swift Sword*, however, and now they were
making their way toward the upper terraces. Sometimes there

was hand-to-hand fighting when they encountered one another or Rhodes's men; sometimes there wasn't. To Zinsser, Wall Water had the nightmarish feel of several insect colonies churned together to provide a mad, internecine doomsday.

It was obvious that Ghost was enjoying his docility. He told himself over and over that there would be other occasions, opposite circumstances. He rubbed the palm sweat from his skin-diving knife on his cummerbund, then padded after her as she slid through a door and down the helical staircase that emptied into Rhodes's bedchambers.

The aftermath of slaughter and the strobing Optimant mainframe baffled them both. Ghost had the maddening self-possession to check the place, while all Zinsser wanted to do was keep running.

"Endgame, New Alexandria ... Hyapatia, Alabaster—this has to be some sort of fuddled fAIry tale," he remarked of the holofield data.

"Not coming from that machine," Ghost countered. Shifting the gun to one hand, she enabled her whatty and moved to the opened Smicker's bust.

"Just how long do you plan to stand here?" Zinsser asked a moment later. "This antique might go on spewing nonsense for hours. Days."

"You're right," Ghost said, taking him off guard. She thrust the memory unit into his hand. "Record as much as you can. We'll delta-V soon enough."

While he turned to the task, she crouched and used her short, flat knife to mark the stone with a pasigraph—an Ext symbol-ideogram message drawing.

"This'll direct latecomers to the boats for extraction," she explained.

"Only if they're Exts," he pointed out, keeping the memory unit trained on the coruscating computer.

"Any Periapt not with an Ext is either a captive or dead, Doctor . . ."

He completed the sentence she'd left hanging: "As you'd be." If instead of going after Ghost he had used the ultimate Pit-fall password he could have regained control of the tethered device and aborted the mission. Starkweather would be hearing his demands now, and Ghost, Haven, and all the rest would be jumping to his tune.

He flicked off the memory unit. "For your information," he began, when a tweedling sling-gun quarrel passed through the spot on which he'd been standing, rebounding from a portion of the armored bust with its broadhead blade snapped off.

Ghost, in Flowstate, was swift and precise. One-handed, she brought up the 'baller, sighted, and fired two measured shots at the houseguard who'd appeared at the top of the staircase. His body, folding back, blocked those behind him from firing.

The realization that the Aquam had meant to kill him sobered Zinsser as few things ever had. While the pom-pommed raiders seemed to have been out for live captives, Rhodes's troops were obviously under no such impediment.

"This way," Ghost shouted, backing toward the terrace doors.

"No, but—" Zinsser was pointing to the other door, in which direction lay the funicular platform and their most direct route to the beach. Then he saw what she'd seen: teams of sling-gunners, crossbowmen, and halberdiers filling the corridor beyond. An Ext in Flowstate with no fear of death might fight her way through, but Zinsser, never. She fired three more rounds that bowled over one halberdier and had his companions hugging the walls or floor.

Zinsser would never know the heights of white-moment fighting she did, but he damn near beat her out the door onto the terrace, avoiding the first ragged return volleys.

In seconds they were back on the familiar promenade, which was now littered with bodies. "This time that inner staircase, down to the beach escarp," Zinsser rasped. Answering signals came from galleries overhead and side porticos. Ghost didn't contradict him.

The drawbridge-thick door, however, barred or bolted from within, wasn't in a mood to cooperate. That left either going back through troops thronging onto the promenade and taking up firing positions above or withdrawing still farther to the private cul-de-sac balcony beyond the rock arch. Zinsser wouldn't have expected Ghost to opt for the choice that left no path of retreat, but she led the way onto the lovers' loge nestled between arch and cliff, threw open the door, and shot the bolt.

"Help me with the pew."

He resheathed his skin-diving knife and gave her back the whatty. Between them they got the stone love seat wedged tight under the decorative doorknob lever.

She extracted the half-used .50-caliber magazine and locked and loaded a full one. Out on Ea *GammaLAW* was under way, trailing smoke, but it was impossible to see if the landing boats were still on the beach.

Zinsser checked his plugphone. "Communications frequencies are still jammed. What're you doing?"

She was up on the low wall, running her long fingers across the salient of granite that protruded through the stronghold fortifications. "We can't stay here." She tilted her head to study the heights. "Bullets won't save us if the Aquam throw down stones or nets."

Zinsser could see that the crag's overhang, higher up, would shield them from attack from above once they were on it but not from sling-gun fire from the loge itself once the Aquam broke out onto it.

"You'd better do it barefoot," Ghost advised, gesturing to his dancing pumps.

By the time *GammaLAW* had surged clear of the aquaculture tangle and crewmen lowered over the bows had cut away fouled lines, netting, and wreckage, the smoke screen the ship had made had all but dissipated. Quant chafed at the delay but had no intention of dealing with additional antiship missiles while dragging a bridal train of waterfarming flotsam.

In the meantime he steadfastly refused Daddy D's near demand to get reinforcements to Wall Water. All commo was still jammed, and no one had any idea what a rescue force might face. Almost everything had been blown to junk by the *Jotan*'s spasm attack. Even Quant's personal WIGcraft gig and *GammaLAW*'s two launches had been pressed into service on picket duty, and they'd all been nailed by the aerospace weapons platform before it went down. Nor was there a single functioning aircraft aboard—not so much as a helipod.

All the same, Daddy D was ready to lead a party ashore in the rigid inflatables. Quant maintained that the immediate need for the RIBs was search and rescue on Lake Ea, and even Delecado couldn't argue with that priority.

The dispersed smoke screen left behind it a changed lake. The familiar lights of the picket ships and CAPflights were gone, but some smoldering wreckage and burning volatiles remained on the surface. Illumination night candles and lanterns on Wall Water's ramparts had burned out, but other fires lit the stronghold in a dozen places.

Lookouts aloft had begun to pick up signal blinkers, a half dozen and more, strewn across the face of Ea—SOS beacons from downed pilots' flotation vests, boat crews' life jackets, and survival rafts. A/V signals were the only way *GammaLAW* could tell floating survivors from the aquaculture clutter and battle wreckage.

Lookouts reported what was thought to be a capsule lifeboat snagged in or moored to the nearest beacon. Quant eased his vessel that way at quarter speed as he circled in on Wall Water once more. The bottom shallowed out under the beacon, but he could at least eyeball it, perhaps even put out a tethered ROVer. If there was any sign of life, he could use RIBs or even a Science Side raft to make the pickup.

But if there was no indication of survivors or if things at the stronghold suddenly went critical, search and rescue would simply have to wait. He couldn't leave Haven's party twisting in the wind while he spent the night trolling around.

He raised Delecado on the captain's battle circuit. "Tell your sharpshooters that I don't want any Aquam getting within a thousand meters of us."

"In that case you'd better take a look at what's standing out from shore," Daddy D returned.

It was the teamboat the *Edge* had chased away earlier, emerged from where it had moored in the shallows and making straight for the blinking beacon and the capsule lifeboat. Torches and other onboard lights had been lit. With visor imagery Quant could see the figures treading endlessly in the capstan cage tiers, being driven by bullyraggers with nettle lashes and coal-heated knouts. The galleon-size teamboat's railings were now fortified with bales, pavis shields, and sandbags, and the arms and armor of its embarked fighters were easy to make out. The weight of improvised defenses had it riding low and wallowing, its decks nearly awash.

At once a change in its upperworks caught Quant's professional eye. "Those bloodthirsty lunatics," he muttered.

There were clear and severe rules against unnecessary conversation on the bridge—and, worse, distracting the captain—yet Gairaszekh couldn't help saying, "A frigging ramming rod?"

Quant called for spotlights, and within moments the floating openwork mill was lit up like center stage. "A frigging Roman *corvus*, Mr. Gairaszekh," Quant amended.

It was a ship's boarding ladder straight out of the Punic Wars but bigger: a timber gangplank with a low railing, held suspended at a slight angle from a supporting pole by a block and tackle at its upper end. From under the extended end stuck an iron spike a half meter long, meant to penetrate and hold fast to whatever decking it encountered. The whole business was mounted high enough to let the Aquam reach the *GammaLAW*'s decks or perhaps the engine test area provided that they were willing to storm uphill.

"Tonight," Quant continued, "we're the Carthaginians."

"Synaptshit," the lee helmsman mumbled, shaking his head in disbelief.

"Put a tampon in it, sailor," Kilobar Keeler warned softly.

Quant had a sudden doubt. What if there was hidden shrewdness to the sortie? Aquams were feudal but savvy enough to suspect that most of LAW's resources in the Eyewash system had been lost. The SWATHship herself had been spilling thick smoke, and the indigs might have concluded that she'd been damaged or had a critical malfunction.

That left the mystery of how the Aquam, with little in the way of fighting vessels and no history of water battles to speak of, possessed and fielded an innovation from the mass galley-fleet engagements of more than three millennia earlier.

Quant took another look at the *corvus*—the "crow," probably named for its forged iron beak. Slotted toward the bottom so that it half straddled its supporting pole, it was built to pivot crudely according to the position of the enemy craft.

"He's making straight for that beacon," Gairaszekh reported. "Gonna grab our adrift."

"Like hell he is," Quant said.

CHAPTER
FORTY-TWO

Zone wove through the Wall Water grounds at a fast tactical lope, his 'baller ready. It was a savory feeling to be on his own and on the hunt: malign triumph and homicidal anticipation, freedom to lash out at will and without consequence, and *fuck* what the politicians wanted— no limits. He nurtured a deep Flowstate certainty that events had swung his way at last.

With *Big Tess* gone, the old rules were obsolete. He felt no regret for the loss of the starship and all its hands. Nothing less could have cleared the stage for a redistribution of power. That it meant long-term or even permanent exile didn't faze him at all. Bureaucracy would be plowed under by the stronger values of survival. No GammaLAW soft-ass would find out about much less fault the sanguine impulse he would vent that night. So long as he wasn't caught in the act. So long as whatever red-handed adjustments he made to the situation were concealed by the night's loosed rabidness.

Commencing with the murder of an Allgrave—step one in Zone's ascension to the title.

His life had taught him that complicated plans usually were a mistake and usually were driven by fear; his intentions in seeking Burning were simplicity itself: hit first, hit fast, hit hard, hit last. Purge any fear of death. Those were the things that had always worked for him.

He would find Burning and corpsify him, along with anyone who might stand with the Allgrave—including Ghost. Toad-crank witnesses if and as necessary. Get back to the SWATH-ship and keep the pot boiling. Without Burning—with Big 'Un Boudreau and most of the other command figures now converted to short-half-life fallout—Daddy D posed the only serious challenge to Zone's promotion to Allgrave. The general was nothing but a shot-out old reserves retread.

His fierce yearning to take by conquest all that Burning had—had but was too weak to use suitably, much less deserve—went so far back that Zone couldn't remember being without it. The possibility of its happening at last was only minutes old.

Concordance was a grave, but Aquamarine was a wide-open game. A few hundred Exts with modern weapons weighed in heavier than hordes of low-tech mudfuckers and mostly unarmed crewies and Science Siders. The underdogs could finally run the pack.

He trotted toward Rhodes's bedchambers, where he'd last seen Ghost; her presence would inevitably draw Burning. Reports of .50-caliber parabellums would have put anyone in the area on alert, so he was trying to avoid contact for the time being. But some kind of commotion was coming from the bedchambers. As he worked his way closer, he smelled strong hardball propellant in the corridor connecting the bedchambers to the throne room. The mess there told him that heavily shod Aquam fighters had recently crowded through. He was watchful entering Rhodes's suite, even though the indigs hadn't posted a rear guard.

One thing was plain: somebody had been doing some archeohacking of Smicker's bust and some hardball shooting as well. Oddly, though, one Manipulant had been shot up with something he couldn't even identify, an armor-piercing round, for all he knew. It had melted clear through the brute. Puzzling and therefore irritating.

He was considering the missing science modules, the dead Manips and Militerrors, and the absence of Ghost, Mason, and Zinsser when he spotted the withdraw-for-extraction pasigraph carved into the stone floor. He recognized it as Ghost's by the wavy line she had used to express the water icon. The likelihood that Burning was with her made Zone's teeth lock in anticipation.

Edging out to recon the terrace, he saw signs of battle on the distant promenade and what looked to be houseguards clustered at the far end where it cul-de-saced but no LAWs. The houseguards were jumped up about something, but they were crowding farther east around Wall Water's face instead of backtracking to the bedchambers.

He heard gunshots, but there was no making out their source. With the grandees' praetorians coursing through the place and no lead on Burning, it was time to go. He could only hope that a revenge-hungry Aquam would take the Allgrave out.

But two things needed doing before he left.

First he set his whatty on a control box and let it scan the blur of data issuing from the Optimant bust. HorrOrgazm, Dooms-Data, Endgame . . . He knew the words, especially the last one, which was connected to some apocryphal cure to the Cyber-plagues—a key to regaining power over all the Pre-Plague artificially alive machines. The readout was suggesting that Endgame was connected somehow to New Alexandria, obviously to the Optimant lighthouse there. He thought about it as he moved on to his second task.

He dug in one of his pouches for the class II demolitions kit he had brought along in place of medical supplies. Haven and Burning would have scatted in their skivvies if they knew he was packing a quartered spool of Oblitex-7 and four detonators. But events had shown how 'cess-headed Haven's peace-and-plenty approach was. Aquam were like anybody else; they'd get with the program once they got a boot up the ass, not before.

The charges were dark and flexible, like so many half-meter hanks of sticky gray polymer cordage. With no way to tell what the radiant computer's weak spots and vulnerabilities were, he simply pressed the det cord into convenient junctures and fissures where explosions would exert the most force.

Since friendlies were still in the area, it should have been SOP to leave the disarm features in place just in case some Ext happened by. But Zone removed the disarms and enabled the detonators' trembler function. Nobody was going to save the computer or avert the explosion.

Destroying it would eliminate any worries about the mud-fuckers accessing it. Maybe the Optimants had a line on weapons capable of subjugating worlds or stamping out the Roke. A man with such knowledge could rule the stars, and power of that sort was reserved for people like him.

He thought about the lighthouse again—and about Endgame. He would have to get his ass to New Alexandria, delta-V, even if it meant commandeering *GammaLAW* to accomplish that. Yes, New Alexandria would have to suffice for a start. If he was foiled along the way? Fuck it.

He lived for the fight, after all.

Burning crashed through the upper branches of a whiffty tree, took a bough beating in the middle tier, then managed to slow himself by catching handholds. A branch hit his right shin so hard that it would have cracked bone if not for his reinforced kneeboots. Brief handholds wrenched him around, and ultimately he ended up with his behind and one leg wedged into the crotch of three limbs.

Branches above him jounced and jolted to Souljourner's arrival. She was either a more practiced aerialist or, for all her size, just better with heights. The whiffty leaves screened them from the Peelhouse but offered no guarantee that the pom-pom-wearing raiders wouldn't take potshots.

Burning extracted his behind from the tree crotch and began to shinny down the gnarled, pebbly bole. He could hear voices raised in argument at the Peelhouse dome shutters, but no one came crashing down in hot pursuit. It showed good sense on their part, though they were bound to try to pick up the chase again.

All freqs were still jammed. "Which way to the dungeon?" he asked as Souljourner was moving down the tree, her legs flashing white in the fitful light of cressets.

"Why go there?" she asked. "Won't your band have returned to their boats?"

"If they weren't in the shuttle." Burning glanced at the lake. "They may be somewhere along a line roughly between the garden and the funicular car. I want to check Rhodes's bedroom first!" That was where Ghost had been headed with the pilfered cybercaul. "What's the quickest way there?

Souljourner pointed. "The bedroom is along that loggia. To the funicular is through the arch and down the stairs, then around to the left." Her tone made it clear which she preferred.

She wasn't about to shed tears about scraping Wall Water off her too-tight slippers.

Burning understood that his immediate duty was to Haven and the shore contingent. More, self-preservation demanded that he light out for the funicular. With the situation in such utter confusion, who could blame him for executing a quick recce of Rhodes's chambers? If refusing to abandon his sister was dereliction of duty, so be it.

"You don't have to come with me," he told the Descrier. "We can rendezvous at the funicular platform." Her hardened jawline and the V-ing of her sun-whitened brow told him to halt. "Then stay behind me and keep your eyes open."

He started off at a fast, vigilant walk; low crawls and silent stalking would eat up too much time. They followed the loggia to a ramp, ascended it to a spiral staircase, then negotiated a rampart outside the chapel. The few Aquams they encountered avoided them. In the distance Burning saw Fabia Lordlady being ushered along by her Unconquerables on a lower esplanade, treating Wall Water as hostile territory.

The roadway across the dam crest was crammed with Aquam, all headed south in the direction of the Laputa landing area. The heavy gunfire from Starkweather's *Jotan* had apparently driven them out of the stronghold.

He'll have us at war with a whole world, Burning thought. If the AlphaLAW wasn't already dead, Burning would vote for keelhauling him until he was.

Burning stooped to pick up vizards and masks discarded by those fleeing or fighting. "We can use these," he said.

He chose one of brass foil that looked like a man in the moon. Souljourner took an etched and painted mollusk shell that gave her the look of a sloe-eyed siren with invitingly pursed vermilion lips. Burning also found a light evening mantle, which he threw around himself to conceal his uniform and the gun in his hand.

Souljourner was familiar enough with Wall Water's layout to steer them clear of authorities and lechers. While domestics, peons, guests, and their attendants wandered or scurried about, Souljourner followed less traveled routes. At one point she hurried Burning into a paternoster to neatly avoid a foursome of houseguards clanking by in double time.

They arrived at Rhodes's bedchambers by way of a staircase used by the kitchen staff. Burning was about to risk a peek when she pulled him back and removed her mask. "No one will think it too odd if I look in," she told him.

He stood to the side of the doorjamb, pistol ready. He was braced for just about anything except the awed gasp that escaped her. Quickly he edged in to glance over her shoulder at the head of Smicker's bust, which had risen nearly to the ceiling, and the flabbergasting data it was spewing into the room.

Inside, they found dead Militerrors and Manipulants. One Manip had been pierced by what Burning could only surmise had been a plasma torch. And why white pom-pom armbands lay discarded there he couldn't guess. A hurried search revealed nothing but corpses stripped of weapons and other gear. The image of Aquams with bloopguns made his skin crawl.

His plugphone remained unusable, and no Ext or Periapt responded to blasts on his field whistle. The smoky stink of the Manip's charred and melted gut evoked memories of Santeria Corners on Concordance. He desperately wanted to shag ass but couldn't—yet.

When he found the curvilinear pasigraph icon, he instantly recognized it as Ghost's. "Listen up," he called to Souljourner. "What's our best way to—no, don't touch that!"

She pulled her hand back from the Optimant computer's main holofield but kept on staring. He could tell by the way she was mouthing the displayed words that she was part of the forty percent or so of Aquams who were literate. "See?" she said, briefly cutting her eyes to him. *"Alabaster!"*

He saw the place name, and then he saw the cords of Oblitex-7 that had been expertly packed into the computer's incandescent nooks and crannies. The disarms had been removed, the trembler functions were enabled, and the timer read four minutes and counting. An EOD team with the right equipment could neutralize the charges, but he had no shot at all.

As to who'd rigged the computer with first-echelon kit explosives, he had no doubt, but he vowed to settle the score before the landing boats pushed. The Aquam could do what they would with Zone's body.

Souljourner was still marveling at the holodisplay that included mention of Alabaster. "Sign off," he beckoned her. "We're vacating."

The final word was lost under a metallic concussion accompanied by a residual blast of vented steam. Mason was right about what he'd seen, Burning told himself. He grabbed hold of Souljourner's hand. "Get us to the funicular!"

"What was that sound?" she asked.

"The starting gun."

CHAPTER
FORTY-THREE

Waving two bloopguns, Scowl-Jowl squinted uncertainly at the Exts and Dextra but refrained from firing. Lod, 'baller lowered, showed the Manipulant an empty upraised palm.

"Hold your fire. We know you stopped the snipers from shooting us. Steady now."

Scowl-Jowl's close-set beady eyes glinted under the supra-orbital bone scarps. Though he spoke only battle-*gullah*, he grasped Lod's meaning and lowered the muzzle of his weapon; then he swayed on his feet. Dark red-green blood was running so freely from his wounds and ripped battlesuit that his trousers were sodden and his opposable-toe combat boots were trickling wet.

Without a Special Troops officer to translate, the Exts were going to have a hard time making the thing understand the evac plan. To abandon Scowl-Jowl after he had fought on their behalf seemed a gross injustice. Dextra was at a loss, so it was Lod who approached the Manip and gestured to the funicular car. "Get aboard! Delta-V, you monstrosity! We're running late!"

Dextra considered Lod, the self-serving little knave who'd dwelled and worked in her Periapt villa for months. Unapologetic shirker and lech, cheerful toady and hedonist, rising to the moment. Proof positive that their situation was grave.

Lod suddenly fell back under cover at the dull thunk and slap of a heavy sling-gun. A quarrel longer than Dextra's forearm found a gap in Scowl-Jowl's battlesuit and buried itself in his back. The Manip went to his knees, dropping one bloopgun while trying to grab the protruding end of the quarrel and yank it out. A second bolt dug into him just above where a human's kidneys would have been.

Two or more Aquams had gained the concrete sentry box and were firing through a cruciform shooting slit. Lod and the others raised their 'ballers and squeezed off .50-caliber slugs, which punched through the mortar and stonework, leaving a wandering constellation of holes and shot groups. No third quarrel flew from the sentry box.

Dextra went to Scowl-Jowl's side, wondering how to render first aid to a creature whose anatomy was a mystery to her. Wix Uniday got there, too, kneeling as Scowl-Jowl tried to regain his feet, free hand slipping in his own blood. Dextra retrieved the bloopgun the Manip had let fall, though it took both hands to lift the giant thing. The weapon was outfitted with a knotted loop of lanyard, which she slung over her head and right shoulder.

Uniday had one shoulder under Scowl-Jowl's armpit, but he couldn't budge him until several Exts pitched in, succeeding at last in drawing the Manip to his feet.

Lod directed them. "Odd numbers, get this Balrog aboard the car. Even numbers, security wheel."

Scowl-Jowl showed good sense by allowing them to help him board the bashed-open funicular. As Exts were setting the internal grabs—the lever brakes—more 'baller shots echoed from a building facing the plaza. Everyone turned to as Zone backed into sight, pausing in the doorway to peg two more shots into the darkness.

The slide stayed back on his automatic, so he ejected the magazine but didn't reach for a new one. Sprinting light-footedly to the car, he snapped his fingers to Strop, indicating his need for more ammunition.

"Board up," he yelled. "Company of mudfuckers right behind me."

Dextra noticed that his wrist whatty had been fitted with an adapter for Optimant systemry, but there was no time to question him about it. Zone took in Scowl-Jowl. "Triage call," he said, chambering a round from the magazine Strop handed him.

Lod drew himself up to his full height. "Just climb aboard, Colonel."

For some reason Zone chose not to contest it. Dextra asked herself what new priority could make him so amenable to shag-assing. As he mounted the platform, however, a foundation-rattling detonation came from above. Zone glanced in the direction of Rhodes's bedchambers with malign pleasure, then ducked into the funicular.

If Zone wasn't a problem, something else was.

"The attendants spiked the cable drum," Wetbar called. "They've got wooden dowels hammered into the main cog-wheels." He paused, then slapped the ballista spear that was protruding from the floor. "This weenie stick's got the car pinned."

Even as Dextra's chest was tightening at the thought of the long climb down the car track, Scowl-Jowl got to his feet again. The Special Trooper grabbed the catapult iron that had penetrated the car and heaved with all his engeneered strength. He made a mewing, childlike noise as his wounds worsened under the strain and blood began to run from him once more. But the barbed titan's arrow began to come free.

Three Exts jumped in to help, working the missile back and forth, and in a moment they had gotten it loose. Two of them heaved the spear clear of the car, while the rest eased the Manipulant down and used their field dressings to control Scowl-Jowl's bleeding.

Dextra eyed the cable drum. "Forget numbers. Everybody pile aboard! And give me a hand up there—no, by the back end." She hastened to a place by the bashed-open rear of the car, where the floor was littered with rubble and shards. She was bracing herself as she heard the ululiphaunts and running feet of Militerrors. "Get ready! You there, stand by those grabs!"

Dextra rested the bloopgun's wide-bore barrel on a bare length of window frame, angling the muzzle down at the windlass. The Exts crammed in, the last few clinging to the sides. She took a deep breath and yanked the trigger, eyes flinching shut in anticipation.

The bloopgun went off with a hollow report and a kick like a grenade launcher. Dextra yelped involuntarily. Some of her fingers felt as if they'd been broken; she'd also stabbed herself in the web of her hand with her opposite thumbnail. But the windlass was intact except for the tip of one pole. She'd somehow managed to miss a target the size of a whirlpool tub that was practically in her lap.

"Gun-shy," Zone jeered.

Swinging to him, she lapsed into Extisms. "Go play with your pipe organ!" She was trying for a better grip on the Special Troop fieldpiece when Lod suggested, "Just pretend it's Starkweather."

Someone else was trying to say something, but she didn't have time to listen. Dextra kept her eyes open and squeezed the trigger. She kept squeezing, feeling as if she were doing a ten-kilo forefinger curl. She was concluding that she'd broken her hand when the bloopgun thumped and jumped again. At the same moment she realized that the background voices had been yelling.

"As you were!"

"Hold your fire!"

"Wait!"

The recoil nearly tipped her back on her rump. A section of the cable drum and the left brake shoe and lever disappeared before her eyes, flung away like pieces of a jigaw puzzle heaved out of the box. Much of the cable itself went, and what was left lay in shreds or severed.

The funicular began to drop down its track, bound for the beach and gathering speed quickly. Everyone aboard was swaying and thrashing. Lod yelled, "You, on the grabs! Don't let the speed get away from you!"

"*Null set,* we're telling you!" a woman shouted back. "The grabs won't hold. We got no brakes!"

Ignoring *GammaLAW*'s Klaxons and a flash-bang warning device fired across its course, the teamboat with its Roman-style storming ramp stood nearer to the adrift picket boat crew member.

Quant got on-line with Spanker FarYore. "Can you give me one CIWS burst past the vessel's side with assurances of not coming anywhere near our beacon?"

"Can do, sir," his gunnery officer affirmed.

Since the close-in chaingun was aft of the superstructure, Quant would have to come side-on to give the teamboat a shot. He thought there might be a psychological advantage as well in dwarfing the Aquam ship. He brought his helm to starboard, ahead one-third and indicating seven knots.

"Gun action portside. One warning burst of fifty rounds off the target's starboard bow quarter. Battery released."

"Aye-aye, sir," FarYore replied.

The CIWS bawled in a vast basso. A sheaf of fast red streaks traveled low trajectories a few points off the teamboat's spade bow, well clear of the 'foil wreckage; 30-mm's chopped up ten-meter-high spikes of water a half klick beyond the indig craft. Quant looked for hasty, even farcical action on the teamboat's decks, but all he saw was some hunching down behind the pavises and barricades. He gave one more PA warning, but it did no more good than his earlier attempt had.

True believers, he thought, then raised Daddy D. "Is your marksman ready?"

"Yassur. What'll you have—an ear? Family jewel?"

"One round through their figurehead will do."

"Yell when you want it."

The figurehead was a brightly painted life-size carving of a woman clutching a stalk of grain and what Quant took to be a loaf of bread. A flurry of activity at the teamboat's starboard side drew his attention, and he got Delecado again. "Belay that last order! General, hold your fire."

"Understood, Cap'n."

Half a dozen Aquams were bent, kneeling, and lying prone at the low gunwale, some holding gaffs and boat hooks. They were pulling up an inert body in a swiftboat crew suit, a black-haired figure wearing a vest whose beacon was dark, either broken or malfing.

It struck Quant that they had known all along what they were doing. They had had him thinking they were going for the wreckage, when all the while they were going for the adrift who was closer to them.

Kilobar piped up. "With the captain's permission, that's Realtime Aqviq, gunner's mate on the hydrofoil *Skate*."

Quant recalled a youngster with coal-black hair—now being held and pummeled by burly, war-clad indigs. The faces of the Aquam—those he could see clearly—were ahowl with elation and triumph, the faces of men who'd laid hands on a feared and loathed enemy. He felt his jaw clench. They haven't known us long enough to hate us like this, he told himself. What the hell was going on?

He was trying to think of some way to get Aqviq back when the blows turned into savage pummeling. The young man was held fast on his knees in spite of his struggles. Fists and sword pommels sent shudders through him. There looked to be some conflict among the crew regarding the beating, but a knob-kerry strike to the back of Aqviq's skull put a sudden end to the bickering.

"General Delecado," Quant rasped. "Three warning rounds, tracer ammunition, into the teamboat's wooden figurehead. Fire at will."

The Aquam flinched away from the boomer rounds that split and splintered the carving, only to shake their weapons at *GammaLAW* all the more angrily. As Quant was hailing them through the PA again, somebody pulled Aqviq's fine black hair back and took his scalp with a sawing knife.

Quant saw very clearly how the lad's features drooped after the anchoring of his face was severed. Abruptly, his expression went ancient, dead, and woebegone all at the same time.

Argument aboard the teamboat recommenced as Aqviq disappeared under a rain of kicks, blows, and hacking. The quartermaster of the watch was cursing in a monotone, when Gairaszekh bit out, "Quiet on the bridge!"

A lookout reported flame on the teamboat, and Quant numbly shifted his focus. He knew what men and women all over his ship were thinking: *Sink them! Kill them!*

A mangonel had appeared on the upperworks behind the *corvus*, and off to one side some sort of local Greek fire was alight in a cauldron. The teamboat came on, paddle wheels churning, straight for the wreckage, the beacon, and another adrift.

"Gun action, starboardside," Quant told FarYore. "Target the catapult on their topdeck. Destroy the boarding ladder, too. Battery released."

The CIWS reached out again, highly accurate. Depleted transuranics blew the targets apart in explosions of tarred wood, rope, leather, and wrought iron. Some of the Aquam around the mangonel and the *corvus* were caught in the fusillade; when hit, they simply came apart like exploding meat.

Quant hardened his heart against both pity and joy. The *corvus*, its mast, and the mangonel shook, then came apart in a nimbus of fragments and disappeared. Pieces of the upperworks deck were flung high as well. Everywhere on the lumbering millship, including the slave tiers, people howled. On *Gamma-LAW*'s bridge there wasn't so much as a grunt.

In an instant liquid fire was leaping high and racing across the teamboat's open deck. It poured down the sides of the super-structure and through planking onto those below, including the shrieking wretches trapped in the capstan cage tiers. Pitch-sealed timber caught quickly; smoke started pouring up from the work spaces.

Whoever was manning the sweeps in the stern threw the helm hard over to port, perhaps because the fire had landed on him. The logy teamboat heeled over as it turned, and its low spade bow dipped under the wavelets. Overloaded and ill manned, it went awash and plowed under. The men who'd killed Aqviq were dumped, armor and all, into the surging lake water, clawing uselessly at the surface.

Quant had studied similar ancient sinkings, but he was astounded at how fast the teamboat went under. Tossing away weapons and tearing hysterically to be rid of armor, men were scrabbling up the tilted deck to stay above the waterline.

None of it, however, seared itself into Quant the way the sight of the slave tiers did. Silhouetted before creeping flames, figures heaved and tore madly at the bars as the decks slid under, trying in vain to thrust themselves through impossibly narrow gaps between wooden uprights. Quant watched men and women break their bones and peel the flesh off themselves in a ghastly animal frenzy to avoid being dragged and drowned in a cage. The cam feeds showed him their agonies as if at arm's length; even without a directional audio pickup, he heard the screams.

It was over in moments, yet it went on forever. The water under and around the teamboat was too shallow for the SWATHship to heave close in to render assistance. Some

Aquam stayed afloat or bobbed back to the surface, but the greater part took their place in the great aquaculture food chain.

Quant eased *GammaLAW* in as close to the *Skate*'s wreckage as he dared, but acoustics, lookouts and the rest located no survivors or bodies. The beacon turned out to be flashing from an empty life vest.

Finally, Quant turned his helm toward shore just as another concussion came rippling out from Wall Water. This one was metallic, heavy as a main battle tank hit by an airdropped engine block, and attended by a shrill, venting hiss. Even as he panned his cam feed and zeroed in on the beach below Rhodes's stronghold, Quant knew what had happened.

The hydrofoil *Edge*, which had gone ashore with Haven's party, had been tied up alongside a quay. Now it was holed forward and settling bow first as crew members scrambled around on it. A ragged white jet from a protected casemate in Wall Water was dissipating in the Big Sere dryness.

Claude Mason had been right about the telltale trace of water vapor he'd seen during his preliminary visit to the stronghold. Perhaps the same genius who'd come up with the *corvus* and the catapult had provided the grandee with yet another novelty—a steam-powered cannon.

CHAPTER
FORTY-FOUR

Zinsser clenched his fists at his sides to stop his hands from trembling at the idea of climbing the granite salient. "Ghost, come down off there," he said, somehow without making it sound pleading. "Mucking about will only get us killed." She was using her 'baller's beer-can-size scope to plot a course across the rock face. When she didn't respond, he added, "The flares will go dark soon, and *then* where will we be? There's a perfectly honorable tradition called surrender."

"I've already *been* a POW," she shot back.

Zinsser tried to quell his dismay with the thought that being held hostage in her close company might have its compensations, but the idea of clambering across the sheer hardstuff in the indifferent light from flares and illumination drones petrified him. It was a long fall to a lower rampart or beach.

"Do you think you're proving how *staunch* you are? Better a live bargaining chip than a dead—"

He interrupted himself as something came rippling and flaming out of the darkness to smash on the paving in a burst of fire, glass, and scraps of brass—a lamp turned into a Molotov cocktail by an Aquam high above and to the left. Zinsser did a frenzied bound onto the wall as Ghost spread four rounds into the night.

A solid concussion at the door told them that a battering ram had been improvised. Door and stone love seat bracing held but wouldn't last long, so Ghost put a .50-caliber through the thick wood, eliciting yelps from the other side. The ramming subsided momentarily.

Zinsser scowled as he wrenched off his handmade dancing slippers. "Do you realize how far away the nearest competent shoemaker is?" he said in elaborate dismay. He was about to cast them aside when she told him not to.

"You'll need them later." All precision and strength, Ghost began edging out along the face of the naked rock. "Know how to climb?" she asked.

He considered the question while he crammed the supple slippers into his cummerbund, next to the skin-diving knife. "Does a little bouldering in my student days count?" He stood at the very end of the wall, feeling the heat of the flames behind him. There were gongs, shouts, and occasional gunshots from far off.

"Do just what I do," Ghost said. "Concentrate. Don't let fear get the better of you or you won't be able to deal with the rock."

Willing his palms to stop sweating and his shakes to vanish, Zinsser ventured out onto the rock. In times past he had been trapped while cave diving, slashed and gnawed by a pod of tritons, and stranded at the bottom of an eleven-kilometer trench by a malfunctioning submersible. He knew how to invoke the calm that was the only chance of survival.

Even so, Ghost only had time to reel off basics as she made the easy traverse along a hand-span ledge to the salient angle. It was straightforward, something adventurous Wall Water children might do on a dare.

"Let your hands and feet carry your weight and keep it centered over your feet. Keep as much of your feet as possible in contact with the rock."

He was certain that she detested having to nursemaid him. "Remember, you'll be failing Burning if you don't talk me through this."

"One move at a time, not two or three," she said, ignoring his attempts at levity. "Look *down* for footholds—deliberately. Apply weight to make friction work for you. These are the handholds: cling-hold, pinch grip, like this. Hand hook—lets you rest your fingers if you have to."

She showed him as she moved; he watched, the words stirring decades-old memories.

"Thumb's your strongest finger; *always use it*." Ghost shifted along easily. The end of the ledge petered out, and the sharp angle of the salient waited. "Come out here so you can see how this is done. Lean slightly away from the rock. Keep your hand-holds between your waist and shoulders if you can."

Cold at night even in the Big Sere, the hardstuff was gritty and coarse, abrading his palms and soles and digits. The slanting light from the descending flares and hovering illumination drones was adequate, but the flares were already even with him, floating down slowly on their powered helivanes, and the drones wouldn't last much longer, either.

Ghost was easing around the salient while Zinsser closed the distance, emulating her clumsily and taking careful note of where her left hand was anchored with a ring grip as she leaned out of sight.

"Move into my place after I negotiate the angle," she said a moment later. "There's a hold on the other side, just about my shoulder height and arm's reach. Footholds, too. We'll have to stem a little bit, then jam and chimney. That'll get us to the next esplanade."

"Speak Terranglish, goddamn you! 'Jam'! 'Stem'!" Preparing for the move, she didn't seem to hear him. "How'd you like it if I flung jargon in your face?"

He was silenced by sounds of parting, grinding wood. Thick halberd blades were chopping at the arch door and levering it away from the jamb and hinges. When Zinsser glanced back around, Ghost was gone.

His version of prayer was his own: strictly for times of crisis. He squeezed off a burst transmission to the infinite, a terse reminder that since it expected so much of him, a more fitting level of help was in order.

Holding the ring grip as she had, he made the traverse around the acute angle; it was easier for him with his longer legs and arms. But when he saw the opposite face of the salient, he almost went back. Death by sling-gun dart or torturer's irons notwithstanding, the face seemed to be as featureless as a Wall Water rampart, up, down, and straight ahead.

He could just discern Ghost in the artificial half-light. She was three meters away in a corner of rock, one foot folded beneath her, sitting nonchalantly on thin air.

Thinking back to their near sexual encounter in the Empyraeum, he said, "Does this qualify as one of those erotically charged extreme moments you pretend to enjoy so much? Because the *only* way you'll get me to follow you out there is by promising something more than escape."

"Pile off me, suet butt!"

Dextra's immediate problem was Scowl-Jowl, whose tree-trunk legs, draped across her, seemed to gain weight every time the funicular car jolted or the creature tried to move under the weight of other bodies.

"Off, I say! You're crushing me!"

She goosed Scowl-Jowl with the barrel of the bloopgun; that was something even a giant could understand. Wounded though he was, the Manipulant did an inverted bridge, holding other jumbled bodies up while Dextra wriggled free.

The tramway walls were whizzing by. If the Exts at the grab levers were right and the brakes were gone, there would be nothing to halt the car until it careened into the crash barrier bumper on the beach platform. Dextra imagined a glass candy dish hitting a ball peen hammer.

"Hang ugly on them fuckers," Zone growled, making his way to the levers with rawboned strength and angry agility.

The floorboards had been partially bashed away by the Aquam ballista iron and further ripped up when Scowl-Jowl had extracted it. Through the gap, Dextra saw that the multi-ply leather brake shoes had been worn away, exposing hand-wrought iron over wood. The self-adoring Rhodes splurged on hedonism but obviously cut corners on basic maintenance.

The grab levers themselves were stopped from grinding metal to metal by limiter pegs. With Zone's strength added to the first Ext's, one peg snapped off; the worn iron face of the grab met the metal banding of the wheel, shrilling like a steel rasp being planed down and spitting metal fragments and sparks onto the blurring track bed. Smoke rose, only to be snatched away by the speed of the car's descent.

Lod and two more Exts broke the opposite limiter peg, but that brake was in even worse shape, the metal itself already worn through. Like a grindstone through plaster, the wheel banding began eating away the wood, setting it aflame in seconds.

Still the car slowed somewhat. Dextra heard a voice yell "Jump for it!"

But no one did—not with sling-gun bolts, pikes, and throwing hatchets suddenly crisscrossing in the car's wake. A rock flung off one of the overarching footbridges barely missed.

The grabs were almost gone now, and the car had plenty of track to regain its speed. Dextra cursed Rhodes for skimping on something as cheap and essential as brake shoes, then clutched at inspiration: *Shoes!*

"Lod!" she yelled. It was a long shot; she'd need help even to try, but . . . "Give a hand here!" Dextra scooched around on her bottom, full skirts catching on glass and splinters, and hiked herself to where the floorboards were mangled open. Then she began prying off another board. "Help me get this open."

It gave, but not for her. It was Scowl-Jowl who threw the floorboard aside and wrenched others out as easily as lathing. Muscles swelled the Manip's combat coverall sleeve; his clawed hands gripped and ripped like talon-fingered waldos. Scowl-Jowl's wishbone-nosed, lantern-jawed caricature of a face was suddenly beautiful to Dextra; the strange earthy smell of him was sweet.

"Careful, Dex." Lod had forgotten his deference in the crisis and stood willing and able to help her risk her neck to save his. Anything else would have been a surprise. "Are you sure about this?"

"Not on your life." But she straddled the hole in the floorboards anyway, fingering her special touchpad card. With Scowl-Jowl and Lod supporting her, she managed to edge her farthingale against a crosspiece in the car's undercarriage. Wix Uniday had struggled out from the general crush to help as well.

Forty centimeters under her unsupported backside, track bed was whipping by at sixty-five klicks an hour, plucking and dragging at her skirts. Too late, she considered what would happen if the skirts got wound around the axle, but there was no revising her plan now. Zone and the others shoved what was left of the grabs out of the way. The car instantly gathered velocity.

She positioned her feet as best she could, then signaled the powered stiltboot exo to extend.

It tried, telescoping out so that the stiltshoes contacted both rear wheel bands where the brake shoes had. The trusswork under her gown exerted force up through its frame, pressing the padded farthingale hard into the crosspiece and harder still. The jouncing she took made her feel as if she were in a bad carrier landing, but the stiltshoes continued to bear down on the wheel bands, the articulation conforming to fit to them, almost grip them.

The funicular car began to slow.

It wasn't what the exo had been made for, however. She tapped the override to apply added force, with the half suit ignoring the damage being done to it. The wheels were grinding their way through the soles of the stiltshoes, and vile smoke was wafting into the car. The manufacturer's guarantee that the exo was powerful, forgiving, and stable wasn't hype. Stress forces on the lower-body frame nearly popped Dextra loose, but Lod and Scowl-Jowl held her fast. The car decelerated even as its wheels gnawed at the stiltsoles. What with Aquam snipers and rock hurlers around in abundance, moderate descent had its advantages over an immediate halt.

Exts were whooping.

"Raise some rads, Dextra!"

"Lay that scorch!"

She gritted to Lod, "Would this ... qualify as ... 'hanging ugly'?"

He grinned at her. "Gorgeously ugly, Madame Commissioner."

Dextra's stiltboot soles gave out about the same time the funicular track-bed grade did, and in the end the car eased to a stop just short of the bumper pier that had been waiting to bash it to smithereens.

Fierce heat generated by braking friction was traveling up the farthingale frame, but that wasn't the only reason she wanted to be freed in a hurry. One look through the open door of the funicular convinced her that she wasn't out of the doo yet. The quay and beach were much changed from when she'd come ashore.

Smoke and the smell of gunfire blew across the landing area, and unmoving bodies—Aquam and offworlder both—littered the sand. The hovercraft's engines were revving and its plenum skirt was inflated, but the hydrofoil *Edge* lay with its bow holed through and plunged into the muck. Its foils were still retracted, and its stern was canted toward Wall Water, its waterjet propulsive outlets aimed uselessly in the air.

She heard bursts of automatic weapons fire and harsh and somewhat frayed Periapt voices. Zone, snarling about area control, belabored the Exts and dispatched them to firing positions around the platform and on the beach.

"Write off the stiltsuit and formal," she said. "Just get me out of this rig."

The exo was a total loss, and the gown was shredded and snagged on the undercarriage. Lod and Scowl-Jowl plucked her out of the hole in the floorboards. Wix Uniday toed glass aside so they could set her down.

Lod drew his gold-chased dagger to saw through courses of cross-lacing, skirt ruching, and hand embroidery that had cost by the square centimeter. Uniday, meanwhile, released the latches on the farthingale truss and the leg and foot braces.

Another burst of chaingun fire moved Lod to declare, "I've never had less fun undressing a woman."

Scowl-Jowl brought up his bloopgun as someone heaved himself into the shattered rear of the funicular. "Madame Haven?"

She pushed Scowl-Jowl's wide-bore aside, and the Manipulant relaxed. It was Quant's cross to bear: Kurt Elide. "What happened here?" Dextra asked.

"The balloon went up, ma'am. I don't know why the *Jotan* didn't target us when it splotched all the picket boats and aircraft, but it didn't. Maybe because we were on the beach. Anyway, pretty soon we heard a racket from Wall Water, and suddenly everybody on the beach was slicing at us and shooting darts. A few got past the sentries somehow and into the boats. Started hacking and stabbing like maniacs—no, like machines."

She thought of the Shadow-rat Hiip, who'd committed suicide to avoid capture aboard the SWATHship when she first arrived.

"I think they had the crews spotted, but somebody must've mistaken me for the boat chief, because he was in the clear and got to the *Northwind*'s stern gun tub while I got jumped by the ones who killed the pilot and copilot. They would've killed me next, except that the gun tub opened up—"

"Kurt!" Her warning tone brought him around. "You're babbling."

He swallowed and then continued in a more controlled voice. "We brought fire to bear, retook the boats, and cleared the beach. But they'd inflicted heavy losses. Commo was dead. Then some kind of steam artillery fired through a slit in the wall up there and blew the *Edge*'s bow open. I think something on the steam gun malfed because I heard breaking metal when it shot, and it didn't shoot again. Then the Aquam retreated inside and sealed the doors. We stood pat, waiting for you. There's only a half dozen of us left. Officers're dead. They had the officers spotted as priority targets."

"Enough, I understand," Dextra said as Lod and the Manip hauled her up. She was left in bodice and phase-change tights, with no shoes to give her height, and her dramatic bird-of-prey coiffure was demolished. The spare bloopgun bumped her hip, but she wasn't about to set it down.

She doubted Rhodes had foreseen *Terrible Swift Sword*'s destruction. The attack on the landing boats was more likely something he'd set up in the event some LAW treachery arose, a contingency ambush that had been sprung because of a misunderstanding.

"Kurt, is the *Northwind* ready to leave?"

He was puzzled. "Yes, but the others—the Allgrave, Doctor Zinsser—"

"Don't need us for company, no matter where they are at the moment," she finished firmly, stepping down to the sand. "We're going." Two petty officers were at work on the down-tilted *Edge*. "What're they doing to the hydrofoil?"

Kurt explained. "Setting demolition charges. It's SOP."

"Enough SOP for one night." She turned to Lod. "Get everybody aboard the hovercraft."

Zone gave Dextra a disdainful glance, then ignored Lod and moved the Exts back by the numbers for the *Northwind*.

The hover's weapons stations were manned, and its spotlights played on the stronghold's walls, especially a casemate projection with a dark firing slit—the steam cannon's lair. The

Exts assumed shooting positions behind splinter shields, gun cupolas, and deckhouse armor, looking itchy to get under way.

"Where's *GammaLAW*?" Dex wanted to know.

Kurt pointed to what looked like a fog bank caught by the last illumination drones settling toward the lake. "She laid down a smoke screen when the *Jotan* fired missiles. We heard her Klaxons a few minutes ago. She must've made it."

A petty officer jumped down from the half-sunk *Edge*. "Demo charges armed, timers running—ten minutes and counting!"

Dextra and the able seaman dashed for the *Northwind*. Lod was helping one of the more banged-up Exts aboard.

"*GammaLAW* better be out there," Dextra told Kurt. "It's the only safe place on the planet. Who's going to pilot *Northwind*?"

Kurt looked frankly apprehensive. "I, ah, actually have more cockpit hours than any of the surviving crew, so, that is . . ."

"Just get us home, Kurt."

She stopped, seeing someone moving aboard *Edge*. It was Zone, leaning over one of the demolitions charges—a whopper epoxied between a quad flechette gun mount and the WHOA-suit transport frame.

Dextra pushed Kurt on his way. After a dubious glance he trotted off to make ready for departure. "This is an excess of attention to detail, isn't it, Colonel?" she asked, moving closer to the 'foil's protruding stern when Zone reappeared.

He made a mocking moue. "Would you rather have the mud-fuckers get their hands on the boat and gear, Commissioner?"

"I'd rather not have you removing the disarms. Or are you concerned that a latecomer might get down here and use the signal lights or grab a lifeboat to save himself? The Allgrave, maybe?"

Zone leapt to the sand so that he was between her and the hovercraft. "You think you're a genius, but you're just a slit-wit. You care about Burning so much, stay here and wait for him."

She brought the bloopgun up. "Get aboard *Northwind*. And the next time you address me that way, war hero or no, you go back to the ranks."

Zone chuckled; from him the sound was unnerving. "Shooting a man takes a lot more balls than blowing away wood and cable-car rope, Haven. Besides, you're going to need me after tonight—a lot worse than you did in Wall Water."

She swallowed hard. "You're useful but not indispensable, so don't push it."

"You sure?"

There was something half-formed about his new air of calculation, this effort to fence. It was past time to leave, but she couldn't resist testing him. "That Manip's stronger than you are and probably has a higher IQ."

A wildness came into his face. "Maybe you'll feel different when those longevity treatments of yours wear off. *Tessie* took all your precious geron 'wares straight to hell, remember?"

Dextra hadn't considered it until he rubbed her face in it. The longev equipment and supplies that TRANSCOM had backlogged along with so much other stuff were gone; they were irreplaceable, given the SWATHship's resources. And she'd been experiencing premenopausal symptoms even before the starship made orbit. But instead of letting Zone see how he'd scored, she gave him a derisive smile that cut diagonally, not horizontally, across her face.

"You're losing your juice fast, Haven." Zone persisted, adopting the expression of an arsonist watching an inferno. "Gray hair, wrinkles ... Soon you'll be buckling your belt around them droopy boobs and your vaj'll be smellin' like—"

She pulled the trigger.

swear rono. Haven't. Besides, you're going. Officed the shot ha—a lot worse than you did in Wall Wars.

CHAPTER
FORTY-FIVE

Seeing that Ghost was seated on nothingness, Zinsser had the sense to stop dead and make no move while he was boggled. Then he realized that she was perched on her legs in a chimneying configuration, right hand crammed into the crack where two faces met. The inside corner was what climbers called a dihedral, this one a ninety-degree angle. Her left leg was braced with the shank horizontal, with the knee and sole of her boot wedged in by deformation and friction. Ghost's trim derriere hovered a few centimeters above her left heel; her right knee was pressed against the stone, with the toe of that boot edged on a bit of purchase. She was poring over the next part of the route as if over a tactical map-imaging holo.

"What about it?" Zinsser shouted. "Can I be assured of erotic joy at the end of this traverse?"

"Your next move's with your right foot to an edge exactly where my finger's aimed." She pointed with her free hand.

"Answer my question, damn you!"

Ghost glanced at him. "You *are* a fool. I'm saving your ass again, Doctor, which means that you're back to owing me *two* lives." She paused, then said, "Now, plant your foot where I showed you. Higher. You're almost there."

Zinsser sighed. Good climbing wasn't a brute matter of hunting for holds and lugging oneself along, he reminded himself. Rather—much like seducing Ghost—it involved careful observation and inventive use of opportunities. The unsure light made it harder by a power of ten; the holds to which she directed him looked to be little more than ropy shadows. Yet her curt direction brought him, after two eternal minutes, to where he could cling near and slightly above her.

339

But instead of congratulating him, Ghost said, "From here we descend. Follow my lead."

Zinsser drew a breath as the wind whipped his hair about. If he couldn't control the situation, he at least had to make a gesture. "I'll go first. That way, if I fall, I won't take you with me."

"You *will* fall if I don't show you the way," she countered. "We're losing light."

The glare of the *Jotan*'s illumination devices was definitely dwindling. She was about to resume when a heavy clanking thud and a pressurized hissing reached them faintly.

"Steam engine?" Zinsser said. "A cannon?"

"Forget it. Watch me."

She started down. Supple in the Skills and the Flowstate, she lowered herself, chocking the crack with her fingers, unrushed but unerring. Chimneying with her legs took more care and exertion than jamming had. She went move by planned move, watching Zinsser in between. He took her terse direction without objection, easing down the dihedral a few centimeters at a time.

The slope angled only slightly, but it began widening. Ghost's clipped instructions were all that passed between them until he nearly made a slip.

"What is it?" she snapped.

"My feet are bleeding." He hadn't even noticed how raw and painful they were. Having jammed them on the hardstuff again, he gingerly wiped first one sole and then the other with his cravat.

"There's a knob below," Ghost called up. "We can stop there." The bulb of stone barely provided room for both of them to stand together, clinging to the crack with hand jams. The scents of her breath and body had an erotic power even out there on the rock.

"I want you," he said.

She snorted a laugh and pointed. "That crack goes the rest of the way down the curtain. We lie back to where it widens, then foot stack until it flares. Chimney another bit. Stem that last stretch."

He saw that the final traverse would end in an exit move onto the esplanade—up an overhang as bare as a baby's bum. "With a pass-fail finale?" he asked shakily.

"Far from a finale." She nodded to the lake. "See?"

"MeoDeos," Zinsser said softly.

Far out on the lake the SWATHship was making for deeper water. There were no signs of the hydrofoil or the hovercraft. "*Someone* must've remained behind to rescue us," he said in desperation.

"I doubt it." Ghost's death-scarred loveliness held something beatific. "We'll get back on our own. Be our own saviors." She swung her free arm around his waist and began swaying him in an erotic stationary waltz. "Masters of our fate."

It wasn't a death wish, Zinsser knew; she was careful to keep her hand jam. The thing was, despite his ardor, he doubted he could have gotten a hard-on if the houris of paradise itself had descended and tongue-bathed him from head to excoriated toes. Nevertheless, he ground back against her as much as he dared.

Disappointingly, it was the most unerotically mechanical thing he'd done since experimenting with a headmaster appliance during the voyage out. He pretended otherwise, kissing her deeply, albeit by rote.

When she stroked his inner thigh, he knew he'd fail the next test of passion, so he looked sharply to the nearest drone. "We don't have much time left."

She stopped caressing him and gave him a look he couldn't decipher. "Who does?" Before he could reply, she took up the climb again.

Left to itself, Zinsser's body imitated her techniques of lieback, holding the near edge of the crack with both hands and walking his feet down the opposite side.

"Don't dyno," she cautioned. "One move at a time." Dynos were the high-risk moves of virtuoso climbers, more than one foot and/or hand in motion at once to cross a gap that couldn't be bridged in any other way. But Zinsser hadn't dynoed; he'd merely screwed up.

Time dilated. He didn't let himself think about what would happen if the houseguards figured out where the two of them had gone and raced over to meet them, although the guards themselves might well have been attacked. His optimism went ice-water cold when he saw the last stretch. Purchase there looked like mere bumps in cake frosting.

"That way, then up and exit." Ghost said, leading. "Wait until I reach the wall so I can guide you."

Zinsser suddenly realized how exhausted he was. And so I can't grab you if I fall? he projected.

He expected to see her drop, but she traversed, smearing. It got even worse in the middle of the ledge, which was at waist height, where he'd expected her to get hung up. Ghost pulled herself up until her hands were on the hold and her head was just above it. Then she pressed herself up with the chancy toe-holds she'd gotten, mantling the tiny ridge of stone, one of the most difficult moves.

She had her right palm on the shelf now and her right side aligned along the rock, pushing herself up mostly by the strength of one arm. Zinsser watched, not blinking, as she leaned in, almost touching the granite, then brought one foot up to a precise place on the two-finger's-width shelf. Her left hand claimed the hold she'd been striving for all along. It was almost two meters from her last toehold.

There was still that overhang, however. With the railing of the esplanade so tantalizing at the top, Ghost began tentative advances, only to retreat. Zinsser had to bite his tongue to keep from barking at her to hurry. The blast of an ululiphaunt sounded from somewhere above—houseguards closing in, perhaps. Ghost gave a low chuckle, then did a superdyno.

A super—both arms and her trailing foot all moving at once, a leap for life up along the face of the gritty hardstuff. She hit her holds, didn't quite find them, then did, with one hand and one foot. In seconds she had the rest, executing her exit move with the form and grace of a gymnastic dancer. She looked down from the other side of the wall with pistol in hand.

"Coast is clear so far. Do it now, Doctor."

He took a steadying breath, thinking, At least she'll remember me. He then eased out along the path she'd blazed. Why his ground-meat fingers and toes clung so well to the cliff he never knew; blood wasn't *that* adhesive, and the Skills weren't communicable. He was halfway into his mantling move when he felt one foot begin to slip in its own gore.

"G-Ghost?"

No answer. The ululiphaunts were louder, and she was gone. Shitshitshit, he said to himself. It was monstrous, really, how unsentimental, how unreachable she was. He felt himself losing balance. No way back and not quite enough leverage to raise himself. Just bad luck, plain old bad luck, which was always what killed people, after all.

The Embedded Way that Purifyre, Essa, and the rest traveled was a route like no other.

It was marked not so much by signs, merestones, and way posts as by people—interlocking and sometimes overlapping networks of them, webs of them accessed or avoided according to the needs of a particular journey. The Embedded Way was an underground transit system of sympathizers.

Intermittent clashes still racked Wall Water, with houseguard and Militerror reinforcements slowly getting the better of the various grandees' praetorians. Purifyre's own raiders, who'd been carrying out harassing attacks and sabotage as well as trying to take Visitant hostages, were withdrawing, making what diversionary trouble they could.

The first leg of the Embedded Way had Purifyre's band following an apprentice pipe artificer who'd worked installing the steam system Purifyre had designed for Rhodes. In actuality Purifyre had sold Rhodes on the idea of the new weapon the pipes served. Rhodes had been too inflated with his own alleged inventive powers and visionary genius to realize he'd been steered.

The 'prentice led them down a darkened service stairwell that connected the distant kitchens to both the throne room and the bedchambers. Doors that gave access to it from the kitchens, several guard posts, and other places had been secured from the inside with wrought-iron hooks, jamb spikes, wedges, and similar devices that had been prepared in advance.

They went with heads pulled low to avoid dashing them on the mean ceiling; they'd even practiced that detail. The burden of the unconscious Claude Mason and the Science Side modules didn't slow them unduly.

They went through a concealed trapdoor that wasn't on the

plans the master masons had given Rhodes's castellan. In the maze that followed the ducting for the great gyn the pipe fitter and his coworkers had built, there were distant hissings and bangings and the broil of venting steam. Warned by lookouts, they made detours where necessary, passing through crypts and along a cistern inspection catwalk. The battle above didn't touch them.

They could have left Wall Water unobserved if they'd had to, but part of the infiltrators' planning had been done expressly to leave Purifyre free of suspicion. His status as Human Enlightenment *rishi*, his credibility among the grandees, and his access to Wall Water were resources of tremendous value.

His party exited a basement storeroom and made its way to a gatehouse guarding what once had been the ground vehicle ramp leading up to the dam crest roadway. The gatehouse was held by a reinforced troop of houseguards bolstered by a quartet of Militerrors. The soldiers were as apprehensive about who might try to fight their way out as about who might try to fight their way in.

"We of the creed are not bloodletters," Purifyre told them. "Even to save our own lives, we shun strife."

"It's all a berserk crush on the roads, *rishi*," the houseguard in charge warned, "in all directions."

"Better that than dying at Visitant hands—or Aquam."

The houseguard called for the Human Enlightenment party to be passed through, but a Militerror sergeant objected. "How do we know they're not assassins?"

Reverberating across the lake from the huge Visitant trimaran, they heard a ripping groan like the breaking up of an icebound river. The offworlder din made the soldiers even more jittery.

"If you can swear to protect us from bare steel and skyfire, we'll gratefully remain right here," Purifyre offered.

The houseguard officer was a believer but was altogether ignorant of Human Enlightenment's secret agenda. Purifyre had presided at the consecration of his home village's shrine a year earlier. "I said pass them through. Let them find what refuge they can—unless anyone thinks they're Visitants."

A useful dupe. Purifyre had long ago gotten over his shame at using and betraying the houseguard's sort. The Militerror backed down, and Purifyre's group headed for the mad press on the dam crest road. They would have to get south across the bottleneck, but that, too, had been planned for; they would arrive at the Trans-Bourne on schedule.

In the same vein, Purifyre's insiders had known that the houseguard's post that night would be this gate, making the man an unwitting portal on the Embedded Way.

The clack of the bloopgun's firing mechanism startled Dextra. She hadn't realized that she'd raised the weapon and pointed it at Zone. But no bolas round diced him into bloody giblets and bone shards because the drum magazine was empty.

It had been so *easy* to pull the trigger, though—when she had always believed that it wouldn't be. Zone's malicious joy in verbally debasing her had overwhelmed her self-control.

He smirked at the pinging echo of the hammer's fall on an empty chamber. "Planned to take me off the roll call, hmm? Didn't notice the selector was up, no bullets?" He snorted. "Don't worry about it. At least you proved your heart doesn't pump fruit juice."

She had the distinct impression that he was purposely letting her know that he was exercising restraint, feeling his way along some larger and newly subtle strategy. He reached to caress her face as if she were some nube he could frighten into putting out.

She stood her ground but leaned away. "You'd have to kill me." She saw debate behind his eyes and would have given anything to hear the nature of the dispute.

They both heard her name being called. Lod was standing down the beach holding a boomer, its sling over his shoulder to steady it. The battle rifle looked immense in the little man's hands. The muzzle was pointing at the ground but angled in Zone's direction.

"Time to wave a fond farewell to exotic Wall Water, Madame Commissioner, Colonel."

To confirm it, there was a hiss of live steam from somewhere inside the casemate, muffled yells, and hammering. Dextra stepped around Zone, sand straining through the feet of her tights.

Zone moved his hand away from his pistol. His next remark was cut off by a tremendous weight that dropped out of the sky to pulverize part of the quay and a floater tied to it. Lod and Dextra ducked reflexively as yells came from the hovercraft.

Zone was unruffled. "Mudfuggers finally realized they can drop rocks on us," he observed, his upper lip lifted a bit with the trenchant humor of it all. He glanced at Dextra. "Like I said, you're gonna need me a lot worse after tonight."

Dextra narrowed her eyes. "If anyone has the potential to be a lot worse, I'm sure you're it, Colonel."

CHAPTER
FORTY-SIX

Somewhere above him Zinsser, trembling near the cliff face, heard Ghost say, "Lean in, Doctor. Bow your head to the rock."

He was so relieved that she hadn't deserted him that he made the obeisance without protest. The subtle shift changed his center of gravity with agonizing slowness. He didn't even mind the shredding his forehead took as he slid it up along the granite. His arm came shakily to full extension, and with his length of leg he found it relatively easy to raise his foot to the toehold she'd used. His muscles thrummed and his raised left knee went into sewing-machine-needle spasms, but he managed to mantle up, bracing himself for that last awful superdyno.

Waiting for him was a mollywood pennon pole Ghost had wedged between the esplanade wall fretwork and the cliff. Harrowing as it was to make use of the pole, it felt like strolling a sidewalk after what he'd been through.

The climb had taken them around to the eastern face of Wall Water, where, but for the dead and the dying, the esplanade was clear for the moment.

A ululiphaunt whined again. Ghost nodded to where a footbridge spanned a chasm that contained tailwater diverted from the dam. The bridge led out of the stronghold and into the jumbled headlands. "Once across, we can beat our way down to the lakeshore."

Zinsser pulled his slippers back on, trying to ignore the torture they inflicted and mulling how close he'd come to dying. Ghost didn't so much as spare the rock a glance before starting off.

He was too grateful to be alive and too intent on remaining that way to object. His rock-grated feet felt like ground raw meat, but he didn't care. His attention was riveted on the foot-bridge. They stepped around the dead and dying.

Not twenty meters along they spotted the broken, mangled body of a Manipulant. Ghost looked to the ruined dungeon. "This one must've fallen."

Its bloopgun was nowhere around. The body looked to have been stripped by someone who knew nothing about combat coveralls or offworld equipment. The Manip's gullet had been gratuitously chopped open, possibly with its own cleaver-hack-knife, which was gone. So were compass/locator, medpouch, and bolus rations.

The scavenger had missed or had not been able to get the safety clasp open on a lower thigh pocket. In it Ghost found a grenade whose capsule shape, markings, and raised symbols identified it as an incendiary.

"Starkweather was *looking* for trouble," Zinsser sniffed. "Blithering incompetent."

They'd nearly reached the footbridge when drums and ululiphaunts sounded and a company of houseguards charged into sight with weapons ready and guidon flying.

Ghost pulled the pin on the grenade, let the spoon fly, and lobbed it over her shoulder as she and Zinsser dashed onto the bridge. Seconds later the night was briefly driven back by orange-white flames mushrooming high behind them. Zinsser couldn't resist a look. Seeing the foot span blocked by fire and the baffle-ment of the houseguards was sheer delight.

Then Ghost's yank at his arm almost brought his feet out from under him. Across the chasm scores of Fanswell's Fanatics—mobilized from their bivouac—were advancing to attack. A solid phalanx of them blocked the far end of the span and a good deal of the hillside beyond. On the other side of the incendiary blaze, meanwhile, the houseguards were taking up shield lock with sling-guns and poleaxes protruding.

At a kind of pergola at the middle of the bridge Ghost pushed him to shelter between a planter and a curving mollywood bench. From the Wall Water side came the whapping of sling-guns as broadhead quarrels began ranging in. Hunkered down, Zinsser tried his plugphone, then gave it up as a lost cause. He checked the planter behind which he lay prone and peered over the edge of the bridge to the tailwater stream far below.

"Put the gun down and fill your stockings," Zinsser told her. He hadn't even put his own stockings back on; now he began to shake them out.

She sounded more irked than confused. "Fill them? With what—and what the hell for?"

He tapped the planter. "Gravel and sand. We'll need twine, too." He nodded at the braided aiguilette looped at her right shoulder. "That'll do—two lengths for each of us." To see his plan dawn on her was a novelty money could not buy. "We have to jump, Ghost." His lips cracked, drawn back in a triumphant smile. "You see that, don't you?"

Ghost spurned the chasm with an offhand glance. "Too shallow."

"No. It's stagnant but deep. They raise delicacies for the stronghold down there. I viewed the SAT imagery."

She shook her head. "It's a seventy-meter fall. We'll tumble. I'd rather die on my feet."

"Endlessly maddening woman," he muttered.

She knew the hidden danger of his desperate plan. From that height falling human bodies would almost inevitably wobble, strike headfirst, land flat, or twist around. The only safe way of hitting the water was the one against which human anatomy and aerodynamic factors militated.

"I *don't* wobble," he said grandly. "I've done this before." Then he told her how. "We must enter feetfirst, ankles locked or crossed." He didn't mention that he'd done it as an undergrad, on a dare, from a height less than half this one.

Ghost measured off and sawed the tough cord while he finished filling his stockings with handfuls of the desert amalgam soil scooped from the planter. She spared him a glower, then drew off her socks and did the same. Her feet had more calluses, scars, and deformations than Zinsser would have pictured, and he briefly wondered what the rest of her might look like unclothed.

When his socks were weighted with what felt like three kilos of amalgam, he started pulling them on. Grinding into his minced-meat injuries, the sand was pure agony. He took one of the aiguilette lengths from her and began tying off the stocking just above his ankle.

"Pull them taut!" he told her. "Cut the circulation off; it doesn't matter. But make sure you use a slipknot or you'll be fish food."

She'd secured the 'baller and was rapidly filling her socks. Her boots were slung by the pull-on tabs from two pistol belt keepers.

Zinsser edged backward to the brink on his belly. Gaps in the uprights afforded ample room to slide down and out into the night.

"Doctor, exactly *what* are they raising in that water?"

He fumed. "What *would* it take to get you to call me Raoul?"

A frown was her only response.

"All right," he said, blowing out his breath. "They're not raising anything that uses sling-guns or cutlasses. Is that good enough for you? Now, hug your chest as you go down. Angular momentum outriggers only make you tumble." He paused and grinned. "Give us a kiss for lu—"

Without rancor she pushed away from the bridge like a swimmer off a raft. He cried out in surprise as he watched her drop into the darkness, Hussar Plaits whipping, weighted socks dragging her upright.

He knew a moment's regrettable hesitation, a low impulse to hear a reassuring splash before he committed himself to the drop. Then pride reasserted itself. This was his stroke of genius, after all. He alligatored backward and shoved off before he could reconsider.

Zinsser had the distinct sensation of having jettisoned his stomach. The tubular deadweights of sand and gravel pulled him feetfirst down through Big Sere air that suddenly felt icy. The fall seemed to elongate his body. He inhaled and exhaled, then took another breath and held it.

Hugging his chest, he waited while the air snake danced around him in celebration of his fall.

Aboard the *Northwind*, Dextra got another pointed lesson in how things had changed.

When, at dusk, she'd come ashore to the sounds of "The

March of the Siamese Children," the hovercraft had been a ship-shape military vessel. Now it looked more like a triage room and charnel house. Exts were seeing to their own wounded and the naval personnel who could still benefit from attention. Bulkheads and decks were spattered with blood and pocked with bullet holes from close-quarters fighting. LAW dead had been shoved behind deck structures and under cabin benches, and if there were body bags aboard, no one had taken the time to find or fill them.

One dead boat crew member had fuzz on his upper lip instead of the mustache he'd been trying for. His face wore the expression she'd seen so many times as a war correspondent: wide-eyed, open-mouthed surprise without signs of anguish or pain.

Another siege-gyn boulder crashed onto the beach from the ramparts, flattening two catch-sorting tables and a small aquatic fertility shrine. She wished suddenly that she had attended more of the briefings on Wall Water's fortifications. Would they be pouring burning fish oil next?

Kurt Elide manned the pilot's seat, while a prepubescent-looking seaman apprentice sat in the copilot's chair. Dextra made a spinning motion in the air with her forefinger, the one she'd seen the boat crews use. "Rev it up! Time for 'The Shag-Ass of the Siamese Survivors.' "

The plenum skirt was inflated, and the lines were cast off. Kurt brought up the rpm, engaging the fan-jets and easing away from the quay. But where she'd looked for *Northwind* to accelerate quickly, it strained to make headway. The seaman apprentice was screaming. "I told you we should've gotten a running start on the beach!"

Dextra teetered over to clutch the back of Kurt's chair. "What's wrong? Pour it on!"

"The hump!" he said through locked teeth as the *Northwind* made for the channel with agonizing slowness, limping along between aquaculture-rigged sandbar islets and moored water farming punts, fenboats, and barges.

Dextra stifled her groan. The hump was the low wall of water piled up in front of the bow by the forced air a hovercraft rode. It resisted the vessel's movement in a waterborne start, increasing in resistance as more force was exerted, until at a certain point the vessel breasted it and could pick up speed. There would have been no hump if *Northwind* had slid down onto the lake from the beach at speed; having started from the quay, however, there was nothing to do but muscle forward until they jumped the hump.

A stone block the size of Dextra's desk crashed through the end of the quay. Water shifted the half-sunk *Edge*'s bow even deeper, but the wave wasn't enough to help *Northwind*'s predicament.

A sustained blare issued from the quad 'chetterguns in the stern tub, even though they were unlikely to find much to target in the battlements of Wall Water. Dextra seized Kurt's shoulder, then froze. He was heading straight for a sandbar aquaculture work site, a spit barely above water, cluttered with a spiderweb of mooring lines, drying seine nets, and sorting tanks. "Kurt, you'll get us hung up!"

"Critical water!" was all he had time to holler.

Northwind went slewing up onto the mud and coming through an ungainly turn, snagging lines, uprooting stakes, overturning a vat, and sideswiping long racks of seedlings. Dextra was flung back against a bench as Kurt crowed, "Critical water!"

Dextra recalled the phrase now: extreme shallows or a beach's edge where the hump disappeared and a hovercraft could get up enough headway to overcome it.

Northwind suddenly slid out over the water, in effect jumping the hump. Thrust that had accelerated it only slowly against the hump now shoved it forward briskly. Crew members were screaming at the top of their lungs from sheer release, while Exts gazed back silently at Wall Water, searching for targets or a signal from their abandoned comrades.

"Radar's picking up the *GammaLAW*," the copilot sang out as Kurt came onto a new heading.

Dextra got a helping hand up from Scowl-Jowl. The hulking LAW soldier set her by Kurt Elide, then went back to hunching silently at the back of the troop compartment.

Dextra stared out at flame and destruction on land and lake. Get past it, she told herself. Start using your head. Figure out a way to pick up the pieces. Aquamarine's now the place where you're soon going to grow old—and eventually die.

So make it count for something.

The funicular had left without them. Its cable drum had been shot to pieces with what Burning inferred to have been bloopgun bolas rounds. He stepped back from the drum's remains with devout caution and gestured for Souljourner to do the same; even a gentle snag on one of the invisible monomolecular filaments could pare flesh from bone in prime cuts, lop fingers off.

There were shot-dead Aquam but no live ones left in the vicinity. A huge arbalest-harpoon lay on the ground, though whatever the thing's origin, it hadn't prevented the funicular from leaving. He hoped that the car had escaped intact, with Ghost aboard. He searched for another of her pasigraphs but found none.

"Is there a stairway to the base?" he asked Souljourner.

She jerked a thumb at the battlements. "Deep inside, where the guards don't walk."

He hefted the 'baller. "Just as well for all concerned."

She guided them to the beach postern door without incident. Instead of a rear guard or rescue team at the quay, there was only the half-sunk hydrofoil *Edge*, holed by what Burning now knew was a steam cannonball or shell.

Night was a pall over the lake, though through it he could discern the running lights of a fast-moving boat, perhaps the hovercraft *Northwind*. He hoped again that Ghost was aboard.

He thought that the half-sunk *Edge* might offer a lifeboat or RIB, but on hoisting himself up the transom ladder and onto the canted deck, he saw that one end of the capsule of the compressed lifeboat had been jaggedly shot away. Because of LOGCOM's misplaced priorities, there were no flotation suits, either.

Crew-served weapons had been stripped or disabled, and this time he wasn't at all surprised to find Oblitex-7 charges primed and counting down. There was just time enough to locate life vests and try his luck in one of the fenboats or coracles before someone in Wall Water got steam artillery pressure up for another round.

He heard halloos and ululiphaunts; the source was out on the water, beyond where one of the aquaculture sand spits was in disarray, gear and paraphernalia flattened, as if a cyclone had blown across it. There was an Aquam barge out there with what resembled an immersible pipe organ on the stern, and there were war canoes paddled and crewed by fighters who'd spent a lifetime doing it.

The indigs were waving torches and rush lights and shaking boat hooks, machetes, and fishing spears at him. If he and Souljourner swam for *GammaLAW*—wherever she was—the Aquam would be on them before their hair got wet.

But ducking back into Wall Water wasn't an option, either.

"The sally ports!" Souljourner called out, hauling herself onto the hydrofoil's deck. Houseguards and Militerrors were mustering. Sling-gun missiles were already zipping in, wide of the target at such long range.

Burning was about to tell Souljourner that her chances were better with Rhodes—that he was off for a swim of uncertain duration and she'd better get clear of the 'foil's demo charges—when he realized that a likelier bet was looking him right in the face. The destruct charges were displaying their final seconds when he paused the countdown, tapping carefully at the touch-pad epoxied between the stern quad-flechette mount and the WHOAsuit gantry. Too bad there were no buttons to pause the sortie squads of Aquam who were working themselves up to attack fervor, Burning thought—too many to stop with .50-calibers and sonics together. At a single blasting note from a res-onat-o, they launched themselves at *Edge*. Thickets of steel and torchlight came at him to choruses of inarticulate killing rage.

"What now?" Souljourner demanded as he left the destruct charges' touchpad and sprang down the canted deck for the hovercraft's bridge and cabin compartment. "We must flee!" She was scared but not weepy. Considering all they'd been through, he figured she just wasn't the crying type.

War cries from the Aquam charge were getting louder fast. Agile in the Skills, he slid, duckwalked, and swung his way into the pilot's chair. There he punched up displays the way he'd been shown on orientation cruises back during the Miseria Isle training. The engines in their watertight compartments powered up—*staunch*.

Sliding his thumb along a row of touch tiles, as if running it down a keyboard, brought the turbopumps revving high, like eager williwaws. The rear viewscreen showed him two lines of attackers in echelon coming at the 'foil's stern out of the smoke and mist.

There were other measures that would have been smart, such as tying up at the quay again, but there wasn't time. He simply drew down all four water-jet throttles with splayed fingers. The turbopumps raved and shot lake water out the stern jets at more than six thousand liters a second.

The four-abreast gushers described flat arcs, intersecting the ranks of Aquam and digging *Edge*'s holed bows deeper into the shore mud. Ea's wavelets surged up over the cabin windshield and sloshed against the watertight bulkheads forward as the picket boat shuddered, sounding as if it were about to come apart.

Burning heard something snap forward but couldn't take his eyes off the rear screen. The turbojets pumped a heavier volume than water cannon or fire hoses; the slewing of the 'foil under their impetus played the four outport streams like automatic fire. Washed back the way they'd come or just flattened, the indigs disappeared under a wall of brackish lake bilge. Some tried to run, but the panning jets caught up with many, lifting them off their feet and sending them flying. Tables, nets, and anything else in the streams were batted far.

As the angle of the deck increased, water began rushing into the cabin. Burning heard an ominous grinding from the intakes, then a terrible screeching and whamming as lake mud fouled the engines. The jets spit, gushed again for a second, then quit altogether. He swamped to the hatch and made his way aft along the deck, climbing as much as walking. Souljourner was braced at a disabled missile, watching as he passed her by. He slapped the WHOAsuit's clear-foredomed armored egg of a head.

"I'm walking home in this. You're welcome to come, but it might be smarter to stay behind."

Crude diving bells were something the aquaculturalists used, but she eyed the WHOAsuit dubiously, thumbing the draw-string pouch at her throat. He supposed that the WHOA wasn't a reassuring sight: 220 centimeters tall, 200 baseline kilos of mass, grossly humpbacked with the bulge of its mission-adaptable space, its hands a tool chest of pincers, effectuators, and multipurpose blades.

"This is underwater armor?" she asked. "A walking diving bell?"

"Exactly, a walking diving bell."

He tapped tiles to get the power-assisted rig warming up, then began flipping open the lockdowns, hitting external controls to crack the hardsuit for entry. With no one there to work the hoist, he'd just have to walk it over the side.

More Aquam were showing up in longboats and on rafts. They were close, but he could be well submerged before they reached the quay. He got the suit three-quarters freed up, steadied by one clamp on its left arm and a last one on its left leg.

Burning braced himself with one foot on the gantry and opened his collar and the first two buttons on his blouse bib front for some air. The suit's cranial dome's seals made a kissing pop, and it swung up and back. The dorsal bulge was vacant; its most recent cargo, a multisensor mapping and sampling package, was somewhere on the Science Side for retooling. That left a large ovoid space with only a few brackets and connectors occupying it.

Power levels read at fifty percent, but that would do fine; he wasn't planning a day at the bottom of a midocean trench. There was an emergency backup propulsion unit bolted to the hardbody's back, small twin underwater hydroturbojets, their turbines driven by molten-lithium/H_2O reaction. Having learned that piloting the ungainly suits under that kind of power was for underwater top guns only, Burning hoped he wouldn't need to do that.

He pulled himself up, getting one leg over the circular dome collar, then stopped as Souljourner gripped his thigh.

"Burning, walking under the water can't be as bad as what the grandee will do to me if I'm retaken now."

"Whatever you say. But I'm warning you, tight quarters." There was a backrest separating the pilot's space from the dorsal bulge; he lifted it off its posts and tossed it aside.

Seeing the interior, she swallowed but didn't waver. "I'm to be your rucksack rider?"

"That's about it."

The slightly prognathous jaw set. She gave him the sideways head tic that was in Scorpia the equivalent of a nod, then kicked off her split-seamed slippers and pulled herself onto the suit rack.

With his guidance, she squirmed around to lower herself into the WHOAsuit feetfirst, gathering her skirts up around her bodice unselfconsciously, baring strong pale legs and ample hips. Lectures had agreed with barracks rumor that most Scorpian women didn't wear lingerie, but Burning got direct confirmation as she eased herself into the suit waist deep, standing on the narrow crotch saddle.

The chunk of sling gun bolts hitting the Edge's transom brought him back into *zanshin*. "Squeeze back."

He was up and around in one move, entering the suit and getting his feet down the heavy boots on the first try, then pulling his arms down after him and inserting them into the WHOA's arms. Because he had to sit as far forward as he could, the minimal saddle wasn't much help.

Souljourner had snuggled herself into the dorsal bulge in a modified squat, her coccyx nestled into its curve. Her heels rested on its rim, while her feet were canted to either side of Burning's waist, left toes on the air recirc panel, right on the back of the sonar control box. Her knees were drawn up under her armpits, her breasts flattened against his back. As he leaned back to check his displays, her hands settled on his shoulders, and he felt the warmth of her breath on his neck above the open collar.

The interior of the hardsuit smelled like strong Science Side disinfectant. He went to undo the last clamp with the right-hand waldo and almost wrenched his arm from its socket; the suit wasn't completely on-line. A moment later it answered his movements perfectly. He hit a chin switch, and the ellipsoid of ceramic glass that was the dome descended and sealed. Air circ kicked in, breaking the sudden silence. Diagnostics showed no problems.

Freed from the gantry's clasp, he took his first faltering steps, moving carefully to avoid squashing Souljourner. Conforming to his back, she tensed her muscles to keep from having the breath driven from her. His blouse, already damp, was quickly sodden with their sweat.

Its gyrosystem possibly confused by shifts in Souljourner's weight, the WHOAsuit didn't feel as responsive as the ones in orientation had. However, the suit had the strength he remembered. Water was rushing up the deck as the *Edge* shifted again. He lumbered down the tilt of the nonskid and into the lake. The suit helped him stay upright, artificial muscles compensating for its clumsiness. Jostled, Souljourner grunted softly by his ear.

Chinning the external audio pickup brought in a distant, indistinguishable uproar. Something whanged off the outside of the dorsal bulge, drawing an unhappy "mmm" from Souljourner—a sling-gun dart, he knew, because others were zipping by him. But he couldn't chance looking back, afraid that he'd end up falling headlong if he did. Instead, he waded quickly into the water, leaving the suit's running lights off, the better to disappear.

✎ FREE DRINKS ✎

Take the Del Rey® survey and get a free newsletter! Answer the questions below and we will send you complimentary copies of the DRINK (Del Rey® Ink) newsletter free for one year. Here's where you will find out all about upcoming books, read articles by top authors, artists, and editors, and get the inside scoop on your favorite books.

Age _____ Sex ❏ M ❏ F

Highest education level: ❏ high school ❏ college ❏ graduate degree

Annual income: ❏ $0-30,000 ❏ $30,001-60,000 ❏ over $60,000

Number of books you read per month: ❏ 0-2 ❏ 3-5 ❏ 6 or more

Preference: ❏ fantasy ❏ science fiction ❏ horror ❏ other fiction ❏ nonfiction

I buy books in hardcover: ❏ frequently ❏ sometimes ❏ rarely

I buy books at: ❏ superstores ❏ mall bookstores ❏ independent bookstores
    ❏ mail order

I read books by new authors: ❏ frequently ❏ sometimes ❏ rarely

I read comic books: ❏ frequently ❏ sometimes ❏ rarely

I watch the Sci-Fi Cable TV channel: ❏ frequently ❏ sometimes ❏ rarely

I am interested in collector editions (signed by the author or illustrated):
    ❏ yes ❏ no ❏ maybe

I read Star Wars novels: ❏ frequently ❏ sometimes ❏ rarely

I read Star Trek novels: ❏ frequently ❏ sometimes ❏ rarely

I read the following newspapers and magazines:
❏ *Analog*	❏ *Locus*	❏ *Popular Science*
❏ *Asimov*	❏ *Wired*	❏ *USA Today*
❏ *SF Universe*	❏ *Realms of Fantasy*	❏ *The New York Times*

Check the box if you do not want your name and address shared with qualified vendors ❏

Name _____
Address _____
City/State/Zip _____
E-mail _____

daley/gammalaw

**PLEASE SEND TO: DEL REY®/The DRINK
201 EAST 50TH STREET NEW YORK NY 10022 OR FAX TO THE
ATTENTION OF DEL REY PUBLICITY 212/572-2676**

DEL REY® ONLINE!

The Del Rey Internet Newsletter...

A monthly electronic publication, posted on the Internet, GEnie, CompuServe, BIX, various BBSs, and the Panix gopher (gopher.panix.com). It features hype-free descriptions of books that are new in the stores, a list of our upcoming books, special announcements, a signing/reading/convention-attendance schedule for Del Rey authors, "In Depth" essays in which professionals in the field (authors, artists, designers, salespeople, etc.) talk about their jobs in science fiction, a question-and-answer section, behind-the-scenes looks at sf publishing, and more!

Internet information source!

A lot of Del Rey material is available to the Internet on our Web site and on a gopher server: all back issues and the current issue of the Del Rey Internet Newsletter, sample chapters of upcoming or current books (readable or downloadable for free), submission requirements, mail-order information, and much more. We will be adding more items of all sorts (mostly new DRINs and sample chapters) regularly. The Web site is http://www.randomhouse.com/delrey/ and the address of the gopher is gopher.panix.com

Why? We at Del Rey realize that the networks are the medium of the future. That's where you'll find us promoting our books, socializing with others in the sf field, and—most important—making contact and sharing information with sf readers.

Online editorial presence: Many of the Del Rey editors are online, on the Internet, GEnie, CompuServe, America Online, and Delphi. There is a Del Rey topic on GEnie and a Del Rey folder on America Online.

Our official e-mail address for Del Rey Books is delrey@randomhouse.com (though it sometimes takes us a while to answer).